SERPENT RISING

THE SAGA OF VENOM AND FLAME

SERPENT RISING

VICTOR ACQUISTA

LIVONIA, MICHIGAN

Edited by Jamie Rich
Proofread by Rebecca Fischer

SERPENT RISING
Copyright © 2020 Victor Acquista

Published by BHC Press

Library of Congress Control Number: 2020933868

ISBN: 978-1-64397-114-8 (Hardcover)
ISBN: 978-1-64397-115-5 (Softcover)
ISBN: 978-1-64397-116-2 (Ebook)

For information, write:
BHC Press
885 Penniman #5505
Plymouth, MI 48170

Visit the publisher:
www.bhcpress.com

To all truth seekers and Lightbringers

SERPENT RISING

PART ONE
BROKEN

1

Impact…crash…darkness. The bedside table lamp and shattered light bulb lay on the floor, but Serena remained unmoved, without will or inclination to clean up the mess. She stared at the ceiling of her tiny efficiency apartment, lit solely by the eerie neon-green from the alarm clock's LED. The glass fragments glittered, taunting her to get out of bed. Instead, she pondered the much larger mess of her life. She lay still, in a familiar paralysis of apathy. Somehow, a glimmer of hope broke through her complacence; she reached over and forced herself to set the alarm. Tomorrow she had another job interview. Desperation crowded out the apathy. Constricted by overwhelming inner and outer darkness, Serena's breath became shallow. Her dry mouth and mounting anxiety muted her scream at life's injustice into a muffled croak. Tomorrow would come…nothing would change.

Survival. A day without struggle followed by a night of peaceful rest—why did achieving this seem so elusive? Agitated, she threw the bedcovers aside. How much longer could this torture go on? Awake and staring overhead, she felt every bit as broken as the glass shards. Her light within had all but extinguished itself, not unlike the fragile bulb. Could tomorrow be her first step out from the deep dark hole that hollowed her insides? Tomorrow she had another job interview.

She double-checked the alarm setting. Serena's fingertips ached as she desperately clung to the possibility of change.

Reaching into her bedside drawer, she randomly pulled out some meds and dry-swallowed two pills. Serena didn't look to check what they were; she kept four or five different sleep meds stashed there. Not that it mattered. None of them worked. Serena needed to speak to Dr. Jenkins about that. Sleep did not come easily to the twenty-one-year-old woman afflicted with anxiety, plagued by PTSD, her life in shambles.

Sometimes it seemed better to stay awake. Steadily worsening vivid nightmares had been infiltrating her dreams. She tossed and turned, trying to stave off the inevitable, trying to deceive herself that tonight the meds would work. Ensnared between apathy and hope, Serena nestled into a crevice of momentary comfort. Her breathing slowed; the cadence of soft snores interrupted the green stillness.

It felt cold in the cave. Even lying on the sleeping rug, the rock floor was hard. She shivered, more from fear than the cold. Why did her great aunt, her *shibízhí*, insist she sleep here alone tonight? She remembered her *shibízhí* saying with no moon the cave would be black. Serena blinked, but it didn't matter whether her eyes were open or closed; she couldn't tell the difference. Repeating and following her aunt's instructions, she crawled to the edge of the pool then stood up to her knees in the still water. *Keep your eyes open. Keep your eyes open.* Her *shibízhí* had said that was the most important thing, not to close her eyes. But she couldn't see anything. She wanted to be brave; she didn't want to disappoint her *shibízhí*, but she was scared. It was so dark.

That's when she saw something. It was just a blur, a smudge of light. Something glowed and slowly took shape—long and curved, it moved toward her. Immersed in blackness, water up to her knees, the creature moved closer. Wavelets rippled against her small trembling body. What was it? The creature glowed with the shape-shifting form of something. She strained her eyes. It looked like a… "No!" she screamed, shutting her eyes and not daring to move. "*Shibízhí, shibízhí*, help me!" There was no response, and then it touched her skin, curling around her leg.

Serena bolted up, heart pounding and sweating as she reached to turn on the bedside table lamp, but the broken light with its shattered bulb still lay on the floor. Partly yelling, partly sobbing, "Damn dream! Goddamned dream! Goddamned aunt! Eleven years and you still haunt me!"

She steadied herself by taking two more pills. Wide awake, lying in near total darkness and still terrified, she tried to fall back to sleep. Jaws clenched tight, trying in vain to stop her teeth from chattering; she shivered, gooseflesh covering her arms held close against her chest. *It touched me. It touched me. That's never happened before...*

"I note on your resume that you attended the University for three semesters. What was your major?" Her interviewer, Mr. Chalmers, drummed his fingers annoyingly on the wooden desk.

"Yes, that is correct. I was majoring in anthropology." She couldn't stop looking at his overgrown nose hairs.

His bushy eyebrows shot up a bit. "And why did you leave?"

"I dropped out." She felt herself begin to fidget.

"Why?"

"May I speak candidly, sir?" she asked, continuing when he nodded. "Because it was all a load of bullshit."

"Really." Mr. Chalmers frowned, his nose twitching along with the extruding hairs.

"Pompous professors living in their academic world of bullshit not teaching anything, just a big money-making scheme to put kids into massive debt." She bit her lip.

"I see; so you didn't want to incur the debt?" Disinterest settled over his face.

"No. I was on scholarship. I have a genius IQ. I just couldn't tolerate the environment."

"I see; let's move on. You previously worked for MaxxEezz," he fumbled with her resume, "for three months as a retail associate. Can we contact your former employer for a reference?"

"Probably not a good idea." She squirmed and shifted in her chair.

"Why is that?" The drumming stopped.

"I left because I was tired of my boss trying to put the moves on me. I told him I wouldn't sleep with him, and when he continued to pester me, I left. Their

HR department didn't buy my sexual harassment allegations. It might be awkward to contact them."

"How about this job at Zip-N-Go Convenience? You were a cashier; that requires some customer service responsibilities."

"That didn't work out."

"How so?"

"One, they were insensitive to my medical condition, and two, they wanted us to lie to the customers to try and get them to buy more junk food snacks, soda, and other overpriced garbage."

"You have an underlying medical problem?"

"Technically, you are not allowed to ask me about that, but since I brought it up, I'll lay it out for you. PTSD—Post-traumatic stress disorder—and no, I was not in the military and no, I don't want to talk about it any further." She knew she was sweating. She desperately needed to take some more medication.

"You know here at Delitz, we have a very progressive HR department." He studied her a moment, "We also require arm tattoos to be covered and no facial piercings; although, one earring per ear and a single nose stud are acceptable. What makes you think you can be an excellent hostess and employee?"

"I'm bright and I'm honest and willing to work hard."

"I can see that, Miss Mendez. We do have other candidates who have applied, so you can expect to hear back from us in a couple of days."

"Thank you!" She stood and muttered to herself, "That's pretty unlikely."

"Did I just hear what I think I heard—something about pretty unlikely?"

"Correct. You're not going to call. You're not going to hire me. I'm too in-your-face, and you probably can't wait for me to leave."

"Miss Mendez, why exactly are you here?"

"To continue my unemployment benefits, I must actively demonstrate a search for new employment. My counselor suggested this. I thought it could work out. It isn't my dream job in all honesty, but I thought it could put me in a position to reenter the employment rolls. Besides, I really do need a job."

"Miss Mendez," he stood, "I appreciate your candor, but let me give you some unsolicited advice. The world runs on dishonesty. You might keep that in mind at your next job interview."

❖   ❖   ❖

"Bombed another interview," she thumbed a text to Bryson, pretty much her only friend. She had managed to calm down a little.

"What next?" read his instant reply.

"Dunno." She sighed. "Investigative reporter for the weird and inexplicable? Poster child for the underachieving dysfunctional?"

"LOL. Glad you haven't lost your sense of humor or sense of determination. Maybe you can try stand-up comedy." There was a pause while she tried to think of something witty. A second text followed. "Going to meeting tonight?"

"Absolutely"

"Great, news to share, tell you later, hang in there."

"Later"

As she bicycled home, she wondered what news Bryson would spring. Had he hacked into the Pentagon or something? The guy was a genius, really a super genius. In the dictionary, next to the definition for genius, there could be a picture of him. Same picture next to super geek nerd—lanky, unkempt mousy brown curls, thick glasses. And, he was a hacker. He had won some speed coding competitions in his teens and finished MIT at age nineteen with degrees in software engineering and ancient history through a cooperative exchange with Harvard. He had patented some obscure switching technology and encryption coding software before finishing grad school at twenty-one and got recruited to work for Silicon Valley and then the government. That had lasted a couple of years until he quit working for the evil empire. Now he lived off-grid near Taos. She held her own given their mutual interest in anthropology and ancient history, but she couldn't keep up with him on the computer front. But he did have an edge—a photographic memory. They had met at the same group meeting as tonight, "Meta-conspiracies Uncovered."

When she got back to the small apartment on the outskirts of Santa Fe she called home, she made herself lunch and listened to her voice mail. Her outreach counselor at unemployment wanted to know how today's interview had gone. The book she requested on Mayan prophecies was ready at the library. Dr. Jenkins' office called to remind her of tomorrow's appointment. She ignored the calls from the vultures and scavenger bill collectors trying to bleed a bloodless stone and went to her tiny bedroom to catalog her prescriptions and determine what needed to be refilled.

There wasn't a speaker for the meeting, so they went around the room sharing the latest on different conspiracies and how they all connected. Jonas, one member of the group, was working on a lead dealing with chem-trails, geoengineering, and the use of HAARP. "You control the weather and you control the food supply. We need to expose this!"

"Speaking of food supply," Hannah, another member, chimed in, "there is a rally next month to get passage of GMO labeling and fight agribusiness. I'll email you all the details. We need to fight these bastards."

A pretty typical meeting colored by anger, paranoia, and a feeling of disempowerment well beyond David vs. Goliath ensued. Other than commiserating, little was actually accomplished.

"So, what's the connection? How are all these cover-ups and conspiracies related?" Bryson posed the question to the group.

"It's the military-industrial complex," someone shouted, "just like Eisenhower warned us."

Serena answered, "It's the cabal; the 0.1% of the 1%; they control everything, and they manipulate everything and everyone to suit their evil interests. We are at their mercy."

"I think you are close to the actual connection that joins all the problems and all the answers." Everyone listened intently; they all respected Bryson and his obvious intellect. "It's information, or rather misinformation, or even disinformation."

"What do you mean? Explain it." Ted asked on everyone's behalf.

"From ancient history to now, powerful individuals and groups have manipulated information, used propaganda and misinformation to confuse people, keep them ignorant, suppress dissent, and maintain power. This is nothing new. Look at what they did to Galileo, the Inquisition, Mary Magdalene, the Salem witch trials, Hitler's Ministry of Information. Shall I go on?" Heads nodded. "Now with technology and the World Wide Web it's orders of magnitude worse. People are inundated with information, the majority of which is distorted. It's not the information age so much as the disinformation age. How can people make truly informed choices when they are fed a steady diet of lies?"

"So, what you're saying," Serena spoke quietly, "is that control of information throughout history has manipulated public perception, shaped public opinion, all to advance the agenda of the powerful and influential."

"Pretty much. I would say that's the connection among all these conspiracies and cover-ups; that and the intention of keeping people ignorant, of withholding the truth," Bryson agreed.

"So, at an even deeper level," Serena interrupted animatedly; she'd just had an epiphany. "At the deepest level, it has to do with truth." She always considered herself to be totally honest and had deep respect for the truth. "It isn't so much a problem of powerful people and secret cabals and how they manipulate information to suit themselves. The real problem is that people cannot determine what is true and what isn't true."

Serena's insight energized everyone in the room. When the side conversations grew louder, Bryson cut in.

"Yes, Serena, I think you have gotten to the heart of things, or should I say," his blue eyes twinkled, "to the truth of it all." The room erupted in laughter.

"It isn't funny. What can we do about it? No offense," Ted said, turning toward Hannah, "but attending a demonstration isn't going to get to the truth underlying the failure to label."

Hannah responded, "You're right; you speak the truth." More laughter followed. "Maybe we need a technological answer, a technological solution. Google is supposed to connect everyone on the planet with information, but if it's misinformation, or people can't figure out truth from falsehood, Google actually makes it worse."

"Well, that's because Google is part of the problem, not the solution. Technically, they wind up amplifying the noise to signal ratio. But we don't have to figure it out tonight. Let's all give some thought between now and next meeting as to how to help people determine truth." It was Bryson who somehow seemed to have become the leader for their meeting that night.

"Wait." Again, Hannah spoke. "How about an app?" A bit of laughter quieted as they realized Hannah was serious. "Really! A phone app, a computer app—something to enable the user to tell if a bit of information was true or false. That would totally disable anyone who was trying to withhold truth and give power back to the common man."

No one replied. Small talk and chairs scraping the cracked linoleum signaled time for the meeting to adjourn.

"Did you know that the Visigoths founded Spain and Portugal?" They were seated in Starbucks. As Serena enjoyed a macchiato, Bryson expounded in typical fashion. "They were a Nordic tribe, along with the Ostrogoths from the area of present-day Eastern Germany. The Ostrogoths defeated the Huns but eventually were absorbed by the Lombards, another Germanic tribe, while the Visigoths went on to sack Rome. Hundreds of years later they were defeated by the Moors, but eventually they fought them off and established the Kingdom of Asturias which subsequently became Spain and Portugal."

"Well, I knew there was quite a bit of Goth influence in the region culturally, but I didn't know the connection." She savored her brew. "But surely the news that you hinted at in your text is more significant than your revelations about the Visigoths."

"Oh…almost forgot, another patent got approved today." He repositioned his glasses to the mirror indents atop his nose.

"Bry, that's awesome! What does that make, eighteen? We should celebrate; I'll buy the next round of coffee."

"Twenty-three actually and still counting; no way you're buying. Brilliant but impoverished you are." This last bit he said in Yoda-speak. "Tell me about your job interview."

"Not much to say." Serena recounted the details. "I'm too honest and it comes across in the interview. People have a hard time with it. Above all to thine own self be true. What can I say?" she shrugged.

"Yeah, no shit."

"The interviewer did say something interesting. He wanted to give me a little advice and said more or less that the world runs on dishonesty."

"He got that right. It's like what we were talking about at the meeting. Speaking of which, I liked your comments and how you saw through to the deepest truth."

"Thanks! It's a blessing and a curse." She smiled. Bryson always seemed to lighten her burdens.

"I also like what Hannah suggested—an app. It's all ones and zeros; what if one represented truth and zero represented false? I've got to think about it." He gazed into her gray eyes. "What's your next step?"

She looked down. "I don't know; the nightmares are getting worse." She told him about last night's dream.

"When is your next appointment with Dr. Jenkins?"

"Tomorrow."

"Maybe you need to go see your great aunt. Maybe you need to go to that cave to confront some kind of a demon. Maybe that should be your focus. Why don't you talk to your psychiatrist about it?"

Serena locked her eyes into his piercing gaze and said nothing. Part of her trembled at his suggestion. A droplet of sweat gathered over her eyebrow piercing. She would have wiped it, but a momentary paralysis seized her. Scrambling for tranquilizers, she downed them with a gulp, but her mouth remained dry with anxiety. Visiting her tormentor sounded like a bad idea.

2

The waiting room was crowded. Twice a month Dr. Carla Jenkins saw patients at the community health center. Not surprisingly, there were quite a few mental health issues among this group of economically disenfranchised; psych patients filled the waiting room. The tired and abused furnishings with ripped upholstery reflected the tired and abused occupants; lives in chaos and disarray, they stoically waited their turns. Serena fit right in. When her turn finally came, she was glad to leave the unpleasant smell that permeated the room.

The medical assistant took her four near-empty prescription bottles. "Could you ask Dr. Jenkins to give me a three-month supply? That way I can save on the co-payment," Serena asked hopefully, but the assistant's face gave her all the answer she needed.

"I'm certain she won't—too great of a suicide risk or potential to sell your prescription on the street. Just take a seat here, the doctor will be in soon."

"Right." She had barely spoken when the harried assistant, who didn't wear a name tag and had all the personality of a brick, exited. Serena perused the magazine rack—nothing was less than two years old: *Time, National Geographic, Popular Mechanics,* and *Sports Illustrated.* "Hmmm," she said out loud, "Which do I prefer—learning about football predictions from two years ago, or world events? It's a difficult decision; perhaps I should flip a coin." Sarcasm was a skill she had honed long ago, mostly for self-defense. A sharp tongue packed more punch than her 105 pounds could muster with her fists. Of late, even this had moderated; her idealism eroded under the assault of her marginalized life. In some ways, she hated this growing apathy. Even Dr. Jenkins' almost maternal encouragement couldn't penetrate Serena's growing indifference.

She selected the *National Geographic.* Despite the torn cover, the table of contents remained intact and the lead article on the Aborigines sounded potentially interesting. She had nearly finished the article when a knock preceded Dr. Jenkins' immediate entry. How the psychiatrist managed a smile puzzled Serena, but the fifty-plus woman seemed unperturbed by the chaos in the clinic. She clasped Serena's file, refreshed herself on elements of the record, and began to take notes. The clinic still used paper as a computerized system previously planned got axed with budget cuts.

"So, how have you been doing?"

Serena gave the psychiatrist an update on her PTSD symptoms, her use of meds and their effects, her recent failed attempts at getting a job, and finished by talking about her sleep, or more appropriately, her lack of sleep because of the nightmares.

"They are getting worse, and I must admit the poor sleep puts me even more on edge than usual."

Dr. Jenkins flipped back several pages. "Yes, so you have been telling me for the past three months. Your dreams are worse, more intense and detailed and naturally more frightening." She paused, "Why do you think that is?"

Serena shrugged, "I don't know, you're the psychiatrist."

Dr. Jenkins didn't immediately answer; instead, she put the chart down and stroked her chin a few times before she asked, "Would you stand up a moment and look in the mirror?" As instructed, Serena gazed at her image in the wall-mounted exam room mirror.

"What do you see?"

"I see a petite, brown-haired young woman, a bit androgynous looking with a few piercings and a lot of tattoos." She paused then added, "How am I doing so far?"

The psychiatrist ignored the quip, saying only, "Look past the physical to the mental and emotional image. Tell me what you see."

"This is uncomfortable."

A stern look met her response. "Try harder!"

"Okay, I see a pretty messed up person who has achieved little with her life despite being smart. I see someone who had a very traumatic episode when she was just an impressionable young girl, traumatized by someone she trusted. I see myself in all my miserable and messed up attempts to get my life together and I rely on medication to get through the day." She felt her voice rising but caught herself, took a breath, and looked at the doctor. "I thought you were supposed to help me feel better. In case you haven't noticed, this is not helping me to feel better."

"Precisely."

"What?"

"I said 'precisely,' and I meant it two ways—a double entendre; you should find that appealing. You can sit back down again, since honestly looking at yourself causes you such discomfort, a bit surprising since you hold honesty so near and dear."

Serena wanted to protest, but she found herself strangely relieved to have spoken so directly about herself and was curious by her doctor's intensity and the new approach.

"I said 'precisely' because you saw through to some of the mental and emotional turmoil that I also see, but there is more to peer through. I also used the word as a way to communicate that I agree with you that I am supposed to help you feel better. Now if you are up to it, get back in front of the mirror and listen to what I have to say when I look at you and tell me if you can see it as well."

The young woman felt paradoxically both reluctant and filled with anticipation gazing at her own image as her psychiatrist continued.

"Aside from your almost absurd physical similarity to that actress who starred in the movie, *The Girl with the Dragon Tattoo*—not the American version, the Swedish version; if you haven't already, you should see it, if you can bear subtitles. I don't remember the actress's name, but it doesn't matter. It's even more curious that a dragon is a winged serpent since obviously your nightmares involve a snake, but I'll get back to that in a moment.

"You are correct in your analysis of your native intelligence as well as your failure to succeed in life, which you relate to your PTSD. And yes, your great aunt was someone you trusted, and she broke your trust by leaving you alone in that dark cave at the tender age of ten. You left out that you have trust issues as a result, but you can see the connection."

Dr. Jenkins waited as Serena nodded. "Here's some more of what you left out. If you look deep down into the darkness within, we can hopefully shed some light there. You have used this difficult life event from your past to cast yourself as a victim and you play the role well. You have trouble with drugs and alcohol because you don't want to face that reality or to challenge that self-image. It's the same reason you dropped out of school. You have had a series of meaningless relationships in part because of the trust issue I just mentioned, but more so because you see yourself as messed up and don't want to inflict yourself on another person. Your baby brother died in a tragic auto accident when your mother was driving you to, of all things, a psychiatry appointment. Your parents split up afterwards which you harbor resentment and confusion about. Did they blame you? Do you blame yourself? Everyone wants to blame your great aunt."

Serena listened; her mouth felt dry making it difficult to swallow, but everything the doctor said rang true.

"It all boils down to something quite simple really. Can you see it?"

As Serena stared at her image, she tried to pierce through to the truth at the center of it all. Something was there, at the very center, but it was covered in darkness, concealed by something she herself had woven. Timidly, she imagined herself pulling back the cover to reveal the truth she'd tried so hard to ignore.

A small voice spoke. "I'm running away." It was as obvious as the nose on her face. "All these years I've been running away. All those years ago, I got broken and I've been so scared, so scared by everything, and I have just been running away from my life."

A tear rolled down Carla Jenkins face as she tenderly grasped Serena's hand and stood beside her. Serena watched the psychiatrist's image next to her own in the wall mirror.

"Yes, that's what I see too." Her voice grew quiet. "I know that must have been hard for you, but I think you'll be feeling better. Sit for a moment; there's just a little bit more I need to say."

As Serena sat back down, she felt lighter somehow. "I do feel better, kind of more comfortable in my own skin."

"I'm glad; it just seems we have been rehashing the same thing over and over during the three years since I first began treating you." She laughed. "One of the definitions of insanity is doing the same thing over and over again and expecting a different result. Today, we took a different approach." Seeing her patient nod in understanding, the doctor continued. "Now back to the snake." She pulled a textbook off a shelf in the exam room. "You see this symbol? Do you know what it's called?"

"Yes, it's a Caduceus; it's on a lot of medical advertising."

"Correct. The two intertwined snakes are a sign of healing. Snakes and serpents have a long history of representing not only healing and rejuvenation, but also wisdom. I'm sure you have come across some of this in your anthropology studies."

"A little."

"One other thing, caves can seem scary because they are dark and full of unknowns, but they are also places of shelter. In some creation mythology, the womb of Mother Earth is represented by a cave. We have demonized serpents and you have demonized your great aunt, but you never heard from her why she brought you to that cave. Maybe she had a good reason."

"What are you saying?"

"I'm saying maybe it's time for you to confront this demon instead of running away. I think you should go see your *shibízhí*. I think it would go a long way to your healing the brokenness you feel."

"That's kind of funny." Seeing her doctor's puzzled face, Serena added, "Bryson told me the same thing yesterday."

As the psychiatrist shelved the medical book, her face looked very earnest. "You should look up the word 'synchronicity' as it relates to Carl Jung. These kinds of occurrences, which you might call 'funny,' are serious. They are symbols and messages that happen all the time, but we often overlook them. They are quite serious, and you should pay close attention. I am even more convinced that you need to see your great aunt."

At that, Dr. Jenkins looked at her watch and began to exit adding, "The sooner the better."

Alone in the exam room, Serena stood up and stared again at her face in the mirror. She sighed and watched her lips as they silently whispered, "She's right."

3

The voice mail broke in after only one ring. "You have reached Bryson Reynolds, please leave a message."

"Hey, it's me; I've got a big favor to ask. Can I borrow your car for a couple of days? I can leave you mine. You'll be pleased to know I'm planning to go to Arizona, to the reservation where my great aunt lives. I don't think my car can make the trip; four-wheel drive is probably a better alternative on the reservation roads. Anyhow, give a call back either way."

Of course, if Bryson wasn't keen on the idea, it was the perfect excuse not to go. A conflict over this surfaced and she immediately felt the need to take some meds. *Doc seemed awful certain that I should do this ASAP. What did she say about Jung and synchronicity?* As she settled into her only comfortable chair, waiting to hear back from Bryson, tablet parked on her lap, she started to search on the net for more info.

She became totally engrossed as she dug into Jung's assertions. He believed there was a relationship between universal energy and the space-time continuum and synchronistic events, that seemed to be causally unrelated, actually were connected at higher levels of reality. It boiled down to a postulate claiming, "temporally coincident occurrences of acausal events" did have synchronous connections at higher levels of reality. In his book, *Synchronicity,* Jung described an event that demonstrated such a connection. It absolutely fascinated her.

As an analytical psychologist, Jung wrote about a session with a patient who revealed a dream she had the night before. In that dream, she received an expensive jewelry item in the design of a golden scarab. As she relayed the dream to the psychoanalyst, he heard something tapping on the window where he saw a large insect. He went to investigate, opened the window, and let the insect in. When he captured it, he noted it was a gold-green scarabaeid, similar in appearance to the golden scarab the woman described in her strange dream. This unusual occurrence led to a therapeutic breakthrough. Jung concluded this was no mere coincidence.

Serena respected Dr. Jenkins, so for the psychiatrist to claim both she and Bryson mentioning the need to see her *shibízhí* represented some kind of synchronicity wigged Serena out a little. She recalled both had used the expression, "confront her demon," and that was the part that freaked her out so much. What if there was some real demon, the creature in her dreams which she knew was a snake or serpent but could never come out and actually admit to herself? She shuddered and at that moment her phone rang; it startled her.

"Bry here, I got your message. That's fantastic! I'm glad you will finally get to the bottom of this stuff. So, when are you planning to leave?"

She sighed. "Dr. Jenkins recommended I go soon and not delay. I don't know, I feel a little conflicted but right now I'm thinking maybe even tomorrow. It's not like I have to go to work or have better plans. Do you know anything about synchronicities?"

"I'll let you use the car on one condition."

"Really! What's that?"

"I'm coming with you. No way I'd let you head out on this adventure by yourself. Don't you know Indian reservations are dangerous? Not that I can offer much protection, but a twenty-one-year-old woman by herself might be asking for trouble. They have their own laws on reservations; they are separate jurisdictions."

"I will not even try to talk you out of coming along. It will help to have someone to share the driving and to talk with." She added, "And the protection, of course."

He laughed. "Besides, I don't think my legs can fit in that little Fiesta you drive."

Breathing a sigh of relief, she said, "Thanks, Bryson; you really are a good friend. I'll buy the gas."

"Not a chance. I've got plenty of money and you don't so case closed."

"I owe ya big time."

"Now, you asked about synchronicities. I take it you refer to events such as the appearance of the scarab beetle while Jung counseled one of his patients and which he described as temporally coincident occurrences of acausal events. Furthermore, Jung postulated that such coincidences are connected at higher levels of reality. A meta-reality underlies and explains this acausal parallelism."

"Are you pulling this out from your eidetic memory bank?"

"It's in the bank now. I just pulled up the Wikipedia citation while we spoke. Damn interesting! Why do you ask?"

"It will be a long drive. I'll tell you all about it along the way. Is tomorrow okay?"

"I don't see why not. It's not like I have to go to work either. I figure about a seven-hour drive. How about you show up around 7:30–8:00 so we can get an early start? Should I pack anything special?"

She felt tempted to say something about garlic, a crucifix, and anything else he could think of to fight demons, but she kept the thought to herself. "Nothing special… I really appreciate this! I'll see you tomorrow."

A fog clouded her mind for the rest of the day as she prepared a pack with a change of clothes and a few personals. More than once, she caught herself muttering to herself; at other times, she trembled. She made sure to pack all her meds. For a moment, she panicked. *What if she doesn't recognize me? It's been eleven years since she last saw me and I was just a little girl then.*

In her closet, she found it at the very back—an old shoebox with family photos. Many times, she had wanted to burn the photo she now stared at; her hands shook. She, just a little girl in jeans and a T-shirt, a big smile on her face, with her *shibízhí* showing a stern lined face in traditional Navajo garb and piercing eyes. Then, she almost lost it as she rummaged to find a magnifying glass. Placing the picture on a flat well-lit surface, she focused the magnifier over her aunt's brooch and shuddered. It was a large beetle! *OMG, what am I getting in to?*

Something even stranger happened that night—she slept without any nightmares. Serena could not recall the last time she had slept peacefully through the entire night, but no dreams, nothing haunted her sleep. She woke feeling well rested and strangely determined.

❖   ❖   ❖

She was certain Bryson knew she had arrived, not by the pleasant crunch of gravel as she slowed her car but because the guy had thousands of dollars of security, all subtle and hidden. When she approached the front door, his voice greeted her over a speaker.

"C'mon in, PTG; it's open." PTG was his nickname for her. It stood for ponytail girl, a name he still used even though she had cut off her ponytail a couple of years ago.

She held out a bag with two cups and a couple of scones from Badass Brew, a local coffeehouse with a name that said it all. "I come bearing gifts." She smiled. "It's the least I can do."

"Good thing you're not Greek. Nothing like some Badass Brew to kick-start the day. Let's drink it here; it's still early, so we should have plenty of time."

Nibbling on her scone, she looked around. From her seat in this breakfast nook, everything looked rather ordinary, modest even. The main part of the house, which was hidden from this vantage point, looked more like mission control at NASA: banks of monitors with screens showing satellite locations, weather conditions, and who knows what else. Bryson had explained it to her once until seeing her eyes glaze over he simply summarized,

"There is a lot I can do here and remain covert. I've got my own power, the satellite dishes I can use not only to track but to bounce signals off of weather satellites, military satellites, and so on. I can pirate signals, scramble and randomize my IP addresses, etc. I have dummy accounts all over the world that are nearly untraceable. Other than my overly large solar array, my footprint is minimal, almost invisible. And that's the way I like it and intend to keep it."

When he had shown her the mainframe, almost equivalent to a supercomputer, down below ground in what the builders had thought was a generous wine cellar, it felt cool. She remembered he had made her put something over her head and wear a gown and gloves. There had even been a negative pressurized antechamber to prevent dust—totally high tech. He hadn't shown her to boast or show off. She had asked, and he obliged. Most of it she really could not grasp the full utility for. From her view, Bryson was absolutely a do-gooder, and in her heart she knew this was how he felt he could do the most good without serving someone else's agenda.

"Snowman, why do you have so much hi-tech security?" The question just blurted out of her mouth between sips of coffee. Her nickname for him had nothing to do with snow and everything to do with Edward Snowden.

"That's a long story; it's something else we can discuss on the car ride. We should probably hit the road."

Once they'd finished breakfast, they packed up the car, a white Subaru Legacy Outback about four or five years old. That was another thing she liked about Bryson—despite being wealthy, he was anything but pretentious. He claimed he was shy and didn't like to call attention to himself.

Activating the security system, he smiled and commented, "You never know when it might snow." Considering this was June, their hottest month in the high desert, she understood his meaning.

Entering the car, Bryson programmed the navigation assistant and Serena took the wheel. "I'll tell you what; I'll go first since you're driving. When we switch, you can tell me about your great aunt and the synchronicity stuff you mentioned yesterday."

"That's great." She smiled. "But don't tell me anything too top secret. If I ever get tortured, I don't want to spill the beans." In the corner of her eye, she saw that he didn't find her comment funny.

4

"I n all honesty, there is a lot about me you don't know. Even more troubling, there is stuff about me that I don't know." He adjusted the passenger seat position to full back.

They were on route 570 headed Southwest toward Espanola. "I'm all ears."

"For one thing, your cave dreams with the snake somehow draw me in. When I was eight years old, I got bit by a snake and almost died. They gave me antivenom shots. My parents said that's what saved me. I was in a coma for days. When I woke up, I had a photographic memory. No one could explain why. Before that, I had been just a normal kid, smart but nothing spectacular. After that, they started calling me a child prodigy. Strange, you would think I should be afraid of snakes, but I'm not."

She nodded but offered no comment, so he continued. "I went to special schools in New York where we lived. My parents were well off. My father worked for a multinational corporation doing international financing; they did business all over the world. You probably thought most of my money is from my patents and work I have done myself, but I actually inherited most of it. Reynolds International is a Fortune 500 company and I'm sure you've heard of them. My father was head of one of their finance divisions and he was also a bank vice president for one of their subsidiaries."

"I knew your parents were dead; you once told me they died in a plane crash. I don't see how this ties in to why you're so concerned about security."

"I'm getting to that." He sighed. "The bank's headquarters were in Switzerland, but they had offices throughout the world. My father often flew to Zurich and London, although he was based in New York. Sometimes my mother traveled with him to a few of these destinations—she had grown up in a small town in Idaho and hadn't traveled much before she met my dad; that's another story, how they met and all.

"When I was thirteen, my father had a trip to Zurich after which he had meetings in Singapore. My mom had never been there, and he rarely traveled to Asia, so they thought why not use the opportunity to have a little vacation." He grabbed a water bottle and took a few gulps. "They never made it to Singapore; their plane crashed. It was a private corporate jet and they never found any wreckage."

"I'm sorry, I didn't realize you were only thirteen when they died. That must have been hard, not having any real closure."

"It gets better; or should I say it gets worse?" An uncharacteristic grim look marred Bryson's face. "At the funeral, a man I had never seen before and never saw again gave me an envelope very surreptitiously and whispered I should open it later. Inside was a note from the State Department, signed by the Secretary of State expressing condolences. There was a medal for honorable service. I still have it along with the letter; unmistakably, there was something clandestine about the whole thing."

"Wait a minute; are you saying you think your father was a spy?"

He shrugged his shoulders. "Seems pretty plausible; what would you think?"

"I don't know—sounds suspicious. Do you think someone murdered him?"

"There's more so I don't want to answer that just yet.

"The estate lawyers handled financial things and I wound up with a lot of money," he continued. "I don't have any brothers or sisters. My mother's sister, Dottie, got a lot of money as well; that was her only sibling. She was living in New York at the time, but less than a year later, Aunt Dottie and I moved to New Mexico. I was still attending special schools and didn't spend a lot of time here, but it became my legal residence. I remember what she said when we moved: 'It's safer there.'"

"It doesn't sound like she was talking about street crime in New York. Did you ever ask her about why she made that comment?"

"Plenty of times, but she always refused to talk about it. It's strange!"

"I'll say. She still doesn't want to discuss it?"

"My Aunt Dottie died. She never married but there wasn't anything suspicious about her death—leukemia. By the way, she lived off-grid as well and had a lot of home security including guns. When she passed away, I was only sixteen and again I inherited a good deal more money. My Aunt Dottie was pretty frugal; that she claimed came from growing up poor in Idaho.

"I would like to say that the story ends there, but there's more, and it's more than peculiar. You may be getting a sense about why I am concerned about security and surveillance. It actually provoked me into studying software programming, especially encryption. I don't have any guns, but I'm all for a Taser and always carry one." His hand dropped over his front pocket.

"Hold it right there." She pulled into a fast food lot. "That coffee has given me a badass bladder screaming for relief."

When she returned, he took a sip of water. "Where was I? Yeah, I got heavy into coding, won some speed coding competitions and apparently got myself on the radar in regard to programming skill. In retrospect, that's not where I wanted to be. I worked for cybersecurity for a big Silicon Valley firm that did a lot of contracting for the Department of Defense. That led to recruitment by good old Uncle Sam. I didn't like what I saw, so you know I left after less than two years. I'm not violating any oaths telling you this by the way."

Serena nodded. "Don't worry, nothing you've told me thus far would land you in jail for treason even if they water-boarded me to extract the intelligence." She smiled, but again noted he did not.

"This shit is not funny; believe me, and I don't think they would stop at waterboarding. That's why I am deliberately leaving certain things out but let me finish; I'm almost done.

"When I worked at DoD, I had mid-level security clearance which gave me access to certain things; more importantly, I could get into certain secure servers. My security clearance and access improved after I transferred to NSA. I was always interested in learning everything I could about my parents' plane crash, but everywhere I searched using everything at my disposal for release of public documents, contacting the company where my father worked, even pulling strings with relatives at Reynolds—everything came up with next to nothing. I always believed the investigation into the crash was superficial at best."

"So, you think there was some sort of cover-up?"

"Absolutely! Anyway, I developed some code, almost impossible to trace back to me, and began to poke into restricted databases. I found a file on my father and the plane crash, but I couldn't open it and I couldn't save it to try to open at my home. If I could have just opened it, my photographic memory could have stored the info, but no such luck. When I went a second time, the file had disappeared, not a trace, like it never existed. You can say whatever you want, but I came to my own conclusions. Somebody is hiding something and if that somebody ever comes looking for me, I want to be hard to find and as prepared as possible.

"Long story, but there you have it." He drained the last of the water and she watched as his prominent Adam's apple slid down and back up his long neck. He looked drained as he crushed the plastic bottle.

"Wow! I had no idea."

5

They were passing Abique. Serena loved this stretch of road—Georgia O'Keeffe country where the landscapes and the skyscapes were spectacular, a marvel to behold. Lost in a reverie of natural wonder, a message beeped over Bryson's cell breaking the spell. He pulled out his phone, a look of concern etched on his face.

"Trouble, Snowman?"

"Can you pull over for a few minutes?"

She watched, not asking any questions as he reached to the back seat, got his backpack and pulled out his laptop, another phone, and a bag with computer chips. Bryson used the other phone to set up a mobile hot spot, downloaded something to his laptop from the phone which messaged him, then worked diligently. She could see how intently he focused and continued watching as he then uploaded commands, hit send, and then powered down his computer. The final step was the most intriguing as he replaced the SIM cards in both phones. A smug smile graced his face which somehow looked more geeky than usual. He packed up his gear and placed his backpack on the rear seat. The entire scene lasted less than ten minutes.

"Okay, we can proceed."

"Would it be out of the question for you to tell me what just happened?"

"Not at all. Simply put, I got a message that a bot had penetrated an outer firewall on one of my overseas servers."

"That doesn't sound good."

"Don't worry, not a serious threat as far as I'm concerned. In fact, I know all about the compromised security and specifically allowed the breach. It takes a reasonably sophisticated attack to get through, but I am more interested in how it was done and who might have done it."

"You're kidding, right? You are saying this server is out there as bait?"

"You can think of it that way. That at least is one purpose. Anyway, I had to quarantine the infiltration and restore the firewall. I could program the server to do it automatically, but I am more interested in seeing if they track the message and the upload. That's why I changed out the SIM cards. The download went to one phone's identification." He held out the receiving phone. "The upload came from a different location. Missoula, Montana if I'm not mistaken. I'll analyze the attack back home to decide if the SIM cards are still any good. I had you pull over because we had a good signal to set up a secure hot spot and I didn't want any broken connection."

Serena stared at him with even more respect. "You obviously know what you are doing. I guess that's how you remain a ghost. I'm impressed!"

"Actually, PTG, I am readily visible, but only as far as I want people to see. Too invisible is an immediate red flag. So, I have a credit card which I use for gas, groceries, and an occasional sundry that I order online. But I use cash frequently and charge up prepaid cards with cash for big purchases like sophisticated hardware. I want to appear pretty normal to anyone who scrutinizes my habits, where I go, what I spend money on, etc. I'm not paranoid, but I like to stay a few steps ahead of the bad guys."

After several miles of silence, he spoke again. "I'm not saying you should or you shouldn't, but you might want to have me deactivate the GPS locator in your phone. It's an easy way for outside parties to track you. Another thing, I would avoid Facebook, Instagram, Twitter, and pretty much any social networking. The data being collected on you and about you is mind-boggling and most people are giving it out without a second thought."

"You're right." A momentary pause followed before she added, "It would probably be worthwhile mentioning it to our conspiracy group, maybe even give a little class demo on how to deactivate tracking. Don't want anybody tracking us."

"Good suggestion. How about we switch?" As Bryson adjusted the seat position to accommodate his long legs, he looked at their location. "Another five hours and we should be there. Is that enough time to tell me about your aunt?"

"Well, I'll have to talk fast... Hah! In truth, it's pretty brief. My *shibízhí*, that's the Navajo word for a paternal aunt, was the sister of my father's mother. My grandfather was Mexican. He took his wife, my father's mother, from the reservation. I gather that caused some hard feelings, but truthfully, my *papi* never talked about his family other than his aunt; as far as I know, she's his only living relative. My grandparents died before I was born. Papi didn't seem all that close to his aunt, but I think she gave him some sense of being connected to his roots. Sometimes she would come and visit with us, stay a few days and leave. Once a year, we would go to visit with her."

"What was she like? What do you remember about her?"

"I liked her; she had a sort of composure and strength and seemed very wise. It's hard to say how old she was; when you are little, everybody looks old, especially if your skin is all creased from being out in the sun. And believe me, her skin was really creased; I can show you a picture later. My mother didn't care much for her; I almost think she was afraid. Back then, and this sure has changed, I wasn't afraid of anything.

"My *shibízhí* never married. She seemed to have some special status, a healer or something. She knew a lot about plants and botanicals, and I loved just walking around with her. She had stories about all the different plants and animals and taught me quite a lot about Navajo culture. Most of it I've forgotten, or maybe repressed, but I think she got me interested in anthropology, myths and cultures. I remember one thing she always used to say to me—'Someday, my little *ch'osh bikq'í*, someday all these things you will understand.' She always sounded so mysterious when she said it too."

"It sounds mysterious. What does it mean?"

Serena giggled. "*Ch'osh bikq'í?* That means lightning bug."

Bryson laughed in response then thought a moment. "Hey, that's a kind of beetle too. You're still going to tell me more about synchronicities, right?"

"Sure, but let's do one story at a time." She continued. "In the summer when I was ten, she asked if I could stay with her on the reservation for a week. I don't think my mother was too thrilled about it, but I think both my parents thought it would be great to have a week together for just the two of them. At the time, I was really excited." Serena halted; a lump caught in her throat.

Bryson looked over at his friend to make sure she was okay. "I take it we are getting up to the cave part of the story. Are you sure you're all right?"

Nodding, she composed herself and continued. "It was both the best week and the worst time of my life; at least, that's how it ended. Until the last night it was great. We hiked to different spots on the reservation. She talked to me about different aspects of Navajo life, stories about so many different things. We slept out under the stars. I wanted to move to the reservation and live like a true-blooded Native American. The next to last night, we stayed at a little shelter she had made; *Shibízhí* said it was a power place where the earth spirits crossed near the surface. I can't say for sure, but I remember having strange dreams that night—dreams with talking animals and spirits. When I told my aunt, she just nodded, and I remember exactly what she said.

"'They come to prepare you. Tomorrow is very special.'

"That was it, exactly what she said and nothing more. When I asked what she meant, she just looked at me, raised a finger to her lips saying nothing, but made a faint hissing sound."

"Wow, I thought my story was intense, but you got me beat. I almost can't wait to meet your *shibízhí*."

"The next day we hiked a few miles to a spot near a big cottonwood tree. It was solitary, not a single other tree anywhere near, and I thought that was a little strange. I can still see the tree in my mind with its strange bent limbs. My aunt said it stood as a guardian. When I asked her what it was guarding, she pointed to a rock outcrop and told me there was a cave opening between the rocks; it was a sacred cave and I would sleep there that night.

"As you can imagine, I thought that was totally awesome until she said I would sleep there alone while she slept close by under the tree."

"Were you afraid?"

"At first I wasn't, until it came to dusk and we went into the dim cave. There was a pool of water and I drank from it. Water in the desert is special, and this was the most beautiful water I ever had. My *shibízhí* had a burning bowl and lit an herb mixture; I know some of it was tobacco because she told me that was one of their sacred plants. The whole cave had a weird dark smokiness at that point. She gave me a Navajo rug and said it had been her grandmother's, that it contained special sleeping magic, and that when I got tired, I should just go to sleep. If I woke up, I should go and stand in the pool and remember to keep my eyes open. She said it would be very dark because there was no moon that night.

"I was a little afraid when she left, but there was still some light and I was already feeling tired, so I figured I would probably go to sleep and see her in the morning. I trusted her.

"Again, I remember exactly what she said—'Do not be afraid, our Mother Earth has blessed you and this cave belongs to her. You are safe here in her arms.'

"She kissed me and left. I was all alone. I still wasn't too afraid, so I lay down, stared at the cave ceiling and eventually I must have gone to sleep. When I woke up it was pitch black and then I was terrified, but I did just what my *shibízhí* had told me. I crawled over to the water and stood up to me knees. After that…"

Bryson saw the ashen white look and beads of sweat on Serena's face and forehead. "That's okay." He reached over and held her hand. She squeezed back. "You don't have to tell me the rest of that part. You told me the latest dream just a couple of days ago."

She inhaled and exhaled deeply, and the moment seemed to pass. Releasing his hand, Serena muttered, "Right, yeah, don't need to go over that part again." The sip of water did nothing to moisten her dry mouth and tongue. For a few minutes they drove in silence until Serena picked up the story. "There isn't much else anyway. My aunt came to the cave, lit a candle, calmed me down, and I tried to go back to sleep next to her under that big cottonwood. When she took me back home and my parents heard she had left me alone in a pitch-black cave, there was a big argument with a lot of yelling, mostly between my parents. I just remember my *shibízhí* looked very sad; she didn't say much. My folks broke off all further contact with her and that was the last time I saw my aunt.

"I think you know the rest—how my parents blamed my *shibízhí* for traumatizing me, they blamed her for messing up my life and then kind of blamed me for my baby brother's death. They really were not a happy couple to begin with and things got worse. After they split up, I lived with my mother, but truthfully, we did not have a close mother-daughter relationship. It's funny, but now when I think about it, my great aunt was really the only adult I felt close to as a child growing up. I should talk to Dr. Jenkins about that. Anyway, when I turned eighteen, neither of my parents wanted to have much to do with me so I have pretty much been confined to screwing up only my own life."

"Why do you say things like that? You had some early childhood trauma, some tragedy, and it sounds like a dysfunctional home life. You're smart; you're pretty; you shouldn't put yourself down so much." Then he added, "*Ch'osh bikq'i.*"

Serena wasn't sure, but she thought she felt herself blushing. "Thanks, you're a good friend! Do you mind if we just drive for a bit? I'm feeling a little talked out."

After a few miles, Bryson offered, "How about some music?"
"Sure."

He turned the audio on and selected from his mpeg library—the best of the Beatles. As *Sergeant Pepper's Lonely Hearts Club Band* played in the background, she looked over and saw his huge grin extending all the way to either side of his thick glasses.

"Very funny! Did you think I would conclude Beatles' music was another synchronicity? Or are you just subtly telling me you want to hear more about Carl Jung?"

"I can listen to Beatles' music anytime, but to be imprisoned in my own car, forced to drive in silence when I am sitting next to such a talented weaver of tales—patience is not my strong suit."

"Okay, you win." She turned down the volume. "Dr. Jenkins said caves can be scary, but they are also places of refuge and protection and that although we think of snakes as evil, in many instances snakes represent healing and wisdom. She then suggested I go and see my aunt, but she said the same thing about confronting a demon as you had told me the other night. That's what led to her connecting the dots as a synchronicity. Which reminds me; I have to show you this picture because there is another synchronicity."

As she reached to the back to gather her pack and rummaged to find the old photograph, Bryson spoke. "I was doing more reading about Jung since our conversation, especially about archetypes. It sounds to me as though your *shibízhí* is a sort of wise woman archetype, a priestess or healer of some type."

"You could be right, but I haven't done the scholarly research you have. Okay, Mr. Genius, what kind of archetype are you?"

"Oh, that's easy. I know I don't look the part, but when I was young, I was big into swords and quests and stuff. When I got an alchemy stone playing *Zelda,* I thought I was the cat's meow. Try not to laugh, but I am most definitely a warrior archetype." He looked at Serena waiting for her response but missed her suppressed laughter.

"Got it! I was afraid I left it behind," she exclaimed triumphantly. "Here, look at this picture. Look at my aunt's brooch; I swear it's a beetle. This photo was taken just when we started the week together that I told you about. That's gotta be a synchronicity."

Bryson grabbed the old picture, studied it a moment, then nearly swerved off the shoulder. "That's your aunt?!" He slammed on the brakes and pulled off the road, held the photo and just stared at it.

"WTF? Yes, that's my *shibízhí*. And that's me," she pointed, "the cute little girl."

Bryson turned to Serena totally serious as he looked right at her. "Do you remember me telling you about getting bitten by a snake and being in a coma?" She nodded. "I have seen this woman before; I cannot forget her face and even if I didn't have a photographic memory, I would not forget her face. When I was in a coma, I had a lot of strange dreams and she was in all of them, singing, chanting, speaking in a language I couldn't understand. That was her, I'm sure of it. When I told my parents about it, they just said it was hallucinations. How can this be? Serena," he grabbed her hand again, "how could this woman that I will now see later today be the same person who came to me when I almost died?"

"I don't know. It seems like a very, very powerful synchronicity." She held his hand and looked into his blue eyes. "I guess you have some questions of your own to ask her about."

6

They tried to make small talk—the weather, movies, politics, but they kept coming back to the same topic. How could it be that Serena's Navajo great aunt, whom Bryson had never met in person, had appeared in his dreams when he was comatose? They tried to listen to music. For a stretch, Serena relayed some of what she remembered from one of her anthropology classes she had taken on Southwest Native American culture; that seemed to be a good distraction. A hundred miles later it still made no sense. The tenor of the trip had taken an even more serious tone, accentuated by ominous thunderclouds massing west, directly in view as they pulled off the road to refuel and grab lunch. But the unspoken questions weighed on Serena's mind. How did her aunt connect to Bryson and what role did she play in his life? What purpose underlay the cave experience that till now seemed to have caused a death of sort in the wise woman's niece? And, most mysterious of all, was there a link between Bryson and Serena that neither understood?

They traveled past Shiprock, located on the Navajo reservation but still in New Mexico. The entire reservation spread over parts of four states which included Utah, Colorado, and Arizona. They were headed to Kayenta, in northern Arizona, still about an hour and forty-five minutes away.

"Do you think we're in for some rain?" Serena picked at her lunch; they had stopped at a no-name burger shack adjacent to a gas station and sat outside.

Bryson looked around and noted the wind had picked up. "Doubt it. This will probably blow over us. Unusual for rain this time of year, not to say it wouldn't be welcome. I look at weather patterns along with my satellite tracking." He had finished and got up to stretch his long legs. "I'm gonna use the restroom and pick up extra bottles of water so why don't you chill for a few before we head on."

"Well, Mr. Weatherman, looks like you were right." They were back on the road with Serena behind the wheel. Sunshine and blue sky filled the windshield as they continued west, now on Rt. 160 in Arizona, just past Teec Noc Pos.

"Have you figured out how we're going to find her? You don't have an address or anything, do you? Do you even know your *shibízhí's* name?"

"It's on the back of the photo. Kayenta's not that big and people know one another. We'll ask around; I'm sure we can find her."

Bryson flipped the photo over. On the back, still legible even through faded ink he read, "Ooljee and Serena, summer 2008". Turning the photo over, he studied it some more, then shook his head. "You look so happy in this photo."

"I was…" They drove the next hour in silence.

"We're here." She parked along a stretch with a few stores. "It looks quite a bit built up from what I remember." They stopped in a few establishments, showed the picture, but had no luck even though the folks were friendly. Serena simply said she had a great aunt who lived here, but she hadn't seen her in over ten years and didn't have an address.

"Do you know what clan she's from?" a middle-aged woman named Dorothy asked. Serena didn't know. "Why don't you try the tribal police? Captain Forrest Nez has been here a long time. He would probably know. Or try Angie in the Trader's Way."

"Where is that?" Dorothy turned her head to the right and pursed her lips. "Thanks!"

"What was that?" Bryson looked a little confused.

"What?"

He mimicked the head turn and lip motion.

"Oh. It's rude to point. She was just showing me where the shop was located. Look, here we are." Instead of pointing to the storefront sign for "Trader's Way," Serena made an exaggerated puckering and kissing motion with her lips.

"Got it." He nodded.

"Oh, and another thing, when you talk to people, try not to look directly at them. That's another thing I remember my aunt telling me is rude. I'm sure many young Navajos don't abide by the old customs, but I don't want to disrespect anyone."

"Got it. No staring, no eye contact. I'll just let you do the talking."

They entered a small and neat shop. As they scanned an assortment of jewelry, beadwork, and some pottery items, an older woman approached them.

"We're looking for Angie. We hope she might help us find a relative."

"You have found Angie; perhaps she can help. *Ya-ta-hey*."

Startled a moment, Serena replied. "*Ya-tah*," then turned to whisper to Bryson, "it's the traditional Navajo greeting."

The elder woman smiled slightly. "How can I assist; who is this relation?"

Serena explained that she was looking for her *shibízhí* whom she had not seen in over ten years and added that she didn't know the clan, but she did have a picture.

Dressed in traditional garb, the shopkeeper had a refined elegance. As Serena retrieved the photo, the woman stood by patiently. There were no other customers in the shop, so she gave the two visitors her full attention.

Placing the photo on a jewelry display counter, Serena said, "I am the little girl in this photo, and standing next to me is my *shibízhí*; her name is Ooljee."

When the elder woman took a quick look at the picture, she gasped, visibly upset. She rushed over to open the door. "You do not speak that woman's name!"

Confused by the complete change in countenance and seeing the shopkeeper by the open door pointing with her lips indicating that they should leave immediately, Serena took the photo. As the two left, the shopkeeper stood sternly at the door. "*Tł'iishtsoh*!"

They exited, not sure how or why they had offended the woman, but they thanked her, and Serena asked, pleaded, "Do you know who we could ask?"

Angie had softened a bit, she looked more afraid than anything else and eager for the two to leave. "Try Captain Nez, at the Tribal Police." Her stance made it clear that she had nothing further to say.

"That was very weird! I'm just saying. Do you have any idea what just happened in there? She looked a little spooked," Bryson stated.

"I don't know, Bry. I can only handle so much intrigue in one day. Honestly, I need to take some meds. A shot or two of tequila would be even better, but alcohol is forbidden on the res." They returned to the car and got the directions using Serena's smartphone—less than a mile away. "It's been a very strange day already and something tells me it's going to get worse."

7

They parked in the lot for the Navajo Tribal Police, Kenyata Substation. The building looked fairly dilapidated, but there was a sign in front: "Moving to Public Safety Facility this Summer." Inside the station, they needed a moment for their eyes to adjust from the bright sunlight. At a desk behind a counter, a woman, possibly a receptionist, looked engrossed in her work. To her right, a man dressed in a khaki uniform stood photocopying something. His back was to them, but he looked to be in his mid to late thirties, same as the woman.

"May I help you?" the woman's voice greeted them. Her name tag said, "Suzie Yazzie."

"We are hoping to speak to Captain Forrest Nez; is he available?"

She looked back at an office behind her, through a glass side panel. "He's on the phone. What is this regarding?"

As Serena explained their quest to locate a relative, she took out the picture but held it back a moment. The man at the copier had stopped copying and listened intently. Suzie Yazzie took the photo, looked at it for a moment, but said nothing. She brought it back to the uniformed man, whispered something and motioned with her lips. She and the man turned, and he met Bryson and Serena at the counter.

"I'm Officer Cuch…Sam Cuch," He held out his hand and smiled. Two teeth were missing. "I'm sorry, the woman you're looking for is no longer here."

Serena's mind raced. *What did that mean, no longer here? Had she moved? Was she dead?* Before she could ask, the office door behind Sam Cuch opened and a much older uniformed man, built like a tree stump, stepped out. His badge read, "Captain Forrest Nez."

Officer Cuch spoke rapidly in Navajo to his superior officer and showed him the photo. He motioned toward Serena, said something and they both laughed while Suzie nodded silently.

"Okay Sam, I'll take it from here." Captain Nez lifted a section of counter and invited them to his office. He shook their hands with a firm handshake; he looked like a man who had seen a lot, much of it not good. Serena immediately liked him. They settled into the only two chairs and looked at the cramped space full of papers, reports, a map on the wall, and an old computer. He pulled a manila file from a file drawer behind the desk and withdrew a paper and a large envelope with the words, "Serena Mendez."

"We appreciate your time today, Captain. I have a few questions, but if I just might ask, what was so funny out in the front office?" Serena paused.

"Oh, I should apologize, Ms. Mendez. Officer Cuch thinks you are too skinny to be Navajo and Suzie apparently agrees. But in truth, there is nothing today that should bring amusement."

He showed them the paper he had withdrawn from the file, a sketched drawing, a rather remarkable likeness of Serena. As she sat in front of him, her jaw dropped in amazement; he added, "She said you would show up eventually. And when you did, I should give you this." Handing over the thick envelope, the one with her name on it, and Serena's picture, he said, "I'm sorry to have to be the one to tell you this; your *shibízhí* lost her wind… By that I mean, she is no longer alive."

Captain Nez continued to talk, but Serena heard none of it through her stunned disbelief. She grabbed Bryson's hand, swooned, leaned forward and her head bumped the surface of the desk as she lost consciousness.

"Suzie, Suzie, can you get some water? Our guest has fainted."

Bryson gently stroked her face. "Hey, PTG...it's okay...it's okay." He faced the Captain. "I think she's coming out of it."

Sipping the water, color returning to her ashen face, Serena composed herself. "Captain, I'm sorry, but did you just tell me Ooljee passed away?" She swallowed.

The Captain cringed. "Please, Ms. Mendez, it is best not to say the name of one who has crossed to the spirit realm. In our tradition, this is best; especially for one such as your great aunt. Many thought she was *tł'iishtsoh*."

"That's the same word the shopkeeper at Trader's Way used. What does it mean?" Bryson asked. Serena looked almost back to normal, so he sat back down.

"Angie? Yes, that would be a word she spoke; I hope you did not name your *shibízhí* in her shop."

"Too late," Serena replied.

He chuckled. "She is probably burning sage and doing a cleansing ceremony as we speak."

"She didn't look happy; actually, she looked a little scared. I didn't mean to offend her."

"Some believe you invite the spirit of a dead person to the place where you name them. The word means ‹dragon.' Most of the time, it refers to an unpleasant old woman and is not complimentary. In your aunt's case, the true meaning went much deeper. A dragon is a winged serpent. Many here believe she was a serpent worshiper, a witch of sorts, maybe even a skin-changer."

"Wait a minute. Please, Captain, slow down. First you tell me my aunt is dead, now you are saying she was a witch. Just so you know, I suffer from PTSD and this is really hard for me." Despite sips of water, her mouth remained dry.

Bryson chimed in. "It's true, Captain Nez, she is on medication. Perhaps we can find out a little more about when and where the woman I won't name lived and died."

"Yes, yes, of course." The burly officer continued. "She used to live close to town, but about ten years ago, she moved out twenty miles or so, closer to Shonto, not too far from the Navajo National Monument. She lived in a hogan there, pretty remote, sort of a recluse. There's a trading post in Shonto and I know she left some pawn there, so you should make sure to pick it up. I used to visit every month just to check on her; she was old; it's in my district."

Serena stood and looked out the grimy window. "When is the last time you saw her?"

"Four months ago, I stopped by. That's when she gave me that envelope and picture." He motioned with his lips. "When I went by three months ago, I found her lying outside. It was strange because I always remember her meeting me inside, tea usually already made as if she expected me. Anyway, can't say how long she had been dead, being out there in the hot sun and all. I would guess a couple of weeks; hard to say. Another funny thing, the crows, vultures, coyotes—nothing had picked at her. Out here, that's a might unusual."

"What did she die from? Was an autopsy done?" Bryson asked.

The captain's broad shoulders shrugged. "Don't know. No sign of foul play; everything in her hogan still intact. Unless something looks suspicious, the Feds—they have jurisdiction for homicides—don't care; it's a tribal matter. All the better Feds weren't interested. We view autopsies as a desecration. Just so you know, she got a traditional sacred burial; I made sure of that."

"Thank you, Captain Nez, for that kindness. Is there any chance you can give us directions to her hogan?"

"Better yet, I'll take you there. I've got to head out to Shonto anyway and it's just a brief detour."

"One last thing, Captain." Serena held the sketched likeness of herself in her hands. "I hadn't seen my *shibízhí* in eleven years. How do you figure she could draw this picture?"

"Ms. Mendez, I've been at this job near forty years and I've seen quite a few things I can't explain. In this instance, I can tell you only what I think. You can believe me, or you can think I'm crazy; it's not going to change what I believe." He paused and made eye contact with Serena before saying with all seriousness, "I don't think your great aunt was a witch." He shook his head. "I think she was a dreamwalker."

They got up and left the office together.

"Suzie, I'm off to Shonto; you can reach me on the radio."

Heading to the parking lot, both feeling dazed, Bryson turned to Serena. "When did you say your nightmares began to get worse?"

She looked past her friend, past the buildings and sparse trees to the mountains far in the distance. "About three months ago."

8

F ollowing the NTP patrol car proved to be easy; the well-paved road had hardly any traffic.

"I'm sorry about your *shibízhí* passing—sorry for both of us, since I had some things I wanted to ask her about myself."

"Maybe she'll come to you in a dream." The sarcasm in Serena's response hung for a moment. "Sorry, I didn't mean that. I just…I just don't know what to think. What does it all mean? I feel more confused than ever!"

"Who knows? I will say this trip has my brain working overtime. Maybe we'll figure it out and maybe we won't, but right now it's a big puzzle and we don't have enough pieces." Bryson paused and glanced over to see Serena absently gazing out the passenger window.

"Ahem, earth to Serena, do you copy?" Seeing her turn toward him, he repeated, "Like I was saying, we don't have enough pieces to this puzzle." He made an exaggerated kissing motion with his lips toward the large brown envelope on her lap. "Duh!"

A smile broke across her face as she slapped the side of her head then held the envelope up as if it were some prize or treasure. "Not too subtle, are you?" Carefully, she began to break the seal but noted it had already been opened then re-taped. "Someone has already opened this."

"That's troubling. What's inside?"

Serena removed the contents—a letter, a green-colored candle, and a deerskin pouch. Opening the pouch, she noted dried leaves and other plant material. Taking it to her nostrils, she inhaled. "Hard to say, could be for tea, maybe some kind of incense; smells nice." Closing the pouch, she examined the candle—four or five inches tall, green, wider than a taper candle but not as wide as a pillar candle. She sniffed it, noted no smell and just shrugged her shoulders.

As she was putting it on her lap, she murmured aloud, more to herself than to Bryson. "Now that's different." Looking closely at the wick, she saw two intertwined threads, one black and one white. "I've never seen a wick like this, have you?" She passed the candle over to Bryson and he studied it, careful to keep a hand on the wheel.

"I'm not big into candles. Can't say that I've seen a wick quite like that; I agree that it's different." He gave it back. "More puzzle pieces, I guess. How about the letter, what does it say?"

She held the fine linen stationary, the kind you find in a fancy store, the kind with matching envelope and paper. This time the envelope was unsealed. Gingerly, she unfolded the letter within and read the flowing script aloud:

Dearest Serena,

My little *ch'osh bikq'í*, that you are reading this means I have lost my wind. There is much I would have liked to tell you before my passing. It will be much harder for you to learn these things—things about your sacred blood, about why Creator Mother and Father have sent you.

I am sorry for the sleeping time in the cave. I meant it as an awakening time, but you were not yet ready to awake. Now it is long past that time but still not too late. It is I, my *ch'osh bikq'í*, who bears the blame and I am deeply sorrowed by all the pain this has caused.

I have left something for you in my hogan, something very important, but I can only share this with you after you sleep and awaken. You must return there. It must be on a night of no moon. Burn what is in the deerskin pouch, burn it all. Use a burning bowl from those I keep. You can light your candle, but it must be dark when you sleep. Take my rug, the one of our ancestors; you will remember it. Stand in the water. Keep your eyes open. Do not let fear close your eyes or your heart.

Be careful, *ch'osh bikq'i.* There is much darkness that wants to swallow your light.

Shibízhí Ooljee

A tear rolled slowly down Serena's face landing on the fine linen paper. She carefully refolded the letter placing it back within its matching envelope and returned it, along with the rest of the contents, to the much larger envelope. She sniffed back the moisture beneath her nose, searched around and found a tissue. Drying her nose and her tears, she confidently and cheerfully exclaimed, "Well, that explains everything!"

Following a sharp turn off to the right onto Rt. 564, a sign read: "Navajo National Monument 10 miles." Five miles later, the patrol car made another right onto something less than a road and more of a dirt trail. Hills, piñon, and juniper flanked either side providing a rugged, picturesque beauty. After another couple of miles, Captain Nez slowed and pulled over. Ahead, they noted a walking trail, perhaps a herder's trail.

"It's a hundred yards back this way. I'll show it to you; you can get your stuff later if you plan to stay."

Up and over a small hill, nestled at the top of a ravine, solitary with nothing but the wind, they came to a hogan. It was traditional Navajo style, domed and mud-covered with a central smoke hole. The door faced east and the sun, illuminating from behind the dwelling, shone toward towering rock formations to the east. Adjacent to the structure lay a small clearing with a wire pen, probably for some sheep or goats, and an outhouse further down the trail. Quail squawked, startled to see them.

Bryson inhaled the clean pine scent and gazed at the orange-hued rock formations. "It's absolutely majestic!" He turned to look at Serena, to gauge her reaction.

She beamed. "I've been here before. The hogan wasn't here then, but we slept in that same spot where it is. My *shibízhí* called this a power place."

Captain Nez, who had kept a respectful silence, now spoke. "Yes, she certainly picked a good spot. Anyway, look around, stay if you want. There's no lock on the door. Here's my card in case you need to call me." He stepped forward and handed Bryson the card. "The cell coverage around here is a little spotty, but if you don't have a signal just walk in the direction we left the cars and you should get something. When I'm in Shonto, I'll stop at the Trading Post and let the owner know you'll be by to pick up your aunt's pawn. His name's Charlie Big Ears; trust me, you'll know him when you see him. Is there anything else I can do for you folks? Again, sorry about coming all this way looking for your *shibízhí* and me having to…having to be the one to…having to meet you under these circumstances."

"Thank you, Captain. You've been very kind. There is only one last question. Where did you find her?"

The burley officer walked a short distance, stopping between the tiny corral and the hogan. "She was right about here, face down." He stopped on a cleared level patch.

Serena stooped down and picked two purple flowers and a flat rock. Walking to the spot where Captain Nez stood, she gently placed a flower on the ground, whispered, and secured the blossom with the stone. Standing, she gave the other flower to the officer. "Thank you again."

He seemed touched by the gift. They shook hands and he tipped his large cowboy hat. "Pleasure!" Then he added, "You two be careful. The reservation can be dangerous. Believe me, I know." They listened as his heavy frame walked down the path receding from their sight and into silence. A few moments later, they heard a car start in the distance and drive away.

Both exhilarated and frightened by the sense of aloneness, she sighed. "That's where it is." She pointed with her hand, not her lips, to the ravine, roughly headed northeast to an arroyo.

"That's where what is?" Bryson looked in the direction she pointed but nothing stood out.

"The cave. I wasn't sure how to get there, but now I know." She looked northeast, her eyes unfocused, recalling a memory, speaking softly, her great aunt's answer to her child's question. "About two or three miles…we follow the wash and then come to an ancient cottonwood…the guardian…"

"So, you're going to do it? Go visit the cave?"

"I don't know. I'm scared, but I feel I have to. I can't explain it; something is drawing me there." She laughed. "Hah, probably like a moth to a flame. She said it had to be a night with no moon. I have no idea when that is."

"Three nights." Bryson noted the look of surprise on her face. "Okay…I looked it up."

She sat on the ground looking at the flower beneath the stone she had set, twirling loose dirt with her fingertip. Shyly, without looking up, she asked, "Would you?"

"Stay? Keep you company?" Awkwardly, he parked himself next to her on the flat ground. "Are you kidding me? Weren't you listening when I told you I am a warrior archetype? Geeky protector boy wouldn't let you do this alone. I'm here for you, girlfriend."

She shifted position to her knees. Just tall enough to comfortably grasp his shoulders, she leaned forward and kissed him on the forehead. "Thank you!" A big grin lit her face. "I'm still scared, but having a warrior nerd protecting me, I feel much safer." She jumped up, brushed off dirt, and added, "C'mon, let's go check out the hogan."

9

Upon entering the hogan, Serena immediately noticed two things. First came an assault of dust stirred by every movement; loose dirt invaded every crack and crevice—unavoidable in this high desert and requiring daily sweeping of the clay floor and walls. She scanned the hut for a broom, happy at the thought of a distraction, a task to occupy her mind away from the discomfort of returning to the cave. There, tucked against the wall, she spied a broom and almost breathed a sigh of relief until her gaze continued to the two walking sticks leaning adjacent to the broom. One, carved in the likeness of a snake, immediately returned her thoughts to the impending encounter. There was no escape.

"Dusty in here." Bryson stood within the structure admiring the construction; he had never been in a hogan before.

The other features striking Serena were a cool temperature and something more infiltrating the living space. Beyond the coolness, a sense of calm flowing energy permeated into the structure itself. Just as her fear and anxiety had welled up a moment before, those same fears were now swallowed into the peace and serenity of this space, a sacred space, a power spot.

"Can you feel it?" she asked her friend, who seemed oversized for the height of the ceiling.

"Yes, nice and cool in here. I'm surprised considering how hot it is outside."

"No, that's not what I meant. Can you feel the calm and the power?"

He stood there, eyes closed, searching, then drawing upon something deeper than the physical. He inhaled deeply and in the soft light within the hogan he replied, "Yes. Now I feel it. There is an energy within that feels comforting, a sense that no matter what is happening outside, here, within these walls," he stood in the center with arms outstretched and turned 360 degrees, "all is right here in this space."

The knowing smile and the gentle nod of her head spoke her agreement. Then curiosity got the best of them both as they examined the contents of the hogan. A shaft of sunlight had angled its way through the smoke hole. As they moved about the home, dust lifted, drifted, and danced in the beam adding to the surreal magic of her *shibízhí's* home, a place that portrayed a blend of traditional and unusual. The narrow beam of light, a focal point, illuminated only a small piece, a sliver of the mysterious Navajo woman.

Scanning the contents, they noted the central woodstove for both cooking and heating. A cast-iron pan and pot, a kettle, a kerosene lamp, tongs, and a poker—it all looked thoroughly ordinary. Many pegs, some with clothing or other household items, similarly spoke of nothing unusual. A table with a woven basket nearing completion lay with adjacent strips of sweetgrass and willow. The unfinished work, now with three or more months of dust settled over it, left the impression of unfinished business. An assortment of other baskets, pots, and jars concealed their hidden contents. They saw several gallon water bottles; most were full, others waited to be refilled. Sheepskins and rolled bedding lay ready to be unrolled along one section. Burning bowls and some herbs, an animal skull, gourds, a large feather, and some Kachina dolls lay shelved on the south side. On the north side, a hunchbacked dancing *Kokopelli* hung silent with drums, a rattle, and a small flute on a shelf below. In silent respect, they each absorbed aspects of the woman who had lived here, reaching out and feeling her spirit.

Suppressing the urge to sneeze, Serena walked up to Bryson who stood intently studying the west wall where a series of artifacts were on shelves or hung arranged in a circle with a single item above. This arrangement, both unusual and surprising, drew her attention, called to her.

"What do you make of this, Bry?"

"In a word, different. I don't mean any disrespect, but it's weird." He reached for his cell phone. "I'm going to take some pictures of each of these, do a little research when we get back."

"Good idea. Can you text them to me? I left my phone charging in the car."

They examined each in sequence starting with the top. A symbol, half-sun and half-moon in a yin-yang fashion with two snakes, one white and one black, each swallowing the other's tail, encircled the inner sun-moon symbol. Light emanated from the snakes' bodies.

"Ever seen anything like this?"

She shook her head. "Nope."

"How about this one?" Under the sun-moon-snake drawing was a framed picture—a Black Madonna with Child, both haloed in light. She held a green candle in her left hand, and there was writing in the hem of her colorful robes. Three other male figures were also in the painting and a scroll with writing on it that looked like Latin lay at the Madonna's feet. An inscription below read: "The Virgin appears to the Guanches."

"Who or what is a Guanches? Was your aunt religious?"

"I don't know. It sounds Spanish, almost like those cowboys in Argentina, Gauchos."

"I don't think so." Moving to the right, he pointed to the next one. A small statue on a shelf, one of those Hindu Devas with six arms who seemed to be dancing, hard to tell if it was male or female. Snakes surrounded the dancing figure. "Definitely Indian, but definitely not Native American."

"Very funny. At least I kind of recognize that one, Shiva or something. This next one," she continued in the circular sequence, "looks really primitive." She examined the brightly colored mask. "Wait a minute, I saw something recently that looked just like this." She muttered to herself, going over her memory banks.

"Got it; saw this in an old *National Geographic.* It's a ceremonial Australian Aboriginal mask."

"C'mon, you can't be serious! Well, let's go with it for now. At least I know the next one. No question this is Aesculapius." He pointed to a carved white marble statue of a classic Greek holding a staff with a snake coiled around it. "The snake staff gives it away. Most of the Ancient History I studied was Western Civ—Greece and Rome. They considered him a demigod of sorts, big into healing. That's why the medical profession uses a caduceus symbol, two snakes wrapped around a pole with wings. Have you seen it? You know what it is?" He took a picture.

The shaft of sunlight had passed. In the diminished light, Bryson didn't notice her color drain, but he heard her slight gasp.

"Sure do."

"Are you okay?"

"Oh yeah, just another synchronicity. Could be I'm getting hypoglycemic or something."

"Do you want to stop? We have plenty of time to look at these later."

"No, it's only two more. Let's finish now, but I have to say, my brain is suffering from information overload. It just seems the more I see, the crazier and cloudier it all becomes."

"I agree. I'm not even trying to process or figure this out anymore. Anyway, this next one is easy. It's Isis." He pointed to a typical Egyptian style glyph depicting a goddess figure.

"How do you know?"

"Her name is written below." He pointed and directed her to some writing, faded but legible. "How about this last one?" The final wall hanging completing the circular arrangement revealed a snakelike human head piercing through a sun motif of some sort.

"Looks Mesoamerican to me. I don't know—Peruvian, Aztec, Mayan, something like that. If I had stayed another semester at University, I planned to learn more about South and Central American culture. I'm sure we can track it down."

"I bet you didn't know your great aunt was a world traveler. Looks like she has Europe, Asia, Africa, Australia, and North and South America covered." He stepped back. "I can tell you one thing: I'm not surprised she creeped people out, snake worship and so on. You got to admit, this is some pretty weird shit."

"I know. I'm getting second thoughts about the cave. I'm wondering what I'll find there—get swallowed up by some serpent demon or go in and never come out."

Bryson couldn't tell if she was serious at that moment. Neither could she.

10

"I don't really feel like doing any more investigating. As it is, I feel like a little kid who opened a thousand-piece puzzle box, but the cover picture was gone, so I don't even know where to start." A big sigh followed. "I'm almost too tired to eat."

"No problem. I always keep a few power bars in the car. As for those puzzles, I always tried to find a corner piece and work from there." He looked around. "Problem is, this hogan is round."

Serena managed a tired smile. Bryson exited to get some things from the car and she mustered enough strength to scout out whatever provisions remained in the home. She found a few staples like salt, spices, some flour, and oil. Bryson came back carrying her phone, their packs, and a guitar.

"I found these." She held up deer jerky.

He held out protein bars. "I've got these. We'll be fine."

"A guitar; I didn't know you played."

"Well, you might want to listen before deciding whether or not I can actually play." A mischievous, boyish grin erupted on his face. "Let's go outside to eat. When I was walking back from the car, I noticed the setting sun in the west lights up the eastern sheer cliff face and formations; it's spectacular."

The red, orange, and pink hues forming the skyscape and the rock scape displayed nature ablaze at its finest. She snapped a dozen photos, including some of Bryson. Serena enjoyed his quirky sense of humor and just hanging out together. Beneath the glory of the Arizona sunset, she munched on deer jerky and a protein bar, while the stress and fear of the unknown subsided.

She yawned. "Hey, I thought you would give me a serenade."

"I'm just waiting for more darkness to make sure my singing scares off any lurking animals or evil spirits."

Nestling on her back, she watched as stars poked out in sparkles. The Milky Way gradually emerged as Bryson tuned his guitar. Then he began—"An oldie but goodie." He smiled and sang Don McLean's *American Pie*. When he finished, he ventured sheepishly, "Well, what do you think?"

Sitting up and placing her hands over both ears while pouting she proclaimed, "That was positively terrible! I'm sure we'll have no denizens from the underworld visiting tonight." When they both laughed, she added, "Good thing Captain Nez is twenty miles away or he might come and have us evicted." She jumped up. "Be right back."

She disappeared into the hogan only to return a moment later with a drum and a rattle. The two improvised a folk music Native American jamboree fusion of sound, laughter, forgotten verses, solos, and made-up lyrics. The singing magic continued indoors as Serena spread out a sheepskin and a blanket, put the native instruments back, and listened while Bryson lullabied her to sleep. *His voice isn't half so bad… I'm lucky to have such a good friend.*

Seeing her closed eyes, slow breaths, and detecting a faint snore, Bryson put his guitar down and retrieved his laptop from his pack. A Wi-Fi hot spot later he searched the internet, whispering to himself, "Can't rest until I at least find a corner piece."

"Hey, sleeping beauty, how did you sleep?"

Stretching, she recalled sleeping in this same spot eleven years ago, a happy little girl getting ready for a grand adventure. Now, she felt like a broken young woman, confused, but feeling ready to claim her birthright. "Great! No bad dreams!" She pounded her bedroll. "I always liked a firm mattress." Standing, she began to work out the kinks in her neck and back. "How about you?"

"Not bad." He stomped the ground. "I hear you on the firmness of the sleeping accommodations. I stayed up late doing a little research and I've learned some fantastic things."

"Hold it right there." She motioned a time-out. "I don't even begin to wake up until I have coffee."

"Excellent idea; let's go to Shonto. I'm sure they'll have coffee at the trading post. We can pick up stuff for later and throw it in the car cooler. And, we can talk to Charlie about collecting your great aunt's pawn."

After cleaning up as best they could, they hit the road, reversing direction from the last leg of their journey yesterday and making careful note where the turnoff was. Back on route 160, they followed signs and onboard navigation to the trading post. Serena looked it up and learned a few details—it had been around since 1915; there was a gas station, native crafts, supplies, etc.

"I don't care as long as they have coffee." They pulled over. They could both smell the coffee aroma as soon as they stepped out of the car. She inhaled. "Ahhh, heaven!"

Inside, it didn't take long to figure out who the owner was. Charlie Big Ears was everything advertised and then some. Serena tried not to stare; fortunately, his facial bones were long and lean. Although Charlie assisted two patrons, as soon as they walked in they heard hushed whispers and the other customers left.

Bryson leaned forward to Serena. "I guess the news is all over the reservation. The witch's niece is on the premises. Better gather your children and infants." While she glared at him, a look that told him to "be quiet," he added, "Remember, speak no names."

She began, "You must be Charlie. Did Captain Nez stop by yesterday saying a relative of someone who died a few months ago might come by?"

"Yup."

Serena extended her hand, accepted a cursory handshake, and continued. "I'm Serena Mendez and this is my friend, Bryson Reynolds." The proprietor nodded; one got the feeling he was a man of few words. "Well, we were hoping to collect any belongings left here. The Captain said you were the person to speak with. But first we want to shop for supplies and have some coffee."

He pointed with his lips. "It's self-serve."

They shopped, gassed up the car, bought bacon, eggs, hot dogs and some rolls, iced tea, and ground coffee. They enjoyed muffins and a second cup of the self-serve which wasn't nearly as good as it smelled.

Before checking out, Charlie went to a back room and returned with a large manila envelope. He spilled the contents onto the counter and read off a separate index card, presumably an inventory list. There were some beads, a bracelet with a leather band surrounding a simple hammered silver center, a pair of turquoise earrings, several turquoise stones, and a few other sundries.

Serena knew enough to ask; she put it delicately. "Did the woman who left these items here owe any money to the store? Is there a balance we need to settle?"

"Nope. All settled."

"Good. Then I guess we need to pay for our things today." After a brief pause, she asked, "I am just wondering, can you tell me what these things are worth?"

The proprietor poked at the stones with a pencil, giving them the feeling Charlie Big Ears did not want to touch any of the deceased woman's possessions. He detailed their approximate values. He was far from loquacious, but he spent the most time with the turquoise stones, explaining why they were of high quality. They looked at each other quite surprised to learn a few were over a hundred dollars. Since their bill for gas and supplies came to $78.54, she offered to trade him a stone he had just appraised at $90.00.

"Trade?"

"First you claim, then Charlie trade."

Serena gathered everything back into the envelope then found the stone to trade and handed it over. Charlie grunted his approval. As they carried their packages out of the trading post, she saw Charlie Big Ears's reflection in the storefront glass door making the sign of the cross.

"I kind of get the feeling he was glad to see us leave and to be rid of my *shibízhí's* possessions."

"Ya think!"

"Can you believe it? I just collected an inheritance of over $700."

"Well I should give you some money for free lodging."

"Not this time, boyfriend. What do you want to do today? D-day isn't until tomorrow night."

As they passed a sign promoting the "Navajo National Monument," they both shrugged as if to say, "Sure, why not, it's only a few miles away."

"I suppose I should go to the cave this afternoon." A forlorn look appeared, as though a thundercloud had suddenly blotted out the sunshine. She looked resigned, not excited. "Need to make sure it's still there."

Bryson had held his excitement in for too long. Abruptly he blurted, "I'm thinking there are more puzzle pieces there in the cave, but wait till I tell you what I learned last night."

"Stop. Hold it right there. I am officially declaring a moratorium on figuring all this out. I just want to relax and have fun." She didn't mean that to sound as cross as it did.

Sheepishly, he asked, "Can I just say one little thing? I'll save the good stuff until after the cave." Seeing her relent, he added, "You know that last artifact we looked at? You were right, it is Mesoamerican. I found an exact picture of that stone carving on the internet." There wasn't any response, so he continued. "It's Quetzalcoatl... He was an Aztec demigod... It means 'feathered serpent.'"

She knew Bryson wanted a more enthusiastic response from her. She knew that given her interest in anthropology she should be curious. She knew she was being selfish. But at that moment, she felt overwhelmed. The beginning of a shaking tremor and dry mouth pointed to signs of mounting PTSD. The best she could muster was a very halfhearted, "That's nice." Fortunately, the entrance to the monument greeted them; she desperately needed the distraction.

11

It was interesting enough for both of them. Neither knew much of the ancient history and cultural roots of this area and there was a lot to learn. They took a self-walking tour. The lands here, etched by sand and stone, wind and water, felt worn and ancient, undisturbed and uncontaminated by modern society. These Pueblo peoples were among the first, carving their sandstone, mud-mortared, and rock dwellings into the cliffs, a remarkable blending of man and nature so as not to disturb the spirit of the land. They farmed the canyons by growing corn, beans, and squash—the Three Sisters—and they hunted wild game as they lived in harmony with Mother Nature. Land, animals, plants, rocks, sky, and water were all sacred, the elements of balance which the Puebloans made sure not to disturb.

The Hopi, whose reservation is contained within the Navajo Nation, were direct descendants. The two visitors learned of the Hopi sacred snake dance ceremony, a ritual over eight days long to call forth the Mother's tears of rain to bring fertility to this harsh desert climate. The more nomadic Navajo or Dineh, moved here centuries later, but always recognized the sacredness of this area. To the Dineh, the Hopi and other Ancestral Puebloans were the Anasazi, the Ancient Ones; though, some traditional Navajo trace their ancestry back to the prehistoric cliff dwellers through clan ceremonies and oral histories.

This site of cliff dwellings for these ancient peoples had been abandoned around AD 1300 during a prolonged drought. This was long before Franciscan missionaries from Spain brought the Catholic religion to this region, a forerunner to European imperialism and conquest. Yet Hopi legends tell a different story of why they abandoned the site. Stories speak of a spiritual quest, a battle between the Snake Clan inhabiting this area of the Navajo National Monument ruins, and the Horn Clan who forced them out.

While the walk and historical diversion had lifted Serena's spirits, everywhere there seemed to be reminders of snakes. She commented on this to Bryson, who, recognizing her need for space and a time of preparation, had walked with her as a silent companion.

"Everywhere I go, both asleep and awake, it seems I get messages about snakes."

"Ever since I was bitten, I have always been sensitized and notice snake things too. You're right; there have been a lot of messages and you would have to be blind, deaf, or in denial not to recognize that." They were hiking on the outskirts of a small aspen, fir, and spruce forest, a remnant from the last ice age twelve thousand years ago. The land itself felt old.

"Look." She pointed to a hawk gliding in descending circles, silent on the wind. They both watched the bird's flight. Returning to Bryson's observation, she wanted to hear his thoughts. "What do you think it all means?"

"Well, I have been trying to connect the dots, but a lot is missing. Still, what I say now might sound very unscientific, but you asked me what I think." Serena just stopped and looked at him, so he continued. "You remember Dr. Jenkins said something about snakes being associated with wisdom? I think these reminders are messages and the snake symbols are heralds telling you something is about to happen. I can't tell you why, and trust me I've been thinking about it, but I think your cave experience will be life-changing in a good way. It's kind of like when a snake sheds its skin. I think that's what is going to happen."

She took her time before answering. They were now on a trail headed back to the visitor's center. "I like your answer. It sounds unscientific, but I think there are things science doesn't understand. I'm not talking about religion here so much as limits to scientific understanding. What happened in that story about Jung, and the synchronicities we have experienced these last few days— how does science explain them?"

She pointed to a small snake and sun petroglyph set against a rock facing. "There is a lot I don't understand, but I like your answer for two reasons. First, I think you might be right; there is a strong sense of spoken truth in what you said, and it resonates with me. I can't explain it and I'm not even going to try. But understand that is pretty scary unto itself—to think you are on the threshold of having your whole life change. Truthfully, it scares the shit out of me."

"Don't think too much." She stopped, and a puzzled look in her gray eyes asked him to explain. "There are some things you can't think through, you just have to live though; you have to turn your mind off and get rid of the perception filters and need to analyze. You know, just go with the flow."

She nodded. "I like it. The second reason is that it gives me hope." A mischievous grin erupted as she blurted, "Here we are on Hopi land and I hopee you are right."

Although she was obviously pleased by her little wordplay pun, Bryson didn't smile at all; instead, he grabbed her arm; his face and blue eyes showed anger. "No! Hope is the wrong path. It's a myth, a carrot we dangle in front of ourselves thinking things are going to work out. That's just sugarcoating fear. It's a grand deception, this fear masquerading as hope." He released his grip, but his voice carried no less intensity. "You must trust. When you trust, you do not need to hope. There is no fear when you trust." He reiterated in Yoda-speak, "Trust only…no fear."

The truth of what he had just said resonated so powerfully, reverberating and echoing in the canyon where they stood. They both felt it; then Bryson broke the spell.

"Bring lots of toilet paper."

"What? Where did that come from?"

"I was just reacting to your comment about getting the shit scared out of you." He winked. "Better bring lots of TP."

"Very funny, but you missed part of the point of what you just said. Miss Fearless is going to be the embodiment of trust going with the flow. So, no reason to be a scaredy pants, but just in case, I'll bring some anyway."

They returned to the car, made sandwiches, and enjoyed a mini-picnic lunch. During an uneventful drive back, Serena indicated she had changed her mind about going to the cave today. Tomorrow, they could go there together, and Bryson would know where to come look for her in case she didn't return. Fatigue drove her decision; they had hiked under a merciless sun.

"I might take a nap when we get back."

"That was one of Einstein's secrets—power nap to recharge the brain. Sounds like a good idea."

There wasn't much to carry in—a few items that didn't need to remain in the car cooler. As they entered, Bryson immediately stopped. "Don't touch anything."

"What's wrong?"

"Someone's been in here since we left."

"How can you be so sure?"

He touched his forehead—"Eidetic memory." One at a time he pointed to three or four items such as his guitar and some notes he had left arranged on the table. "They're close, but not quite the way we left them. Someone's been snooping."

"Are you absolutely sure?" His look left no doubt about his certainty. "But why would anyone want to do that? Everyone we have met except for Captain Nez seems to want to have nothing to do with my aunt." She did a quick inventory. "Well, it doesn't look as though anything's been taken. Again, why would anyone come looking here, shift stuff around?"

"Don't know. I have the same question." Bryson sat down. "But I remember in the letter your aunt wrote that she said she left something important for you here. I also remember that the big envelope had been resealed. I'm just speculating, but I think someone wants something and thinks it's hidden in the hogan. That's the only explanation that makes sense to me given the information we have."

Serena had to admit it was a plausible hypothesis. It made her uncomfortable and uneasy, not the kind that an extra dose of trust could dismiss. The hogan felt safe, protected, a haven of sorts. Thinking someone uninvited had invaded this little sanctuary disrupted the very essence of what the structure embodied—a violation of this refuge.

"What do you think we should do? There isn't even a lock on the door. What if they come back?"

"Not sure. I've got to get some things out of the car. I've got ideas, but you'll have to ask me again tomorrow."

Partly as a way to think about something else, Serena gathered wood and used the small fire pit outside to prepare for cooking later. It was too hot to use the indoor stove. She mixed flour and water into a dough and said she would try to make a special treat along with hot dogs and beans. Once she finished, she lay down to nap. Bryson had returned with a tackle box that had an assortment of small electronic parts and supplies. He had also set up a solar charger and had plugged his computer in. Given the physical and mental effort of the day, Serena surprised herself and managed to sleep. She had found the Navajo rug given to her *shibízhí* by her aunt's grandmother. She recalled the weave, a traditional Navajo design. As a ten year old, it reminded her of a turtle shell. It was silly, but somehow thinking of sleeping on top of a giant turtle was almost as good as not thinking at all. A couple of hours later she awoke, thirsty but otherwise feeling refreshed in body, mind, and spirit.

Bryson had lit the fire while she slept, and the wood had burned to a nice bed of coals releasing the embedded piñon scent. She cleaned the cast-iron pan, got some cooking oil, and flattened out the dough.

"Fry bread? That's one of my favorites!"

"Yeah, mine too. Problem is I haven't made it in a hundred years which, when you think about it, is kinda dumb since it's pretty easy to make."

The rest of dinner prep was a joint effort figuring out how not to burn themselves or the food as they shifted the pan and pot over the grate and turned hot dogs with a stick. The iced tea refreshed them, a nice change from tepid water. Much like two young kids, they roasted marshmallows and told stories around the campfire. They even managed to brew cowboy-style coffee, storing some in a thermos cup for tomorrow morning. Good food shared among friends and a fire goes a long way to dispelling any fears. Calm had returned, but was it the calm before a storm?

12

Day three of their adventure began much like day two except they had warm coffee and muffins to wake their brains up. Personal care took longer. They had more than enough water but had only brought one change of clothes. It hadn't occurred to them to hand wash something yesterday and leave it for the sun and fresh air to work their magic. Instead, they laughed and made fun of themselves. She called him "smelly boy" and he called her "stinky girl"; each time they used the names it stayed funny and they laughed. They mimicked Hollywood Western Indian-speak.

"Me great big smelly boy think stinky girl no like him no more."

Deep exaggerated inhalation. "Me no smell you because stinky girl's nose too full of stinky girl."

It eased the tension, helping the day to pass. Bryson drove into Kenyata. He wanted to see if they had some things but didn't want Serena to know specifically what he wanted to buy. She stayed behind giving the hogan another sweep to get herself mentally prepared.

"I should be back in a couple of hours max. Is there anything you need?"

"Uhh…more deodorant?" Sunlight glistened off her grinning teeth.

Not to be outdone, Bryson took out a pad and paper and began to write while announcing out loud, "Stinky girl need heap lot of deodorant." Then raising his armpit and sniffing, he said, "Maybe smelly boy need some too."

As she watched him drive off, with a big smile on her face she thought to herself, *laughter, the foolproof antidote to all my angst! Hey Mr. glowing snake, I am just going to laugh when I see you and give you a nice little snaky lick.* She stuck out and wiggled her tongue.

Bryson seemed pleased when he returned. About forty-five minutes later he called her over to showcase his talents and creations. "This," he held up a small egg-shaped saucer thingy with wires attached to a D cell battery, "is home security at its simplest."

"That's funny because it looks like a battery-operated egg, sunny-side up." She watched as he shook his head.

"The unbeliever doubts, but make no mistake, this device combines a 180-degree-view security camera with digital storage that is motion activated. It will not be easy to conceal, but it will show us if anyone decides to snoop around when no one is here."

"Well, I'm impressed! Why didn't you just buy a lock?"

"No, that wouldn't help. We want to know who the enemy is. I need clandestine footage. Then I can use facial recognition software and hack into government data files to find out who the bad guy is. Pretty elegant really since who would expect it? Lock could mess that all up."

"Damn, you are smarter than you look. And, just so there is no mistake, you look pretty damn smart." She noticed his blushing cheeks.

"Next creation…drumroll please."

Serena leapt up, grabbed the instrument, and drummed.

"Ladies and gentlemen, allow me to razzle dazzle you with this." He now held up a turquoise earring, one from her aunt. "This might look like a perfectly ordinary earring, but that is only to the untrained eye." He quit the huckster voice and said with all seriousness, "I embedded a locator chip. If you keep this on your person, I can track you. Now, I am not stalking you, but we deactivated your phone GPS and anyway, you can drop your phone or lose it and then there is no tracking capability."

She took the earring and put it on. "How does it look?"

"It's perfect. I don't think you're going to have any trouble tonight, but just in case, I would like you to wear it. If you don't come back, I'll be able to locate you. This brings me to my last item, which I didn't make." He held up a Taser.

"A Taser?"

"This is a really good law enforcement-quality device. Don't let the small size fool you. This would incapacitate a Neanderthal caveman, should one happen to come by there while you sleep. I know what I said about trust yesterday, but it bothers me knowing someone might be watching us in general or you in particular. I've got another one of these." He patted the front pocket of his jeans.

❖   ❖   ❖

A late afternoon meal seemed to make sense; this way Serena would not have to worry about dinner. She packed up what she figured she needed including the turtle rug, an extra blanket, water, and the pouch with the incense. Holding up a roll of toilet paper, she smiled to herself as she placed it in the pack. She selected a nice burning bowl from several on a shelf and put it next to her green candle and a lighter. She finished with the Taser and a kitchen knife that she threw in for good measure. She admitted to herself that the last two items gave her a sense of security. A flashlight completed her outfitting.

They each carried a couple of plastic water gallons to fill up in the pool at the cave. Bryson found some leather lacing and tied the empty containers to the back of her pack. He demonstrated how to pad her neck and drape the full containers balanced to either side. Leaving the hogan, she stopped in the entryway and examined the two walking sticks; both were too short for Bryson. She selected the carved wooden snake, a small act of defiance.

"Did you set up the weather station?"

Bryson had to think a moment to make the connection. "You mean in case of snow? Oh yeah, the Snowman has it all set. I positioned the clay pots and arranged them so you can barely see it."

The terrain wasn't rugged, but it required some climbing. Although their destination lay two to three miles northeast, they figured an hour and a half or so, which should give Bryson enough time to return in daylight. Serena, too absorbed in the task before her, just focused on putting one foot after the other in determined pursuit of her trial. Bryson sensed her withdrawing.

"I see it!"

Bryson squinted, adjusted his glasses, and spotted it too. Easily still a mile ahead stood a solitary tree. "Yeah, I see it too—the sentry or guardian tree you told me about."

During the final half hour of their trek, the tree loomed larger and larger until they were upon it. It looked ancient, twisted branches supporting an enormous canopy of leaves; a charred lightning scar disfigured a section of the trunk. This tree had seen many storms, droughts, and flash floods since the time it had been a sapling. It had outlived the folly of countless men and stood now before them, a watcher, silent with unspoken wisdom.

"That has got to be the most magnificent cottonwood I've ever seen. How old do you think it is?"

"Very."

Her one-word answer concerned Bryson. He knew Serena well enough to understand that when she tried to keep a lid on her PTSD, she got very quiet. *This must be hard for her, like putting someone who fears confined spaces into a locked closet.* Looking over he saw she looked no less resolute.

"The cave should be there." She pointed to a rock outcrop with a large crack, more of a gash about twenty yards away. "You may have to squeeze through. It's narrower than I remember, but I guess I was a lot smaller then."

They passed through an opening, quickly descending ten feet. Crouching down, Bryson wriggled forward and then he was in. He moved a few steps so he could stand up. In the dim light, he saw Serena; she appeared lost in some memory. As his eyes adjusted, he saw the pool, roughly in the center of the cave but continuing to the back wall. He couldn't judge whether the water continued below and beyond the back wall of rock. Cool absolute stillness permeated the cave's air and water; the only sounds, echoing slightly, occasional foot shuffles and their breath. Bryson noticed Serena's rapid breathing.

"Hey, PTG." He stood right next to her, towering over her petite frame. "You okay?"

She nodded, sighed, and unpacked a few things. She lay out the rug and blanket, along with the flashlight, kitchen knife, and Taser. On a waist-high rock at the edge of the pool, she set the burning bowl, emptied the deer skin pouch into the bowl and put her candle and lighter adjacent. Taking her empty water jugs, she and Bryson filled them as well as the two he carried.

Cupping his hand to sample some, he grunted, "Good water."

After wriggling their way back out of the cave, the sun hurt their eyes. As they ambled back to the tree, he surprised her when he spoke to it, asking it to watch over her that night and then apologizing before breaking off a twig and handing it to her.

"Take a little piece of the guardian in with you. He'll protect you while warrior boy is gone."

She managed a weak smile, touched by his words and gesture. With a hug and a kiss, she said, "I can do this… I'll see you tomorrow." Then she watched as his lanky frame sauntered off and the crunch of his footsteps receded and disappeared in a howling, gusting wind. To the west, the sun burned strong with another two hours before dusk.

Returning to the cave, Serena took the two gallons of water outside, pouring the cool liquid over her hair, her face, and her body, washing herself in some ritualistic ablution. She leaned against the cottonwood facing west, allowing the sun and the wind to dry her. She reviewed her conversation with Bryson yesterday, the one about trust and going with the flow and why she shouldn't try to overthink things. She reviewed every detail she could recall from being with her *shibízhí* and everything she had learned in the last two and a half days. *She loved me. There is no way she would put me in danger.*

As a ball of orange lit the distant cliff faces with soft hues of pink and red, she drew comfort from the thoughts of trust and love. She felt strangely calm. A lone coyote howled in the distance. It was time.

13

She sprinkled corn pollen on the Navajo turtle rug; her aunt had told her that was for good luck. Serena took the twig and placed it beneath a blanket roll supporting her head. The cave had been dim; now the scant light rapidly faded. Snapping the flashlight on, it surprised her to see how little it did to illuminate her surroundings. The weak beam pierced into slices of darkness. She lit the candle; somehow, it provided much more illumination. A steady light burned, but the rare sputter and flicker produced shadow creatures dancing on the walls.

When she fired the incense, the cave quickly filled with a strange blend of scents. The smoky intoxication swirled, making new shapes, patterns, and shadows upon the surrounding rock and stone. The effect mesmerized her and soon she felt overpowered by the desire to sleep. After blowing out the candle, she lay down and watched the fading incense embers burn to a final curl of smoke. The embers were extinguished. Blackness engulfed her. She tried to see her hand waving before her face, tried to see the cave walls or ceiling, but immeasurable darkness surrounded her. Grabbing and holding the twig, she tried not to think. Somehow sleep overcame her.

Sometimes at night she awoke petrified, completely unable to move, muscles paralyzed, surrounded by darkness around her, not nearly as terrifying as the darkness within, a black and empty abyss, a place where no light shown at all and engulfed her soul. Dr. Jenkins had called her paralysis a hypnogogic state. Serena called it a black dream—a place where the colors, sensations, and dream images were themselves swallowed by the utter darkness. On this moonless night, in the dark cave, dreams and waking both trapped her in blackness. She tried to call out to her *shibizhi* for help, but her arms, her legs, even her voice were all powerless. She couldn't force even a squeak from her throat. Impotent, she lay there trembling inside, but not shaking. She had never felt so afraid as this—the scariest night terror, a black dream with silent screams enveloped her, surrounded her, choked her. Though she screamed, no sound came forth, both light and sound rendered powerless in this blackness. No one came to help. She was alone.

When the horror passed, Serena willed herself up. Drenched in sweat, she stripped naked and crawled into the water where she stood knee deep. *Keep your eyes open… Keep your eyes open.* It became her mantra. Repeating it steadied her. She had a toehold to stand against her fear. *Keep your eyes open… Keep your eyes open.* She reached up with her hand, invisible in the darkness, to make sure her lids were open.

Then she saw it. It started as a blur, a smudge of light, somewhere back where the water and wall ran together. It seemed to glow and slowly took shape, long and curved, it moved toward her gracefully, undulating, almost tentative in its approach. Watery ripples brushed against her legs. Instead of fear, she felt curious as this creature approached. It was a snake, a luminous form swimming toward her. When it touched her leg, rather than recoil, she looked down and marveled at its beauty, its grace; a power emanated from its curving, swimming form, almost electric. As she peered downward, she saw a second snake in the faint luminescence. This second snake, long and black, coiled around her left leg. Where had it come from? Had it come up from the earth below or had it somehow crawled down and come out from within her? This second snake, so much a part of her that she could barely feel it, wrapped around her leg, gliding along her body, calling, drawing, pulling the luminous snake toward her with a dark magnetism. As the light snake fixed itself around her right leg, Serena felt its energy pulsating, glowing. The two snakes coiled around her, a serpentine dance up and down her body, at times intertwined with one another. It was a love dance! Serena felt herself entranced as she undulated with their bodies in joined caresses. Transfixed, absorbed beyond her previous fears, she could not say how long the two snakes embraced. In a final joined movement, they curled as one around each leg, up her abdomen, chest, then down her neck, along her back and slowly disappeared, entering into the base of her spine.

She arched upward, her whole body electrified, on fire; every part of her—arms, legs, fingers, toes, tongue, nipples, scalp—tingled and scintillated alive with energy. The entire cave felt like it was pulsating with energy and she was just a part of the cave, the rocks, the water. Everything felt alive, each cell in her body aware and somehow awake. She looked at herself in the water, at the same time feeling as though she herself was part of the water. Serena saw her reflection—an auric etheric glow enveloped her, shimmering and radiating. The hypnotic light show continued as time lost all meaning.

Slowly, the altered state faded, and Serena reentered a normal physical plane. Surrounded once again by darkness, she felt for and found the candle which she lit to bathe the cave in candlelight once more. She stood back in the water, almost hoping the serpents would return. When she peered downward, she noticed it, a glint of metal perhaps three feet ahead from where she stood. As she stepped forward, she could see a metallic object easily made visible by the candle's light. What could it be?

Groping with her hand, she felt the object and retrieved it from the pool's bottom. In her hand, she held a ring with a key and a tag, much like a dog tag. There were letters of some sort, but in the dim light she could not decipher them. Stepping from the pool, she held the treasure close to the flame and read the tag aloud, "*Ch'osh bikq'i*…dig under stove." She held the tag and attached key and muttered, "She did hide something in the hogan."

Laying back down on the Navajo rug she felt the strength of the turtle that had carried her thus far. Clutching the metal keyring, she fell back asleep. She awoke as dawn brought the light of a new day into the womb where she had slept.

She quickly packed her items and left the cave. Pausing to hold her hand against the ancient cottonwood, she gave thanks, adjusted her pack and water jugs, grabbed her walking stick, and headed back. She couldn't wait to tell Bryson. About three quarters of the way back she stopped to check her pack; in her haste, she'd forgotten the candle and burning bowl. No problem, she could return later or tomorrow. Secrets had waited long enough, and answers lay with the key she carried.

14

With heightened awareness, the breeze, the sun, the trees, the birds all filled her senses. She could not recall ever feeling so alive. About a half mile to go, she smelled it and stopped just long enough to confirm. Drifting on the wind, mixed with the sweet smell of burning piñon, the unmistakable scent of fresh coffee and a hint of bacon beckoned. Serena practically sprinted to the hogan, the gallon jug in each hand felt light as cotton candy.

Bryson, busy frying potatoes, greeted her with a relieved smile. "I see a cave troll did not take you prisoner; either that or somehow you managed to escape." Then he added, "I guess everything turned out okay."

Her forceful squeeze surprised them both. Serena didn't know what to do first—tell him about her experience, dig for treasure, or have some coffee and breakfast. Sensibility prevailed; she started with coffee and a bite to eat.

Between sips of cowboy-style brew and mouthfuls of food, she told Bryson the details. As she spoke, he typed at his laptop keyboard.

"Slow down, you're going to choke. Besides, I can only go so fast."

She composed herself, gulped a last morsel, and poured a second cup of coffee. "By the way, thanks for preparing breakfast—you are awesome! What exactly are you doing?"

He tilted the screen so she could see. "This is a little game I call 'connecting the dots.' I assign tags to certain things you describe and add it to my data file. I've been doing the same thing with the note your aunt already wrote to you, things in her hut like the Aboriginal mask, things we learned from Captain Nez. They're all pieces to the puzzle. For instance, you mentioned a black snake and a luminous snake. Your aunt said something about sacred blood. I tag all of them. I also make other speculative, more hypothetical tags. With what you just told me, I've made a tag called 'mystical experience,' but I code that differently. I have similar speculations about 'bloodline' and 'DNA.'"

She watched as nests of colored boxes appeared and moved in different organized patterns across the screen. "What will you do with it all?"

"This processor is too weak and the connection too slow. When I get back, I'll run correlation analyses and other database sorting tools to try and connect the dots. I'll search lots of different data depositories. Part of it is similar to the way a reference librarian will data mine, but I use original algorithms. Depending on what I find, I might do other types of tags with clustered information and speculation. I call those meta-tags. Anyway, that's how I play 'connect the dots.'"

"Very impressive! Are you ready to play a different game? I call this one 'dig for buried treasure.'"

Behind the outhouse they found assorted gardening tools including a shovel. Bryson had a multi-tool with a screwdriver that he needed to loosen the stovepipe. The cast-iron stove felt as though it weighed a few hundred pounds, but they moved it easily; Serena could not believe the energy running through her veins.

"Have you been working out at the gym or something? I don't know, you look and act different—stronger, more kick-ass if you know what I mean."

"Strong coffee brewed with that good cave water—must have special minerals."

"Maybe we should go get more," he suggested.

"Have to. Somehow, I managed to forget the candle and bowl. We can get as much water as we can carry, Gunga Din." The look on her face spoke volumes—quit talking and start digging!

A distinct sound of metal on metal clinked. "I hit something." Hardpack clay doesn't yield easily; it took ten minutes of serious exertion, but their efforts were rewarded when Bryson held a metal box.

They moved to the table, tense with anticipation and saying nothing. The key Serena had found in the cave slid right in and Serena removed the contents: another leather pouch, another letter, and an unusual necklace. Finely crafted silver and gold shaped into a snake coiled around a candle with a halo of golden light; nothing about it looked Native American.

"I've never seen anything like this; it's beautiful!" As she held it out for examination, sunlight streaming from the east reflected in tantalizing mystery.

Bryson snapped some photos. "This will be fun to research."

The skin pouch held dozens and dozens of gemstones, well over a hundred. Many of them were turquoise and most were larger than the ones Charlie Big Ears had appraised, but Bryson had been to enough native jewelry vendors around Taos to recognize amber, jasper, and lapis. Some he didn't recognize. "Whoa, I don't know, PTG, but if I had to guess, I would say these are easily worth fifteen to twenty thousand dollars."

Wide-eyed, mouth dry, and hands shaking, she looked back at him but said nothing as she picked up the letter. The writing and linen paper were the same as before:

> Welcome child. You are now initiated into the Sisterhood of the Light. You have taken the first step to be that which is in your blood, Guanche blood, the blood of a Candelaria; few of us remain. The Candelaria are Lightbringers serving truth and healing to illuminate, restore balance, and mend that which is broken. You must complete the Circle to come into the fullness of your power.

> In all places and among all peoples, there are brothers and sisters who serve truth. Some serve as truth keepers to make sure the light is never extinguished. Some are healers, others are dreamers who walk the world of both spirit and matter. Ooljee is such. Until you complete the Circle, your gifts are unknown. Those whose blood is strong are speakers of truth. Many great sages speak this wisdom through time because these truths are beyond time. The great avatars throughout the history of men and women are the Lightbringers. They shine the light of truth where darkness cannot hide.

> Creator Mother/Father, the Light Singer, shaped light and sound to bring life into being. Light and sound are the energy between matter and spirit, the energy of creation. The sun and

the moon dance—man and woman, black and white, light and dark; it is all the song and the dance of matter and spirit.

Darkness is upon us. All light creates shadow. So it is and so it has been since the beginning when the two snakes split, the time of breaking.

You are a warrior woman in the battle between truth and illusion. The deceiver, teller of lies, and all that follow him seek to hold the power of knowledge. Knowledge of what is true and what is false.

Ooljee wishes she could be your guide, but my flame has gone dark. You must go to the Naga Sanctuary near the Temple of Mansi Devi. Find our sister Nalini Kumar; she will instruct you. Go soon, my child, and be ever wary.

Seek the truth. Remember, you are Candelaria—a Lightbringer. You are the candle, as yet unlit, but the blood in you is strong. The candle is the vessel. The wick of unity must be lit for your truth to shine. You must complete the Circle.

Light seeker, light keeper, light speaker—may you burn brightly…

Free the truth… Be the truth… A light for all to see… The truth shall set us free…

A drawn serpent and candle symbol, the same as the necklace, closed the message.

Setting the paper down, her voice small, she asked, "Bry, what do you think it all means?"

He paused his furious typing and tagging. "Holy shit, Serena; there is some serious symbolism and messaging going on here! This is awesome, way better than *Zelda*! Don't you see? It's a quest and you are a chosen one. I'm serious; I'm not fooling around when I say that. You have a destiny to fulfill and it's way bigger than we can figure out with the information we have so far."

"I don't understand—Candelaria, Guanche blood, go to India—what is she saying?"

The scared deer-in-the-headlights look didn't slow him down. "Oh, that's just the beginning, warrior girl…I mean woman. I already know about the Candelaria and Guanche connection. I wanted to tell you the other day, but you asked me to wait. That Black Madonna picture over there at the top of the circle." He motioned toward the arrangement on the wall. "That's not just a circle, it's obviously *the Circle*, the one your *shibízhi* keeps referring to. The painting depicts the Virgin of Candelaria appearing to the Guanches, the people native to the Canary Islands. The natives there are genetically different from other places in Spain and Europe—many have blue eyes, gray eyes…ahem," Serena batted her eyes to show she was listening, "blond hair. My preliminary research even says they might be genetic remnants from Atlantis. Wouldn't that be cool? I've only started digging into all this, but I'll also mention their language seems to share a lot of similarities to Dravidian, the language of ancient India. Oh, another thing, their island Tenerife has a huge volcano, Teide, sacred to the natives, kind of like Mt. Olympus to the ancient Greeks. Legend has it that the volcano imprisons the God of Light and Sun there."

Seeing now that she looked overwhelmed, Bryson tried to curb his enthusiasm slightly. "I'll stop there but for one last thing, then I promise to give you a chance to absorb all this new information. Written around the hem of the Virgin of Candelaria's robes are seven messages that no one has yet decoded; their meanings are a total mystery… What do you think of that?"

Serena sat staring at the Circle of artifacts; all her energy and excitement sucked into a familiar sick feeling knotting the pit of her stomach. "I think I need to go find my pills."

15

"Is this channel secure?" A crackle of static followed.

"Of course."

"Status report."

"She hiked out about three miles from the witch's hut, spent the night in what looks like a small cave. It's hard to say; there's a slit in an outcropping of rocks. She left a while ago in the direction of the hut."

"The man with her?"

"Bryson Reynolds, we ran the car plates. He stayed behind, but I can't say now since I've been following the girl. I'm still here at the cave."

"And you searched the serpent's hut?"

"Only three times, did you read my report?"

"Yes. I still don't understand how an old woman stood up to your questioning."

"Next time, you can question her yourself. Oops, that's right; she no longer walks among the living. Too bad you're not a spirit walker." Static as he got no response. "Look, what do you want me to do?"

"Search the cave. Maybe you'll find something. Live in the light!"

"May the light protect you." The radio went silent.

16

Everywhere and everything around her screamed to Serena that she needed to get started—do something and begin her journey. It was too much! She shut down with only one thing on her mind—*I've got to get the hell out of here…the sooner the better.*

Stalwart Bryson understood. He packed up the car and set the surveillance. There wasn't any footage from the brief period they had been away yesterday. Clean up went quickly as they bagged all their trash for disposal back home. If they hurried back to the cave, they could still make it to Taos by 8 or 9 PM.

Serena's pace brought them to the cave in just over an hour. Rather than squeeze past the narrow opening crevice, Bryson waited near the entrance. That's when he heard her scream and saw her rush back out.

"Bry, there's someone inside!" White and shaking, she repeated, "There's someone in there…and I think he's dead."

Talking like a hero seemed easier than demonstrating the bravery required at that moment, but Bryson managed to say, "I'll check it out." With Taser in one hand, he wriggled through the crevice and downward to the cave opening. After he entered and waited for his eyes to adjust from the bright glare to the dim cave interior, he spotted a body about ten feet in. In the low light, the blue of the man's face looked a shade of gray.

"It's okay. He's dead; it's safe to come in."

Serena followed, locating the bowl and the candle which she lit for better illumination. "Bryson, it's Officer Cuch…from the Tribal Police!" Although no longer in uniform, the death grimace exposing his two missing teeth left no doubt.

"Don't touch anything!" Carefully cataloguing the scene in front of him, Bryson began taking multiple pictures using the flash on his phone. Each momentary flash gave the entire scene a macabre strobe-illuminated effect.

Sam Cuch lay face up, a tourniquet drawn over his left bicep caused disfigured swelling. Two puncture wounds were evident over his upper forearm, but that wasn't what caught Bryson's attention. Further down the dead man's arm inked a very distinct tattoo—a serpent with a small pyramid over its head with a central eye, similar to what's on the back of a dollar bill. He took some extra pictures of that.

"What are those?" Serena pointed to a set of dark goggles next to the dead man.

"Night vision glasses." He took photos of those as well, careful not to disturb anything. "Listen, we gotta get out of here."

"We can't just leave him here."

"We gotta go, like now." The urgency in his voice left no room for debate. "I'll explain outside. Forget about getting more water. The sooner we leave the better."

Making their way out, Bryson said nothing until they reached the safety of the big sentry tree. "Looks like he died from a snake bite. Did you see the puncture marks and tourniquet?" He watched her nod. "Obviously he was following you and must have gone to search the cave after you left."

"Okay, that sounds plausible, but why leave him there? What will we tell Captain Nez?"

"We don't tell Nez anything. Did you see that radio strapped to his belt? I wager someone knows he was following you and knows about where to find him. I wouldn't trust Nez or anyone. The sooner we get off the reservation the better I'll feel." He started to jog.

Serena thought Bryson was overreacting; she couldn't quite figure out why he seemed so spooked by the whole thing; although, finding a dead man, who they both knew the identity of and concluded was probably watching them earlier, felt more than a little creepy. When they paused to catch their breath, she confronted him.

"Hey, what gives? I've never seen you like this. Is it the dead man, us being followed, or something else?"

"Remember I told you about my father's funeral service?" He looked right at her. "Remember I told you a man I had never seen before and not since gave me a package, the one with the medal and a letter from the State Department? Remember that? Did you see Officer Cuch's tattoo—pretty unusual, right? Well, that man at my father's funeral had the same tattoo!"

"What! Are you sure?"

"Positive! It was hot that day. He had a sport jacket over his arm and it concealed the envelope. When he gave it to me, his arm flashed right under my face. I can still see the picture of that mark in my mind's eye."

"Shit, shit, shit!" Serena spoke. "These aren't synchronicities, Bry. Something is going on and we are just seeing bits and pieces. I have a feeling whatever it is, it's big—way bigger than we know."

"PTG, you got that right. Something is going on…and I intend to get to the bottom of it."

"We should probably stop at the Kayenta substation, so I can leave Captain Nez my contact information in case something happens at my *shibízhí's* hogan."

"I have a better idea. We should let them know we're leaving. This way they'll know we're gone, and it sort of invites them back in where we can record any intruder. I've got a dummy number associated with an abandoned property, but the calls forward to an answering machine I have at my home. It prevents certain undesirable tracking. I'll give them that number. Besides, you will be out of the country for who knows how long."

"That's smart; I wouldn't have thought of something like that."

"Believe me, I'm just warming up," he muttered. "I'll handle everything at the police station. You stay in the car and keep the engine running."

Suzie Yazzie explained Captain Nez was out. She offered to have Bryson speak with the officer on duty who just that moment came from a back office to the front reception area. He was the spitting image of Sam Cuch, "Hello, I'm Officer Dan Cuch, can I help you?"

Bryson kept his cool. "Damn, you look just like Sam Cuch. He must be your brother; I met him the other day."

"Identical twins." He smiled, showing a full set of teeth. "He's off today. How can I help?"

He explained that Captain Nez had taken him and his friend, Serena Mendez, to the home of her great aunt. "Serena didn't know she had died. Anyway, we are headed back and Serena thought she should leave Captain Nez her contact information in case anything happened at the hogan. She's out in the car; it's been a rough couple of days." He scribbled a name and number on a piece of paper and handed it over.

Officer Cuch took the paper and glanced at it, saying, "I'll see that he gets it."

Back in the car, Serena asked, "How did it go?"

"Come into my parlor said the spider to the fly. Let's see if anyone takes the bait. We set two traps—the phone and the camera. In the meantime, keep your earring on and the Taser handy." She fingered the turquoise earring. "Oh, by the way, Sam Cuch has a twin brother, carbon copy except for the teeth, name of Dan. If I was really thinking, I would have bugged him; I'll have to think a little better from now on."

After an hour speculating and trying to assemble all the crazy pieces thrown out in the last three days, they agreed to stop trying. The drive back seemed a lot longer than the drive there.

While Serena dozed, Bryson's mind operated in overdrive. *I've got more questions than answers, but I will damn sure get to the bottom of this shit.* He looked upward. *Dad, what the hell were you involved with?*

PART TWO
SNAKEWOMAN

17

S he found her seat and settled in for the flight to New Delhi. Considering Canada and Mexico were the only foreign countries she had
been to, Serena decided she might as well be traveling to Mars. Unbelievable
as it might seem, there was a direct flight from San Francisco lasting only sixteen hours. Bryson suggested it, having lived in San Francisco. Recognizing the
strong tech ties between India and Silicon Valley, Air India obliged with a direct
flight to Indira Gandhi International Airport. Then she had a 3.5-hour train
connection to Chandigarh in northern India, flanked by Pakistan to the east
and Nepal to the west. The Mansi Devi Temple Complex lay situated on a hill-
top near Chandigarh and the Naga Sanctuary was nearby. The Hindu statue in
her aunt's hogan represented Mansi Devi, Shiva's daughter—the snake goddess.
Despite her trepidations about the many hours of travel, and flight and train
connections, Serena's fears focused on what waited for her in this far-off strange
land. It had been a crazy week, and this seemed to be her first opportunity to sort
out the events since leaving the reservation. Air India seemed an almost insignif-
icant new experience as she reviewed the last week.

On the drive back, Bryson had convinced her of a few things. He would
front her ten thousand dollars and work on getting her gemstones appraised in
Taos and Santa Fe. She agreed and settled all her outstanding debts. She further

agreed to wear the earring at all times, not that she needed convincing given the strange events on the reservation. He also copied her passport. If hers was lost or stolen, he could get her a replacement much quicker; his connections among the hacker community assured him the fake would pass customs and TSA. Imagining potential threats left her unsettled, but "an ounce of prevention," she reasoned, was prudent. He also gave her two additional SIM cards for her phone and downloaded a Tor browser to her tablet; the latter randomized her IP address giving her a layer of anonymity. His final security measure involved a secret code of sorts. If she was ever in trouble, she could message him and include some facet of the weather. Bryson didn't know what he would do if he learned she was in danger, but somehow, the covert messaging instructions brought a measure of comfort to them both.

He picked her up at her apartment and chauffeured her to the airport in Albuquerque for her flight to San Francisco. He had brought her a gift of sorts to take along. Holding up a pack of American Spirit cigarettes he once again adopted the huckster voice. "Ladies and gentlemen, this may look like an ordinary package of cigarettes, but do not let your eyes deceive you." He flipped the top back to show eighteen cigarettes—two missing but otherwise nothing unusual. Then he explained they were dummy tops, just the upper ten millimeters showed; beneath he had concealed a Taser. By pressing over the "S," the electrodes would eject though the two missing slots.

"Don't pack this on your carry-on. Unless you want to send me a weather report from jail, put these both in your luggage." The second "gift" was pepper spray. "Pack them right before you check your luggage and unpack them as soon as you get your stuff from baggage claim. Airports are not safe, and you are traveling alone." Somewhat unconvincingly he added, "I'm sure you'll be fine and have a wonderful time while enjoying outstanding weather."

Their shared experience drew them closer. His goodbye hug and kiss seemed to linger; she liked that. Bryson reminded her to call or text when she arrived in New Delhi. He would be in Denver then, meeting with his uncle.

"Haven't seen him in a long time, not since a cousin got married four or five years ago. He's very important in the family business, travels all over the world, has a meeting with the governor or something to discuss a business opportunity, wants to catch up. I won't fly, not given what happened to my parents, so I plan to overnight in Denver."

"Drive safely, Bry. I'm not sure when I'll be back, hopefully no more than a couple of weeks. I'll stay in close touch." The door slammed and she wheeled her suitcase as the Subaru pulled away.

In San Francisco she had to claim her luggage from her domestic flight and recheck it for her international flight in a different terminal. Serena clutched her boarding pass, passport, and purse; she reminded herself to take some medication prior to boarding. TSA had been a breeze. The agent commented on her unusual necklace, reminding her she would need to remove it to avoid setting off the metal detector. He chatted a moment while noting her final destination was India and he wished her safe travels. The meds she had taken kicked in with the desired effect. Fifteen minutes after ascending, she fell asleep.

After watching her clear the metal detector, TSA Agent Riesman, pretending to need the restroom, had one of his colleagues take over his station.

"Serena Mendez just passed through security."

"You're sure it was her? Can you confirm that her final destination is New Delhi?"

"Yes, New Delhi. I remind you that my job is to verify identities. Unless her passport is fake, or she has an identical twin with the same name, it was her. Besides, she had on the flame necklace."

"You've got to be kidding!"

"Do I get extra compensation for that additional information?"

"You get what they promised you—no more, no less. She's Li's problem now; that's his jurisdiction. We'll make his people aware. You did well."

"Live in the light."

"May the light protect you."

Meaningless conversation with her seated passenger neighbors, food with more curry than she cared for, several bathroom breaks, and fitful naps characterized her lengthy flight. When she finally landed, she bought a colorful headscarf, cleared customs, and followed the signs to baggage claim. Everyone spoke English, a testament to British imperialism.

As she prepared to text Bryson and let him know she had arrived safely, a man holding a sign caught her attention. There, amidst several presumed drivers holding tablets and signs with people's names, this man's sign read, "Serena Mendez." Discomfort gripped at her stomach, her "Spidey sense" clued her that possible danger lurked. Serena's awareness had sharpened since her experience in the cave. Donning the headscarf and easing toward the back of baggage claim, she called Bryson.

"Hey, I was going to text you but decided to call instead. Made it in safely. What time is it there?"

A groggy voice answered. "Just after midnight."

"That's weird. It's 11:30 AM local time—twelve-and-a-half-hour difference. Flight was long, but I need to ask you something. Did you arrange for someone to pick me up?"

"No. Why do you ask?"

"There is someone here at baggage claim holding a sign with my name. He looks like a driver trying to connect with a traveler. I didn't tell anyone my plans. Even at the Naga Sanctuary, they don't know I'm coming."

"Listen. Pick up your bags. Unpack the special gifts I gave you and get the hell out of there! Take a taxi to the train station. Don't linger. Call me from the taxi."

Ten minutes later she called back. "I'm in the taxi and as far as I can tell no one is following."

"You're positive you didn't tell anybody your destination?"

"I told my neighbor in the next unit that I would be away for a while, but I never said where I was going. Besides, she's about seventy years old, always trying to mother me, beyond suspicion. Who would want to follow me? I'm just barely a grown-up with disabling PTSD."

"I don't know who and, just as important, I don't know why. Could be human trafficking, but I doubt it. More likely has to do with your great aunt; the tattoo on the dead officer might hold a clue. Could be your necklace; I haven't been able to find out much about that. I'm working on these dots but haven't connected them yet. If you bought your plane tickets using a credit card, someone could have tracked you that way. That's pretty basic hacking but doesn't answer who or why."

It dawned on her, like an eruption of light into blackness. "It's me."

"What?"

"I can't tell you why, but I just feel the truth of it in my bones. They want me, and without sounding too paranoid, I don't have a clue who 'they' are."

"Go on, there is a certain conviction in your voice, the same I heard when you spoke a deep truth at the last conspiracy meeting."

"It's something about my blood or bloodline, Bry. Candelaria—that's the clue to work on. I'm sure of it. Either they want me for something, to help them in some way, or…" her voice sounded small, but certain, "or they are afraid of me."

"Maybe you should come home until we can get a handle on this. We don't know the whos, the whys, the purpose or motives. Until then, the level of risk, how much danger you might be in—it's impossible to calculate."

"No. I'm not coming back until I meet Nalini Kumar at the sanctuary. She might have some answers. I might be small, but I'm smart. I think I'll be okay."

"You might be very brave or very stupid, but for the moment, I'm going with option one."

She smiled. "Stop worrying. Remember, trust… I think we're almost at the train station. Before I go, I don't want you to feel the whole conversation is all about me. How was your meeting with your uncle?"

"The condensed version is he offered me a job, actually lots of different jobs. Research for the company, hook me up with contacts he has in the government, something at Sandia labs totally cutting-edge, help me start a nonprofit—that's just a few possibilities. I struggled to diplomatically tell him I thought everything about the Reynolds family of companies and businesses were part of what's wrong with the world—government in bed with multinational corporations. Bottom line, I turned him down."

"What was his reaction?"

"He kinda laughed at me, kinda scolded me, and then said something a little strange. He said, 'You're just like your father.'" A pause followed before Bryson made his point. "Then he said, 'And look what happened to him.'"

"Bryson. I don't like the sound of that." She paid her taxi fare. "I have an idea. Here are two more dots to enter into your matrix. Whatever the name of that corporation flying the jet your parents died in, put that into your database for further analysis. The other dot to run correlations on: 'Reynolds!'"

A light went off in his own mind. "I like the way you think, PTG; I like the way you play my little game of connect the dots."

"The problem is what if you don't like what you find out? You could uncover something ugly."

He ignored that last comment. "Be safe, you're not in Kansas anymore."

"You watch out too," she giggled, "I'm too far away to protect you."

He hung up. Bryson walked barefoot, plopped into his desk chair, and stared at a monitor. "Let's see just what I find out..." he muttered to himself.

18

An uneventful and monotonous train ride to Chandigarh followed. The rocking and swaying along with the repetitive sound of the wheels on the tracks lulled her. After watching the quaint countryside for ten minutes, she closed her eyes and soon fell asleep. Her tablet recharged as did she. Two hours later, stiff but rested, she had a snack and felt renewed. Local time: almost 2 PM.

Chandigarh looked to be a fantastic city—capital of Punjab and Haryana, internationally renowned for its architecture and urban design. She smiled learning the city was named in part after Chandi, an Indian warrior goddess. *Here I am, a young warrior woman in the city of a warrior goddess,* she mused, but this was not her final destination. The railhead was less than a thirty-minute drive to the Naga Sanctuary. Perhaps she would have time during her stay to visit highlights of this city dating back to prehistory and now with modern infrastructure. Known also for its dense banyan and eucalyptus, one of the many things she longed to explore in this, India's wealthiest town, but these explorations would have to wait. She was on a mission and needed to hail another taxi. *Almost there...*

❖   ❖   ❖

The driver turned right down a tree-lined single lane dirt drive. A stone archway with a bronze cast sign in Sanskrit lettering with the English below in much smaller letters identified this as: "Naga Sanctuary." He drove to the end where a fountain of cascading rocks and water stood, and the road curved gracefully to a circular drive. The car stopped, and the driver unloaded her baggage; he gestured to a small building and announced, "Your destination." As he collected his fare, he added, concern evident in his voice, "You do not look the type. I hope you find whatever it is you are seeking. Be careful."

Oh my, I thought a sanctuary would be a safe place. Standing in front of a clear administrative or entry building of some sort, she looked around before entering. A path led to an iron gate, beyond which she caught glimpses of what looked like a courtyard. There were many flowers, some statues, and a large bell within her rather limited view. This was obviously not a tourist attraction; she doubted it was even open to the public. It reminded her of an abbey where she once spent a weekend retreat, where cloistered monks tried to teach meditation skills to people with PTSD. It hadn't worked for her, but the abbey had been memorable.

The door creaked slightly as she entered. There were seats, cushions, books, potted plants, but surprisingly few decorations. A faint smell of incense filled the room; a curl of smoke rose from a small burner. Behind a counter, a woman stood with her back to Serena, arranging fresh flowers; she seemed to be singing to them and appeared to be in no hurry to even turn around. The woman wore a deep saffron-colored robe with a bright red hem; the colors made the flowers look drab by comparison. Her shaved head reflected a hint of sunlight coming through the many windows. With uncharacteristic patience, Serena waited.

Still yet to turn around, the woman's voice asked, "Do you seek the truth, child?" and then she resumed her soft singing.

"Actually, I am looking for one of the sisters here, Nalini Kumar. Someone directed me to find her…but it's a long story… I have traveled some distance." She waited, expecting a response, but the woman continued with her singing and flower arranging. A surreal, time-warp feeling began to grow when Serena realized she had not answered the woman's question. "Yes, of course I seek the truth," she said, adding, "the truth shall set us free."

The woman's head nodded and her singing stopped. "An answer wise beyond your years... The sister you seek is no longer here." Then she turned around.

Serena gasped. Where the woman's eyes should be, only milky white globes filled her sockets. Between her sparse eyebrows, a red *bindi* fashioned as a small eye met her gaze.

"Many seeking truth are blinded by illusion."

Her initial surprise melted as Serena not only studied the woman but also the message in her words. The face was impossible to date or try to guess the age of. An aura of wisdom surrounded the strange woman. Serena suspended thinking, closed her eyes, and acted purely on instinct and intuition, overcome by a deep stillness, as unmoving water over an endless depth. Time suspended.

"The same illusion which binds our freedom." Serena didn't recognize her own voice.

"Your light shines brightly, sister. Long has it been since a Candelaria has visited our sanctuary. But time also is an illusion."

"The time of darkness and shadow is not."

Whether it was a howl or a cackle of laugher erupting along with the smile embedded upon a thousand wrinkles on the old woman's face, Serena could not say for sure, but the sound broke the mystical binding and again physical reality ensued. She faced the blind woman.

"Will Nalini Kumar be back anytime soon?"

Another howl of laughter followed and the woman said, "This child, we do not know. She visits with Sisters of the Black Serpent in Egypt...but her daughter is here. Come, I shall take you there. I am called Anshula." Milky orbs looked at the incense burner where the cone had just extinguished. "Good time to leave. Besides, I am all out of cones and prefer the fresh flowers for now."

How the woman knew the incense had just burned down and how Anshula navigated with complete ease and certainty despite her blindness did not occur to Serena as she tried to keep up with her escort in the flowing yellow robes. The old woman was spry. As they entered through the iron gate, the full splendor of the courtyard defied description—flowers in staggering colors, strange trees, statues of Hindu goddesses, serpent statues, more fountains, stone and wooden benches, walking paths, and the large bell Serena had previously seen. Women, similarly dressed in bright yellow kaftans, some completely naked, and all with shaved heads appeared to be in yogic meditation on a grassy spot. A breeze tickled wind chimes. Small housing units, almost like bungalows, flanked two sides of the courtyard haphazardly. Larger buildings were at the far end. Serena guessed they might be communal dining or meeting halls of some sort. Beyond that she could not say.

Serena almost did not know where to look, there seemed to be so much to absorb, but the entire picture conveyed a sense of peace and tranquility—an enclave of sanity in an otherwise insane world. In the distance, ever watchful and majestic, stood the foothills of the Himalayas.

"Yes, I know, it is beautiful, is it not? I still see it, not as well as before, but in my mind's eye, the beauty never fades… Be careful."

Serena froze. A large snake, that she was pretty sure was a cobra, slithered in a sunny patch on the path ahead.

"We have many snakes here. They sometimes do not take well to strangers." She stopped just before the snake, leaned forward a moment then motioned for Serena to lean next to her. Lazily, the snake flicked out its tongue a few times then returned to soaking up the sunlight. "Once they get to know your smell, you should be perfectly fine and in no danger. That is why I chose to lead you here."

They diverted to a small path and stood in front of one of the small dwellings. "This is where Nalini's daughter Dharani lives; no doubt she is expecting you." At that moment, the door opened, Anshula clasped her palms together, bowed, and withdrew.

Dharani stood in front of the open door. Her dress and shaven head looked identical to everyone else on the sanctuary grounds. A smile and a small red *bindi* lit her face as she embraced the traveler. "You must be Serena Mendez. Mother said you would visit, but she did not know when. Welcome, sister!" Seeing the necklace, the gold and silver candle and snake adorning Serena's neck, she suddenly looked frightened. "It is true then. You should never wear your mark in public, sister. It is a grave danger, especially for you who number so few."

A momentary shadow crossed Serena's consciousness as a chill descended. Her necklace suddenly felt tight, constricting her neck and making it difficult to breathe. She steadied herself and pushed back a clawing fear. As a cloud momentarily blocks the sun, the sensation passed, and warmth returned.

Small, cozy, and sparsely decorated, Serena scanned the environment. In some ways, it reminded her of her great aunt's hogan though the architecture was totally different.

"I have so many questions."

"I am sure you do. As well, you must be weary from your lengthy travels." Dharani's demeanor, so calm and tranquil, immediately set Serena at ease. "Would you like chai?" Her impatience at wanting to know answers immediately melted away, and she gladly took a seat. *Chai first, answers later. There really is no reason to rush.*

19

S erena almost didn't know where to start; she sought answers to so many unknowns. Rather than start by asking, she thought it best to start by telling. Over the next hour, while sipping chai and nibbling on some sweets she did not recognize, the young woman recounted the story of her life to date. Dharani rarely asked questions or interrupted; instead, she sat intently listening; her dark brown eyes conveyed deep understanding. When Serena described her first encounter in the cave as a young girl, she sensed in her listener not surprise, but disappointment that the experience ended as it did. Serena left nothing out, including the circle of symbols in her *shibízhí's* home, the recent return to the cave, and the dead man including his tattoo. When appropriate, she showed pictures to her hostess, images captured on her cell phone. She finished by recounting her trip here, including the man with the sign in baggage claim. At this last piece, Dharani looked concerned.

"You are certain none knew of your journey here other than your friend Bryson, whose trustworthiness is beyond question?"

"Yes, I am sure. I hoped that perhaps you or your mother somehow knew I was coming and sent the man to pick me up."

"No, child. Ooljee and Nalini were moon sisters; occasionally they journeyed together during the night, but your great aunt, your *shibízhí* as you call her, was not certain you would ever come. My mother had planned to be here. If she'd known the time of your arrival, it is she who would be serving you tea now." Dharani rose and disappeared for a moment to a back room before she returned with a sketch of Serena, identical to the one Captain Nez had in his office. "Mother left this with few instructions other than to prepare you for your next chakra opening."

"Next chakra opening? Wait a minute, so you have no idea who that man might have been."

"I have a very good idea who that man works with or for. This will come with more discussion as you learn the history of the great battle between light and darkness, moon and sun. All this follows the second breaking. To speak of this now would be to start the story in the middle. There is time for the telling, so you understand and know the truth. For now, I will only say that you are safe here."

"Can you tell me about the Candelaria?"

"That too is part of the telling. I sense your impatience. This is good and bad as the desire to seek the truth in you is very strong; it is part of your Candelaria blood. But there is much false knowledge which needs to be undone and this takes time. Opening your next chakra is crucial. Those are mother's instructions."

It was not the answer she wanted, but she had traveled far to this place upon instructions from her elder. Wisdom and patience prevailed. "I've heard of chakras, the energy centers or vortexes, but I really don't know anything about them."

"Come, let us walk while your energy becomes more in tune with our sanctuary. This land is sacred, and walking will help to connect you. Tonight, there is a shared meal. This will give you the chance to meet the acolytes here as well as those who study our Shakti yoga. We are known as the master teachers of this path to enlightenment. This would be good training for you as well. Here you will learn much about your chakras as well as many other things to help you on your journey."

As they both rose to exit, Dharani paused at the door looking toward Serena's feet. "It is best to walk barefoot to let nature tickle your feet with her energy."

Barefoot and with no hurry at all, the two women strolled through the paths and the grass as soft sunlight on the leaves and shadows danced before them. Birds and insects sang amidst fragrances, subtle and changing on the shifting breeze. Everyone greeted them with respectful *Namastes,* and all had the same peaceful, tranquil ways which aligned with the serenity of the Naga Sanctuary. For the first time in her life, Serena actually felt serene and completely one and at ease with her surroundings. Her initial fear of the many snakes evaporated like a dewdrop greeting the morning sun. PTSD felt like something foreign that had been purged or removed, much as one might remove a pricking and painful thorn followed by an immediate sense of relief. Immersing herself in this newfound freedom, Serena felt concern for nothing beyond the present moment.

Sensing her visitor's calm receptiveness, Dharani began. "The chakras are your own connection to the different spirit vibrations; they connect you energetically to different states of being which exist within the universe. They are open or closed to a lesser or greater extent. The more open, the more connected you are. In the cave, the mystical male snake opened your root chakra to join with your female snake who called to him. You are now more connected, and here, as we walk, you can let the energy which roots you and connects you to the energy of the physical plane flow into and out of your root chakra."

The truth of this did not need further explanation. Through the soles of her feet, Serena felt the very connection Dharani described. "But there is more. Your third chakra, through which the energy of fear travels into and out through your navel, has opened, too. And your fourth, the heart chakra where love flows most strongly, is also more open than when we first began our walk. These things I can not only sense, but see in your aura, the energy field surrounding you which itself has different layers. I do not ask if you feel these things as I see them and only speak their truth."

It almost seemed incredible, but all that Dharani explained only gave words to communicate something Serena knew. Having this spoken validated what she was feeling. "Please continue; you skipped over the second chakra."

A faint smile along with a gesture to sit on a stone bench followed. A fountain splashed nearby. "The second chakra is very powerful. Beneath it your kundalini energy lies coiled like a snake. The second chakra is the gateway to release this energy. When the kundalini snake awakens, it travels to open all the seven chakras. This is the next step on the journey of the Circle in the pictures you showed me. For this, we must await a visit from our Reverend Mother, the wisest in our order. She is also a *shaktipat,* a Guru or enlightened master who can awaken your kundalini through spiritual transmission. She travels among our several sanctuaries. Word has been sent to her of your arrival. It is perhaps better that Nalini is not here since it was Reverend Mother who sent her away, but this story goes to the fifth or throat chakra. Finishing with the second, the kundalini also connects to the sex energies of the body and the universe. Especially in the West, they confuse this. Shakti yoga is our method of controlling the sex energy and using it, even transforming it to open the other chakra centers. All this is only words to you, but as you study and practice, an inner knowing will blossom. While I can describe the rising of the kundalini serpent to you, it is only when you experience this awakening that you will begin to truly understand the power."

They rose to continue their stroll. Serena had lost all sense of time or questions, wanting only to hear and learn more of the chakras. "The fifth chakra lies in the throat. My mother Nalini believes our Sisterhood should be more involved in speaking the truth rather than just keeping it to ourselves. This too relates to the history following the second breaking which you will learn about. The Reverend Mother does not agree with mother but grew weary of her call to stop remaining silent. The Black Snake Sisters in Egypt are masters of the fifth chakra, much as we are masters of the second, so Reverend Mother sent her there to learn more." It appeared Dharani laughed to herself at the drama of these two elders; her eyes sparkled with merriment. "Finally, there is the sixth chakra which is also called your third eye." Touching the middle of her forehead, she explained, "When this opens, your thoughts and perceptions of reality are clear, and you can see the spirit in matter. Last is the crown chakra which itself is separate from our physical nature." Dharani put her hands over Serena's head. "When the crown is fully opened you are connected to pure consciousness. At this sanctuary, only Anshula and our Reverend Mother, when she visits here, have reached this level of awakening."

"Anshula, the blind woman who took me to your home?"

"Believe me, she sees much more than you or I, sister. She is a day-walker and lives fully in the spirit world while remaining here on the physical plane. She finds it amusing."

Serena was about to ask a question when her hostess remarked, "That is enough for this day. It is now time that we gather for food and fellowship." At that moment, the large bell chimed three times.

20

B ryson felt pleased with himself. Serena appeared to be safely tucked away for the moment, at least judging from her calls and reports. His research uncovered steady new information about the battle between light and darkness, an allegory for truth and falsehood. Connected associations among the various pieces emerged. He now had several meta-tags dealing with secret societies. By luck, happenstance, or synchronicity, their conspiracy group had a speaker lined up in a couple of weeks—an expert on the Illuminati. The "All-Seeing Eye" in the pyramid topping the snake tattoo suggested a Freemason or Illuminati theme, but he couldn't trace it any further. Maybe the speaker could.

The phone number he had left at the Tribal Police resulted in three calls: two from Officer Dan Cuch, a third from a party identifying himself as Charles Godfried; the number given was a Chicago area exchange. Reverse phone lookup confirmed the number as belonging to Charles Godfried, but there were no listings on social media, nothing in several other data banks confirming or tracing the name, number, and location. Conclusion: probable pseudonym.

Research on the necklace had thus far blanked—nothing on jewelry, antiquity, religious artifacts, or other avenues he investigated. He sent the picture with an inquiry to Sotheby's through an anonymous, untraceable email. The response from a Monsieur Rene Dubufet seemed intriguing—he had never seen such a piece but had heard of the Candelaria Cult, that was the language he used, and he would contact a curator at the Vatican Museum who might have additional information. Background check on Rene Dubufet confirmed him to be a legitimate employee of Sotheby's. Today, Bryson had received a follow-up message:

Dear Sir/Madam,

Today I received information regarding the Candelaria Necklace you previously inquired about. My contact at the

Vatican indicated it is extremely rare. I have taken the liberty of communicating with a private collector who has expressed interest in other esoteric artifacts. Arranging an exchange with this potential buyer and with you as a consignor would require negotiation. We would, of course, need to verify the authenticity of the item and to ensure that acquiring such a piece was done legally. Please do not interpret this last statement as in any way suggesting impropriety.

As I am sure you understand, we would require the standard commission; although, there may be room for negotiation as we are merely facilitating a private sale and not an actual auction. Also, the final purchase price could affect our terms as well. The piece I would estimate at this time, conservatively, as worth eight million pounds which is over twelve million US dollars.

Shall I make arrangements with the firm representing the interested collector for viewing and authentication? I trust the party you represent wishes all to be handled with the utmost discretion and I assure you that we at Sotheby's fully understand the requisite considerations.

Please advise as to how you would like me to proceed or assist in any manner. We thank you for considering Sotheby's as an exchange agency.

Very truly yours,
Monsieur Rene Dubufet

Whoa, that's a lot of tacos! I wonder what Serena will think when I send her this—probably that I'm messing with her. Got to figure out a way for her to keep it safe. They had both learned that the Candelarias had almost been wiped out in the Middle Ages, so it seemed a good bet that anything having to do with the Candelarias could put her at risk. For the moment, he hatched a new plan. He responded to the message with a vague, "I will convey this to my client and shall communicate pending their consideration." Then he set to work establishing a new "sticky trap" as he liked to think of this bit of cyber-espionage.

A short while later, Bryson admired the new listing on eBay with a slightly altered photoshopped image of the Candelaria necklace. The account for this listing was, of course, bogus and untraceable, but he could see if any interested parties followed the listing. Initial bid he set at fourteen million dollars while chuckling out loud. That would be sweet!

As he drove to Santa Fe with plans to pick up Serena's mail, he considered possibilities for protecting the necklace. He rejected shipping it back to the US but wondered about a safe-deposit box in a bank vault in Chandigarh; an international bank would probably be best. Then again, the sisters at the Naga Sanctuary might have ideas as well.

Arriving at her apartment complex, he rang the neighbor's unit, and Mrs. Trujillo answered. Bryson got the feeling she rarely left the apartment as he watched her slowly use a walker to move from the door to the kitchen table.

"Serena reminded me to thank you for helping to keep an eye on things for her and to collect her mail." He reached down to scratch behind the ears of Mrs. Trujillo's cat rubbing against his leg.

"No problem. She's a good girl. Like to see her with a nice young man." She eyed Bryson to gauge his response as she put together a few pieces of mail and a catalogue, wrapping them all with a rubber band. "Looks like Oreo thinks you're a good fella."

He gave another scratch to the black-and-white cat and picked her up, holding her as she purred. Bryson almost didn't hear what Mrs. Trujillo said next.

"Not like them other fellas."

"What was that? I'm not sure I heard you."

"Yer too young to be hard a hearing. Wait till you're my age. I said," she raised her voice, "not like them other fellas."

"What other people? Did anyone come by looking for Serena?" He watched as the old woman nodded.

"Oreo didn't care for 'em very much either, tried to scratch one of them."

"So, there was more than one? What did they want?"

"Snoopin' around I can tell you that. Wanted to know where my next-door neighbor had gone and when she would be back. They were all polite, both of them, smiling and being pleasant, but ole Maria," she struck her breast, "can smell a rat, just as well as Oreo." She followed with something in Spanish that Bryson couldn't understand but it sounded like a curse.

Bryson put the cat down and Oreo returned to brushing against his leg. "Did you get their names?"

"Course I did; wouldn't be much of a watcher if I didn't learn something about who was snoopin' around what I'm watching." A self-satisfied grunt followed as she handed him the mail. "One was named Dan, didn't give his last name—Native for sure. The other was blond-haired, blue-eyed, mid-forties—wore a suit, no tie. Didn't like him. Charlie something. Give me a minute... Godfried, that's it. Charles Godfried, I could tell he wasn't from around here."

Bryson's eyebrows flinched. "Mrs. Trujillo, that was real smart of you to get their names. If anyone else shows up, please give me a call." He left her a number. "Don't give any information about Serena."

"My little Serena's not in any trouble, is she? They weren't bill collectors or some drug dealers, right?"

"No, she's not in trouble." He stood to go. *At least I hope not,* he thought to himself... "You're doing a great job and thanks a bunch." He shut the door. *This isn't a game, Snowman, my friend might be in a lot of trouble.*

Not entirely sure how best to handle security for the valuable necklace or for his close friend, the solution to one problem came on a text message from Serena that included a few photos. So as not to text and drive, he pulled over and studied the selfies of Serena—bald-headed in a saffron robe trimmed in red with a mysterious smile. He texted back, "Driving, have news, will call later... Bald women are sexy!" He finished with a wide-eyed emoji and hit "send."

21

The last few days had been incredible! The Naga Sisterhood began to shed light on many of the mysteries she and Bryson were trying to piece together. The first breaking, as Dharani termed it, essentially referred to creation of the entire manifest universe—out of darkness (the black void of complete nothingness) the entire universe of matter and energy came into being represented by light. This caused an illusion of duality, of separateness, but it is all just spirit incarnating as energy and energy incarnating as matter. Dharani explained the vibrational frequency of spirit becomes progressively denser as it forms matter, but everything in existence is all part of the same spirit. Thus, duality represents an illusion, a falsehood, the first apparent separation from unity as the actual reality beneath the illusion—the first breaking.

In truth, this creation story was not new to Serena; she had heard this sort of thing before. It was the story of the second breaking that totally intrigued her. It so enthralled her that she had accepted an invitation to enter as an initiate, shaved her head, and accepted an acolyte's robe. She had also started her training in Shakti Yoga. Her instructress, Shanti Desai, explained it was necessary to have at least the basic skills to control the kundalini energy once it activated. Her teacher was aptly named—Shanti translated as "the tranquil one." Serena had never met anyone who seemed more peaceful and completely one in the moment. Everything the woman did had a perfect grace with no wasted motion or energy in her movements. Serena simply enjoyed being next to her instructress, watching her move, absorbing her presence. Fortunately, she displayed unfailing patience with her new pupil—one who lacked discipline of body and mind. Serena spent most of the day with Shanti learning breath control, postures, asanas, mudras, mantras, and chants. The instruction sessions were private. There was so much to learn.

Serena continued to spend time with Dharani and lived as a guest in her household. Upon her formal initiation, Serena would be given living quarters in the communal home. Dharani herself apprenticed to Bhilangana, the chief archivist/librarian for their entire order, not just this sanctuary. Everyone called her Bili which seemed kind of funny to Serena. The archivist was 102 years old though Serena would have guessed she was at most in her seventies. Dharani explained that until her formal initiation by the Reverend Mother, the library would be off-limits to Serena, but eventually she would spend time there learning the secret truths that their order had devoted themselves to preserving. Her hostess briefly explained about the second breaking, but most of the truths stored in the library dealt with the falsehoods perpetrated and spread through history as a result of the second breaking. Dharani also assured Serena that she could complete the Circle training here at the sanctuary with some travel to other locations for more advanced study. It might take a few years.

That seemed to be a small problem. She had not included that detail in her communications with Bryson and admittedly, she felt inner conflict. Never in her life had the young woman felt more at home than being among these women at the Naga Sanctuary—this sisterhood. Her PTSD symptoms had all but vanished in the brief time she spent here, barefoot, practicing yoga, on a strict vegetarian diet. Never had she felt so laser-focused with the intention of perfecting her breath, her postures, etc. And she thirsted to learn the truth of this world. This seemed to be part of the very fabric of who Serena Mendez was at her very core. And here at the sanctuary, her thirst could be quenched.

Yet, there remained a part inside her head, a little voice that echoed precisely what came across looking in the mirror of Dr. Jenkins exam room: "I'm running away…"

Serena sat with her tablet summarizing notes. She would email these to Bryson so that he could abstract relevant parts to tag. Her notes also functioned as a journal to refer back to. She took separate entries on her yoga progress but kept these to herself.

Much of the history before the second breaking has been lost. There were other earth species dwelling on the planet. Whether they started here, or their origin was extraterrestrial, no one can say for sure. A great civilization lived in the Pacific—Lemuria. No records were kept as the Lemurians, inhabitants of the continent of Mu, were telepathic. They were highly spiritual and lived in accord with nature. According to Dharani, even their physical forms were less dense, their skin was greenish brown, and they primarily lived underground. A group traveled from Lemuria to establish a colony in the Indus Valley. Standard history dates this to 7,500 years ago, but Dharani explained it was much earlier, perhaps as much as 100,000 years ago. Mu was destroyed; why or how is not known.

The remaining Lemurians were few in numbers. They bred with prehistoric humans. This marked the beginning of the second breaking. Many of the hybrids were unnatural; some were beasts. Interspecies breeding upset the balance of matter and spirit, corrupting the DNA. Not all the hybrids failed; however, the joining caused a subversion of spirit to matter. The resulting hybrids lusted for worldly satisfaction through sensual gratification and power. Physical desires took precedence over spiritual pursuits. Many of these hybrid lines rose to dominance. While the Lemurians and these more successful hybrids taught early prehistoric humans the basics of civilization, they maintained control by genetically preserving their hybridized bloodline. This has continued to this day. Still, this corruption was only the beginning.

Another great civilization lived in the Atlantic. Their technology went far beyond what we know of today. They had mastered flight, including spaceflight, mastered gravity and how to create massive structures. We know them as the people of Atlantis. At a point in their history, there was a battle for control. This we know from ancient Vedic texts, most of which were destroyed in the flood that occurred much later. Dharani explained to me that many details were in a translated text in their library, "The World Out of Balance," part of my required reading. After a prolonged conflict, many Atlanteans were cast out. The defeated moved to different areas and began to rebuild. Most of them concentrated in the region of Sumeria. We know this from clay tablets. To the Sumerians, who were hybridized with Lemurian DNA, these Atlanteans were like gods and goddesses. Most were tall with fair skin; they came from the sky with knowledge and power including how to manipulate genes. Mixing their seed with the natives further contaminated and corrupted the DNA. More beasts—giants and other humanlike creatures were born of this advanced hybridization program.

The development of humanity's natural genetic blueprint was designed to result in growth and evolution and a gradual unfolding of spiritual truth. This would gradually move us past the first breaking and back into unity consciousness. The consequences of the genetic alterations made spiritual ascent very difficult for a hybridized human and gave the purebloods enormous power and control. For most of humanity, genetic lines had been corrupted from the original design, causing us to remain handicapped in rising past the material to the spiritual plane. Another battle for control of the Atlantean continent, fought primarily by armies produced by the genetic breeding program, ended in near total destruction of all civilization. This battle corresponds to the time of the great flood.

"More tomorrow, this is as far as I've gotten." As she hit 'send' on these compiled notes, her cell rang. "Hey, Bry, I just sent you a long email. You are not going to believe some of the incredible things I am learning."

"Yeah, well you might have a hard time with the things I've learned. I hope you're sitting. Some of it's good, and some of it not so good. Which do you want first, the good news or the bad?"

"Let's start with the good."

"Well, that necklace your *shibízhí* left you is worth at least eight million pounds."

"You're joking right? Eight million dollars is more money than I can imagine."

"No, I said eight million pounds; that's over twelve million dollars—just a bit more to stretch your imagination."

An uncomfortable tight feeling grew in Serena's pit. "OMG, Bry, you are stressing me out. What am I going to do?"

"No problem, PTG. I got it figured out. It turns out, you did most of the work by sending me those selfies. By the way, I have to come up with a new nickname for you since PTG doesn't work anymore. What do you prefer, Rich Bitch or Baldie Beauty?"

"Very funny! How about you stick with PTG for now?"

"Right. Okay, here's my suggestion." Bryson explained that he had contacts among the hacker community in India. Using one of the pictures she had sent, he could make a false Indian passport with a fake name and identity. She could use the passport for identification to set up a safe-deposit box in an international bank in Chandigarh. Their passport ID check procedures are nil, so she should easily be able to get the necklace secured. He could get her the fake ID in as little as two days. The only thing she needed to do was send him a name.

"That's easy. My great aunt's name, Ooljee, means 'moon' in Navajo. The Hindu name Chanda means the same thing. So how about, Chanda Patel? It's got a nice sound." Serena could not argue with the reasoning and sensibility of Bryson's plan. She didn't like the rest of his report which was all about what he learned from the phone calls to the number he had given Officer Dan Cuch and how this connected to the suspicious visit with Mrs. Trujillo. Now there was a man from Chicago after her as well.

"Do you think they were just after the necklace? Do I have to sell it and hire bodyguards? I don't know what I should do."

"I hope that's all it is. I think you should stay put for now. No need to hire anyone just yet; warrior nerd here is working on more traps." He decided not to give her any details.

As she hung up, Serena noticed only one thing. Nausea, anxiety, and irritability crept from her stomach up to her brain and filled everywhere in between. For the first time since arriving, she medicated. Yoga couldn't handle this. Medication beat meditation.

22

Night. Sleep eluded her. Serena quietly left Dharani's home and walked the sanctuary grounds. She felt no snake fear; fear and doubt of a different sort stalked her. Was staying here a grand cop-out? Who pursued her and why? A fork in the path lay before her; conflict and indecision weighed heavily upon her. A solitary figure stood motionless, silhouetted by a crescent moon and night clouds. It was Anshula. They greeted one another with a ceremonial bow.

"My child has a shadow of darkness in her aura. What troubles you, Serena?"

The enlightened elder listened. They sat in the lotus position on a grassy spot, two women bound in sisterhood. Beneath the milky orbs, Serena imagined a bemused twinkle as she unloaded her fears and her conflict. Strange how just sharing this with another soul somehow eased the burden. The entire time Anshula sat as though this was the only thing of importance at that moment, listening with the intensity of a blind person who hears and sees through to naked truth. At last, she spoke.

"In the great battle we fight, sacrifice is required. Your struggle is not running away; that was your past. Your struggle now is running toward. Whichever path you choose requires sacrifice. The decision is yours. One does not serve truth without courage. You are a Lightbringer. When the time comes, you will be ready."

Serena knew the wise woman conveyed deep wisdom but would not point to one path. "Stay a while here, sister, practice your meditation and be filled with the stillness of night."

The young woman focused her breath control. A deep meditation ensued, and she went to the world between dreams and wakefulness. Dim. Just a sliver of moonlight. Sitting in perfect stillness, she saw herself, embodied in soft light. The intensity grew until her light consumed everything. The meditation ended. Calmly, she rose and returned to her guest bed. She knew what to do. Sleep followed easily. In the distance, Anshula continued to meander the sanctuary gardens; laugh wrinkles and a smile creased her aged face.

Two days later, a package arrived by express delivery addressed to her, care of the Naga Sanctuary. It wasn't the photo she would have chosen, but Chanda Patel looked very Hindu in the official faux passport. A cryptic note from Snowman advised she not use the name in any further email, phone, or texts. He added, "Miss you…"

I guess I need to venture back out into the real world. Dharani accompanied her. They both dressed in identical robes with red and yellow scarves covering their heads. On the way there, they passed the Mansa Devi Temple. Though less than two miles away by a back road, it surprised Serena to learn the Naga Sisterhood had nothing to do with the temple at all.

"Occasionally, we go for a ceremonial service or may sometimes attend a festival, but we think they are more of a tourist attraction and a distraction."

"Distraction?"

"We do not worship devas, gods, or goddesses. Religion, and in more recent centuries science, just another religion of sorts—these things are full of false beliefs. We worship truth and this cuts through many false beliefs."

Spoken truths such as these confirmed to Serena that her decision to stay and complete her training was the correct one. *And the truth shall set us free.* The power in those words grew in her mind.

"You should attend the next festival. It's in just a few days. I'll bring you. It is important for you to understand the people and culture of India."

At the moment, there seemed to be more pressing and important things for Serena to understand; she expressed this to Dharani.

"Yes, yes, I know; you want answers to so many questions. You are impatient, sister. There is much that I can still tell you, but our library is really where you need to seek your answers. Yet, all this must wait. Shanti has asked that you spend all of the next three days together with her so that she can prepare you for Reverend Mother's visit. Shanti says your mind gets too distracted by all the new knowledge I am sharing with you; it slows your yoga training." She laughed. "I told her we both have a good student, but her instruction was more important for the moment."

"Three days? Only three more days and my kundalini serpent will be released? Do you think I will be ready?"

She laughed again. "It does not matter what I think, sister. If Shanti is your teacher, I am sure you will be prepared... Oh look, we are at the bank."

On one side of the street stood a branch of the Bank of Baroda, India's International Bank. Across the street, Serena noted Citibank. Why that seemed funny to her, she couldn't say, but she felt that a Hindu might prefer the Bank of Baroda, so they proceeded.

The bank personnel were extremely polite. Apart from the endless paperwork, everything went well. A cursory glance accompanied the presentation of her passport. Serena had already strategically practiced her signature for her false identity; she signed multiple documents. A half hour later, she and Dharani exited the bank with the valuable necklace safely secured.

"In truth, sister, when you arrived at my door wearing the necklace, I was very surprised. I am glad, and I am sure it relieves you, to have put it in a place of safety. It is most beautiful and most rare indeed."

"Why is that? What happened to the Candelaria?"

"Despite what I promised Shanti, this much I will tell you. Long have the Candelaria been persecuted by the Brotherhood of the Sun and all their factions. The Luminaria, we who are lighted by the moon, our Mother, also have many factions. Our Order, The Naga Sisterhood, is but one of those Luminarian Sects that serve the light of truth. Nalini, my mother, grows now on a different branch—the Black Snake Sisters in Egypt. Only the moon has the power to block the light of the sun. Your branch, the Candelaria, was broken many years ago."

While Serena pleaded for more information, Dharani only said, "Sister Shanti will be most displeased with me. Clear your mind. I will show and tell you more after Reverend Mother opens your next chakra. Many more answers are in our archives. Bili will show you, even better than I. You must be patient."

Upon arriving back at the sanctuary, Serena found Shanti. The next three days she stopped thinking in order to train intensively. Her body was doing things she never thought possible. Her mind presented a different challenge; there she remained a stubborn novice.

The morning of her planned initiation Serena woke at dawn and went outside to stretch and greet the sun. She felt famished. The mental and physical discipline required of her during the past three days had left her hungry. What she really wanted was a cup of strong coffee, but that was not among the offerings at the sanctuary. Dharani broke the news—today Serena must fast as part of her preparation. Water was permitted, and also tulsi tea. This herb, made from the Holy Basil plant, had purifying properties.

As she sipped her tea, eying some delicious cakes with desire, but committed to fasting, she inquired about what to expect.

"Do I have to swear an oath or something, pledge my firstborn child, drink blood, cut my palms, or sacrifice an animal?" Humor helped to dispel the hunger.

"You are silly today, sister. What you speak of is seen in Bollywood and your Hollywood. Though," her voice grew serious, "such things are said of the Dark Brotherhood initiations."

"So, what happens?"

"You will drink a mixture of medicinal roots and snake venom with a small amount of snake blood. Do not fear; the snake is not harmed in the gathering. The mixture is quite bitter. Although the drink is not essential, it prepares the nervous system for the *shaktipat's* transmission. All the Sisterhood will be present."

"That's all?"

"When the Reverend Mother is done, you should stand. Try not to fall. It is the first test of your control. Shanti will be displeased if you are unable to stand. No more can I say. Each person's experience is different. Some things cannot be explained in words."

After a second cup of tea, she dressed for the day, glancing first in a mirror. The bald head no longer surprised her when she gazed at her own reflection. New muscles, a toned and fit appearance, and an erect posture all replaced what she had previously viewed—a slightly hunched over, petite but not toned body. Serena liked what she saw. All her piercings were gone, but she continued to wear the single turquoise earring. Dharani said she needed to remove it for the ceremony, but the sister would return it after the initiation.

The yoga exercises today remained light. Shanti indicated her pleasure at Serena's progress. As the acolyte held an especially difficult posture, an unfamiliar sister approached. Though her garment was no different, Serena immediately knew this to be the Reverend Mother. Shanti bowed in respect and her student followed suit. She and Reverend Mother whispered a few things that Serena could not overhear, and moments later the head of the order strolled with the soon-to-be newest initiate.

The Reverend Mother was much younger than Serena expected—mid-fifties at the most. There was an aura of power about the woman, an energy that drew Serena in. This woman could outshine any corporate president or head of state. When she looked at you, it was more looking through you, stripping you naked with no place to hide. Yet, she seemed totally and completely down-to-earth. She asked Serena questions about her childhood, her Ooljee of whom the Reverend Mother had heard, and laughed at some silly story Serena shared about being a child afraid in a cave. By the end of the walk, it felt as though the two had been friends for years.

"Your light shines brightly, sister. We are honored to have you among us." These words almost baffled Serena, more so when the older woman bowed to the young woman. She rose and kissed her gently on the forehead. "You will do fine, sister."

Immediately, a shock ran through Serena's spine. Her soles tingled, pins and needles erupted on her fingertips, the roots of the hair no longer on her shaved head burst into flame. She swooned, mute in amazement. The arousal lasted less than a minute then subsided. Reverend Mother winked and glided away. "Time to milk the snakes."

Rejoining Shanti to resume her exercises, all Serena could think of at that moment—*Try not to fall, try not to fall...*

The ritual began. Near sunset, sisters arrive in silence, motioning that Serena should follow. They escort her to a building well past the courtyard nestled in a grove of trees. A fountain within cascades in clear water. Candles illuminate the room. Sisters strip her, bathe her, and dress her in a delicate gown. She guesses the material to be an exceedingly fine silk. Ribbons of black and white adorn the gossamer fabric with half-moons and half-suns dyed front and back.

They lead her down narrow stairs to a chamber, illuminated by a single oil lamp set on a stone table with a solitary stone bowl. All the sisters are present, about twenty in total. Shanti takes her hand and directs Serena to drink the contents of the bowl. Bitterness invades every taste bud on her tongue. Shanti removes the gown and Serena stands naked. The Reverend Mother steps forward. Serena kneels, not daring to look at this High Priestess, an enlightened presence looking at, looking through the young initiate to the kundalini within. Soft chanting fills the room. Serena does not understand the Hindi words. As the Sisterhood sways gently, a sleepy almost trancelike feeling begins to affect the young woman. The room disappears; all the sisters glow in luminous light. The Reverend Mother sparkles in scintillating effervescence. The chanting subsides, and she speaks.

"Who vouches for this initiate who wishes to be part of our Naga Sisterhood, part of the Luminaria who seek to keep the sacred light of truth burning; who vouches for her?"

The chamber remains silent.

"Who vouches for Serena Mendez?"

An uncomfortably long silence ensues until Anshula speaks. The elder sister so enjoys this ceremony; she has the right for first vouching. To her, this presents a source of great amusement. Serena recognizes the old woman's voice.

"Anshula vouches for her. Please get on with it, my bladder is not as young as it used to be."

In the dim light, Serena cannot tell if the Reverend Mother frowns or smiles. All the sisters as one voice their agreement. She leans forward and kisses Serena in the middle of her forehead.

Immediately, the jolt running through the young woman's body nearly overpowers her, but she manages to remain kneeling. Every cell of her body seems alive, bursting with life force. Waves of electricity run up and down her body through to her fingertips and toes. The room blurs, dizzy, blinded, nothing to focus on, light shooting through the room, she herself the source of light beams and flashes and she can see each individual sister, their luminescence, their light energy.

"Rise, Sister of the Light."

For a moment, Serena remains kneeling, powerless to harness the energy she feels. *Breathe…focus…breathe.* She can't stand. *Breathe…focus…breathe.* She does not stand; instead, she leaps to her feet erect and steady.

Serena did not see the smile on sister Shanti's face as a strange, unfamiliar, but all-consuming burning seized the acolyte's pelvis.

23

Serena awoke unsure of what had happened after the ceremony; the memories were vague, dim. She recalled that someone had placed a robe on her, the one that she wore every day. She remembered much hugging and laughter. All the sisters went outside. They sang; they danced. There was food, but Serena wasn't hungry. She had so much energy. She was sure her *shibizhi* was there…or was that in a dream?

This morning, the burning in her pelvis remained—more of a throbbing. She had a terrible headache. Dharani was nowhere in sight, so she fixed herself some chai and breakfast and left to find Shanti. Her teacher stood balanced in a torturous asana, composed and tranquil as ever. She greeted Serena while balancing on two hands with her legs bent back, soles of her feet resting upon her head.

"How do you feel this morning, sister?" Shanti asked without breaking her position.

"Apart from a bad headache and extreme burning in my pelvis, I feel great. I've never had a urinary tract infection, but I imagine this is what it feels like."

Shanti burst out laughing uproariously, completely out of character, lost her balance, and rolled on the grass, tears streaming over her light brown skin. "You are so funny sometimes, Serena, that even I cannot control myself." She stood. "That is your kundalini, sister. It stirs within and yours is very restless. You did well last night. Upon your transmission your fire lit all of us. It was truly most beautiful."

"So, this burning throbbing misery down here," she pointed to her groin, "is what I asked to have released by activating my second chakra?" The instructress nodded. "What am I supposed to do now?"

Trying not to laugh at her student's naiveté, she said, "This is the practice of Shakti yoga, sister. Over time, you will learn to control and harness this energy to charge all seven chakras. This takes time; you must be patient. Trust me, you are off to a wonderful start."

Serena sat on the ground next to her yoga master, looked down between her legs, and sighed. "I can tell this is going to take a while. What do you suggest for today?"

"For today, child, I suggest you take the day off. It is best to let your energies settle on their own; there is no rush. Tomorrow we can start some new exercises, but you already know the basics. Besides, I promised sister Dharani not to keep you. She so very much wishes to show you our library. There are books that explain how to train the kundalini energy. Reading and study are an important part of mastery." She resumed her previous asana and Serena left, heading toward the library.

She had never been inside the small building. Inside, it looked fairly typical—shelves and stacks of books and periodicals, cozy reading chairs, an old book kind of smell. One of her sisters thanked her for last night and reported that Dharani waited below on the second level. She pointed toward a stairwell; Serena descended.

This second level seemed much more businesslike—books, desks, workstations and tables, a few computer terminals. Several sisters nodded toward her as she entered, and Dharani appeared from behind a book stack speaking in a hushed voice. "I thought it best you sleep extra after last night. Come, we have much to discuss." Randomly, she pulled a book from a shelf and went to a back-room office shutting the door behind her.

"Last night was wonderful; you did well, sister! There is so much here I wish to share with you."

Serena felt her sister's excitement and energy, but her response, "I'm all ears," didn't convey much enthusiasm. At that moment, she felt distracted by the burning down below. "Umm," she added. "I'm having a little issue with my kundalini."

Dharani nodded knowingly. "Someday I shall share with you the experience of my awakening. But for now, let me explain to you about our archives." She held out the book she had taken from the shelf, *Ophiolatreia: Serpent Worship*, by Hargrave Jennings. "This is a good one. Not one of the required readings, but still I recommend you read through it someday."

She continued by explaining how the material covered in each book had a commentary section attached where sisters of the order had clarified the underlying mistruths and falsehoods. There was also a section devoted to additional information about the author. For this particular book, by way of illustration, she explained that the book, published in 1889, had many historically correct facts about the presence and history of serpent worship throughout human history. Two sisters reviewing the material commented upon this. Both were long dead but had attested in the comment section as to the historical accuracy and truths contained. They further exposed the primary untruth revealed in the author's work. He associated the serpent worship, myths and symbols from

many different cultures, with the male phallus by asserting that all the snake worship was merely a metaphor for phallic worship.

Somehow, phallic worship was not the ideal subject for Serena to be
thinking about at that moment as sexual energies made it difficult for her to pay
close attention. She practiced a breathing technique and listened as the librarian
continued.

"Comments about the author show that he was a well-known Rosicrucian
and Freemason. These associations immediately make the book's argument
suspect, since both orders trace back to the Brotherhood of the Sun. Such factions
are masters at manipulating truth into falsehood, misdirecting and controlling
the interpretation of factual evidence." She shut the book. "So, you see, much of
our work in preserving truth rests in uncovering lies and falsehood."

The Naga Sisterhood had a lot of work to do sorting through historical
accounts, new publications, expert opinion, and so forth to determine truths
and distortions of truth. "Most of what you have learned has been altered and
distorted in ways to serve the purposes and goals of a few very powerful groups.
Many of our required readings explain about these groups and their hidden
agendas." She shuddered.

They went another level down. This entire floor was apparently devoted
to sacred religious texts such as the Upanishads, Bible, Koran, Talmud, Tao-
Te-Ching, etc. This level contained all the major Holy Books and thousands of
other sources such as scrolls and tablets. Most were copies. The work of interpreting and discerning truth from falsehood, which the Sisterhood had engaged
in over the thousands of years of their order's existence, Serena guessed amount-
ed to millions of hours.

"How long have the sisters been doing this work?"

"Our order has existed for over ten thousand years. There are several
books that detail this; they are required reading. First, I suggest you start with
The Naga Sisterhood Origins and History; it is excellent, but there are others.
These are on the next level. Come, let me show you."

As with the last two levels above, there were desks, tables, a few computers,
and a few sisters all scattered amidst thousands of volumes. It was more of the
same—books with commentaries by sisters on the contents and the authors.
"Upstairs I have a list of all the required books—one hundred twenty at last

count. But I also want to show you this particular book that I have told you about before." She located and withdrew one of many copies of *The World Out of Balance—The First and Second Breakings.*

"This book itself is incomplete. Nearly all copies of the original Sanskrit scrolls were destroyed, but what information has been preserved gives details about how the world came to be, how humans came to be, and how both people and the world are broken." She held out the book for Serena to see. There on the cover, a familiar image stood out—a black snake and a white snake in a circle biting their tails and enclosing a balanced half-moon and half-sun.

Serena exhaled. "I've seen that image before."

"Really?" Dharani replied, surprise evident in her voice. "Where, when?"

"In the hogan where my *shibízhí* lived." Serena took out her cell phone, scrolled to find the image, and showed Dharani. "That reminds me, here in this picture of the Virgin appearing to the Guanches, there are words and phrases, seven to be precise, that no one knows the meaning of. Are you aware of them? Do you know what they mean?" She showed first the picture, then the list of words and phrases Bryson had sent her separately.

"No, Serena, I have not seen these words, but perhaps our eldest sister Bili has. We are headed down to see her next in the last level below. It would be good to ask this of her. This question goes well with a little present she told me she has arranged for you."

Nothing had prepared the young acolyte for what lay below. It was noticeably cooler; she didn't mind as she still had some heat issues in her own below area. She noted a hum of sorts from different electronics and other equipment. This lowest level had printing and copying machines, even a book binding machine, computer servers, modern digitizing and scanning equipment. A half-dozen sisters studiously worked to digitize microfiche, all under the watchful eye of the senior archivist.

Impressed, Serena surveyed the modern operation with a mixture of incredulity and complete amazement as she uttered, "OMG, who organized and arranged all this?"

Bili looked up. Apparently, her hearing had not suffered despite her 102 years of age. She smiled with a measure of pride. "You know, little sister, I haven't just been reading all these years."

Serena didn't know what to say. She hadn't spent much time with Bili, who generally wasn't around and seemed mostly to be talking to herself. She gathered that Bili spent most of her time here, performing archival tasks. The eldest sister suspended her supervision, and they followed her to a back office.

"I have prepared a special gift for you, Serena; something to honor your commitment in joining our order." She handed over a copy of a book, *The Candelaria Fellowship—A Flame Extinguished*. The cover showed a drawing, similar in design to the necklace, but the colors were different—a black snake coiled around a green candle.

She accepted the book with reverence and glee.

"It's yours to keep; I copied it myself. The original is extremely rare. I had not read it myself until Dharani's mother researched it. Sister Nalini has done a fine review. You can read her comments in the back section. I bound them all together. I'm afraid the story is not a happy one."

Dharani spoke. "Sister, there are words written in association with a picture that involves the Candelaria. Do you know their meaning?"

"I know of the words, but not of their meaning. This is a mystery. There is so much we do not know." With that, she got up to resume the copy supervision.

Serena clutched hopefully at the gift, thanked Bili, and bowed. The anticipation of finally learning about her Candelaria past quelled the restless kundalini. She turned to Dharani. "Have you read this?"

"I have, sister. I have. It tells a sad story, one that has been common for many of the Luminaria. We of the Naga are fortunate to survive as we do, but many who serve the light have lost their lives in our charge to maintain the truth and the freedoms born of truth. Did sister Shanti release you for the day?"

"Yes, she said you wanted me in the library."

"This is so, but I have shown you enough for today. If you can wait to read your gift for another few hours, I offered to take you to the Mansa Devi festival. You should go so you can learn more of the people here. I can drive you and pick you up. The festival is fun. You will enjoy it. You can even find coffee there."

That last piece of information was too tempting of an offer to refuse. Serena brought the book to her guest quarters and gathered her fanny pack which remained concealed beneath her sister's robe. "Two hours, that should be enough. If it's not too much trouble, could you pick me up from wherever you drop me off?"

24

I t reminded her of street festivals back home only much larger—more vendors, more events such as dancing and singing, more food, and many, many more people. It wasn't as large as a state fair, and there weren't any animal exhibits. She almost didn't know where to start, but Dharani told her where she could buy coffee. She smelled it before she saw it—a small tent, more of a tarp with two café-style tables, six chairs, and a sign that read "Starbucks Coffee Here." That worked for her!

Strolling around, *grande* in hand, she absorbed the festive atmosphere. Many attendees wore typical Western-style clothing, but many more wore traditional dress. The colors, the jewelry, the hair—for a moment, just a moment, she missed her tresses. It passed.

A large gathering stoked curiosity, demanded an investigation. On a stage danced twenty performers in beautiful vibrant kaftans and scarves in varying intense colors, many with flower garlands draped around their necks. They began to weave in unison to Hindu music as a vocalist chanted then sang. Serena had no idea what he was singing about so she asked the person next to her.

"It is a snake song to Mansa Devi." The responder seemed surprised that Serena, dressed as she was, did not know this. "We call for her protection." The bobbing and weaving continued as Serena moved with the music, picking up the chants. It was fun; she thoroughly enjoyed the atmosphere, all the while thinking to herself about all the beautiful people here making such beautiful music.

The dance ended. She strolled along and looked at some beads and other trinkets, then she noticed another gathering, smaller but well attended. As she moved to get a better view, there he was—an authentic snake charmer.

Head wrapped in a large orange turban, a woven basket set before him, the performer sat cross-legged on a small rug. The music coming forth from the flutelike instrument, a *pungi* someone told her, was mysterious, haunting. Serena moved forward to get a better look. As he played, a snake's head appeared and slowly, the snake rose. It was a cobra spreading its regal hood to the delight of all those watching.

As she watched the snake and listened to the hypnotic music, she became entranced, falling under the spell of the *pungi*, undulating much like the snake rising from the basket. The burning sensation in Serena's pelvis returned and grew to a fiery blaze. She felt incredibly aroused as she listened, completely hypnotized by the performer. She did not hear the "whoosh" over the sound of the wind instrument, but a gasp erupted behind her as a man ten feet away collapsed and the crowd reacted. The din of the crowd further masked a second "whoosh" as a poison dart struck the snake charmer and he collapsed to the crowd's surprise, dismay, and concern. People rushed to assist the musician. A tall man grabbed her arm firmly.

"You are in great danger here." Gripping her arm tightly, the stranger muscled her forward. "Come, we must leave at once."

Under his strong grasp she couldn't reach into her fanny pack to get her pepper spray or her cigarette Taser. She looked at her abductor. His skin was too dark. His nose was too broad. He was tall, even taller than Bryson. She sensed a sinewy strength in his lean muscular body. Surely, he could overpower her, but strangely she was not afraid.

"Who are you? Where are you taking me? What danger is there?"

"Serena Mendez, you must trust me."

The accent was British, but not an Indian accent. "You're not Indian. You're Australian." He smiled, showing the biggest teeth she had ever seen, perched beneath his broad nose. "A native, Aborigine if I'm not mistaken."

"Correct. G'day, mate. How ya going? The real deal, mate, but right now, we've got to get you out of here. Undoubtedly there are more than the two I darted to sleep."

"Who is after me? Is this about the necklace? I don't have it anymore."

He released his grip. "No, this is not about a necklace, though that is one of several dangers and why I was sent to protect you. Those people," he waved back to where they had stood a few moments earlier, "they are very bad! They seek young women to trade in the sex markets. A pretty girl such as you, especially with an awake kundalini spirit snake, you are a great prize to people such as those. This is why I had to act as I did."

"But who are you? Who sent you to protect me?" They were well beyond the crowds of people and walked at a slow pace. He towered over Serena, dwarfing her small body.

"My name is Beangagarrie Brindabella, but this is too big to say with the mouth, so you can just call me Mr. B. When you get to know me better, my friends call me BB. A man called Gurumarra, the man I serve, sent me here; he is my Chief. Among my people, he is a great shaman."

"But how did you know where to find me?"

"Gurumarra had this knowledge."

"Where did he get this knowledge from?"

"I do not know for sure. I think it is from another shaman, a woman called Ooljee."

"Your Chief is friends with Ooljee? She is my great aunt."

"I did not say they were friends, but come child, there will be plenty of time to share these stories." He opened the door to a car, and she entered as he started the engine.

"What do you mean? You're taking me back to the Naga Sanctuary, right?" She reached in her fanny pack to remove her weapons.

"Serena Mendez, your Naga Sisters are among those I am sent to protect you from."

25

7 AM. Bryson checked his email noting the quick message from Serena sent five hours earlier—midafternoon her time. "Feeling great following last night's ceremony! Library is totally awesome. Going to a festival at the Mansa Devi Temple. So many things to talk about. Will call you tonight." *Sounds as though things are going well.*

Long day planned. He needed to stop and pick up mail from Mrs. Trujillo. He also planned to strategically place a surveillance camera in Serena's apartment. Bryson had two state-of-the-art video units—motion activated, digital storage. The second unit he planned to place in the hogan, replacing the rather crude and bulky one he had scrapped together with one more compact and sophisticated. He threw together a day pack including lunch and snacks. He faced a minimum thirteen hours of driving plus the setup of the two cameras and two breaks to stretch the legs. If he left soon, he could still make it back home by night.

No new visitors had been to Serena's apartment. Nothing unusual in the mail. He raised the volume in his voice to speak with Mrs. Trujillo. "Happy to report our little girl is just fine. Still not sure when she plans to return." He scratched Oreo behind the ears. Bryson trusted Mrs. Trujillo. *She might look feeble, but the woman is definitely not a slouch. I'll bet she was a force to be reckoned with in her day.* Camera setup including testing took less than fifteen minutes and he was back on the road.

The fraudulent listing on eBay had four parties following the necklace. No bids, but that was expected. It took minimal digging to trace information about the parties. One traced through to an IP address and server in Rome; he assumed this somehow connected to the curator at the Vatican that Monsieur Dubufet contacted for information. There was a listing routed through Singapore; best guess some Indonesian entrepreneur looking to copy the design, maybe try to pass a reproduction off in the black market. Another interested party came through London, possibly the private collector mentioned in the Sotheby's communication. It was the fourth follower watching the listing that drew his interest—Chicago area. *No surprise there. Mr. fake Charles Godfried or I'm back in first grade. I'll take the listing down in a couple more days, see if I score any other hits first.*

By 9 PM he still hadn't heard from Serena; he wasn't overly concerned till her text came through. "Some rain clouds at the festival but storm cleared. Call me when you can." A moment later he pulled over to make the call.

"Everything okay?"

"Bry, I almost don't know where to begin, but short answer is I'm fine."

"How about you start somewhere near the beginning? The more I know, the better I can hopefully work through things."

What followed focused on her experience opening her second chakra. Serena minimized the throbbing, burning, tingling aftereffects carried over into the next day, but Bryson gathered the whole thing as rather intense. The library setup, how the sisters archive, analyze, maintain, and organize the life's work of their order impressed Bryson. He now had an idea of the magnitude and scope of their work, and some new avenues to pursue.

Serena continued her story with the festival leading up to the snake charmer and her rescue by the mysterious Mr. Beangagarrie Brindabella; she had to spell it out; he asked her to text him the correct spelling, so he could do some research. Same thing with Gurumarra, the Aborigine Shaman Chief.

"He saved me from human trafficking! Not that I think I would have made a good sex slave anyway." Her attempt to make light of this fooled no one. "I had to leave the book behind…it kills me Bry. I left it in my room." He wasn't sure, but it sounded as though Serena was crying.

"That's okay, PTG. What matters is you're safe. Do you have your passport, your credit cards, and your special smokes?"

"Yes. I even have both passports. They're in my fanny pack along with my tablet; thank God I didn't leave that in my room."

"Don't worry about the book, we'll figure something out. Again, what's most important is that you're safe." He lowered his voice so that it was barely audible. "Do you trust him? This Mr. B guy, do you trust him?"

"I think so…I mean, yes I do. Sometimes you just get a feeling about someone."

"Remember the Circle? Your aunt's design had the Aboriginal mask. Remember? I think this is all going according to plan. I think Australia is where your next chakra opening is going to happen. It's just a gut feeling, Serena, but I think this is the way your *shibízhí* planned it."

"I hope you're right, Bry… I hope you're right."

"No, remember hope is just sugarcoated fear. Be fearless. Have trust."

"You're probably right, but at this moment, I sure wish I had put meds in my little pack. I could use some right about now. Gotta go, will call you when I have more info."

"Be safe and g'nite, girlfriend."

He had no plans to stop in Kayenta or anywhere along the way other than for a pit stop. Constantly reminding and reassuring himself that his friend would be safe occupied his mind the entire time. The miles wore on. He could not be in touch with her during travel across a large expanse of ocean, but he could periodically track her by satellite two or three times daily via the tiny earring transmitter. Lots of pirates operate around Indonesia. In international waters, lawlessness rules the seven seas. Despite his bravado talk about trust, Bryson worried. It seemed incredible to consider what had transpired over the last few weeks with his friend from the Navajo reservation to India and now off to Australia. He almost couldn't believe it himself. Another message alert on his cell— an attempted hack got through the second firewall of the computer in Missoula he routed through a server there. *The hackers are getting smarter. I might need to take this route down soon.*

Research on the ever-growing database of factoids continued to accumulate along with associations. The Brotherhood of the Sun connected to the Brotherhood of the Snake, but details of this association had not yet surfaced. Serpent worship and symbols lit up throughout his data which he used as a mapping program to generate points of connection. Serpent dots lit up all over the map from ancient history to modern times. Candelaria references and connections remained elusive. Some evidence, more speculation, that Quetzalcoatl might have a connection to Atlantis. Dravidian language roots connected ancient India and the Indus Valley to the Naga Sisterhood. Where chakras fit in, the sleuth did not have a firm idea just yet: seven chakras, seven mysterious words or phrases hidden in the Virgin of Candelaria image—possibly relevant?

Codes, code-breaking, unravelling tangled connections and finding intersection points—the task seemed to get more difficult instead of easier. Still with only one corner piece of this giant puzzle, Bryson gave himself a headache working the details, looking for the obscure both among the obvious and hidden below the surface. Then he zoomed out from the big picture and tried to focus his mind on one single tiny piece—Chicago. *What the hell is in Chicago?*

Midafternoon, the hogan looked just as he remembered it, saw it in his mind's picture image. The still unlocked door stood closed, but the broom placement just beyond the entrance was different. *I doubt it moved itself.* In the pervasive dust and fine dirt infiltrating the structure, it appeared someone had used the broom to cover their tracks. The video footage would confirm or deny his suspicions. He collected the equipment, hooked up his laptop and ran the video. Pay dirt!

Officer Cuch and a tall blond-haired, blue-eyed chap had been to the hogan. They pointed a few times to the stove; apparently Bryson and Serena had been careless in leaving some loose clay. The two men had moved and replaced the cast-iron stove after poking the area recently dug. He would study the footage more when he got home. Smiling contentedly, Bryson watched on his screen as the blond man picked up some of the pottery on the shelves for closer examination. Bryson retrieved these items, careful to wear gloves. With any luck, he could pick up prints and cross-reference these with some facial recognition analysis. *Mr. Godfried, your days of anonymity are numbered.* Concealing the new surveillance unit represented no challenge at all. Concealing his tracks required a little more finesse, but leaving the hogan, Bryson felt the time and effort were all well worth it. The Chicago connection might soon have light shining down upon it. He raced home.

26

"What do you mean? Why do you say that?" Serena objected to Mr. B's claim to the need to protect her from her Naga Sisters.

"Serena Mendez, there is much you do not understand. There is much I do not understand, but this I know—you are not meant to illuminate a library."

"Go on; explain…and you can call me Serena."

"India is a passive country. It is fine to practice your yoga and seek enlightenment, but the Naga Sisters see your power. They do not seek change but only to be holders of truth. It will take you ten years to complete your training if you remain with them."

"Who has told you these things?"

"As I have already spoken, Gurumarra has sent me on this mission and this because of Ooljee."

"My great aunt Ooljee is dead."

"And she haunts Gurumarra in his sleep, sometimes when he is awake. He calls her a spirit nag." Mr. B shook his head as though laughing to himself.

"So, is this about me and my destiny?" Sarcasm came through loud and clear. "Or is this about your Chief getting a better night's rest?"

He winced. "Serena, if you do not trust me and my mission, perhaps it is best we turn back now." He noted her silence, seeing her think, sulk, weigh out the options. "There is much I do not know, but this I can say—a candle projects its light to the surrounding space. If the space is small, only a small area is lit. I am told you are like a giant candle, one who can shed a great light. Among my people, we talk of the dark times eventually ending. Books are good, I love books, but you are one about whom books are to be written, not a caretaker of history."

A long sigh followed a long silence; the young woman digested what he had just said. She did not ask for this responsibility, did not want this burden, but she felt committed to completing the Circle. She reached a decision.

"Where are we going?" The question could have been "Where are you taking me?" but she had decided to trust this stranger.

"We are driving to Digha; it is on the Northeast coast of India. It is a twenty-six-hour drive. From there we take a boat to Northwest Australia. Such a journey will take at least eleven days. Then we find Gurumarra."

"What do you mean, 'Then we find Gurumarra?' You don't know where he is?"

"He is called 'The Wanderer.' We will locate him when the time comes. For now, we should find a secondhand store to buy you some clothes."

Serena looked at her cell phone, seeing it down to 5%. "I need to buy a phone charger."

They stopped to eat in Bareilly, bought a cell charger in an electronics store, and a few items in a secondhand store. She also found a duffle backpack that Mr. B approved of. He said in Australia they would do a lot of walking and pointed out not to buy more than she felt comfortable carrying. The shop did not have much of what they would require for the end part of their travel, but she was off to a good start. As she changed into a T-shirt and jeans, she had the unmistakable sense that she was shedding one skin for another.

She called Dharani, but if her sister's fears about the acolyte's disappearance were high at the beginning of the call, they were accentuated by the end of the call. She insisted that this was an abduction, and that Serena was in grave danger. Even Mr. B's phone assurances that the trip to Australia was only temporary did little to convince Dharani. Yet, the girl's stubbornness prevailed; the call ended uncomfortably, but with plans to remain in touch.

By 11:30 PM they found lodging outside Jaunpur; both were exhausted by the events of the day. Serena did yoga to still her mind and stared at the blank ceiling overhead. Mr. B snored from across the room, but the sound and rhythm of his breathing calmed her. *He is on a mission. I too am on a mission. It started as an adventure, but it is more than that. All my life I have run from myself and now, just like Anshula told me, now I race toward something.* Just what that something was, her purpose, what Beangagarrie Brindabella had spoken of, her great aunt, the Naga Sisters—it all danced in her head and sleep remained elusive despite her exhaustion.

It seemed she had only just dozed off when Mr. B shook her gently. "Come, child; we need to resume our journey." His voice was a deep baritone, very steady. The orange of early dawn lit the sky. "You can sleep more in the car." Doubtless, he too felt weary, but she surmised he drew strength from some inner source.

Serena never liked long car rides, and this was by far the worst ever. Sixteen hours including breaks to stretch, refuel, and eat. Her guardian, protector, abductor—it seemed her opinion vacillated—did all the driving. He was not the sort of man who sought conversation, but when asked, he obliged without difficulty. They exchanged life stories. Serena's seemed brief, even when detailing the most recent events of the last few weeks. All the while he listened; he was a good listener, but occasionally he asked astute questions.

His story went on for hours. Oral tradition and storytelling were part of his native culture. As she listened, it wasn't long before she understood him to be the most fascinating and erudite man she had ever met. At fifty-five, he certainly was among the wisest. Early in his youth, Mr. B had distanced himself from his Aboriginal heritage, preferring the glamour of Western culture that had infiltrated and conquered Australia. He excelled academically and eventually went to England to study at Oxford on scholarship.

"In many respects, I felt happy there. Modern civilization offered comforts, benefits, status far lacking in the village where I had been born. The allure, the seduction that academic achievement offered, London as a modern city with all its amenities—these thoroughly entranced me. I look back now and understand how this happened, though at the time I was naïve, maybe even blinded by ambition. Still, I enjoyed a certain happiness, albeit shallow and nothing more than a veneer, a polish giving sparkle to something hollow beneath." Serena looked over to him and saw sadness as he relived this part of his past.

"I obtained a degree in biology and then a PhD. I was interested in reptiles, so I majored in herpetology, but I also saw how much progress was occurring in genetics, and how this field was only in a new infancy of potential discovery. So, I became an expert in this rather narrow niche combining herpetology and genetics. To my good fortune, the film *Jurassic Park,* an international blockbuster, suddenly made my field very sexy. Research dollars poured in, I lectured and taught at the University. By all measures, I enjoyed what the West would call success."

"My research uncovered some startling results. A portion of reptilian DNA we sequenced appeared dormant. There was a similar sequence in human DNA which appeared active. Was this a coincidence? I published papers. It seemed odd after the papers came out, but I since have learned why; it became difficult to publish. More research, though impeccable, found only rejection among prestigious journals. Then my research funding dried up almost overnight. Confused, I doubled my efforts. I had recently married a beautiful woman, I needed to provide, advance my career, climb the ladder." In some ways, it seemed as though he talked out loud to himself rather than to the young woman seated next to him.

"Still, I persisted. Some colleagues advised that I turn to other research areas; they named a dozen such promising directions in genetics, but I was stubborn. I managed to get another paper published, and this only resulted in ridicule from my colleagues. They claimed my conclusions about human and reptilian DNA were the stuff of science fiction. I could not understand any of this. Why was this happening to me? By the time I uncovered the reasons it was too late." Mr. B produced a hanky to wipe the tears now welling. "Kalinda, that was my wife's name...such a beautiful name for such a beautiful woman. She died in a mysterious accident. She was five months pregnant at the time with a baby girl." He looked over at her. "She would have been about your age now." He handed Serena the hanky. They both wept.

A few miles of silence, deep mournful breaths and native aboriginal expressions followed. Serena did not ask him to translate. Conversation lapsed, then the story continued.

"You see, young lady, I was just too stubborn to understand and to open my eyes and see what lay behind all this. It seemed there was nothing left for me in England, at the University, in my research. They had withdrawn even my previously published papers. My funding was gone. At first, I became a pariah in the scientific community, then something worse—a nothing. I was no one, and no one wanted me. All the glamour and glitter of my Western life had evaporated, like a dewdrop vanishing with the rising sun. No, that is too pretty, more like a hangover from too much partying and excess finally subsides and it leaves you asking yourself, 'What happened?'"

"What happened?" The story completely enthralled and saddened her. "Who did this to you and why?"

"There are powerful people, powerful interests, secrets that I might have discovered, and these were behind my fall. Still, ultimately, it is I who did this to myself, but it took me a long time to realize that.

"In any case, I returned to Australia. I sought answers from the wisest man known to me at the time—Gurumarra. He was not Chief then, but still was known to be a gifted shaman. I was not spiritual, but Gurumarra opened my eyes." Glancing at his companion, he said, "You will like him when you meet him."

"What did you learn from him?"

"I am still learning from him. He explained about the two snakes and their great battle over the moon and the sun, between darkness and light. He explained how men and women, but mostly men, desire the power and things which typify Western culture, that these seductions are but one method of mind control. He explained how these predators, these shadow shapers, infiltrate the mind and fill it with lies, falsehoods, desires and passions. They use fear and anger—emotions paired with thoughts, and they create illusion. In truth, it is a delusion and has been this way throughout history. In modern times we talk about such ideas as ego structures and ego identities. It is all a prison of the mind, shaped and controlled by only a few who benefit from enslavement of the many, those of us who buy into the delusion. And we do so willingly. I did."

He drew a deep sigh. "But child, there will be much time to discuss this further as we sail forth over the sunny sea. I will tell you of my own spiritual growth and where I now dedicate my energy and my gifts. There is much more to my story. At some time in the telling, perhaps you can then call me BB."

As they drove, she looked though the passenger window at the picturesque Indian countryside—in many ways unfamiliar, but in other ways not unlike so many places over the globe. Serena felt small and the world much bigger, a vast expanse of humanity with hopes, fears, and desires somehow stuck in a hamster wheel that someone else had devised and the hamsters merrily engaged. She could not get the image out of her brain.

All the while she also felt deep respect and compassion for the man driving next to her. Unquestionably, he was a man of science and a man of letters, educated and erudite, but there was so much more. She sensed it. Her companion was also deeply spiritual, grounded, connected. He suffered from no illusions or delusions about the world and his place in it. He saw the sacred and the profane along with their mirrored reflections everywhere he looked. In short, he was probably the most well-balanced and authentic human being she had ever met. He carried a deep joy and a deep sorrow in the container of his body, mind, and soul. And he offered her his friendship, freely and willingly in the simple calling of his name, a bond between them.

"BB?" She asked. "Can we pull over at the next place, so I can use a restroom?" She added sheepishly, "You can call me PTG. Only one other person calls me that. It stands for 'ponytail girl,' though you would never think that now." She rubbed her shaved head. Past his enormous teeth, revealed beneath parting lips, a deep baritone laugh rumbled forth. Serena had never heard music so sweet.

27

B ryson had done some digging and gave Serena his findings through an email exchange. Beangagarrie Brindabella had been a respected genetics researcher who fell into disfavor over some controversial assertions and more or less dropped off the radar about twenty years ago. Gurumarra had no hits through his search engines which Bryson thought was a good thing; anyone shady would have been exposed and written about somewhere. Bottom line, he had basically found nothing that Serena didn't already know and certainly nothing to suggest a problem. His cyber-sleuthing included a trip to the hogan and analysis of video footage, along with fingerprints he had transferred to a biometric sensor. He scanned databases for a match. The Snowman felt confident he would identify the Charlie Godfried mystery man and get a true ID on him. Bryson told Serena that he missed her, and he reminded her to be careful.

The long drive was taking a toll on them both. BB insisted on all the driving; the only explanation that made any sense to Serena was that he felt responsible for her and therefore must drive her to their destination. It seemed chauvinistic to her. Though the man's stamina seemed endless, when the car lurched, and she saw him jerk to wakefulness, she thought he would relent. Instead, he withdrew a small tin from a pocket and pinched some dried leaves that he chewed then discarded. The mission continued; dusk, then nightfall confined the two as they drove on through monotony. She powered down her tablet and took a nap.

"Wake, child. We have arrived."

Disorientation took a moment to subside. She looked out. They pulled into the parking lot of a rental car agency; it remained open 24/7.

"Gather your things. We can walk to the marina; it's only about a kilometer."

Still groggy, she followed BB's instructions. "What time is it?"

"A little past 11:00; soon we can both relax. But you need to remain close. I am not familiar with this area and do not know what dangers we might encounter."

But Digha this time of night was quiet, a sleepy ocean-side resort.

An occasional streetlamp, haloed in a seaside night-mist, and random strings of bulbs lit the vacant marina. Docks with many boats in various shapes and sizes—sailing vessels, catamarans, flat-bottomed party boats, small skiffs, and yachts, stood open or canvased in the different berths. Colorful flags stood motionless in the thick air. Wavelets lapped the sides of the floating assortment. Salt and seaweed filled her nostrils; it had been years since she had smelled the ocean. Serena inhaled deeply. Offshore, strands of music and laughter from a large pleasure craft drifted over the calm waters.

From the shadows, a hidden voice spoke, "It is right this way, sir." Footsteps and a man emerged from the darkness, himself darker than the night. "We've a small motorboat to bring us out to the *Miranda.*"

Mr. B embraced the stranger. "It's good to see you, mate." Serena couldn't understand what followed next in musical Aboriginal language. In the darkness, she watched two sets of teeth and four eyes until she heard BB say, "Sorry about the late hour, mate. Are we ready to launch?"

"No sooner than having you and our guest aboard."

"Apologies." BB turned to Serena and the two men stepped toward her. "This is Serena Mendez… Serena, this is Anatjari."

"It is a pleasure to meet you, Miss Serena." The respect and deference in his voice surprised her as he lifted her duffle. "Please follow me."

"I am pleased to make your acquaintance." It sounded formal, she was not sure how Australians did the greeting ritual, but she felt relieved when Anatjari's smile stretched across his broad face. In the meager light from the closest electric bulb, his teeth, the second largest she had ever seen, glinted as they all moved briskly down a wooden dock.

Moored in the final berth bobbed not a motorboat, but a dinghy. To her novice eyes it looked little more than an inflatable raft. Then she realized it was for transport to and from shore. Moments later Anatjari undid the ropes, pushed off from a wooden pylon and started the outboard. Water splashed her face and the noise of the engine cut through the stillness of the night as they navigated toward two points of light—the *Miranda,* anchored some distance offshore, impossible for her to gauge. Ten minutes later they transferred to the main craft, a 36m yacht; they hoisted the dinghy using a winch of some sort. Serena tried to get oriented. To her, this looked like a luxury liner. An older man stepped forward.

He and BB grabbed arms and embraced. "Yarramundi, I cannot think of a better man than yourself to bring us safe passage."

"Beangagarrie, I am honored to have you aboard our vessel." He turned toward Serena. "And most honored to have you aboard as well, Lightbringer." She stood, not sure what to say, unaccustomed to being a guest anywhere, much less a guest of honor. Confused, yet pleased at the same time, she shook Yarramundi's outstretched hand and thanked him. "Come, let me show you to your quarters. In the morning, when the sun has risen, I shall give you a tour. You must be tired from your land journey. The sea," he looked out to the vast expanse of black night and water, stars twinkling overhead, "will take the weariness from your bones."

He escorted her down wooden stairs to a lower deck; BB followed. The room disoriented her; the quarters resembled a hotel room with a double bed and dresser complete with a bedside table and lamp, a large-screen TV and en suite amenities. This type of luxury was outside her life's experience. The captain, obviously proud of the accommodations that he could offer his guest, left while assuring her breakfast awaited in the morning. Eying the bed longingly, she remembered to first email Bryson, unsure when she would next communicate, but assuring him she was in good hands. She lay back, certain this now represented a dream, but in minutes she herself was dreaming. Serena did not wake when the yacht's engines stirred to life; the constant low drone and gentle rocking provoked a deep sleep.

Shafts of sunlight streamed through the cabin window. She pinched herself and spoke out loud just to verify that she was indeed awake. She showered—a wonderful and sorely needed surprise. *I am sailing somewhere on the Indian Ocean taking a hot shower. Can this be real?*

But reality sometimes exceeds any preconceived ideas. In Serena's case, she had no preconceived notions; this unfolding experience remained completely foreign to her, outside any frame of reference. She stepped out into the salon, also on the lower deck, where she had seen a dining table with chairs. Immediately, heaven greeted her in force. Easily balancing her small frame against the rocking motion, inhaling deeply and gloriously through flared nostrils, a welcome smell enveloped her. *Coffee!*

"Good morning, Miss Serena." An unfamiliar voice spoke. "I am Iluka Napanangka." He looked similar to Anatjari, only lighter skinned with more laugh lines on his face. "My mother and father are upstairs on the main deck. Anatjari is now sleeping. He piloted our craft during the night and now rests. BB too is still asleep. I trust you rested well. What can I prepare for you to eat this morning?"

"I'll start with some coffee. It smells incredible!"

Serena learned that Australians were rather elitist when it came to their coffee. Each cup is brewed individually. Much like a barista, her host/cook/crewman had mastered the art. What he produced with its rich crème of foam was possibly the absolute best coffee experience of her life; so much better than

American coffee. Scones, an omelet, fresh fruit, juice, and several additional cups and Serena felt in love with life and in total enjoyment of the moment.

Iluka showed her the kitchen and the brewing machinery. He proudly fingered the dark Indonesian beans, a premium Sulawesi Toraja dark roast. "Even blacker than my brother," he joked. They had picked up ten twenty-five-pound sacks when they refueled near Jakarta on the trip out.

She learned all about the kin relationships and the family ties uniting Mr. B with Iluka's own family that operated this charter service. They traveled at Gurumarra's beckoning, a clan duty that they were happy to oblige. She gathered that the kinship ties uniting them were an important part of their society. She recalled this also from the fortuitous article she had read while waiting for her last appointment with Dr. Jenkins; that seemed a lifetime ago.

"How did your brother know where and how to find us last night? He seemed to know we were coming right when we did. Mr. B doesn't even have a cell phone."

"Yes, to you this must seem strange, but to my people, we find it strange that you lack this ability, or at least do not practice it. What you do not practice you tend to forget."

Then she remembered something she read in *National Geographic*—Australian Aboriginals can communicate certain things such as danger and location through a type of telepathy. "You are talking about telepathy, aren't you?"

"Yes, some Westerners have explained it as such. We all come from oneness and in this sense, we share the same mind. It is more like learning to tune into the same frequency; especially with members of our own tribe or family, we share a type of connection through the one mind."

Serena found this to be incredible, but Iluka explained further. "Have you never had the experience where you are thinking about someone and at that moment they ring you up? I'm sure you have heard about mothers' sensing by intuition that their child is hurt or in danger; or maybe you have read about identical twins feeling and sharing pain when one gets injured. It is much the same. Call this telepathy if you want. We all have this ability, but in most people it remains latent, asleep. Australia is a big island and only sparsely populated. We native peoples have managed to get by quite well, uncorrupted by the White Man. We never lost this sharing of the mind." He added, "And it extends well beyond just the mind of people to the consciousness of all things. Gurumarra can explain better. You should ask him about this. It is all something long since forgotten by Westerners."

BB joined them, and Serena had a fourth cup of the marvelous Sulawesi brew. The three went to the main deck where she met Takariya Napanang-ka—wife, mother, first mate, and Serena would later learn, executive chef. Yar-ramundi, whose name meant "deep water," gave her the full tour and details about their ship.

The *Miranda,* a luxury yacht with four cabins and a crew of four, came equipped with a range of toys such as snorkeling and scuba diving equipment, fishing gear, thousands of movies, air-conditioning, satellite phone, even an inflatable swimming pool. The ship launched eight years earlier but had been completely refitted last year. She hailed from Kimberley, Australia, her home port. Booking a charter such as this stretched the limits of her imagination. What did it cost? She decided not to ask. Who among the rich and famous, the wealthy elite, had slept in the same bed she now occupied? On open water, they cruised at twelve knots.

Tour done, BB and the captain engaged in private conversation, the crew attended to chores, and Serena found herself alone. A steady breeze left her cool, but she had been warned about the fierce sun this close to the equator. It was only mid-morning and she needed to clear her mind. Yoga, with its challenging asanas requiring steady postures and balance, presented special challenges on the deck of a moving ship. As she focused, she harnessed the kundalini energy, at first wild but gradually tamed into control. Her entire body, mind, and spirit felt alive with vibrating, pulsating energy. Now seated in lotus position, a deep connection to earth, water, and sky filled her being as she entered meditative stillness.

Evening began with a fantastic meal: several courses, fresh seafood, the names, spices, and preparation all new to Serena, and all absolutely delicious. All highlighted by laughter, storytelling, and the comfort of family, for the crew had readily adopted her as one of their own, a sister lost long ago and now reunit-ed with her kin. The cuisine highlights of the Naga Sisterhood, namely tea and vegetables, and their reserved camaraderie could not compete. The grand seduc-tion of peace, tranquility, and the fountains and gardens of the past weeks paled to the majesty and freedom of the open sea. Spectacular night vistas beckoned, and the raw power of the ocean swallowed her in its infinite expanse. For the moment, she reveled in the escapism, the pampering, and the sheer indulgence gifted to her by the crew of the *Miranda* and the sanctuary of the sea.

28

Her second day at sea Serena contacted Bryson by satellite phone, but the conversation was brief by necessity. He cautioned that such calls were easy to intercept and not to worry as he would follow her course through the earring transmitter. He had identified Charles Godfried as Claus Gorman, formally working US military intelligence as an army operative. This information was a little worrisome. The prints matched along with the video image, but nothing in particular in his file seemed concerning, and nothing tied him to Chicago. Bryson continued searching HR files for Chicago-based companies that might require high-level security, as well as gas station video since just about everyone fills up a tank. There were thousands of gas stations and he had nothing to help him narrow the search. They agreed to keep contact to a minimum during the ocean transit.

Each day, she practiced her Shakti yoga. Balance and strength along with her stamina in holding difficult poses improved. More importantly, her discipline in guiding the kundalini energy, restraining and unleashing it according to her will, advanced dramatically. Nothing competed with her practice. Her sun-exposed skin displayed a vibrant tan. Seeing her own image reflected in the waters of the inflated pool, she hardly recognized the person looking back.

On day six, she spotted a land mass in the distance—Christmas Island. They were making excellent timing and had traveled more than halfway home. Anatjari and Iluka were especially pleased; they both missed their wives and children. Typically, they stayed away for only two weeks; already, this trip had lasted almost three weeks.

Yarramundi chose this port to refuel. Piracy near the Indonesian coast was rampant and during the ocean transit to India, they had a close call. The details made for one of many dinnertime stories and now they laughed. At the time it was less funny. Christmas Island is a territory of Australia. With just over two thousand inhabitants, it is world renowned for its biologic diversity and natural beauty. Most of the island is a protected natural park. The local flora and fauna, spectacular in their color both on land and along the reefs, are a natural wonder. The annual red crab migration of over one hundred million animals is unique to this small ocean island.

"It is a shame we are not here in November," BB spoke, "that is the time of the crab migration. I have seen it and still sometimes cannot believe what I witnessed. It is unfortunate we do not have more time here. There will be a chance to snorkel along the reef if you like, but you might prefer time back on land. If you go, be on the lookout for the robber crabs." He chuckled. "Some are almost as big as you." He chased her with pinching motions of his slender hands.

A tropical island paradise awaited. BB underestimated the size of the robber crabs; they were gigantic! A frigate bird startled her by puffing out its crimson red gullet. She learned they could stay aloft a week at a time. Red-footed boobies flew, hopped, and squawked. She squawked back. Snapping photos with her phone—birds in flight, crabs on land, colorful plants, ferns, orchids, flowers she could not name, and insects flying, buzzing, crawling—everywhere she turned seemed to display a sight to behold. She marveled at this wonderful playground and the warm, friendly people who greeted her. Exhilarated, yet mournful at how little time they had to spend here, she returned to the appointed rendezvous. Iluka met her.

"It is most beautiful here. My wife and I love to visit with the children. You should hear how they jump and scream when a red crab tickles their toes." In her mind the image and sound flashed with a momentary connection.

She surveyed the island paradise. "Someday I will return here, maybe even to listen to my own children."

He looked at her and nodded. "This is a good place."

Two days out from home port she sensed the change. All her senses seemed more acute since her kundalini release. The air moved differently, with an unfamiliar heaviness. The smell of the wind had changed along with the countenance of the crew. The captain and his wife huddled, listening to the marine forecast, checking the radar and sonar. Cyclones could occur any time of the year in this part of the Indian Ocean. Storms at sea are common and the crew, as well as the ship, had weathered many such storms.

Yarramundi looked worried. He called a meeting for passengers and crew. "We've got a bit of a storm headed our way." He pointed to a slight gray smudge visible on the horizon. "I've changed course to try to run around it, but it might get choppy, even a little more than choppy." A moment later he produced life preservers. The wind had noticeably picked up.

"BB, you and Miss Serena best head below deck while we ride this out." He handed each of them a life preserver then winked. "Just in case, the Captain likes to play it safe."

Serena placed the bright orange vest with the major floatation portion straddling her neck and looked toward the stairway to go to her quarters on the deck below. The heaving and motion as the *Miranda* sliced through the growing waves caused an unfamiliar nausea to start inside her belly. The sky suddenly grew dark gray.

"Best get moving, child. This will get rough." The captain's voice pierced through the wind.

Mr. B led the way. Twelve steps stood between decks connected by a wooden stairway with sturdy metal handrails. She held on tightly to keep her balance. This differed from yoga. On the fifth step, the boat pitched upward to crest a large swell. She leaned back and almost felt her back against the upper stairs so steep was the boat's climb. As it crested the wave, she straightened, completely unprepared for the ship's decent down the back of the swell. Her shifting center of gravity and the boat's downward pitch threw her forward violently. Losing her grip, she lurched, scrambled for purchase, screamed, and flew over the remaining stairs. That was the last thing she remembered. Blood pooled beneath the bleeding gash where her head struck the lip of the last stair. The downy stubble of a few days' growth on her scalp stained red as she lay motionless.

"We may have found her," Mr. Chung reported to his superior. He stood erect. They spoke in Chinese.

Dr. Kenseiko Li stood with his back to the speaker. He looked out an office window of blackened glass; Singapore's skyline stretched out before him.

"Who?" Li's quiet voice shouted with authority that could not be challenged. The large office displayed a quiet and refined elegance—nothing overdone, everything in the correct measure, much like its occupant. At this hour, the space appeared dim, a result of the dark reflective glass concealing his company's skyscraper. Dr. Li remained silhouetted and spoke to the window.

"The American girl, we think we have located her." The voice came from behind him.

"I am intrigued, continue."

"A woman by the name of Serena Mendez, an American, has been hospitalized at the Royal Darwin in the Northern Territory following a boating accident. She is in a coma. A rather tense air-sea rescue broadcast on the news media. AMSA Search and Rescue dispatched a helicopter in the middle of a cyclone. One of our contacts released the name to us."

"Sounds rather dramatic… Go on." He looked at the gray patch staining the top of his left hand.

"We were able to infiltrate the hospital's firewall. There is not much information. She apparently had been in India, joined an Ashram or something, maybe a cult of some sort. Then she met a man who claims to be her guardian, and he was taking her to Australia by sea. His yacht was in a storm, she fell, injuring her head, and has been in a coma since."

"Do we know anything about this man?" He shifted his weight to the right, onto his clubbed foot, causing his entire frame to shift slightly to the side.

"No sir, the boat is registered to a couple operating a charter service."

"And I presume you have checked their bookings?"

"Of course. This block of time has nothing scheduled."

"Good. Continue your research. We will need a sample of her blood. I trust you can acquire this."

"Yes, Dr. Li. I shall get to work." He bowed, readying to be dismissed.

"Stay in the light, Chung."

After Chung had closed the door, Li hobbled to his desk, retrieved a remote and used it to draw the blinds. Even the late afternoon sunlight hurt, only one of the ways his body was beginning to fail him. He picked up a glass paperweight—a globe representing the earth, and absently studied the blue-green glass. *She is close. Almost in my own backyard. If she is the one, we will be much further along than even I had hoped.*

Serena awoke in the neurosurgical unit at the Royal Darwin Hospital in northern Australia. She surveyed first her body then her surroundings. Fingers and toes moved slowly. She reached for her head; it hurt everywhere she touched. Bandages covered stitches which she could not feel but guessed from the intense pain were concealed below. A neck collar restricted her movement, but from the corner of her eye she saw someone. Even with blurry vision, the height was unmistakable.

"Where am I?"

BB's concerned and sleep-deprived face came into view. He held her hand and softly spoke to her. "You took quite a bad fall, child. We thought we might lose you. You are at the Royal Darwin Hospital and you have fortunately woken up from surgery. Do you remember anything?"

She tried to sit up, wincing instead at the throb intensifying in her head and her neck rebelling at the effort—*not a good idea!* "I remember a storm. After that it's a blank."

"That was three days ago, Serena." A nurse came in, glad to see her patient awake; she took a set of vital signs.

"Did you say I just had surgery?" Things seemed to take a while to register, her thoughts moved molasses-like through a muddled brain. "Did I break something?"

His laugh spoke relief not merriment. "Were it not for the life preserver around your neck, you likely would have broken that. You suffered a concussion, a nondepressed skull fracture, and a nasty gash on the scalp from which you lost a good deal of blood. Fortunately, not so much that you required a transfusion, but you will be weak for a while. Oh yes, and a nasty neck sprain, but the collar is more a precaution than anything else."

"Then why the surgery?" Her brain seemed to be working better already.

"You had some internal bleeding, under the skull but over the brain. It is common with head injuries, or so the doctor explained. He called it a subdural hematoma. It was large enough that you required surgery to remove the collection of blood." He smiled. "But the doctor says you should make a complete recovery and be brand new in a week or two. I was worried that you might have permanent damage, but he assures me that you will be fine."

"Happy to hear that." The throb in her head lessened to just barely tolerable.

"If you feel tired, you should rest. I will remain here at your side," BB added.

"What about the crew; what about the *Miranda?*"

"All safe back in port in Kimberley. It's not that far, perhaps 1,800 kilometers. They feel terrible about your injuries but are pleased to learn you are recovering."

A cheery young man in scrubs entered the room carrying a red tray with tubes and needles; his name badge read "Jonathan Stewart."

"Serena Mendez? Hello, I'm Jonathan, here to collect blood." He checked her wristband, gave her a squeezy thing, and placed a tourniquet around her arm. Satisfying himself upon examination of her arm about where to make his attack, he swabbed with an alcohol wipe, donned gloves, and apologized. "Sorry, just a small poke and it will be over."

The needle prick felt like nothing compared to her head which throbbed more with each squeeze of the foam ball.

BB eyed the phlebotomist. "Jonathan, Miss Mendez is already through with her surgery. Her chemistries and other tests were fine. Why do you need four more tubes of blood?"

"I don't know, sir. I just do as I'm told. I draw the blood, not order the tests." He removed his paraphernalia, Serena thanked him, and he exited, every bit as cheery as when he entered.

Two days later she held her discharge instructions; they cautioned against any lifting or bending, advised her to drink plenty of water, absolutely no alcohol, no driving, and stitches out in one week. The black and blue adorning her face made her look grotesque, but she was happy to be released, and fortunate to be alive.

29

I t was pretty dicey. Tracking Serena's progress over the Indian Ocean, the rapid diversion on a new heading ending at the Royal Darwin Hospital, coupled with the severe weather he followed by satellite and marine forecasts—they all pointed to some disaster. News reports of the air-sea rescue accomplished by the brave men and women of the Australian Maritime Safety Authority search and rescue team confirmed his suspicions. The media exposure compromised everything. Her name leaked—an absolute disaster for someone being tracked and pursued by an unknown foe. Easy to find her for anyone that happened to be looking. Who exactly was looking?

The really difficult part for Bryson was not knowing her condition. "In a coma" sounded ominous to be sure, but when she called him from the hospital and he got the details, especially the part about "expecting a full recovery," he felt relieved. His strong advice to her was to lie low, not leave a trail, and get out of Darwin ASAP. The urgency of determining exactly who Claus Gorman worked for intensified.

He got lucky. The grainy convenience store surveillance video was of poor quality and gave a facial recognition match of only 72%, but a license plate pulled off the vehicle traced back to Charles Godfried. It gave him a possible home address, but it left Bryson feeling uneasy. *Why does this guy make such an effort to cover his true identity?* The nonexistent footprint left by the real Claus Gorman, CG for short, suggested a pro. The man knew a lot about security, and it made it tough for Bryson to track him down. He thought about hiring someone to plant a tracer on CG's car, but that had risks. The breakthrough came from traffic cams; Chicago certainly had plenty. It was tedious but following the vehicle from the available cams led to a probable work destination—bingo!

Baxter Consolidated, LTD was a privately held company; he gathered they worked heavily with the defense industry and military contracting. In the company's phone directory, Claus Gorman had a listing in the security division. Bryson added the company name to his data linking program and within thirty minutes his search algorithm had returned one association—a very disturbing match. Mr. Peter Reynolds was listed among the Board of Directors for Baxter Consolidated—*Uncle Peter! How the hell does this fit together?*

Mr. B drew the curtains and slid the chain securing the door. The media coverage identifying Serena left him uneasy. He had not forgotten her story of the dead man in the cave, the arm tattoo, nor what she had shared from her friend Bryson. Maybe he was being too cautious, but he also knew the Candelaria had been pursued, hunted down, and killed in the past. Why, he did not know, but best to play it safe.

The small Galapagos Motel was located just a few blocks from the hospital. BB had paid cash and used a false name while Serena waited outside the registration office. She looked odd with her head wrapped in a bright headscarf concealing her bandages. Tomorrow he would rent a car. They needed to travel to Alexander Island to meet with Gurumarra, about seventeen hours, but an easy drive down Route 1. He would have preferred to leave tomorrow, when Serena was supposed to be discharged, but the doctor came by midafternoon and said she could go. She was tired and still weak, resting at the moment. As long as they left tomorrow morning, everything should be fine. He felt uneasy but couldn't rationalize feeling this worried. Everything should be fine.

The loud knock woke him. He must have been dozing in the chair. Again, a loud knock, but Serena remained asleep.

"Who is it? What do you want?" He reached for the in-room coffee carafe, the only immediate weapon he could think of.

"Beangagarrie, is that you? Open the door."

He knew that voice, but it had been a long time, at least twenty years. He opened the door only to the length of the security chain.

"Thank goodness, mate. Hurry, I don't know how much time we have."

With some surprise and relief, he greeted an old friend, Djalu. They spoke in their indigenous tongue. The commotion woke Serena.

"What is going on?"

"No questions. Gather your things as quickly as possible and go with this man. I will join you in a moment."

BB left for the motel office, not to check out; he had already prepaid. Instead, he casually asked for directions to a restaurant in walking distance where they could sit and have a nice leisurely meal; he conveyed no sense of urgency. With three recommendations written on a scrap of paper, he joined his friend moments later at the car parked two blocks away. Serena sat in the back seat wearing a hooded jacket and they sped away.

"Would someone please tell me what the hell is going on?"

"Yes, child, we are safe for the moment. DJ can explain our hasty departure."

Djalu, whom everyone called DJ, seemed relieved as they drove through an outlying area. "Miss Serena, everyone here knows of your arrival; it was a big story on the news. I thought the tall man leaving the helicopter after it landed looked a lot like my old friend BB. There are not many of us natives as tall as he and I had not seen him for twenty years." He turned to BB. "We have a lot of catching up to do, mate; maybe we have a shout together later.

"About two hours ago I got me a call from Yarramundi, you know, the Captain of the *Miranda*. He and I sometimes do business together with tourists. I fly them in my charter plane, and he floats them in his charter boat. Personally, I think he makes out much better in the arrangement." After his chuckle ended, DJ continued. "Yarramundi called from his satellite phone; him bein' back out at sea. He says some people called him askin' a lot of questions about "the American girl"—did he know where she was going? Who was the man she traveled with? Yarramundi did not like the questioning; he made up a name for BB to throw 'em off the scent. All he told them was what they already knew—AMSA flew the girl to Royal Darwin."

"Who were they?" She turned to BB. "Who do you think they were?"

"There is more, child. Listen as DJ tells the rest."

"Next thing old Yarri does is call me, knowing I'm livin' in these parts. He thinks I ought to find BB and warn him someone's taken an interest to his whereabouts, if you know what I mean. But no sooner does I hang up the phone when I gets another call, this one from somebody claiming to be the police. He says the authorities are looking for an American girl and he wants to know if I've got a booking or perchance flew her off midafternoon. Fortunately, I've got nothing to keep him talking to me, so when he's done, I start sweeping the area with my mind using our internal guidance way that we Aborigines use to communicate, 'specially if we're kin. All the while I'm thinkin' maybe my old friend here is in some kind of trouble. And I'm thinking if I can find him, pretty damn sure someone else could, so I better get there first, if you receive my meaning." He paused. "Now that we're all here, can you tell your old friend what kind a trouble you managed to get into and maybe DJ can help you to the clear."

Thirty minutes after their unplanned exit from the Galapagos Motel, conveniently located near Darwin Royal Hospital, they did not see the four men dressed in black, communicating on a private band, split up to search three local restaurants.

"No problem, Mate. This is the slow season for tours and drop-offs in the isolated bush. I'll fly you both to a nice secluded camp area I know an hour away and we can spend the night. Tomorrow we'll take a fly to Alexander Island. Now that's beautiful country out there. So that's where the Wanderer is at now? Hard to keep up with Gurumarra; I might even stay for a spell. Still waitin' for him to light up the bulb inside me head." He thumped the side of his head.

For a moment, Serena felt the knock. Her head hurt. Even though she seemed to be recovering, she felt tired of being chased. Fear crept back inside her gut. She didn't have any more pills to calm that beast. She wanted to go home, to wake up and find out she was just an ordinary young woman trying to get by in a crazy world, not some sort of f'in superhero. She didn't know what to do. She called Bryson; maybe he could settle her down; maybe he could make sense of this.

He never raised his voice, made a point never to show emotion; instead, he lowered his voice to a bare whisper. "Mr. Chung, are you saying you do not know Serena Mendez's whereabouts?" The blood test results were most promising, but he wanted the girl, more blood, tissue samples, her ovaries.

"The hospital released her prior to our operatives being in place. We have not yet identified the man she travels with."

"Do you have video footage of this unidentified man?"

"Yes, Dr. Li, Australian media covered the helicopter landing. The footage is blurry, but it includes her traveling companion, the man who claims to be her guardian."

"And the hospital's security camera video?"

"We are still working on obtaining that, sir."

"Bring me what you have."

Fifteen minutes later Mr. Chung stood at attention, sweat beading on his forehead, while Dr. Li reviewed the grainy video. He did not look pleased.

"You are saying you are unable to identify this tall Australian Aborigine?"

"That is correct, sir. We are running the image through several databases."

"Remind me, Mr. Chung, why you are my Chief of Security."

The subordinate, now sweating profusely, stumbled in his response.

"Never mind, Chung." The voice whispered, barely audible. "The man is Beangagarrie Brindabella. His height is tall even for an Aborigine. He is a geneticist. I suggest you find him. I am sure you do not need to be reminded that failure is not an option. At Advanced Bionics, none of our personnel fail. You do understand this?"

"Yes, Dr. Li. I understand this completely."

As he watched the subordinate leave, Li picked up the same glass globe and crushed it in his hand. A rare display of emotion, but no one witnessed his anger. *Brindabella resurfaced after so many years. Back from the dead or perhaps soon to join them…permanently. What are you up to, Beangagarrie Brindabella?*

30

In fifteen minutes, they pulled up to a cabin with an oversized garage at the edge of a field. A bright yellow aircraft stood idle near the garage.

"She's all gassed up; I keep her ready to go on a moment's notice…like now." A broad grin followed. "Just give me five to pack a cooler and use the head, Mate."

Ten minutes later they were airborne. He flew a Cessna 180 aeroplane—single prop, seating for four, and as he put it, "as reliable as a mosquito bite in the bush." This was a late model made in 1980 and had logged thousands of hours of flight time all over the Australian bush. He was certain this plane would still be flying long after he was down under. DJ claimed he could land it on a run field as short as a tennis court, but he was prone to exaggeration.

The engine sound discouraged conversation other than to shout. Below, the unspoiled beauty of the Australian bush stretched as far as she could see. Kangaroos, or were they wallabies, hopped along without looking up as they flew overhead. BB shook her and pointed to a hilly collection of rock outcroppings. "Very famous rock paintings, very sacred to our people," he shouted, and Serena nodded.

Airborne, her fears once again lifted and she felt safe, out of reach and once again energized by the strange new sights and vistas. DJ flew toward Alexander Island. She lost sense of time, but as red and orange hues lit the scattered clouds, a clearing down below came into view. The pilot circled and landed. Just like that she found herself transported literally and figuratively from a scared girl afraid of an unknown beast hunting her in the urban jungle, to a protected haven in the unspoiled Australian wilderness.

"It's beautiful!" She breathed in the pristine freshness.

Given her prohibition against lifting, she sat there while BB and DJ collected wood, all the while laughing, sharing stories, and catching up on old times. She ran through a few yoga routines and felt the best she had felt all day. The added safety of dancing flames soon followed as BB's old friend seemed to magically produce a grate and cooking accoutrements. The blaze dwindled to coals and some unknown scents, quite possibly the gourmet camping equivalent of a feast, filled the air.

"Ain't been to this spot in over a year, but it's still just as lovely as I recall." Stars and the sounds of night creatures filled the air. DJ had dozens of stories about his adventures in the bush, crazy tourists from all over the world, animal stories, plant stories, near-death experiences, survival in the wilderness. No doubt he was both resourceful and entertaining.

Her belly full, lying back gazing at the Milky Way, the coals still warming her face, Serena finally asked the question dogging her from earlier today. "BB, who are the people after me and why? It makes no sense!"

"Ah, child, but it does make sense, at least to me. But to explain I need to tell you more about the stories of creation from our land and this place. Understand that the Aborigines have the oldest culture of all known peoples and dating back at least sixty-five thousand years, maybe one hundred thousand or more." A rich orange glow bathed his face. She drew close to listen, the latent anthropologist in her now wide awake.

"I am a man of science, but before science, people came to understand the world differently and sought meaning and shared understanding with stories and symbols. This war between science and spirituality is silly nonsense; they are just different methods for explaining reality. In our tradition, before man walked was Tjukurrpa, the Dreamtime. The Great Rainbow Serpent Kalseuru awoke from within the earth and moved across the flat land creating the rivers and mountains. From his belly or her belly, because the Rainbow Serpent contains and is both male and female, all the plants and creatures spilled forth and they remain here till this day. In this sense, it is still the Dreamtime, even in the present, because the present contains the past."

She nodded her understanding and he continued. "There were many early peoples, before we came to the land. Some were spirit peoples like the Mimi, small and thin, who taught us how to hunt and make fire. They are long gone but their spirits are still in the forests and among the rocks, especially the cracks and crevices. The lizard god, Mangar-Kunjer-Kunja, found two primeval people joined together. He cut them apart and they became the Rella-manerinja, the masters of men.

"I tried in my scientific mind to make sense of this last story, the unjoining of this combined being. This is what actually drove me to both genetics and herpetology, but it was not until Gurumarra explained it to me so that I truly understood.

"The lizard god was not a god at all but from an advanced race living on earth. To the primitive people of the time, he would have seemed a god to them, capable of great things. In the absence of true understanding and lacking record-keeping other than by oral history, this is how they reported it over many generations.

"I believe the unjoining of the two people as told in this story is more about cutting apart the blueprint of our species' DNA and changing it somehow. Why I think this I cannot completely say, it is more of a feeling, the kind of feeling that comes with a deep knowing. I try to explain the science to Gurumarra, but he stops me saying he does not want the science; that is not what is important. In any case, it is clear to me this splitting has to do with DNA. Gurumarra says this action caused a great imbalance and led to the time of darkness. The split beings could not master spirit and matter, somehow a result of the corruption of the intact genetic blueprint. This gave the lizard god, and those who followed, mastery over others. I believe the mastery is best thought of as mind control, a way to manipulate mental and emotional energies and to suppress spiritual growth. Gurumarra uses different language, but I believe he is saying the same thing. As for you, he believes you have the power to mend that which the lizard god broke apart. He does not know how.

"In my case, Serena, I am convinced that my fall from academia and the death of my wife Kalinda are both related to this story of the lizard god. That is why I share it with you at this time. I believe the children of this lizard god, what in some places is called the Brotherhood of the Snake, are responsible. I think it is these same people who pursue you now. But this is something to ask our Chief; he is very wise."

They slept in the open air beneath the night sky. BB's story was not that much different from what she had learned in the Naga Sanctuary about the two breakings. There was no flood; perhaps it did not come all the way to Australia. This Brotherhood of the Snake had come up before. Bryson had it in the "connect the dots" program. Who are they? What do they want? More questions, but this group sounded like a corner piece in this giant puzzle. She didn't know when she would connect with Bryson again, but she made a note to tell him this. She gradually drifted into a restful and dreamless slumber.

Serena watched the sun rise in the east, spectacular in its beauty. She stretched and went through her routine while the men packed and prepared a light breakfast which thankfully included coffee. As they flew to Alexander Island, she succumbed to a deep sense of awe at the natural beauty around her, leaving her immersed in gratitude. *No matter what happens, I will always treasure this night in the bush. Spirit and matter connect here unimpeded, unencumbered, just raw and pure.* Her kundalini energy only grew and magnified, drawing from the sky overhead and earth below. She felt herself as someone else—a force, a light, a fire, a Candelaria!

❖   ❖   ❖

When the bush plane descended, almost gliding into a soft landing, she couldn't understand why. The ocean was nowhere in sight, not even a large lake.

"Why have we landed? I thought we were headed to Alexander Island?"

DJ winked at BB. "We were. And now, Missy, we're here. Welcome to Alexander Island. I can't remember the last time I was here, but it is truly a special place."

BB explained that here legend tells that the Rainbow Serpent slept, coiled in a comfortable oval, carving the two rivers which surrounded a jewel of green. Actually, they were two forks of the Fitzroy River which split and rejoined itself about 80 kilometers downstream.

"Well, that kinda makes sense." She had abandoned any preconceived bias about how these natives could find one another, so she rather matter-of-factly asked, "How far away is Gurumarra?"

The two tribesmen looked at each other and pointed in the same direction then argued about how far. BB said one hundred meters, but DJ said two hundred; they placed a small wager. DJ won easily, the product of living and surviving in the bush. He chided his kin. "You need to spend more time in the bush, my brother."

Nothing prepared Serena for what next occurred. From beyond a grove of eucalyptus trees, a deep voice, one with unmistakable authority, boomed in native Aborigine and BB had to translate. "Djalu, you are as dense as a rock. I hope you had the good sense to bring me some honey. BB is useless when it comes to finding honey and you know I have a sweet tooth." Then followed the most enormous laugh she had ever heard. DJ responded in native tongue and she gathered the answer was no. Through the trees, there he was.

Upon a boulder, idly carving a piece of wood, she had to blink to be sure, sat a man of mid-height and dark skin, whitish-yellow long hair and a beard to match, but that was not the striking part. He wore a ridiculous-looking stovepipe hat and a tattered coat resembling a Civil War era Confederate uniform. She blinked again and he bellowed some more. From this distance, she didn't see any teeth.

"What did he say?" she whispered to BB.

"He wants to know what took us. He says his bottom hurts from sitting on the rock for so long."

The Chieftain rose and straightened; he was slightly overweight. He approached the trio pointing to Serena. BB translated his next words, something about finally being able to get some sleep. Gurumarra motioned and BB quietly said, "He wants you to lift your shirt."

"What?" At the moment, the absurdity of his visage fully matched the absurdity of the unexpected request.

BB clarified. "Just up past the belly. He needs to look more closely at that energy spot, what you call the chakra."

Hesitantly, the young woman obliged, lifting her tee just up to below her breasts, fully exposing her abdomen. The shaman grunted, making a sound that sounded like "Feh," and waved his hand downward, spilling out something in their native tongue. Before BB could explain, Gurumarra said something else, bellowed another laugh, threw aside whatever he had been carving, and strode away. She distinctly heard him repeat twice, "Galinawa, Galinawa," as he raised and shook his hands, seemingly speaking to someone else.

"What was that all about?"

"First, he says that you are very skinny." She re-covered her torso. "Then he says, that the snake in your belly is very fat, and very lazy. I don't know why but he seems to think this is funny."

"What does Galinawa mean and who was he talking to?"

"That is his name for you. I am not sure, but I think he spoke to your Ooljee. Just so you know, this is a very special name. It means 'one who carries the light.'"

She swallowed and the Chief returned, sat back on the rock and carved a new, somewhat larger piece of wood. He muttered something then erupted into another great laugh.

"He says he needed a bigger piece of wood. If he has to, he'll use a whole tree."

DJ chimed in, "Ah, Missy, that Gurri is quite the trip, aye? I think later you and me will go off and find him some nice honey. That oughta get us in his good graces."

31

B ryson peeled back another layer thanks to Monsieur Dubufet. Follow-up correspondence with the Sotheby's agent led to a facilitated
contact with the Law Firm of Darrel, Fulbright, and Worthington—one of London's most prestigious. Bryson had received an inquiry about the Candelaria
necklace directly from Barrister Fulbright. To be contacted by one of the firm's
principals connoted a certain seriousness, reinforced by the facts that the email
origin and routing differed from the firm's normal server and channels. More
than a little curious, the Darrel, Fulbright, Worthington Law Firm had strong
ties to the Rothschild's, one of the most prominent and influential families in the
world. A family coincidently associated with the Illuminati. You didn't need a
genius IQ to appreciate the connections. Everything suggested something more
than "an interested collector of rare religious artifacts," as Sir Dalton Fulbright
had put it in his private correspondence.

Continuing the little cat-and-mouse game he had started, Bryson responded that the owner of the necklace was temporarily out of the country with an
uncertain return. He had notified the owner, intentionally not designating
whether this was a "he" or a "she," and was instructed to delay any viewing
or appraisal until their return from abroad. He apologized that he could not
be more specific but assured the barrister he would be in touch. Rather than
remain anonymous, which seemed rude, he closed his response with a pseudonym, Alex Stark, confident that would lead them absolutely nowhere. He sent
a similar email to Monsieur Dubufet. It was a high-stakes game. The initial offer
had already jumped considerably; Sir Dalton had noted his buyer was prepared
to pay the sum of ten million pounds—nearly fifteen million dollars. *I'm lucky
the special guest speaker for the Mega-Conspiracy Group is giving his presentation
tonight. I might have a few questions to ask.*

A photographic memory had many benefits. As he watched group
members and other interested attendees who wanted to hear tonight's speaker
furiously taking notes, Bryson watched the slides and simply attached the verbal
message that went along. He could probably give the presentation himself after
assimilating the slides and lecture, although his verbal memory skills were much

less detailed. The speaker, a Mr. Raleigh Jones, had clear mastery of the material and gave a detailed, highly informative presentation. The man himself, however, looked chronically anxious, as though at any moment he might be abducted. The paranoia distracted from the overall content, but this particular audience loved it. He spoke about the origins of the Illuminati, their roots dating to prehistory and the so-called Brotherhood of the Sun, their attempts (largely successful) to maintain their bloodlines, about the New World Order and the desire to create a superior human being, Lucifer worship and other rituals. There were supposedly thirteen main families with influence worldwide; the Rothschild family dynasty was among this elite group of thirteen.

Some of the information was new, but several pieces had already come up in the data linking program. Bryson made a mental note of two additional search items to enter: the Bilderberg Group and Bohemian Grove. Upon closing, Mr. Jones received a standing ovation and opened the hall to questions. There were many, mostly about mind control and propaganda, and the relationship between money and government. There were a few questions asking about what could be done to counteract the influence of the powerful Illuminati and their agenda. Other than get the word out, the speaker had no strategy. Clearly, he was trying to follow his own suggestion, and Bryson gave him credit for that. When his turn came, Bryson asked about the Candelaria Cult or Fellowship. Unfortunately, the expert had never heard of this name or society.

After the crowd dispersed, some of the group members who hosted the event stayed behind to clean up. Everyone seemed pretty pumped; this particular talk had drawn the biggest crowd, and more than a few attendees asked about joining their group. Bryson approached Raleigh Jones, thanked him for the excellent presentation and requested that he look at a picture of something to get his opinion.

"It's a tattoo. I'm pretty sure it has Illuminati connections, but I'm wondering if you have any more info." He showed the expert an image on his cell phone of the tattoo on Officer Cuch's arm, the same as he'd seen on the arm of the mystery man at his father's funeral.

"Oh, I think I've seen that before, but I can't give you any details. I have a book at home with pictures of this sort of stuff." He took out his own cell phone and Bryson sent the image to him. "I'll look it up and let you know if I have more info. The different families and their associated connections often use these tattoos, but it really is only for the lower members. The higher-ups generally refrain from these markings. I didn't mention it in the lecture, but another way they tend to self-identify or communicate their brotherhood is through little expressions such as, 'Live in the Light' or 'May the Light protect you.' A lot of secret societies do the same thing. I could probably give an entire lecture on symbols and stuff connected with the Illuminati. By the way, a big thanks to your group for having me. I would love to come back sometime." Nervously, he packed the rest of his things and exited out the back.

Shutting down the lights and locking the door, Bryson felt certain of one thing: *I've got another corner piece to my puzzle. Can't wait to let Serena know.*

32

"So you see, after you've tapped out the spot and cut away some of the tree, you take your little stick probe and poke it into the hole." DJ took the twig and slid it into the tree. "Then, if you picked a good spot, this is what you get." He withdrew the stick, proudly displaying the wiggling white grub on the end. "A nice fat witchetty. Here, you give it a try. Later we'll sauté 'em up for a scrumptious little treat." He popped the still live grub into his mouth, wiped his lips saying, "Better than shrimp on the bar-bee."

Serena took the twig she had fashioned under DJ's tutelage and probed; although, she was pretty sure she would pass on the eating part should she manage to skewer a witchetty. The bushman was amazing; she spent most of her time with him absorbing his vast knowledge of the bush and survival. He'd found a trove of honey in the hollow of a tree and they'd collected some; the Chief squealed with delight when they presented it. If DJ was ever stranded on a desert island, he would put Robinson Crusoe to shame. She knew she had only scratched the surface of the guide's deep well of knowledge about his land, about nature, and how to live in harmony.

"Our Mother really provides us with all we need. You just have to listen and look and learn."

In five days she had learned a lot, and it went well beyond the difference between kangaroos and wallabies. Serena had learned about much of Australia's unique flora and fauna—the marsupials, the koala, kookaburra birds, dingoes, wombats, the list went on. The termite mounds fascinated her. Millions of individual termites used advanced engineering to construct the mounds which they shared collectively in a harmonious society. The spectacular baobab trees, the abundant eucalyptus, and the many ways Aborigines had adapted its gifts to support their needs amazed and humbled her. This ancient people, with their sacred respect for the land and one another, had figured out many things more technologically developed civilizations had yet to figure out.

As DJ put it, not in a prideful way so much as matter-of-fact, "We've been here quite a lot longer than most other cultures. It's just a shame more people are not open to looking at how we get by. You can lead a horse to water...someday he might decide to take a drink."

A routine of daily yoga and hiking had her physically feeling back to normal. She had few interactions with Gurumarra, learning only that their final destination lay farther south, where there was a particular cave with rock paintings from their ancestors, a place of initiation, a sacred place. BB explained to her that the earth had certain energy meridians, ley lines in the common terminology, where the Gaia energy of Mother Earth concentrated. The location Gurumarra sought was important because three meridians crossed there. BB had told her they would arrive on the day when the night would be lit by a full moon, another aspect that had additional significance, though BB himself could not offer an explanation why.

He and the shaman, a *Koradji* in their native tongue, spent most of their time together. Often, Gurumarra seemed to be speaking to someone not visible. BB explained this, saying, "Most people call him the Wanderer because he is always on the move, walking throughout the land. But the true reason, which few understand, is that he wanders the spirit plane, both in the day and during his dreams. He encounters many beings among the spirits and speaks with them. I follow mostly to record knowledge that Gurumarra shares."

She asked BB to find out if in Gurumarra's wanderings he knew the meaning of the seven Candelaria words and phrases, showing these to her scholar friend. Unfortunately, Gurumarra had no such understanding of the meanings but he would ask among the spirits he knew. Later BB reported that the words were very ancient, in a language no longer spoken and long since forgotten. "I am sorry, Galinawa, that he is unable to help more."

Djalu had already refueled and flown his plane, parking the Cessna reasonably close to their destination. He confirmed that it was a location sacred to his people. He admitted being a little surprised that his Chief would bring a non-native there. The guide had hiked back along the river and rejoined them. He brought her to the river, cautioning her about the crocodiles that lay camouflaged beneath the water and warned her that Ginga the crocodile is always looking for a woman he can steal to be his wife. DJ told her the origin story:

"Ginga was once a man, early in the Dreamtime. He fell asleep warming himself near a fire when accidentally the flames lit his back on fire. He rushed into the river to douse the flames, but his back formed blistery lumps. He turned himself into a crocodile, always close to water where he is safe."

Seven days in the Australian bush, stubble of dark brown hair covering the almost healed scar on her head, black and blue marks from her injury faded, covered in a deep brown tan—when Serena emerged at the clearing near the caves late-morning, she almost looked like a wild, forest-spirit . She moved with ease and grace as though this had been her land of birth, and she, one of its many inhabitants, felt thoroughly at home.

She saw the rock formation and the flat stone spread before it, charred by countless ritual fires. BB showed her the rock paintings drawn by their ancestors—animals, stick-figure men, spirit people called Mimis he explained. The walls displayed scenes of the sun and the moon, the rivers and the Great Rainbow Serpent. She could feel earth energy permeating the entire area.

"You can never understand today, Serena, unless you understand what came before. Gurumarra shows you great honor in taking you to this place."

People arrived throughout the day: women, children, and men of their clan. They spoke little to her. The children seemed both curious and shy; at times she heard them whisper, "Galinawa." At sundown, an elder woman arrived accompanied by two younger women to whom she gave directions. All were clad in simple cloth skirts, naked above the waist. They brought bowls with pigments of some sort and a large quantity of white kaolin clay. She watched as they body-painted one another, mostly smearing white with dots and designs of bright red and ochre.

The elder woman, the one with authority, instructed Serena to remove her clothes, and they proceeded to dress her in a similar skirt and to paint her body. She felt but did not see the snake glyphs they traced in coils and curls. She guessed a yellow sun, or was it the moon, now decorated her forehead. When they had finished, they led her to the flat rocks where she stood alone, a circle of the clan kin surrounding her. Night had fallen. Serena tried to register the scene before her.

The flickers of a huge fire, tongues of flame dancing with shadows, cast its illumination on the tribe, their wide eyes and white teeth reflecting flashes of orange, women, men, children in white kaolin and colored markings. Clap sticks in hand, the tribe silently sways and waits. She looks around, mindful of her small breasts, exposed for all to view, fearful of what is about to happen. The old familiar nausea and tightening in her gut momentarily grabs hold and steals her concentration. She searches, catching sight of DJ, clap sticks clenched in his hands and BB, barely recognizable, perched behind a huge didgeridoo. Only the crackle of fire disturbs the silence. Anticipation for the ritual soon to unfold mounts. She can feel the tension.

Gurumarra stands. Gone is the ridiculous stovepipe hat and coat. He is adorned in body paint, necklaces, and he holds the wooden piece he had been whittling and crafting for days. In all ways, his stance commands power and attention. His voice is deep yet musical. At some unseen signal, clap sticks pound in unison, the didgeridoo music begins, giving wind to the voice of the creators. Their shaman begins the telling, his voice full of meaning accentuated by his eyes which convey a deep knowing. Men dance in snakelike fashion; women and children join; others chant. Serena quickly understands this dance tells the creation story of the Rainbow Serpent.

No sooner has the dance and music ended when another story starts with a new rhythm and cadence. Women dance on one side, weaving and curving in unison, while men do a similar dance on the other side creating two circles. This one she could not follow, but BB explained the story behind this second myth to her the following day:

The white snake who was man, argued with the black snake who was woman, about who was stronger, the sun or the moon. The man snake saw the sun's light and warmth and said it was stronger. The woman snake told him only the moon has the power to block the sun. They arranged a contest. The white snake told the sun to leave. The earth became dark and cold and all was in danger of dying till he called it back. The black snake instructed the moon to leave. The earth became covered in water, deep rumblings shook the ground and the earth almost split until she called the moon back. At once, they saw their foolishness and grasped one another mouth to tail to circle sun and moon and forever hold them in place.

The story and dancing finish in one large circle of both men and women with arms locked. They all look at Serena. Loud clapping of sticks and rapid chanting follows and Gurumarra approaches, shaking the carved wooden totem he had crafted. To her surprise, it opens in the middle. He stands over her chanting something undecipherable, waving the totem. Whatever it is he wants to happen does not. For a moment there is complete silence. A full moon reveals itself from behind an ominous night cloud; it casts an eerie light.

The Chieftain steps back, rejoins the two wooden pieces and calls out a command. A new cadence of sticks and wind music begins, and another story unfolds in dance. This one she gathers is the story BB had told her—the story of Mangar-Kunjer-Kunja, the lizard god and how he split the first joined people into two. Something stirs deep in her belly. It isn't a cramp, but something indescribably different. She looks up at the flames dancing among the rocks. In the smoke and flicker, sticklike beings seem to emerge from the crevices. In the trees enclosing this sacred spot, more of the stick figures come and seem to dance among the clan. For a moment, she swears an old Navajo woman dances in the smoky moonlight while shaking a rattle. Again, it grows silent, and the shaman approaches wielding the two pieces of the totem. He stands over her chanting and shouting; the fire roars behind him. The cramping pain, if that's what it is, returns only stronger and then it passes. She gazes around the silent circle to see faces lit with anticipation, some with doubt. Smoke and light and silence play tricks with her senses.

Gurumarra turns with his back toward Serena. When he faces her again, she feels his raw power, and sees that he is angry. She fears him. He shakes the wooden totem, she can see now that the two halves close together over a hollow, a wooden container with carvings decorating all around. She stands in front of him, dwarfed by his size and power. He gives her the two halves placing one in each hand and has her hold them in front of her belly. The cramp returns only this time much worse; she struggles to remain standing. She watches as the shaman turns and pulls something out from the fire. He waves a flaming brand, extinguishing the fire using his hand, and leaves a red glowing ember. She holds her breath as a chanting incantation follows. Gurumarra leans forward and suddenly thrusts the burning firebrand directly into her navel. Gripped and seized by the most intense pain she has ever known, far beyond her worst nightmares, tearing at her insides, lighting her on fire, screaming she draws her hands to her belly, collapses to the ground…and blacks out.

33

The day started off bad. Monitoring his news feed, a report from Missoula left him annoyed. NSA and FBI agents had broken into the home of Mary Carpenter, a forty-five-year-old single mother suspected of being involved in an international cybercrime ring. Bryson felt bad that he was responsible for screwing up the woman's life. Although he was certain they would clear her, at the moment he needed to do computer housekeeping. *I'll figure out a way to make it up to her somewhere down the road.*

Holding his cell, rereading the text for the fifth time, his hand shook. Bryson took a few moments to slow his breathing. He sat down. His day just got a whole lot worse. The message came from Raleigh Jones.

"Following up with you on the tattoo and have information. In the lecture, I showed a slide of just the thirteen bloodlines: Astor, Bundy, Collins, DuPont, Freeman, Kennedy, Li, Merovingian, Onassis, Rockefeller, Rothschild, Russell, Van Duyn. There is a group of affiliated Illuminati families, not top echelon, more like second tier: Disney, Krupp, McDonald, Reynolds. That tattoo image you sent me is associated with the Reynolds family. Hope this helps. Best, Raleigh."

A knife impaled him; the words stood out like a neon sign: REYNOLDS FAMILY. Doubts flooded his mind, swept his emotions. REYNOLDS FAMILY! His father, his uncle—what were they, what are they mixed up with? But the real pain, the twist of the knife in his back, so real that he could feel it, was the uncertainty: *What is in my blood…my genes? Who am I? What am I?* He sat, powerless to stop the torrent of mounting doubt. He swallowed, trying to move the dry lump stuck over his Adam's apple. *What am I going to tell Serena?*

She awoke, immediately sensing that something was different. Probing her navel, feeling gingerly around her belly button, she felt no pain, no burn, no scar. Somehow, she had been bathed and clothed in her normal attire. Raising her shirt and looking down, everything felt and looked normal. She lay on a grass mat; the wooden totem lay next to her on the ground. It took a few moments to register, but she felt at ease, totally fearless. All her life, a dread lingered within—always ready to come forward and show itself. Whatever that longtime companion, that feeling in her gut that pills, medicine, and more recently yoga held at bay—it was gone, replaced by something akin to a warm cozy glow.

Footsteps shuffled, and she rolled over to see Gurumarra, once again sporting his hat and coat, along with a big grin. She propped herself up on her elbows.

"Ah, the Galinawa awakens." He spoke perfect English excepting a pronounced Australian accent.

"You speak English?"

"Of course, this is Australia; we were colonized by the British!"

She stood. "Then why have you been having Beangagarrie translate?"

"Too many questions," BB's voice answered. "Our Chief prefers to spend his time speaking with the spirits and tires from conversing with inquisitive people… No offense intended."

"What happened last night?"

"You see, right away another question." The Chief let out an enormous laugh and continued. "That old snake in your belly, he did not want to wake up and leave. He was coiled tightly inside you and did not want to let go." Another laugh rumbled out, even more pronounced. "But he did not know the power of

Gurumarra, wanderer of the spirit world, a mighty *Koradji* of his people. I had to poke him with the fire stick until he jumped out. He got so scared he jumped right out of his old skin." The laugh erupted again; the shaman was obviously pleased with himself. When he finally settled down he stated, "Yes indeed, most definitely a big fat snake. See for yourself." He pointed to the carved wooden totem.

Seeing Serena's puzzled look, BB chimed in. "He wants you to open the wooden container."

She picked it up and studied the intricate carvings which made no sense to her. Carefully, holding the totem vertically, she first joggled it; she heard something inside. She pulled the pieces apart to reveal a large snakeskin; iridescent scales of green and copper and brown caught the morning sun and sparkled.

"But how?" she stammered. "How…where did this come from…how did this get inside?"

His lips pulled back to a toothless grin and Gurumarra bellowed, "Too many questions." The Chief strode off talking to himself or some unseen guest.

Serena, totally astonished, looked to BB, her eyes pleading for a response. Instead, he merely shrugged his shoulders, flashed those huge teeth, and offered the only explanation she would get. "I told you he is a great shaman. I also told you that you would like him." Before she could argue, he gracefully bowed and left.

Well, someday I'll figure it out, but at the moment, I am dang hungry. There is a hole in my belly like I have never felt before. Other than hunger, she felt great. DJ perched over a small cook-fire. Something smelled delicious. It was just the two of them along with BB and the Chieftain, both of whom had already eaten. The other men and women, present for last night's ritual, were all gone.

She ate ravenously, not bothering to ask what tasted so good. As she slugged a gulp of strong java, Djalu casually said, "Nothin' quite like a bit of yummy witchetty wormies to git your day started." Seeing her abruptly spit out every-thing in her mouth, he laughed, winked, and slapped his hands to his knees say-ing, "Naahh!"

"Okay, good one, but now you owe me; could you please tell me what the heck happened last night?"

"Beats me, Missy. There's a whole lot DJ can't make no sense of." He pointed to his head. "You see this? Dense as a rock; you heard Gurri say so yourself.
Best I can tell you is, I would say whatever went on, I'm thinking it turned out
pretty good…if you receive my meaning."

While Serena finished the rest of the food, whatever it was, DJ said he was
off to fetch some water to put out the fire. He told her it was best she pack up
since they would break camp soon and he needed to get back. By that she figured
they would fly off to somewhere.

Somewhere turned out to be back to Darwin, where they had an International Airport. As they readied to take off, Gurumarra gave her a big hug and
a kiss and told her Ooljee was so pleased she promised to leave him alone for a
while. He laughed again saying, "That one is a powerful shaman. I think I would
have liked to dance with her when she still walked among us. But in the end, we
all dance together. Remember this, Galinawa: in the end we all dance together in
the Dreamtime. Now go; Gurumarra is glad to rid you of that snake. You have
no more fear and your inner snake, what you call kundalini, rises through your
third chakra. May the spirits of sky and earth walk with you."

"Where will he go next?" She addressed BB just before the prop drowned
out conversation.

"Who knows? I don't think even he knows. That is part of being the Wanderer."

As the bush plane took flight, Serena looked out to sky above and around
her, and to earth below. She felt light, almost as though she did not need the
plane to soar. Whatever fears and anxieties had plagued her were gone; her PTSD
was gone. She knew it. She felt it.

Reflecting upon her recent experiences, she realized she had never felt so
happy and unburdened. *The Naga Sanctuary was great. My sisters there embody so
much goodness and discipline.* The kundalini within her stirred from first to second
chakra. *The trip over the ocean was wonderful for the solitude and majesty of the open
sea. But here in Australia, in this raw and untouched expanse of beauty and harmony,
here I think I could live life as fully and fearlessly as anyone possibly could.* Her inner
serpent energy played in her third chakra and she felt it open fully, a fiery furnace

burned within. *But first I must complete the Circle. I am a warrior. I am keeper of the sacred flame. I am torchbearer of truth. I am Galinawa.*

34

D J flew BB and Serena to his home, taxiing the Cessna next to the garage, much as when they had first arrived. The two men conferred and headed inside to make some further arrangements; certain precautions seemed prudent. Serena finally reconnected with Bryson. She had so many things to share.

After lengthy details about what had happened to her, how she was feeling, and the like, Serena got down to business. "Hey, I think I figured out another corner piece to the big puzzle we are working at."

"Really, PTG, I think I have a corner piece too. You go first."

"Well, based on different cultural myths and stories about forces of dark and light battling each other, creation, and so on that seem to pop up in different yet similar ways, I feel pretty certain that the Brotherhood of the Snake/Brotherhood of the Sun is involved and plays a major role. What do you think?"

"That is pretty phenomenal, Serena, considering that you are not using the data associating algorithms I am. It turns out I came to a similar conclusion using an entirely different methodology. I figured the Illuminati as a key piece and they trace their roots back to the same Brotherhood. We are a good team, girlfriend." His chuckle came through loud and clear.

"What's so funny?"

"Don't you see, it's so classic, I just have to laugh."

"What is?"

"Our approaches—they are classic male and female. Bryson uses a rational analytic left-brain way of figuring this out while Serena takes the right-brain intuitive path and we each get to the same place. We are not just a good team; we are a combination of strengths."

"You're right, I love it! Now, tell me about the speaker for the conspiracy group meeting. Did you learn anything? Obviously, some info from the presentation must have helped you in your conclusions. By the way, I will point out that you had help, but I went solo."

The other end went silent. "Bry, are you still there?"

"Yeah."

"What's the matter? You don't sound right."

"Nothing...I'm fine."

"I don't think so, boyfriend. I can hear it in your voice. Lay it on me; I can take it. Remember, we're a team." She listened to his long sigh. Call it intuition, but she wanted to be next to him at this moment, not half a world away.

"I didn't know how to tell you this...but I guess...I guess I should just come clean. The Reynolds family are higher-ups in the whole Illuminati network. The Seeing Eye in the snake tattoo Cuch had on his forearm is the eye of Lucifer, and that particular tattoo is used by people involved with the Reynolds family—*my* family."

His voice sounded constricted; at times he choked up. He spilled it all out including what he knew about Claus Gorman and Baxter Consolidated. Serena listened as he went through all the sordid details and his feelings of doubt about his family, about himself. Through it all, she did her best to be with him even though they were so far apart. He closed with a simple, "Thanks, I'm glad I told you. I feel better."

"Bry, no matter what you're thinking or feeling I can tell you for sure, you are one of the most honest and trustworthy people I've ever met. You're a good guy and I don't mean that in a trite 'nice guy' way; I mean you are doing everything you can to make this a better world. Don't ever doubt that."

"You're a good friend. So, what happens next?"

"I'm off to Greece. That's the next stop on my Circle tour and Gurumarra confirmed it with my great aunt's spirit. I'm headed to the Temple of Hygeia in Epidaurus; I haven't had a chance to look it up yet, so that's all I can tell you. Beangagarrie is researching some of the travel details now; I'll send them to you when I have them."

"Right. I'll see what I can find out as well. Just remember to keep sharp and be safe."

Serena sat meditating, still processing the new pieces of information. Eventually, BB and DJ went over the plan they had devised. Djalu would drive them to a hotel near the airport where he'd made a reservation in his name. Tomorrow, she and BB would taxi to the airport and she would fly first to Perth in Western Australia. From there, she would take an international flight on Qantas Air to Dubai and then connect on a flight to Athens. They had not yet booked the flights and would wait to the last minute in order to minimize the chance that anyone could track her, but they cautioned she would need to be extra careful at the airport in Athens. As for travel in Greece to get to Epidaurus, they hadn't worked out those details yet, but thought it should not be too difficult to figure out. It seemed like a good plan.

Saying goodbye to Djalu was hard; Serena so enjoyed his company, his sense of humor, and just being around him. There was nothing not to like; he typified a man comfortable in his own skin, not pretentious or judgmental. She wondered if it was a cultural thing with the Aborigines. In a very short time, she felt immense respect for the indigenous people of Australia as well as a kinship with them. She promised DJ she would visit and they would do a sort of walkabout together. His toothy grin and warm hug at her promise remained fixed like a photograph in her mind. A taxi brought Serena and BB to the hotel—a nothing special, completely ordinary establishment. They kept a low profile.

Gensu Li strode with a certain air of confidence toward the corner office of Advanced Bionics. While the move from Hong Kong to Singapore represented a compromise of sorts, it was worth it—an honor and an advancement.

"Uncle, I am leaving Singapore for a couple of days."

"I presume for good reason."

Suppressing his self-pleasure and not wanting to appear too eager, he reported very matter-of-factly: "I have uncovered passenger bookings from Darwin to Perth to Dubai and then Greece for Serena Mendez. The tickets were purchased this morning. There is not enough time for me to intersect in Darwin, but with the holdover in Perth, I can meet with her there and return back to Singapore tomorrow. I have already given instructions to fuel a corporate jet."

"Excellent! I see I have made a wise choice in selecting my new head of security."

"Thank you, uncle." He bowed. "Shall I dispatch a second team to Greece?"

"Are you expecting to fail?"

"No, uncle, but good security requires careful planning, including contingency plans." He saw the subtle nod of agreement.

"Notify our colleagues among the Onassis family and request they remain on standby. Give them photos but say nothing about why the girl is valuable."

"Yes, uncle." He was dismissed. *That went well. I don't even miss Hong Kong.*

A tear welled and rolled slowly down BB's face when it came time to depart their separate ways. Serena carried the same duffel she had bought in India; she couldn't even remember where they had stopped on that miserably long car ride. Almost reading her thoughts, standing tall and handing her the bag with his slender hands, he remarked, "Yes, child, we have come a long way together in a very short time."

Her gray eyes fixed their gaze on her guardian and protector. "I don't know how to thank you for being with me during this time of my journey. You are the most remarkable man I have ever met." He had to bend over considerably to compensate for their heights. Tenderly, Serena kissed his forehead.

Wiping away tears, his parting words and his visage stuck in her memory. "You have given me much more than you know, Serena Mendez—both a feeling of having a daughter I lost before I could even hold her in my arms and, more importantly, hope for the future, hope that the dark times may end even in my lifetime, and that I, Beangagarrie Brindabella, might have played a small part." His enormous teeth flashed just a moment. "Be safe, Galinawa, and let the light you carry shine brightly." She watched his tall frame get absorbed into the crowd, shouldered her bag, and went to check in. She had a lot of traveling to do.

The flight to Perth was wonderfully uneventful. She picked up her duffel at baggage claim and figured out what terminal she needed to go to for her international flight, the next leg of her journey. The arrival/departure board showed all the info for her Qantas flight. She had just a little more than a two-hour layover—plenty of time to get through security in the international terminal and to the boarding gate. Ticket in hand, she showed her passport to the booking attendant and placed her baggage to have a claim ticket attached.

"Oh, Serena Mendez...I have a notation here that there is an urgent message for you from a Mr. Brindabella."

She swallowed; BB didn't carry a phone, so she had no way to contact him. "Does it say what the message is?"

"No." The attendant read off a screen. "It says to direct you to room 114B. That's in the suite of offices further down in the terminal. I can have someone take you there." She motioned to a security officer and gave some instructions. "Best to take your bag with you; I hope everything is all right."

Serena gathered her duffel. Normally, this unexpected development would grip inside her gut, but her PTSD had gone. Still, she felt a need for caution.

The security officer was very professional. "It's right this way, Ms. Mendez." The escort ended about three minutes later in the terminal at a suite of offices. "Right through this door, 114B should be somewhere in the middle."

Proceeding to 114B she took a deep breath, grasped the handle, and opened the door. *I hope it's nothing bad.* A single man sat near a window and stood when she entered.

"Ahh, you must be Serena Mendez. Beangagarrie feared you might not get his message."

"What is this about? What is his message?" She faced an Asian man, she guessed Chinese from the accent, late thirties she judged, slightly taller than she, very fit looking. He wore a tailored business jacket over a collarless shirt.

"He says it is not safe for you to travel to Greece. The people pursuing you have intercepted those plans."

Serena didn't like this man. He has a smug arrogance to his manner, but she decided to play along. "What does he suggest?" She sat down to convey an air of comfort, to keep this stranger off guard.

"I am to take you to Singapore. We have a private jet. After a few days, we can then bring you to Greece."

He was lying; she was sure of it. "Thanks, but I think I can take care of myself. Why exactly is it that I need to be in Singapore?"

"Ms. Mendez, I do not give the orders, I merely follow them." He smiled confidently and strode between the door and Serena. "You are coming with me to Singapore. We can do this the hard way or the easy way."

Not showing the least bit of fear, she remained seated. "What is the hard way?"

"I strike you on the head, not far from the scar beneath your very short hair, rendering you unconscious. In ten minutes, some of my men arrive in a company limo with a wheelchair that they bring to this office suite and we then continue to take you to the corporate jet parked in a hangar at the far corner of this airport."

"What's the easy way?"

He twisted a large ring on his finger; she watched as several prongs protruded upward. "This contains a rapid-acting sedative and will spare me from having to reinjure your pretty head. We'll wheel you asleep, rather than unconscious, to the waiting limo… Which do you prefer?"

"Hmmm." She pretended to be weighing her options. "I'll go with plan B." She noted his smug and satisfied face and played her cards. Demurely brushing her hair, channeling some sex energy and slightly spreading her legs, she looked right at him. "I hear Singapore is quite nice."

"Not nearly as much as Hong Kong." He remained standing but did take a step toward her.

Casually, she reached to her duffel. "Do you mind if I smoke?"

"Smoking is prohibited in public places in Australia."

She rummaged through her belongings. "Well, I have PTSD and the smoking helps me to relax. Maybe you won't need to sedate me after all. Besides, what are they going to do, arrest me?" She pulled out her pack of yellow American Spirits.

"Don't you know smoking is bad for your health?" Seeing the brand, he said, "Ah, American Spirit, I've never tried them."

She leaned forward to offer him a smoke, and he took another step toward her. She pressed over the "S." Two electrodes discharged along with some confetti, striking her envoy in the chest. She watched his immobilized form shake violently then fall to the floor.

She quipped, "Don't you know that smoking is bad for your health?"

35

S erena stood over him, removed and twisted the ring to administer the sedative. Thinking through the rest of her plan, she removed his wallet and passport, took photos of his driver's license and ID. Her would-be assailant was Gensu Li. She replaced his items, located and confiscated his cell phone. *I'm sure Bryson can use this.* Lastly, she rolled up his sleeves noting a dragon tattoo, not the medieval sort of fire-breathing type, this was a more Chinese dragon with short wings, the kind you see in a Chinese New Year celebration. She took photos of her detainer. *I'll send it all to Bryson.*

She calmly picked up her bag and got ready to leave when another idea came to her. She removed a few items then took off her tracer earring and buried it inside one of the pockets in the duffel, leaving it in the room. "You see, I am quite able to care for myself." In no rush, she left room 114B with Gensu Li sprawled unconscious on the floor.

She held her boarding pass and passport, confirmed the gate, and walked to the security checkpoint. Fortunately, the line moved quickly. Once Serena was within the secure portion of the terminal, she immediately went to a store with sundry items and purchased a disposable razor and nail polish. She had no intention of taking the Qantas flight, certain that Li or his associates would detain her or even involve airport security on some made-up suspicion. Next, she withdrew money from an ATM. Entering a family restroom further down the terminal, a mother changing her crying infant paid her no heed as Serena shaved the new growth of hair on her scalp, careful not to slice the healing scar. In a stall, she changed into her kaftan, the same one worn by the Naga Sisters, and the headscarf she previously purchased. A circular dab of the muted red nail polish formed a dot in the middle of her forehead. The restroom had now emptied; she threw out her clothes and shoes, slipping on the last item she had removed from her duffel bag, a pair of casual sandals.

Serena Mendez had vanished, and Chanda Patel found a nice quiet eatery where she ordered chai and a vegetarian salad. Seated alone at a table, she felt a sense of freedom, every bit a new woman capable of almost anything. She called Bryson to give him a weather report of sorts with all the new developments, but there was no answer. She texted him: "Stormy weather but forecast good. Need to talk ASAP."

A few minutes later he called. "Sorry, I just stepped out to get the recycle bin. What's up?"

It took only a few moments to give him an update. "So, I'm sending you the photos and info on Gensu. I will need a new flight and I want you to book it. Avoid Dubai as well; just get me to Greece and there is no rush. Do you think I'll have any trouble getting through customs?"

"No, you should be fine. You might want to pick up another outfit, maybe a burqa; that will hide your face even more."

"Good suggestion. I'm going to find a place here that ships international and send the phone to you."

"Take out the battery and SIM card; that will render it untraceable, but pack them in the bag."

"Already done, Snowman."

"I'm gonna have to start calling you Jamie Bond. You are really on top of things. I am very proud."

"And you'll track my bag? I'm sure they'll take it with them."

"Yeah, that was smart too. I don't think it would have occurred to me to do that. I'll charge up your debit card and look into flights, but I won't purchase anything till you confirm. Oh, I'm sending you info on the Temple of Hygeia, just click the link. You're gonna be surprised."

Overhead she heard her name being paged and ignored it with a sense of satisfaction. She found a shop selling clothes; they also sold luggage. She placed a burqa and a second outfit along with a tee, jeans, and footwear in a new carry-on. Entering a souvenir shop, Serena, now Chanda, verified they could ship. She guessed Bryson's head size and selected a genuine Aussie bush hat and a stuffed kangaroo, slipping the phone, battery, and SIM card in the pouch. While making light conversation with the clerk, she addressed the package and paid extra for insurance.

Smiling, she thanked the clerk who smiled back at her. "I'm sure he'll love it."

Next, she purchased a book, a best seller romance of some sort, parked herself in view of the arrival/departure board, pretended to read, and waited for Bryson's call.

Her phone rang. "This is Chanda." She spoke with a mild Indian accent.

"Qatar Airlines Flight number 1912. It departs in three hours. Perth to Abu Dhabi International Airport. From there, you can connect on their affiliate carrier, Aegean Air, to take you to Eleftherios Venizelos Airport in Athens. Shall I book you?"

"Yes, I can see the Qatar flight on the board. It looks as though it's on time."

A moment later he exclaimed, "Done. I'll email you the boarding pass so you have it on your phone. You'll need it at the gate to board."

"Got it."

"You should change out the SIM card in your phone to one of the others I gave you. Do you still have them?"

"Yes, I'll do that."

"In eighteen hours, you should arrive in Athens, but call or text me from Qatar. I'm told their airline is positively top-notch. Have a good flight."

Sitting in an out-of-the-way location, noting that her previously scheduled flight on Qantas had departed on schedule, and her name no longer paged overhead, Chanda Patel rose and made her way to gate 6D. Flight 1912 to Abu Dhabi would board in ten minutes. She downloaded the brochure for the Temple of Hygeia Bryson had sent her the link for, texted him that she was getting ready to board, and pulled up the page with her e-boarding pass. Fifteen minutes later, she powered down her phone, settled into her surprisingly comfortable seat, and educated herself about her next destination.

The Snowman had it right again:

> Nestled in the hills overlooking the great theater of Epidaurus, join us for a relaxing and rejuvenating spa experience in a location frequented by Plato and Aristotle and renowned for its healing traditions. Arrive tired and leave refreshed as the Sons and Daughters of Hygeia pamper you and care for you in the ancient healing methods of Asclepius, Father of Medicine.

Enjoy a daily routine of mineral baths from a volcanic spring, private walking trails under the Aegean sun, common meals to socialize with fellow travelers, and nightly theater showcasing the finest in Greek comedy and tragedy. Receive dream interpretation by our world-renowned Seeress to help you unlock and release emotional blocks. You will experience the full benefits of healing to mind, body, and spirit under the guidance of Asclepius's daughter Hygeia, the personification of health, whose lineage at this temple is unbroken since antiquity.

All meals prepared by our gourmet chef in an eco-friendly exclusive spa. Five, seven, and ten-day all-inclusive packages…

The address, phone number, and web-based booking details followed. *Wow, not what I expected. I wonder what Ooljee had in mind?* She stretched, becoming aware for the first time of some tension in her muscles. She felt safe for the moment and wondered what it would feel like to soak in hot mineral springs. When she awoke, stars twinkled through the plane's window. An attentive cabin crew member had left her a neck pillow, but Serena had apparently fallen into a deep sleep, rewarded now by feeling refreshed and fine other than a crook in her neck. She was already halfway through the eleven-hour flight and it was time for dinner. To her surprise and delight, the food was excellent. After dinner she typed out an email to send to Bryson and a second message for Dharani, assuring her Naga sister that she was safe, and giving a synopsis of what had occurred both en route and in Australia. She would send off both when they landed in Abu Dhabi.

The woman seated next to her did not speak English. Serena used the time to practice manipulating her kundalini up and down her open chakras, feeling the flow of open and unimpeded energy, wondering how it would be different to have all seven chakras open. *One step at a time; these are not the sorts of things to be rushed.* Despite reminding herself of this, she felt impatient; she wanted to finish the mission she started and noted with frustration that she wasn't even halfway through her journey around the world. Not to mention that Gensu Li pursued her and Claus Gorman wanted her as well. She hoped Bryson could figure out why. A certain irony struck her: *All those years I was running away from myself and now I am running away from other people who seem bent as hell on finding me. But this isn't like paparazzi pursuing a famous celebrity; these are bad people who want me for some reason or reasons.* She reviewed every detail she could recall—Li's well-tailored sports jacket, his cocky arrogance, and his dragon tattoo. Serena hoped she never would see him again and that her super sleuth friend could shed light on her would-be abductor's purpose.

The sick feeling in his stomach was not going away anytime soon. He rummaged in his medicine cabinet, found some old antacids and chewed a couple to no benefit. *Great! Now I have this disgusting chalk taste in my mouth to go along with this distress in my gut.* Bryson drummed his fingers on his desk, staring at both monitors.

There wasn't a whole lot available on Gensu Li. Forty years old, lived in Hong Kong, a hellion when he had been in his late teens and early twenties. If indeed all this related to the same Gensu Li, the man had won some martial arts competitions, but then he'd essentially dropped out of sight. What pictures he found looked close enough to a younger version of the ones Serena had sent. None of this seemed particularly troubling by itself.

Bryson flinched and rubbed his abdomen; he drank a glass of water and belched rather unceremoniously—all to no avail. On one monitor, he read it through a second time, scrolling and speed-reading—everything he had collected thus far on the Li family and their Illuminati roots and connections, as well as corporate, government, and military associations. He was sure he would uncover even more as his data linking algorithms searched an ever-widening array of databases.

On the other monitor, he had everything he could find out about Dr. Kenseiko Li, the President and CEO of Advanced Bionics, headquartered in Singapore, the current resting place of Serena Mendez's duffel bag with hidden earring. Kenseiko Li had PhDs in both molecular biology and genetics and currently led the privately held company that was pioneering gene-based cures to diseases and biomolecular "life enhancement" technologies. Their cutting-edge research, or so the company claimed, one day expected to result in gene therapies to halt aging, to enhance cognitive abilities, and a host of other advances. All of Advanced

Bionics funding was through private investment making the company relatively non-transparent and therefore able to say and promote whatever they chose to. There wasn't any way to verify or to fact-check their claims. All their research was "proprietary." It screamed secrecy!

The biography section on the Advanced Bionics' home page listed details that Bryson could verify through other sources. His bio touted Dr. Li's scientific accomplishments and business acumen, tracing his advancement from head of research to the president at Lifesource Enterprises, another private corporation, before its merger with Advanced Bionics. Li became head of the merged companies.

He held the newspaper, yellowed and fragile, although every word stood emblazoned within his eidetic memory. Bryson had forced himself to pull it from the paper files he kept in his office and he glanced at the family photo on his desk—mom, dad, and himself enjoying a sunny afternoon at a beach on the coast of Maine. He didn't remove the photo but knew on the back was written, "Summer 2004, Kennebunk."

The faded *New York Times* headline dated October 12, 2004:

> SEARCH CONCLUDED FOR MISSING PLANE. PROMINENT FINANCIER AND WIFE PRESUMED DEAD. Mr. George Reynolds and his wife, traveling on a private Lockheed corporate jet en route from Zurich to Singapore that disappeared on tracking radar and without a distress call eight days ago…

The story went on for a half page detailing the accomplishments of his father, his family's influence as a wealthy and influential paragon of American industrialism, his mother's accomplishments in her own right as a law professor at NYU, etc. It closed detailing surviving family members. It named Bryson as a young genius; his father's older brother Peter was also named. The article/obituary closed with the following line: "The President of Lifesource Enterprises, Dr. Kenseiko Li, whose company owned the missing jet, expressed his deep condolences to the Reynolds family over this tragic event."

Tossing the paper to the side, Bryson promptly threw up.

36

S erena, still disguised as Chanda, exited her plane and found a display with information about arriving and departing flights. The Aegean Air flight to Athens appeared to be on schedule. She texted Bryson, sent off her two emails, and found a place to buy a new charger for her tablet that would work in Greece. The cosmopolitan airport looked busy but not too congested. Judging from their attire, people from throughout the world scurried past in their suits and jeans, skirts, dresses, burqas, and hijabs, many very colorful. She noted quite a few women, presumably Muslim, had their faces hidden beneath a niqab or simple veil concealing part of their face. She needed to use a restroom and took the opportunity to change again. Her choice of garment, purchased in Perth, turned out to be perfect. She exited in a muted gray and brown full burqa including mesh covering her eyes, the previous nail polish forehead dot removed and underlying skin now back to normal. Her name could just as easily have been Muslim or Hindu; Serena/Chanda now appeared to be a conservative young woman walking to her destination gate in this moderate Arab nation. She blended perfectly into her surroundings but remained wary.

The final leg of her current air connections took off and landed without a hitch. She had no luggage beyond her carry-on and nothing to declare at customs. She offered to remove her veil, but the agent did not feel the need and just waved her through. *So far so good. I just need to call them at the Temple, ask their recommendations for travel from Athens to Epidaurus, and book myself a wonderful spa experience.* She also sent a text to Bryson letting him know that when she had those arrangements made she planned to call him. He responded asking her to check her email right away—new information.

It took a while to plow through the lengthy message—all about Gensu and Dr. Kenseiko Li, Advanced Bionics, and Lifesource. Bryson had even sent a JPEG with the newspaper article. *Ouch! This must have him pretty worked up. Hell, it's hard for me to imagine how he is processing this. How is this all connected? What the hell is going on??*

❖   ❖   ❖

"You disappoint me, nephew."

"She never boarded the flight to Dubai." He kept his eyes down.

"So, where is she?"

"The team that Onassis sent checked multiple flights originating from Perth and connecting through other cities for an entire extra day. They swear she did not arrive in Athens."

"So where is she, nephew?" He flinched momentarily as an errant shaft of sunlight broke through the mirrored glass onto his neck. Quickly, he adjusted the blinds.

"I do not know, uncle, but I will find her. She had help. I will track her down."

"I want that American girl. What is your plan?"

"We have the cigarette package, the one with the Taser." He flexed his muscles, still sore from the shock. "Most of the fingerprints on the package were too large for such a small woman. We are running those prints through our channels. If we can locate her associate, perhaps we can locate the girl."

"Very well; keep me posted…and Gensu, I am sure I need not remind you that I do not like to be disappointed."

Gensu Li bowed and exited saying nothing. *I'm going to find that little fucking bitch…and when I do, she'll be sorry she didn't come with me before.*

In some ways, this last bit of travel seemed too easy. Elena, the staff person at the Temple of Hygeia, not only booked her stay, she put "Chanda" on hold while contacting a shuttle service they recommended and made the arrangements for her. Now she sat while her driver pointed out different scenic and historical details as they drove along the Megara Gulf toward the Argolid Peninsula where the ancient city of Epidaurus stood. The blue waters, intense sunshine, and sea breeze invigorated her. The two-hour drive on land literally grounded her after the lengthy air travel and congestion of Athens. Entering another world and another time, she absorbed all that her impromptu tour guide shared.

Greece had been hit hard during the financial crisis and even more so by the sanctions imposed by the European Union in exchange for debt relief—extortion by the European finance ministers and their governments her driver,

Anastacio, complained—"They are rapists who force their will upon our good people!" But rather than spit or curse, he simply shrugged. "Still, this is Greece, and we have survived many wars and battles." He then launched into details about the Peloponnesian Wars occurring in these very hills, along this same coast centuries earlier. She texted Bryson, knowing he would be jealous given his studies of Western Civilization. Somehow, two hours elapsed.

"Dude, I can see the edge of the Great Theater in Epidaurus—it's totally awesome! You would love it." Then she added, "Wish you were here with me," followed by a smiley-faced emoji. Serena didn't expect a response; it was a nine-hour time difference or about 5 AM in Taos. She paid her driver and left a generous tip for Anastacio, his unemployed wife, and their three children. Fortunately, she had stopped at a currency exchange at the airport and had plenty of euros. He humbly thanked her saying the gods were good to him this day and left her his card in case she needed a driver to return her to Athens when her stay concluded. She thought to herself, *he is a hardworking man, just trying to get by and provide for his family, a decent human impoverished by world bankers and governments—like so many places throughout the world.* He wished her a restful stay in his native country and safe journeys. He drove away. She stood between two Ionian columns, readily distinguished by the curved volutes on the capitals. A sign in both Greek and English read: "Temple of Hygeia—Asclepian Healing Center." Beneath the words she noted a stone bas relief of a bowl and a snake, apparently the symbol associated with this daughter of Asclepius. She snapped photos, slung her bag over her shoulder and entered.

A woman, just a few years older than she, wore a simple white tunic. Her long black hair was pulled back, accentuating her dark brown, almost black eyes whose corners crinkled as she smiled in welcome. "You must be Chanda. I am Elena; we spoke over the phone. You made good timing."

"Yes, thank you—the drive here was wonderful; it was so helpful of you to make those arrangements." Serena immediately liked this woman; Elena exuded a certain warmth and gentle presence. It struck her a moment later—*The woman radiates healing energy. I can feel it!*

"Come, you must be weary from your travels. You have come to the right place. Would you like some fresh fruit or refreshment? Let me show you to your room and the mineral baths. After a soak, you will feel brand new." Elena glided through a back entrance, past fragrant flowers, fountains, and stone sculptures as Chanda followed close behind, absorbing the healing energies surrounding her.

37

B y the time Bryson got back to her, Chanda had changed to Western-style jeans and a light top, been escorted throughout the spa, and had gone to the gymnasium. She learned this was more than just a place to work out. There were indoor and outdoor facilities, all supervised by *gymnastai*—the teachers, coaches, and trainers of athletes. They wore short tunics. All the staff looked remarkably fit. They asked about her fitness goals, admired her lithe and flexible body, and offered to work with her on nutrition and strength training if she desired. For today, she only wanted to practice her asanas. Although in ancient Greece the athletes trained in the nude, that tradition was not upheld at the spa.

"Hey, how's the spa experience, PTG?" He sounded good.

"Bry, I don't care if you don't like to fly, some day we are coming here together. The totality of what is here will absolutely blow you away."

They updated one another. Bryson had been trying to locate anything Beangagarrie Brindabella had published. BB was a geneticist and Advanced Bionics researched gene therapies. There had to be a connection. He felt pleased that Serena had booked only a five-day package. He reasoned that the shorter she stayed in any single place, the less likely any pursuers could catch up with her.

"How am I doing in the money department?"

"No problem, I cashed in a few more of your great aunt's gemstones. There's plenty more. What's on the agenda?"

"I'm still trying to figure things out over here. I gather the director likes to meet individually with all the guests, but I arrived too late today to meet with her, so that will happen tomorrow." She adopted her best imitation of Thurston Howell, III's wife from *Gilligan's Island*. "Well dahling, later today I'm going to have a hot oil massage followed by a mineral spring soak. Tonight, I'm sure I'll have a fabulous meal and then a bit of theater. I do so hope it's a comedy, dahling."

"You crack me up. I just might have to get over my fear of flying."

The hot oil massage, followed by scraping her skin using a curved blade, a strigil the masseuse explained, and a long soak in the mineral baths all left Chanda feeling wonderfully refreshed and rejuvenated. In less than six hours she had transformed from aching muscles, tired from travel and stress, to energized guest at the healing Temple of Hygeia. The meal did not disappoint—better than even the brochure suggested.

The staff, all resembling Greek gods and goddesses, had changed from their basic white tunics, the same unisex garment worn by both the male and female staff, into costumes for the evening performance. Tonight featured a tragedy by the ancient Greek playwright, Euripides. Before the start, an actor explained the role of theater to the Greeks. It represented more than movies or a performance of modern times. The plays brought life to human drama, great themes of challenge, growth, destiny met or thwarted with the gods intervening, laughing, or playing with their human characters. The plays were meant to have the people think about life, the meaning of life, and the forces that shape our lives. Tonight's performance, *Helen,* was a melodrama about the "face that launched a thousand ships" contending with the vicissitudes and whims of the gods. There were more than a few comic elements. In her mind, Chanda tried to imagine how Grecians of the day would have responded. The anthropologist in her felt curious. She lay in her bed wondering what life would have been like in those ancient times. She drifted to sleep thinking about her own still unfulfilled destiny.

A deep slumber ensued. Serena had a strange dream. A large bird with a long curved beak, it looked a little like a flamingo or a heron, flew solo, silhouetted for a moment across the face of a blazing sun. She followed the bird's flight as it landed, alighting upon a rock. A snake lay sunning itself upon the rock, indifferent to the large bird. Without warning, scooping the reptile into its beak, the bird took flight but now it was night. She saw its form with the snake dangling from its beak silhouetted across a full moon. The dream was very vivid; she awoke remembering even the most minute detail.

She rose at dawn, walked the property, and greeted other guests, many of whom she had met the previous night at the common meal and theater. Today would be hot; she felt the warm sunlight on her darkened skin. After a light breakfast, before the heat of the day, she found a secluded grassy spot and practiced her yoga, feet bare and connected to the earth. Kundalini energy flowed from the base of her spine through to her solar plexus uninhibited. The air smelled clean and fresh, delighting her nostrils, filling her with nature. Time passed unheeded; she had no schedule and no deadlines. Though her eyes were closed in meditative stillness, she sensed someone approach. A woman wearing the same simple tunic as the rest of the staff at the Temple and carrying a staff of two entwined snakes crossing several times with wings at the top—a golden caduceus—walked toward her. Serena's spine tingled.

"You must be Chanda. I am Agape, the director. Welcome to our sacred place."

Some things cannot be explained; this applied to Agape—early fifties, classic Mediterranean features with an understated elegance. It was not her posture, her grace, her movement, or her poise. One would not describe her as beautiful in the sense of her physical features or well-proportioned frame. It was her eyes, her countenance, her aura. Quite simply, the woman radiated love. At the metaphysical level, Serena sensed her power and humility—the woman had a presence like no one she had ever encountered, the embodiment or incarnation of pure love. She stared, enamored by the elder woman's being.

"I am glad you have visited us. We are honored to have guests from all over the world. What is it you seek here at our Temple?" She sat comfortably next to her guest, with no agenda other than to determine needs and where healing might be required.

"Where do I start?" It seemed her story had turned into a saga.

"It is best to start at the beginning."

"How much time do we have?"

"As much time as we need." A warm smile accompanied the invitation to tell the story. "Here in Greece, we are fond of long sagas and heroic journeys. Have you read *The Odyssey*?"

Serena took a deep breath. It required nearly an hour for Agape, whose very name means love, to hear the narrative. Serena left nothing out, from childhood to the Navajo reservation, her aunt's Circle, India, Australia, pursuit, near capture, and arrival. All the while, the director listened attentively, at times nodding, at times empathically absorbing some of Serena's fears and pain and suffering. At length, Agape stood up and held her staff tightly. She looked troubled.

"For today, you have given me much to dwell upon. I understand your desire to have the next chakra opened. I cannot promise this to you. I must speak with Melantha. She is our Seeress; I must speak with her about a dream I had many years ago when I myself was perhaps your age. Yet, I remember this dream as though it was in my sleep last night, still fresh in my mind. I share it with you now as I believe my dream and your visit here are connected.

"I stood in the chamber of awakening; it is a sacred place here on our grounds. The chamber was completely dark. Hermes, the messenger god, the god of wisdom, uncle to Asclepius and half brother to Apollo visited me, giving me a candle. It was a strange candle—the wick had a black thread and a white thread wrapped each upon the other. The likes of this I had never seen before. He said I must light this candle in order for the chamber to be illuminated. He left, leaving me in darkness. Now you arrive. I know nothing of the Candelaria, nothing of their history or their lineage, but I see a flame within you, child, something which burns. I must speak with Melantha. Come with me so that you may also speak with her of your dreams."

"Melantha sees with eyes that pierce the veil, the cloud that obscures. Approach Melantha and speak of your night visions, so that I may interpret the messages from the gods."

Serena waited as Agape approached the speaker. She gathered the language Melantha spoke had poetic authority. The Seeress was old, wrinkled, yet displayed a certain vitality. She sat on a stone chair facing a crevice. A misty vapor of fumes seemed to emanate from the crevice. The air smelled faintly of sulfur. Serena surmised this was most likely a volcanic vent spewing gas from deep within the earth, the same geothermic forces heating the mineral baths. Although not herself a student of ancient Greece, she knew enough to recognize a similarity to the oracle at Delphi, Apollo's temple where a priestess inhaled psychosis-inducing fumes and then interpreted signs and their meanings.

Dream interpretations were private affairs. Serena had no idea of the details Melantha and Agape discussed, but when it was apparently over, Agape had a strange look. Leaving quickly, she said, "I must check some things. Tomorrow we shall speak."

The smoke irritated Serena's eyes; they burned, and tears blurred her vision as she approached the old woman. There, seated on the stone chair, vapors billowing from below, she noticed Melantha's eyes were completely scarred over, not like the milky orbs her Naga sister Anshula had; the Seeress's eyes were angry red with a web of scar tissue crossing iris, cornea, and pupil if any remained. She couldn't tell if the old woman could see at all, but a firm hand grasped Serena by the arm, like a talon holding her, drawing her near. "Come and tell Melantha of who visits in the night so that she can prophecy your future."

She fought through the smoke. Serena had not prepared a dream vision for which she desired interpretation. She now understood the dream in the cave, a dream that had haunted her for so long. But last night's dream was odd, still fresh in her memory, so why not give Melantha a go? Although the old woman was more than a little creepy, Serena wasn't afraid; she relayed the dream of the strange bird and the snake.

Melantha cackled, there is no other word to describe the sounds coming from her throat, and then suddenly she fell into a trance. What little of her irises that Serena could see rolled back in her head. Normally, Serena would be spooked by this; instead, she listened as the oracle spoke.

"Ibis is the bird-form Hermes chooses to visit you. He flies from Egypt where he lived before coming to Greece. There his name was Thoth. His beak is the crescent of the moon for he is god of the moon. He braves the power of the sun to pick up the snake. You are the snake. He brings you because you carry the power of the moon, the power to block the sun. You must go to Egypt. Hermes himself visits you to tell you this. Heed him, child; he is god of wisdom. You, child, are a Snakewoman." Melantha began to cough and wheeze violently, but still held Serena in her talon-like grip. "The Ibis beckons...heed his call." Her eyes drifted downwards; the old woman released her hold. Evidently, the trance and dream interpretation had concluded.

"Melantha sees with eyes that pierce the veil, the cloud that obscures. Approach Melantha and speak of your night visions so that I may interpret the messages from the gods."

How did she know about Egypt? Did Agape tell her about my Circle of tasks? Somehow, Serena knew beyond doubt...no way! Melantha drew the advice from a deeper source of wisdom. *One step at a time, girl. One step at a time...*

38

The following morning, a cool sea breeze left jewels of dew upon the moist grass where she practiced. Balanced with head down on both her hands and with legs scissored, she held the pose in focused concentration—twenty seconds…thirty…forty…she did not see Agape watching…fifty…at fifty-six seconds she collapsed, her arms shaking from the effort.

"Good morning, Serena. Your form and strength are quite advanced. I delight in watching."

"Thank you, Agape! I still have much to learn." The director appeared troubled; the fullness of her peaceful and loving presence seemed mysteriously shrouded by something.

"I have learned much since last we spoke. While I do not wish to interrupt your yoga, there are urgent matters to discuss. Come, let us walk together."

Toweling off her sweat and dew, Serena rose and followed, listening to what the elder woman now shared.

"After your session with Melantha, she sought me out to share a dream she herself had the night you arrived; the significance and understanding of that dream had not been clear to the Seeress herself until she met with you. Understand these things, child: in all my time here, Melantha has never sought me out; she is very, very old, at least two hundred years. I am the sixth director she remembers, but there were others she has since forgotten."

Serena said nothing. The two women walked in seclusion and Agape continued. "Melantha dreamt of a dragon from the West, flying to our temple and trying to destroy it, but it failed. A second dragon, more powerful than the first, flew from the East and destroyed the temple. She claims that you are in danger here and must go to Egypt, that Hermes himself summons you there. She says your presence here puts us all in danger."

The shroud troubling this Daughter of Hygeia lifted at this telling and she once again displayed the full loving countenance of her being. "I am sorry to require that you leave, but for our safety and your own safety, this must be. Yet, there is more that I must share."

Without speaking, Serena showed her understanding. How would she achieve the next chakra opening? She wanted to ask; instead, she listened as the High Priestess continued.

"We of this temple are a loose-knit group of many who share origin with the teachings of Hermes. He founded many mystery schools. This story I will tell in more detail. For the moment, know that after meeting with Melantha, I contacted the leader of a sect in Egypt. They still have a school and train in the sacred ways. They are the Sisterhood of the Black Snake."

At the mention of their name Serena chimed, "Yes, I know of them, one of my Naga sisters trains there to learn the ways of the voice. Her name is Nalini, and she is the moon sister to my great aunt, and also a dreamwalker. She is the one who is supposed to guide me; I spoke of her yesterday."

"Yes, Nalini is now a proselyte of that sect. They know of you and your Candelaria heritage. I am told you are in great danger here, that your safety at the Naga Sanctuary was guaranteed, but not so here. They are sending emissaries to bring you to Egypt where they believe they can protect you."

She stopped and faced Serena, placing hands upon both of the young woman's shoulders; a grave look darkened her eyes. "You are not being pursued, child; you are being hunted!"

In the last three days he had accomplished nothing—nada, zilch, donut hole, a total sum of zero. Nothing new to report on his Chicago connection, nothing on Li, Advanced Bionics, his uncle Peter, or his efforts to locate published studies from BB. There was one small thing—Bryson had managed to put off the Sotheby's agent and buyer for a couple of weeks with a lame story about the owner not quite being ready to part with the necklace. *Whoopi doodah, I sure have been productive!* Now, holding the package that had just been delivered, he at last had something to get working on.

The hat Serena had sent fit him well; he wore it as he played with the stuffed kangaroo and shot a selfie video to send to Serena, a stylized geek version of *Crocodile Dundee*. Then he attacked the contents of the marsupial's pouch— the cell phone of Serena's would-be abductor. *Let's see what you are hiding, Mr. Gensu Li.*

"We have identified the fingerprints taken off the package of American cigarettes."

"Good, nephew, I was beginning to get impatient."

"They belong to a Bryson Reynolds. He used to work for the US government. He is an expert in computer code and software security."

Kenseiko Li's eyebrows raised slightly. "That is most curious! It is a name I am most familiar with."

"Would you like me to find and eliminate him, uncle? I will not fail you."

"No, Gensu, that is not necessary at this time. Keep searching for the girl, but in the meantime, I have another assignment for you…"

Upon conveying his instructions to his Head of Security and watching him bow, the CEO of Advanced Bionics drummed his desk, flipped a pen artfully between his fingers, checked the time, and picked up the phone.

"Peter, it's been a while since we last have spoken."

Peter swallowed. "Dr. Li, it is good to hear from you; I trust the light shines upon you."

"Spare me the pleasantries. It seems your family does not tire in its efforts to cause problems, problems for all of us and what we desire to achieve." Dr. Li explained the situation to Peter Reynolds, making it clear that he expected the problem to be dealt with. Li did not get into the full details as to why this particular girl was significant, her unique genetic profile, etc.; these were secrets above the Reynolds family. He merely conveyed that Bryson Reynolds should be able to lead them to Serena Mendez. After they had captured the American girl, he did not care what happened to Peter's nephew.

"Yes, Dr. Li, you can count on me, sir. Remain in the light."

"Trust me, Peter, I intend to, I intend to." He closed the blinds and stood in shadow. "May the light shine on you as well."

Hanging up the phone, Peter Reynolds did not let his concern come across in his voice as he placed a call.

"Claus."

"Yes, Mr. Reynolds."

"I have a special job for you. Expense it to the Charles Godfried account…"
He gave detailed instructions to Claus Gorman regarding this special assignment.

"Yes, Mr. Reynolds, I'll leave no later than this evening."

"Hunted, but why? Did she say why?"

"I cannot answer this for certain, but perhaps you will understand better as I explain more about who Hermes was in the pantheon of gods. First, you must realize that none of these were gods or goddesses…"

The historical details which Agape then relayed began to shed light on mysteries thus far shrouded in darkness. The so-called gods and goddesses were Atlanteans. They possessed superior knowledge and technology and genes; the more primitive peoples of the time looked upon them as gods. Their superior genes resulted in long life spans—hundreds, even over a thousand years. As a result, many different stories about these beings, at times with different names, confuse students of history.

"The men and women of Atlantis suffered from great pride and constantly bickered among themselves. There were shifting allegiances, but few bondings as they preferred to mate with the short-lived men and women we know of today. Apollo himself was a product of mating between a true full-blooded Atlantean, Zeus, and a lesser species, a mere mortal female. The same is true of his half-brother Hermes. They have different names in different mythologies, but they are the same people. Apollo was especially proud, calling himself a sun god. He slew the earth spirit Python, guardian to Gaia, the Earth Mother. Python existed at a higher ethereal plane; Apollo slew Python in order to have a temple for himself at Delphi, a site of great Gaia energy. His son, Asclepius, took the power of the snake guardian and used it for good, to bring healing, renewal, rejuvenation. Asclepius's daughter was Hygeia."

"But the knowledge of Asclepius was only partial. His uncle, Hermes Trismegistus, bore the full wisdom of the peoples of Atlantis. His teachings in the *Corpus Hermeticus* and *Definitions to Asclepius* are ancient sacred texts which share Atlantean wisdom; these provide the basis for our teachings. This staff," she held up her Caduceus, "represents the power of the two snakes. Hermes, under different names, set up mystery schools to teach the ancient wisdom and ways. Atlanteans had mastered alchemy and could transmute matter and energy..."

Agape continued for over an hour, explaining about the gnostic schools that Hermes Trismegistus had founded and how some had been corrupted by those who did not want to share knowledge but to withhold it. "This division became known as the war between serpents. One faction wanted to hold the knowledge secret and use this knowledge to exert power and influence over the ignorant. A second group wanted the knowledge to be available for all. This split really originated much earlier with the Atlantean known as Prometheus, the bringer of fire to mankind. Some say he brought this to elevate the primitives; others believe he desired control over them. In other mythologies, more widely known, Prometheus was called Lucifer, the fallen angel."

It all seemed rather complicated to Serena, but as Agape explained these pieces, it began to make sense.

"We here at this temple and others, where we serve as sons and daughters of Hygeia, have always remained neutral in this war between serpents. We freely give healing to any who seek it. But now, child, it appears this war, as it has continued for thousands of years, has now come to us."

"What do you mean?"

"The Black Snake Sisters belong to a faction who wish to make knowledge known to all. This is in keeping with what Hermes taught; they call him by another name, Thoth, but the esoteric teachings are the same. They wish to protect you. But those in the Brotherhood of the Sun, also called the White Snake Brotherhood, those who wish to keep the sacred teachings to themselves, they seek you. For what reasons I cannot say, but I can say that we cannot protect you."

"But what makes me important? Why me?" Suddenly Serena had a thought, a possible insight or explanation. "Could it have something to do with the Candelaria mystery? Do you know the meaning of these words?" She showed the message to Agape, the seven mysterious words and phrases sewn in the hem of the Virgin of Candelaria's apparition:

ETIEPESEPMERI

LPVRINENIPEPNEIFANT

EAFM IPNINI FMEAREI

NARMPRLMOTARE

OLM INRANFR TAEBNPEM Reven NVINAPIMLIFINIPI
NIPIAN

EVPMIRNA ENVPMTI EPNMPIR VRVIVINRN APVI
MERI PIVNIAN NTRHN

NBIMEI ANNEIPERFMIVIFVE

"I am sorry, Serena; I do not know these words." She continued to study the messages, then examined her staff. "Here on the staff of Hermes are pictured the two snakes; they cross seven times. These represent the seven planes of spirit descending into matter and matter ascending into spirit. They are the seven spheres of transcendence. Pure spirit, which to us is *Nous,* the pure awareness of the creator, transforms to energy and energy transforms to matter as the density increases. In alchemy, we learn to master some of these energies. All healing involves the movement and transfer of energy. We work primarily with physical, mental, emotional, and soul-based energies in our healing practices."

"But how does this relate to these messages?"

"There are seven chakras, and these loosely correspond to the seven vibrational planes. Beyond that, the Rod of Hermes depict wings. Beyond that is pure awareness, pure consciousness. There are seven parts to the messages you show me. Is this coincidence? I think not. If these words contain such knowledge, and one knew the speaking of these words, there would be great power in this. Such power could destroy those of the White Snake Brotherhood.

"Knowledge comes to us in three ways. There is the knowledge we gain from others, from their experience and what they share of those experiences in however they interpret them. There is knowledge which comes from your own experience. This represents a deeper way of knowing. Finally, there is knowledge that comes from the universal truths, a wisdom that is beyond experience. What I say of these seven may be of this last type. The true gnosis is not revealed to me in the fullness of understanding, but this is what my intuition speaks to me as truth. I cannot say for sure what your importance in this great war between these two factions is. But I can say with certainty that you are in danger." She embraced Serena in loving concern. "Your light must be protected. Of this, I am sure."

The two had wandered around the grounds several times. Agape finished, "I shall come to you near sunset; now I must go and prepare."

39

*G*oddamned waste of taxpayer money! He clenched his fists and would have pounded his desk but for the need to show composure and be restrained working in his cramped office. Mike Carson, "Big Mike" to his friends, fumed. The email from Stuart Finch, flagged as urgent, remained open on his screen. Stuart, his Section Chief, was his immediate boss in the chain of command at NSA. Big Mike, a former nose guard for the Nebraska Cornhuskers, formerly a Marine working intelligence, who joined the NSA because he was a patriot, was merely a Unit Chief, supervising a group of analysts who knew more about modern surveillance, computer code, and algorithms than he ever would. Fifty-one put Mike well past his prime. He hated field work, he hated desk work, the staff he supervised were smarter than he was, and he knew it. But most of all, he hated his boss. Stuart Finch—"Finch the Grinch" he called him—never cracked a smile, stingy with praise, all business. Mike had applied for the position that Stuart had been given two years ago, in spite of the fact that Mike had four years more service time. *He is a goddamned insensitive little prick!*

The email basically reminded Mike that Stuart needed a response on "Operation Mesa Gold." Mike had taken yesterday off to recover from his daughter Theresa's wedding. He had programmed an auto response showing he was out of the office. "Why is that friggin' little dickhead bugging me? I've been at my desk for all of two hours!" He muttered it out loud, but too soft for anyone to hear. He suspected his boss was gay, or worse, that he was a Democrat!

Mike thought the whole operation a joke, starting with its name. *Who the hell comes up with these names?* He typed his reply through gritted teeth, "Yes, Mr. Finch, my analyst Roberta Reardon will be informed of her new temporary assignment and report for her scheduled briefing." He followed that email with one to Roberta telling her to meet with him in five minutes.

He collected himself, admitting that he felt more sore than usual. The Section Chief position stood a full two pay grades higher with a substantially better salary. Theresa's wedding was nice, but it was an economy affair. It made Mike feel "small balls." And he still had Theresa's sister's wedding, most likely in a few years, and he hadn't saved a penny.

Last week, Roberta had sent him a preliminary analyst report on some email foreign correspondence she had linked together. She was new to the agency, only six months as a member of his unit and already she showed promise. He liked her, same age as Theresa, a bright future provided the GD government doesn't cut back even more and handcuff our efforts to protect Americans. *Snowden, there's another little prick. We need to find him and string him up by his balls.* He wasn't the least bit calmed down when Roberta Reardon sheepishly knocked on his door.

"You wanted to see me, sir?" Her voice hesitated, unsure about the reason for the summons. She pushed her glasses back—an unsuccessful effort to appear confident.

"Conference room." He pointed, "Nothing to worry about, you're not in any trouble." He saw her immediate relief as the two went to a conference room. He shut the door.

"Nice work on that report you sent me last week."

"Thank you, sir."

"I passed it up the chain of command to our Section Head. Apparently, he sent it over to Homeland Security and now they are planning an op." He rolled his eyes. "Mesa Gold. Listen, I know it sounds like a brand of tequila, but I don't come up with the names. Refresh me again on the details and anything new since your report."

The young analyst proceeded to cogently give him the essentials: a variety of emails from different sources, some traced to India, Australia, and Greece, some chatter about Illuminati, Brotherhood of the Snake, Black Serpent Sisterhood. She was undecided whether it represented a true terrorist threat but had simply organized the traffic and found a pattern. What was new, and possibly significant, was that some of the routing went through the same server connected to the recent cybercrime search and seizure in Missoula; could be meaningless but could be somehow connected. That, in essence, comprised her findings to date.

"Good work. Keep at it. They want you on temporary assignment to be part of a sting operation."

"But I'm an analyst, not a field agent."

"I know, Roberta. Last year the Director," he rolled his eyes again, "decided it would be good for analysts to sometimes head out in the field so that they could see what the outcome of their work is and perhaps get a better idea of what the field agents actually do. It's the same reason why we sometimes have field operatives here in the office, but you've only been here six months. They usually pair with analysts who have been here at least a year." He had to admit it wasn't a bad idea to do the crossover to help the left hand and right hand better coordinate. Seeing his analyst's enthusiastic response as he explained the assignment, he fed off of her youth and excitement.

"So that's it, any questions?"

"No sir, other than when do I leave?"

"You have a briefing at 0800 tomorrow at Homeland. I'll forward you the details. Pack a few things; if you need some extra time, I know it's short notice, you can leave early today, I'll authorize it. Remember to take your ID. Finch said you're going to Taos in New Mexico. I hear it's nice there."

He dismissed Roberta Reardon and went back to his office. *Goddamned waste of taxpayer money! We'll never make America great again throwing good money away.*

40

A small alcove led to the chamber of awakening, a rock-hewn vestibule completely enclosed and lit by oil lamps and a single brazier giving a soft orange glow. Serena sensed a strong sulfuric scent, not unpleasant and somewhat subtler than where Melantha sat, but still acrid. Her eyes teared. A rock basin with water stood in the center; bubbles continuously erupted from below and burst with a vaporous gasp. Earth, air, fire, water—the alchemical elements were all contained within the cauldron-vessel of the vestibule itself.

Standing next to the basin, Agape announced, "The perfume of Pythia." The Priestess closed her eyes and inhaled deeply, swaying and murmuring to herself. "It is intoxicating!" For a moment she seemed to drift off then returned. "Here, child, take the staff, place it in the orifice, and grasp it firmly."

Agape handed Serena the golden Caduceus staff; the lower portion slid into a hidden opening within the center of the basin. As she did this, her kundalini energy roused powerfully in a sudden jolt. Her pelvis throbbed and tingled. The insertion of the rod into the rock orifice of the earth evoked a sexual union. As she breathed the sulfurous mists, she felt woozy, holding the staff to maintain her stance, entering some unreality.

The Caduceus began to vibrate, seeming to come alive in her hands; it glowed with white light as did Agape, whose amorphous body now resembled an egg of shifting lights and colors, an open vortex, centered where Serena imagined the healer's heart, pulsating with radiance and energy.

The entwined snakes seemed to pick up the pulsations and danced with each other in ecstasy. Time had no meaning in this metaphysical realm. She saw but did not see Agape approach; she heard but did not hear the Priestess speak, or sing, or whisper. Hands or arms, or were they serpents arising from the multicolored egg of the healer, moved over Serena's chest and back; the kundalini snakes within her spine rose, called forth into her heart chakra.

Tears streamed from her face, but she remained unaware. She joined into the heart radiance of the older woman who now also grasped the staff of Hermes. The three—two women and the staff—were as one, one with the rock basin, one with the water, one with the scented air, one with the earth, one with all of creation and filled with pure love. Her kundalini from within burst forth in joy, dancing within her heart, absorbing and projecting a pulsating energy of love, love of all things.

Serena could not say how long she drifted on the currents that enveloped them. She felt but did not feel herself gently and lovingly taken from the vestibule into the twilight, through the gardens, past the fountains, and onto her bed. Her dreams were more than dreams, they were exquisite visions of life, of beauty, of goodness, and of love for the oneness of creation. Of all her chakra openings, this was not just the most powerful, it was the most beautiful and the most empowering. The divine mother goddess embraced her, and Serena embraced the universe.

❖   ❖   ❖

"When I look around, the entire world looks different to me. I see the beauty and also the pain and suffering in the other guests here, in the trees and the flowers, in the birds and the animals." Serena stood, sad that it was time to leave the Temple of Hygeia, but realizing her destiny called her elsewhere. She faced the director. The bright morning sun shone upon them.

"You are gifted with a strong kundalini, child." Agape's face beamed. "Now that your heart-space is open and fed with this energy, you see the world as I do, so desperately in need of healing. Our Earth Mother has truly blessed you."

"It is funny, in a way rather ironic." The young woman shared this new insight. "For my entire life I have seen myself as broken, in need of being fixed, in need of being healed."

"Go on." The whirring blades of a helicopter, at first faint, now grew louder.

"But I don't feel that way any longer. I feel whole."

"The words forming the root for the word 'health' are the same as the words for 'whole' and for 'holy.' To be healthy is to be all these things. It is sacred; it is as Hermes understood and taught."

"Yes, I see that now. Even more, I feel it... I know it."

Agape leaned forward looking very intensely and lovingly at Serena, her deep brown eyes locked with the Candelaria's gray eyes. She raised her voice over the sound of a helicopter hovering above and descending. Wind whipped her tunic and hair. "This, Serena, is a true gnosis, the deep knowing of things. With your heart wisdom, you see this and understand. You see and understand that it is not you who were broken so much as the world. The world is broken; you see it every place you look, feel it in your heart, know it in your mind. The world is in need of healing far beyond what we can do at this temple."

The two women embraced, hearts full of love. Serena nodded. "Yes, it is just as you say... Truth! You give voice to the Truth of what is."

"Yes, sister; now go and heal our broken world."

PART THREE
CANDELARIA

41

The wind gusts lessened as the rotors slowed, but the blades continued to spin, a sign that the copter planned to be airborne again soon. A door opened on the black craft, just adjacent to a company insignia: A white pyramid with the words "PYRAMID" running up the left side and "COMMUNICATIONS" running down the right side. Beneath the base read, "Voice of Truth." Serena and Agape drew nearer to one another as a man stepped out dressed in black, wearing a uniform of some sort with a similar insignia for PYRAMID COMMUNICATIONS, and a pale-blue photo ID. He held a drawn sidearm and scanned as he zigzagged around the craft then spoke into a headset microphone. "All clear."

A woman stepped out, dressed in a similar black uniform, but her name tag was pale-yellow. Serena looked at the woman, and immediately recognized the family resemblance. "Nalini Kumar?" The identity was confirmed as the name on her badge became legible.

"Serena Mendez...or should I say Chanda Patel? At last! When Dharani told me you had left, I worried I might never fulfill my promise to Ooljee, my moon sister." She extended her hand adding, "Come, we are on a tight schedule."

Agape appeared distressed and alarmed by the gun and the uniforms, but she still emanated love; she embraced the other women. «Be safe, Snake Sisters."

Serena and Nalini thanked her and boarded the chopper as the idling blades whirred into action. Door secured, they were aloft seconds later. Yelling over the noise of the helicopter, Nalini handed a set of headphones to Serena and told her to tune into channel six. With the headset in place, the effect startled Serena; they must have had good noise cancellation tech because the spinning blades were only faintly audible. She dialed to "six."

"Welcome, my Naga sister. I hope you have been practicing your Shakti exercises." Nalini's eyes crinkled as a subtle smile broke across her tawny face. She wasn't beautiful, but she had the refined elegance and the aura of peace characterizing the Naga Sisterhood. She handed over a bundle of clothes and said, "Here, you need to put these on."

Serena looked over at the other occupants: Youssef Mourad, according to his blue ID badge, had holstered his weapon. The busy pilot had not so much as turned around for introductions.

Seeing the young woman's concern, Nalini added, "This is no time for modesty, child. Youssef has seen many things in his life; he is here for your protection. We normally have two security personnel, but the craft only carries four. He is among our best. That reminds me," she said, turning to retrieve something from a storage bin, a gray vest. "You should put this on as well."

They were flying over water; however, the vest looked odd as a flotation device. Then it hit her: Kevlar! She glared at Nalini. "What's this for?"

"Cairo is a very dangerous place."

She removed her clothes, self-consciously aware that she owned only two bras and they were both back in New Mexico. Youssef did not so much as blink. Moments later, Kevlar hiding the remnants of her femininity, dressed in the uniform of Pyramid Communications, her short fuzz feebly rising over her shaved head, Serena looked asexual, identified as female only by her photo-less name tag, "Chanda Patel" also on a yellow background. Beneath her name, a title: Proselyte.

Nalini took in the transformation and nodded. "Dharani gave us good proportions to size your uniform."

Serena/Chanda felt unenthusiastic as she recalled images of Demi Moore in GI Jane and noting the material felt stiff and scratchy against her skin. *I nev-*

er much cared for that movie. Speaking into the headset mic, managing a slight smile, she asked, "Okay, now what?"

"We have a lot to do between now and Cairo." She handed Serena two folders. "We have one stop in Crete where you can use a restroom while we refuel. I have several things I need to do during the flight." She pointed to a workstation with a laptop computer, a printer/copier, and a shredder, along with some portable file folders. Straps secured all the equipment from movement.

"Wait a minute. What is all this?"

"We're journalists. Pyramid Communications is an independent alternative media company—'The Voice of Truth'—and you are my intern. Read the information in the folders; it's much easier and more complete than having me explain it all. I am sure you will have many questions, as do I. There is much I need to learn about you, Chanda. That is your name while you are with me and while you are in Egypt. For safety reasons, Serena Mendez has disappeared."

Hiking the last quarter mile from where he had parked his car, Claus Gorman could see the residence, just visible through the trees on the property. He studied the terrain through military binoculars. *No problem, gives me the chance to play with another of my toys.* Silently, he unzipped his duffel and set up a small monitor as he viewed the residence from above using video from his surveillance drone. A short while later, satisfied, he hiked in a semicircle around the perimeter, seventy degrees from his current position, and nestled his bag against a tree trunk. The house stood maybe fifty or sixty yards away and likely, but by no means assuredly, beyond the view of any long-range surveillance camera. Besides, he had positioned himself at an angle inconsistent with how an intruder would approach the structure. Still, he felt wary. Working intelligence his entire adult life, Claus Gorman had learned a few things—be cautious and don't underestimate the target.

Shimmying up the tree, he placed a wide-angled video camera and battery pack. He had to climb back down to get his next two toys, both from Baxter Consolidated. The saucer/cone-shaped audio surveillance device measured about ten inches across—easy to hide among the branches, but it had to be positioned properly as it was highly directional. The true beauty lay in the next instrument he held; this was the first time he got to use it in the field. It worked beautifully. He took the phased array microwave emitter and pointed it toward the house. The low-power radar signal from the emitter bounced back into his receiver enabling him to look through solid walls. The first prototype at Baxter had been eight and a half feet. This little gem measured just under two feet. Scanning through the walls rewarded his efforts with the desired view—the image, a little blurry but unmistakable—a desk with two monitors and a chair. It required some targeting coordinates and delicate positioning, but he eventually satisfied himself with the setup of the two high-tech devices. Target now under surveillance, both sound and audio, using the best equipment his company built. Silently, he descended from the tree-perch and packed up the rest of his gear.

Claus hiked back to his vehicle. He felt pleased with himself as he dwelled on a few different thoughts. *Bryson Reynolds is a smart kid, a real pro as far as I can tell. But there are limits to what you can do remotely. Boots on the ground… It's not how these kids like to do things. But I'll take boots on the ground any day.* He glanced down watching his L.L. Bean light hiking boots step one foot after the next, a Colt Python .38, his "snubbie," nestled in an ankle holster. *What the hell, let's see how the new toys work. I should be back in Chicago for dinner. What am I in the mood to eat?*

The information in the two folders was both weird and fascinating at the same time. Folder #1 had markings in large capitals on every page: SHRED AFTER READING. The contents included something that resembled an organizational chart, a password exchange for today, a listing of two safe houses, and a specific schedule set just for Chanda Patel. Before reading any of these documents, she scanned through Folder #2—an overview of the Emerald Tablets of Thoth, and a comparison between the Isis Mystery School and traditions of the Naga Sanctuary. It also contained news briefs for the day. Since the first file material contained little to absorb, she concentrated on reviewing it first, but distraction intervened as Nalini and Youssef conversed on a different channel. Youssef nodded, picked up Chanda's bag, and began examining the contents.

"Hey, what are you doing? That's my stuff!" But the sound of the copter drowned her words. She motioned to the two of them tapping her headset and raising six fingers, then spoke indignantly, "That's my private stuff, what gives you the right to go through it?"

Nalini answered as Youssef waved an electronic wand of some sort, then picked out her phone and tablet. "He is checking for any bugs or items which may cause problems when we go through customs. Trust me; it is for all of our safety."

"Are the location finder GPS components in these devices active?" The gruff voice conveyed strict business.

"No, I disabled them." Her answer surprised the security agent.

"Excellent." He looked pleased. "Everything here is fine." The voice seemed less severe as Youssef returned the bag to the space below Chanda's seat.

She really had no experience reviewing organizational charts. Key information clearly had been left out such as names to go with the positions, although sometimes numbers were assigned. The color-coding on their badges made sense to her now—yellow designated "Order of Isis," blue corresponded to the security personnel for the entire organization. There were three major categories under the umbrella "SISTERS OF THE BLACK SNAKE*." The asterisk specified this title had been dropped and appeared only for historical purposes. Pyramid Communications represented one of the three org chart lines. It had the elements of a media company of some sort—a bona fide address, mobile reporting vans, a helicopter, IT, HR, maintenance, and of course, security.

The other two pieces mirrored each other: Isis Mystery School and College of the Alchemies of Horus. Each of these had an Abbot/Abbess heading the division—no names, just numbers next to symbols Sun 1 /Moon 1 for each of the educational leaders along with a breakdown you would expect from some kind of small institute of learning. Off to the side, there were other related organizational elements; the most interesting was a series of numerically designated safe houses.

She did her best to absorb the information. Prior to shredding the document, she asked Nalini, "If our ID tags are yellow, it means we are part of the Isis division. Do they also operate in the Pyramid division of this organization?"

"It is an astute question. The simple answer is no, not under ordinary circumstances. We are only pretend journalists for this trip until we are safely back at the school. We need to clear you through customs, and it will go more smoothly for the two of us if we are working with the news agency."

Satisfied, she shredded the first classified document and read through the rest. The password exchange seemed rather mundane: "Q: Have you tried the recipe I recommended? A: Yes, I added coconut milk; it was excellent." *Not exactly 007 material, but it seems weird that they would even have a secret password.* The spy parallels continued as she read and tried to memorize the locations of two different safe houses. She had absolutely no idea of how to pronounce the street names, but Chanda had a good memory. When she felt confident, she destroyed these other two papers.

The last item in the "secure shred after reading folder" was some sort of itinerary/daily schedule. For her, today seemed straightforward enough: pick up at the temple in Greece, travel to Crete, land Egypt, arrive Pyramid headquarters, debrief, sleep. Everything had a time except the last item. Everything on the schedule also had a responsible party assigned to be with her.

"Why does my schedule need to be destroyed?"

"We don't want to let the enemy know where you are, where you are going, or who is going with you."

"Right. That makes sense." *I don't know if I'm cut out for this spy stuff!* She reached into her bag for her phone.

"What are you doing?" Alarm sounded in Nalini's voice.

"I thought I would get ready to call my friend Bryson. Looks like we are getting close to Crete and I was checking for a signal."

Youssef shook his head vigorously. He and Nalini spoke on a separate channel. "No calls and no texts. Youssef is right. We have scrambling equipment at most of our locations, so this restriction is just for now. He said you could send an email to your friend, but do not say where you are going or who you are with. He also says he needs to see the email before you send it."

She typed it out on her tablet, angry about all the restrictions, feeling like a schoolchild. Rules and limitations always bothered her and got her feeling irritated. "Bry, phone temporarily out, but should be charged up and ready to go later. All is well. Have lots to discuss next call. Finished up with Agape at the Temple of Hygeia and continuing my grand Mediterranean vacation. Hope you are fine, XOXO." She left it unsigned and handed it over to the security guard; he frowned but agreed she could send it when they landed.

A crackle of static preceded, "It's your pilot. Everyone needs to strap in and stay sharp. We're landing in five minutes. It's breezy today and might get a little choppy." The voice was clearly female—a woman piloted the helicopter; Chanda hadn't expected that.

42

Nalini checked the fit of Chanda's vest and the two women used a rest facility in the hangar. Youssef stood guard outside. *His weapon remains on board the helicopter, but somehow, I don't think that compromises his lethality*, she thought as she freshened up. The washroom apparently serviced a restricted area, not for commercial passengers. A Greek customs official of some sort spoke with the pilot then reviewed some papers including Chanda's passport. Satisfied, he left while the refueling continued. She finally had a moment to speak with the pilot who had removed her headphones. Chanda had a clear look at the woman's face. It wasn't pretty. Multiple healed but brutal-looking scars cut through her visage.

Eyes shone brightly on the pilot's scarred face as she extended her hand to shake. "No names but am glad to have you on board. Our trip has been smooth so far and I expect the same for the rest of the way. The man who just left will help make our trip through customs go much more smoothly. We are fortunate."

Chanda, uncertain how to respond—it all struck her as cloak and dagger stuff from a book or a movie—grabbed the pilot's hand and gasped. She immediately drew back. The hand was fake, a prosthetic.

The pilot shrugged. "Package bomb…helped me to learn to be more careful." She reentered the aircraft, donned her headset, and spoke with the control tower going over their flight plan.

Pyramid Communications' newest faux employee hit "send" on her tablet to provide Bryson with a restricted update and watched as Crete shrank in size below. *All that Minoan civilization…Bry would appreciate this island. All the great history and people to explore and learn about and what do I do? I make a pit stop. What a waste!* Decidedly in a bad mood, she picked up the second folder.

Across the Atlantic, Bryson read through the email out loud with audible commentary on the message. "What do you mean you are continuing your vacation? You weren't supposed to leave the Temple of Hygeia until tomorrow. Did Agape open your next chakra?" The more he read through it, the stranger the whole message seemed. It didn't sound like Serena at all, and the "XOXO" close just wasn't her style. *Something weird is going on, but no mention of the weather, so I have to assume she is letting me know she is okay but can't talk. She also wants me to know she left the temple. Okay, PTG, so where exactly are you?* Tracking the origin of an email through a variety of cyber-routers and switches took all of two minutes for the experienced hacker. *Crete! WTF are you doing in Crete?*

In Chicago, enjoying a late dinner of veal marsala from Leonardo's Pasta Palace, his favorite place for takeout, and not the least bit concerned about the milk-fed, abused baby calf he munched, Claus Gorman felt exceptionally pleased with himself as he listened to the digitized audio from his nest set up that very morning. *Damn that is a nice little unit!* he thought, staring down at his now-bare feet, toes nestled in a plush Persian rug.

A few phone calls later, he dialed his boss. "Mr. Reynolds, Charles Godfried reporting in with some information on the last assignment." He left a number to reach him at and sure enough, the call back came a few minutes later.

"Claus, I didn't expect to hear from you so soon. You have good news I hope."

"Yes, sir. First let me say that the modified R6-40-10 audio device the company makes works great. The positioning is tricky, but if it's properly directed, the audio quality is superb. Anyway, the unit is already giving some intel. It seems the girl has been at a Temple of Hygeia in Greece."

"Never heard of it. Do you know why she is there?"

"Actually, there are three of them in Greece. Don't know for sure; they are just fancy spas—all inclusive, that kind of nonsense. I called all three…had another name…Agape…got lucky since only one of them had a staff person by that name… Turns out she's the director. Our girl has been in Epidaurus."

"What do you make of it?"

"Not sure, but she isn't there anymore… Sounds as though she left prematurely, before her spa experience concluded… Don't know where she left to but might learn more from new intel."

"Great work. Remind me to tell your boss to give you a raise."

"What do you want me to do, boss? Should I contact Li's people and let them know?"

A moment of silence followed as Peter Reynolds considered his next set of instructions. "Not yet. Instead of a raise, how about a nice spa vacation to Greece? I've heard good things about an exclusive place in Epidaurus." He chuckled a moment. "In all seriousness, book Charles Godfried and get over there as soon as you can. Call me from Greece with new info when you have it."

"Yes, sir."

"I trust you can continue to monitor my nephew remotely?"

"Yes, sir." He finished the last bite of his veal dinner and wiped the sauce off his grinning face. *I could use a nice long soak in a mineral spring bath…*

"Get packing. I'll handle Li." As he hung up the phone, Peter wondered to himself again, *why, Kenseiko, why do you want that girl so badly? What is so special about her? Why is she so important?*

43

Every now and then she took a break. The information in the second folder seemed to be almost too much to process all at once. Thoth, ancient Atlantean, the same being as Hermes, had apparently transcribed information onto some green crystalline matrix—the Emerald Tablets. The wisdom contained within these codices—knowledge about spirit and matter and how to transmute energy, healing, the use of harmonic resonances to move matter—went on and on until Serena's head spun.

This sect, the Black Snake Sisterhood, based upon the teachings in the Emerald Tablets, had been founded by Isis herself, prior to the split with the Brotherhood of the White Snake. This Isis Mystery School eventually absorbed a faction of the White Snakes who followed similar teachings contained in the tablets; however, they focused on controlling and transmuting the male *Ka*. This splinter faction originally called themselves the Alchemists of Horus and they recognized the need to balance and harmonize the male *Ka* with the female *Ka* rather than be in opposition, the stance of the White Brotherhood. Furthermore, the Sisters had the actual ancient codices, transcribed onto some miraculous emerald-colored substance that somehow interfaced with the reader's mind, initiating some type of direct transmission of information.

Only the most advanced members of the sect obtained access to the tablets themselves, but some translations were available for the fifteen tablets. She scanned the summaries of the different tablets, but the esoteric, mystical, and spiritual details would require lengthy and time intensive study. Apparently, Thoth established a number of schools throughout the ancient world to share, study, and utilize this knowledge. For reasons not detailed with any specifics, mankind had difficulty ascending along the path of spiritual enlightenment, advancing to understand the interplay of matter, energy, and spirit. Thoth provided instruction and guidance in methods to achieve this advancement to enlightenment. Some ancients apparently usurped the information to use it for personal gain and power. Some of the schools themselves became tools and a means to train an elite group of priests and priestesses, a royalty class that exercised power and control through the misuse and abuse of Thoth's shared wisdom.

It all began to make sense, to come together in an almost incomprehensible manner stretching across eons of human history, dating back to creation itself and how spirit manifest itself into physical form, how the energies themselves could be transmuted, manipulated, and shaped. The energies flowing in and through humans existed in continuum with Gaia, earth energy, and more inclusively with cosmic energy. It was all the same energy, vibrating at different frequencies, amalgamated into different forms.

Insights formulated in her mind. "The sun and the moon dance, man and woman, black and white, light and dark. It is all the dance of matter and spirit." These were the words Ooljee had written in her letter to Serena. On a more intuitive level, the young Candelaria felt on the threshold of gnosis—true knowing, a true understanding of the very fabric of reality. Then it hit her, a light erupting in her mind. The force stunned her momentarily as she stared blankly, without comprehension of her surroundings: *My Circle training is all about unlocking and mastering these teachings! Whoa, it's making a lot more sense. Opening the chakras are steps along a path of mastery.*

"Chanda?" Nalini shook the young woman without response. "Chanda!" She waved her hand in front of her fellow passenger who stirred. "Chanda, you have been sitting unmoving and just staring for ten minutes. Are you okay?"

She took a deep breath. "I…I think so." The words came out slowly, labored, blurry. "I think I had some kind of insight… I don't know, there's a lot to process." Her mind and thoughts cleared. "This information is very relevant; it has clarified some things about my training."

"Your training is one of the things I want to discuss. I am a poor substitute for Ooljee." The voice through her headset sounded tinny.

"Are you still communicating with my aunt? I have so many questions."

Nalini shook her head. "No, child. We walked together in the dream world, but now she walks among the spirits. This is not a place I know how to get to. Tell me about your progress through the Circle."

Serena provided her appointed instructress with a condensed overview, spending a disproportionate amount of time extolling the time spent at the Naga Sanctuary, advancing through to her experience in Greece with Agape.

"Our sisters in India are most wonderful, but they are too passive in this battle between the serpents, too willing to minister to history. The sect in Egypt is more activist, less concerned with history and more concerned with the present, much like you of the Candelaria. Soon, when your fifth chakra is opened, you will better understand the power of the voice."

"Wait a minute, what did you mean about 'much like you of the Candelaria?'"

"Did you not read the book in the library, 'The Candelaria Fellowship—A Flame Extinguished?' I myself did a review. I asked Bili to copy it for you."

With all that had occurred since, Serena hadn't thought much about the book, although she felt it probably had information that would be useful, information that would shed further light upon her mission. "I left it in India. I had just received it but had not read it when my visit to the Mansa Devi festival led to the trip to Australia… Sorry!"

"That is most unfortunate, but I shall prepare a quick summary. This was supposed to be part of your early training. Ordinarily, I would have said you never should have left India. I did not expect you so soon. I plan to return there in a few weeks. I desired to learn the opening words and have the power to unlock your fifth chakra as part of Ooljee's wish for me to instruct you. Yet somehow you have been guided to me at this time. You are much further along than had you arrived after I returned from Egypt. Continue with the folder and I will do my best to summarize the information in the book. The quicker you can complete your Circle, the better for us all." A click sounded in her headset.

The remaining documents made more sense considering Nalini's comments. She glanced over a list of news items and other events from throughout the world with comments by the staff at Pyramid Communications. These were similar in substance to the reviews conducted on archived material in the Naga library, but much briefer in focus and content. For example, she read a news item about conflict in Yemen. The explanation along with this event detailed the real forces behind the conflict and how both sides, seemingly in opposite camps, actually served the same entity that benefited from the conflict regardless of which side won. There were a dozen such exposés. One story, explaining about the destruction of the Amazon rain forest by government-sanctioned multinationals, had a flag attached noting that it would be the subject of a documentary staff was preparing to air later in the month.

Apparently, these news items were distributed by the company through various outlets: the internet, alternative media, etc. Hence, Pyramid Communications labeled themselves the "Voice of Truth" not so much for interpreting historical events, but in a concerted effort to expose the powers and forces shaping world events today. *The members of our conspiracy group back home would lap this up like a thirsty dog. I'm going to send links to Bry with the relevant websites. This company is doing outstanding work and we need to distribute it more widely to help get the word out.*

She thought her brain had filled to capacity, not another neuron available to absorb new information. That was until she picked up the last document in her folder—"Comparison between the Isis Mystery School and traditions of the Naga Sanctuary." Obviously, this had been prepared by Nalini to help her student understand the language used by the two sects to reference the same teachings. Again, the information was fascinating. Totally absorbed, Serena soaked it up.

It started with a quote: "For he that seeks wisdom, also must seek Truth. Truth is the key to open the Kingdom of Light."—Druidic Realms, A Compendium

Many cultures and traditions had knowledge of the Life Force, the vital energy which both animates and sustains all creation. In the Vedic tradition we call this *prana;* in the far East, they call this *chi* or *qi;* in the West, in more modern times, it is referred to as *vril.* No matter the language describing this energy, it is all the same. In the arcane language of ancient Egypt, they called it *sekhem.* For those of us who learned the ways and teachings of the Naga Sisterhood and who wish to become familiar with the terminology used by our cousins in the Ancient Sisterhood of the Black Snake, I, Nalini Kumar of the Fourth Order, humbly provide this comparison.

The seven Chakras, the energy vortexes which interface the energy at the ethereal plane of the subtle body, are identical in the two systems but the word for the path of the seven Chakras is *Djed* in the Egyptian lexicon. No similar word is in the Hindu teachings.

Ida, our term for the pathway up the left side of the spine, is the *Black Serpent* in the words of our cousins in Egypt. This is the lunar pathway of feminine energy.

Pingala, our term for the pathway up the right side of the spine, is the *Gold Serpent* in the words of our cousins in Egypt. This is the solar pathway of masculine energy.

Pranic Tube, in our Hindu teachings that through which the life energy flows, is the *Central Pillar* where the *sekhem* moves within a person.

Shakti, our word for the *kundalini,* does not have an exact correlate in Egyptian teaching but *Neter* applies to subtle energies and powers. Our term *Siddhis,* the expression of yogic subtle powers, is also an expression of *Neter.*

The goal of our teachings at the Naga Sanctuary is to master the *kundalini* energy through the practice of *Shakti* yoga and thus to fully enable the opening of the seven chakras and the flow of *prana* throughout the subtle bodies. The teachings among those schooled in the mysteries of Isis are similar. They use breath, postures, meditation, and other techniques to move *sekhem* to open the chakras and to activate *Ka,* the subtle body energies.

Many other similarities to the two teaching methods exist. That which I humbly provide is only a start to facilitate better study and understanding.

It ended with a quote: "To the darkness of ignorance, respond with Truth. The wise speak Truth. They are torchbearers illuminating as sunlight upon all to dispel darkness."—Hidden Tablet IV, Wisdom and Truth

Placing the document back in the folder, Serena spoke over the chopper blades into her mic. "Why did you finish the comparison with the quote you used?"

Nalini smiled. "Because the truth shall set you free...and you are the flame of truth... You are Candelaria." She handed over another paper, this one hastily titled: "Summary of the Candelaria Fellowship, Past and Present."

Before responding, Serena felt the helicopter bank just as her headphones filled with static, then the pilot's voice broke in. "Look to the left, ladies and gentleman, and see the lights of Cairo. Touchdown in five minutes. Buckle up."

44

KUFM, NPR local affiliate, Missoula, MO: *The FBI today released Mary Carpenter, whose home was raided for alleged cybercrime activities. She was cleared of all charges, herself apparently the victim of a sophisticated cybercrime scheme. In a statement, the FBI indicated they regretted the inconvenience caused to this innocent woman. Her attorney, spokesperson for the victim, stated they were investigating whether to file a suit in federal district court for wrongful arrest and illegal search and seizure. In other news…*

At least something went right today. Frustration ruled the moment. Gensu Li's phone led to just another series of dead ends. Personal contacts, a private gym for martial arts instruction, some Hong Kong restaurants and clubs—there were dozens of phone numbers to trace, but nothing of any substance other than a couple of calls to and from Singapore, all traced to Advanced Bionics. *Damn, I was sure something more would turn up.*

Unexpectedly, something did, but not from a source he expected. The phone rang and on the other end, Maria Trujillo's voice surprised him.

"Is this Bryson?"

"Hello, Mrs. Trujillo, how are you and how is Oreo doing?" He raised the volume of his voice.

"Cat's fine, thanks for asking. You told me to call if anyone else came snooping around Serena's place."

"Yes, that's right." *Maybe today won't be a total waste after all.*

"Ole Maria caught somebody at the door. I'm thinking he may have already been inside her apartment."

"Why is that?"

"For one thing, he had on some purple gloves and looked to me like he was closing her door, not opening it. He stuffed a bag or something in his pocket just as I opened my door."

"Did you get his name? What did he want?"

"I'm getting to that; give an old lady a chance to tell her story… He claimed he was a friend of hers visiting from oversees… Unlikely in my judgment. All I can say is he didn't look honest—beady eyes, Asian looking. I will say this about him—he looked damn well-dressed. Can't think of a single good reason to trust a well-dressed foreigner snoopin' at your neighbor's door who can't even come up with a good reason why he's there."

"Did he leave a name or a number?"

"No…of course not. I would have told you if he did. Anyway, I thought you should know."

"Thanks, Mrs. Trujillo. I'll stop by later to pick up Serena's mail."

The drive to Santa Fe sped by. He stopped to pick up a cat treat for Oreo. Serena's neighbor didn't want to let him go, somewhat relentlessly asking him questions about his availability, reminding him what a nice girl Serena was, wanting to know if she was okay and when she would be back. Diplomatically and politely, he excused himself after forty-five minutes. He entered the apartment.

It needed a good dusting. It didn't take long to transfer the video feed from his camera to his laptop. What he saw disturbed him; he didn't like it one bit. Sure enough, someone had broken into Serena's apartment. It was Gensu Li—no doubt about it. The intruder looked around, listened to her answering machine, and carefully went through some of her drawers and closets, meticulous about replacing everything just as he had found it. He wore nitrile gloves, their unmistakable purple the same as the ones Bryson kept in the entry vestibule storage locker leading into his mainframe room. The intruder did not want to leave any fingerprints. Troubling as this break-in seemed, what bothered Bryson the most was Gensu's exit from Serena's bathroom. He watched as the infiltrator carefully placed a hairbrush into a specimen bag—the kind of thing you might expect when gathering evidence at a crime scene.

Driving home, he kept thinking about the same thing. *There's only one reason I can think of why a hairbrush might be confiscated...DNA. Why do they want PTG's DNA?* The unmistakable connection to Advanced Bionics—a company involved in GENE RESEARCH!—left him sweating. *Shit, shit, shit! This is not good.*

Again, they landed in a spot away from the normal passenger terminals. Chanda noted uniformed security personnel, well-armed. Officials and guards checked their craft and their papers, including her Indian passport. Youssef showed his license to carry a weapon. Chanda remained silent the entire time other than answering that she was starting as an intern at Pyramid Communications. A company sedan waited for them and they finally cleared extensive security checks and were on the road. The driver wore a uniform and had a blue-colored security badge.

"We live in a military state in Egypt."

It surprised Chanda to hear the pilot speak, noting a certain sadness behind the woman's deep brown eyes. "Why do you say that?"

"The military controls the government and the press. There is censorship and propaganda. Most of the people do not realize the depth of the deception. We at Pyramid Communications have a lot of work to do."

Though relieved to have the subject changed, Chanda felt mindful of the vest irritating her skin, reminding her of Nalini's words—"Cairo is a very dangerous place!"

Arriving at Pyramid Communications' base of operations only reinforced that reality. Razor wire decorated the top of a perimeter fence opening at a guard station. A series of concrete barricades needed to be negotiated, a measure of protection against car and truck bombs. They exited, cooperated with pat-downs and explosive detection dogs, and finally were allowed to pass through outer security to the next level of security—electronic retinal and fingerprint bio ID along with keypunch passcode. Beyond this second layer, more personnel carrying semiautomatic weapons stood silently alert and at their posts. They arrived at a building which had no windows—essentially a concrete bunker. She noted some transmission towers and a helipad close by.

Nalini whispered, "The company takes security very seriously."

No shit, Sherlock. Yesterday I was soaking in a lavender-scented mineral bath listening to the gentle cascade of flowing water. She kept the thoughts to herself while managing a weak, "I guess it's for our own protection."

Although it was past 9 PM, food had been prepared. Smelling it, Chanda realized how hungry she felt. Nothing special, some Moroccan stew and lamb koftas; she didn't recognize the other items. The best was saved for last, some honey cakes and Turkish coffee—the kind your spoon stands up in. The honey reminded her of Australia—less than a week had transpired. It seemed more than a continent away, separated by distance and the events of the last 72 hours. She enjoyed a second cup before someone whisked her off.

She remembered pink tags designated the HR department. Someone from HR took her picture, followed by biometric scans, and loaded her data into their system. A four-digit passcode randomly generated as three-one-seven-six got assigned to her, and moments later a new ID badge with a pale-yellow background and a relatively awful photo hung clipped to her uniform. The old ID went to a bin for shredding. "Chanda Patel—Proselyte/Intern" looked official. The HR staff person had never welcomed Chanda or introduced herself while methodically performing her assigned tasks. Chanda wondered if perhaps the woman felt annoyed by having to work late, but it was clear this organization operated with a certain efficiency. The woman escorted her to a room and Chanda recalled the schedule she had previously viewed ended with a debriefing session.

"The work Pyramid Communications does, essentially to expose lies and present truth, places all of our personnel, even the cleaning staff, at risk." Ossam Khoury wore an orange tag; Chanda did not recall what department that represented. He showed her a slide presentation, verified that she understood their security check-in procedures, the importance of destroying any documents designated to shred, the prohibition against taking a phone or other electronic communication off premises, and so on. After answering her questions, Ossam smiled. He seemed like a decent chap.

"Fortunately, you will primarily be at a safe house learning and studying with the Isis sisters. It is much safer there." She felt only slightly more reassured as her debriefing session apparently concluded. Somehow, seeing Nalini gave her a sense of relief. *She's been here for months and looks pretty well-adjusted. She's still got all her arms and legs, so I guess that's a good sign.*

A company vehicle with a driver and a second security operative picked up the two Naga sisters. Chanda noticed the helicopter now stood silent on the helipad. She drew a deep breath wondering how quickly she could get through this next stop on her Circle journey. Thus far, warming up to this new location wasn't happening. The love and warmth that overflowed in Agape's presence seemed a distant memory, in spite of occurring less than a day ago. With what little concentration she could muster, she pulled some energy up her spine into her open heart-chakra. It wasn't enough.

45

Chanda looked at her schedule for the day, the secret password, and the safe house locations before destroying all three. They had printed out via a secure network moments earlier. The last two days had been much the same: an instructress from the school, yesterday it was Moon 6, trained both

Nalini and Chanda in the Isis mysteries of gathering, concentrating, and elevating *sekhem*. Nalini had separate instruction in manipulating the energies through her voice overlying the fifth chakra; Chanda watched. In addition to study, the two women practiced their Shakti yoga and incorporated some of the Egyptian techniques. There was daily training in self-defense; this was not fun. Chanda's body had metamorphosed into a lean, toned, flexible and agile young woman. Whatever this martial art form the Pyramid staff taught, Chanda felt ill-prepared; she was not a punching bag. The free-form techniques seemed to involve a lot of kickboxing—ouch!

The rest of the day, the two students had time for reading. The resident of the safe house, a lovely woman who fortunately was also a good cook, prepared meals. She looked matronly until proctoring a *tahtib* session taught by a younger man. *Tahtib* is an ancient form of Egyptian stick fighting; their docile housemother had been a former national finalist. Chanda learned quickly; still, every blow she landed followed at least four she received.

The house itself blended well among other residences on this street. She learned the main Isis school wasn't in Cairo at all, but closer to Alexandria, out somewhere in the desert. She and Nalini bonded quickly. They discussed their personal histories, other sisters at the Naga Sanctuary, stories about Dharani and raising her without the help of her father, a diplomat who tragically died. Nalini didn't say it, but Chanda suspected someone had assassinated her husband. Calls and other communication with Bryson were permitted. Mercifully, she wasn't required to wear her vest while in the house. She had no reason to leave.

At long last, Chanda learned about her Candelaria heritage. The early origins of the bloodline involved Atlantis, but the time of founding the Candelaria Order was not known for sure. They were a small but powerful fellowship, trained in the mystery school traditions of Thoth. Many of the Candelaria were especially strong in manipulating the voice, projecting energy from the fifth chakra into the surrounding environment.

"I myself have only recently had this energy center opened more fully. Until my next chakra is open," Nalini pointed over her third eye, "the power of the voice is not fully realized." Nalini explained that knowing the words in your mind and powering them from the sixth chakra and into the fifth gave them added force. The greater the kundalini, the greater the force. The mastery involves knowing the words of power and speaking them with power. She then followed with more details. Her voice conveyed reverence.

"This Isis school specializes in the opening of this chakra, much like we in India specialize in opening the second chakra. Moses was an Egyptian who schooled in the ancient alchemies of Horus. He struck a rock with his serpent staff and called forth water. He spoke the words of power and parted the Red Sea. Yeshua, also of this lineage, calmed a violent storm on the Sea of Galilee. He multiplied loaves and fish by speaking the words and channeling his *sekhem*. The voice is very, very powerful!"

"I thought those stories were just hyperbole, myths, and so forth."

"Our gurus unlock and master certain *siddhis*. You see these even today—they levitate and perform telekinesis. *Qi Gong* masters can make fire from the air, split rocks with their hands and a shout. These are not just stories. The voice is very powerful and therefore very dangerous.

"The Candelaria had not only power in the voice, they were true Telesti—the cream of the Gnostics. It was their knowledge of the arcane mysteries that led to them being hunted down, burned as witches, unbelievers, occult practitioners, devil worshipers. Those who feared these Telesti, feared their power, did everything they could to stamp them out, end their teachings. The Knights Templar, the Inquisition, years of propaganda and persecution—the fellowship withered. Some of their teachings remained among the Druids. Even though you carry the genes, the teachings have been lost."

Chanda had questions, but Nalini motioned enough instruction for today. Tomorrow she wanted to talk more about Gnosticism, the murder of Hypatia, and the burning of the Great Library in Alexandria. "When you know of these things, when you know the truth of history, this war between darkness and light takes on new significance. It is then you will understand how this same war continues to this day."

She used the time to call Bryson. Bad news.

"Maria saw him, spoke with him?"

"Yes. She's a little ornery, but she sure is a good lookout. She was right about Gensu breaking in, but don't worry about your stuff. He didn't take anything valuable according to the video footage I reviewed."

"Of course not, I don't own anything valuable."

"Wrong, PTG, you've got a bag of semiprecious gemstones and a rare necklace worth millions locked away in a vault."

"Okay, you got me there. Did he take anything?"

An uncomfortable pause followed, the kind of break when someone on the other end is debating whether they should or should not tell you something, something that might make you worry.

"Bry? Are you still there?"

His voice sounded serious. "Yeah, still here... You wanted to know if he took something. He did: your hairbrush."

Bryson didn't expect her laugh. Rubbing the top of her head, running her fingers through new growth measuring under an inch, she said, "That's okay; I won't be needing that brush anytime soon."

"You don't get it. It's not funny at all, PTG. Your hairbrush has skin cells and hair follicles. Those follicles also contain cells, and all these cells have... DNA. They want your DNA, Serena, they want your genes. Li works for Bionics; they mess around with genes and DNA and now they have yours!" The information sounded dark, ominous, threatening.

She swallowed. "Oh my God! What are they going to do with it?"

"I don't know; and worse, I don't know how to find out."

Serena ended the call and sat. Something else bothered her. In the past, she would push these thoughts aside, usually they landed in her gut and she would take medicine until the thoughts quieted down and she calmed down. Instead, she went within. That's one thing the Gnostics did, she had learned that from research the last few days. They would go inside their heads to examine their thoughts and the workings of their minds. It took a few minutes of focused concentration to see it. How had she missed it earlier?

She called Bryson back; it surprised him to hear from her so soon. "What's up?"

"Remember the letter my great aunt left me, the one that got all this started?"

"Sure, I've got a photographic memory. Would you like me to recite it to you?"

"No, how many times does she mention the word 'blood?'"

"Hold on… I have to read and count; it's harder than walking and chewing gum… four."

"Read me those four sentences."

"Actually, it's only two sentences. Once she uses it three times in the same sentence:

> "You have taken the first step to be that which is in your blood,
> Guanche blood, the blood of a Candelaria; few of us remain.
>
> You are the candle, as yet unlit, but the blood in you is strong.

"Why do you ask?"

"Something happened when I was in the hospital in Darwin. I didn't think much of it at the time, but BB questioned it. I was already done with my surgery. A tech from the lab came to draw blood; he was unusually chipper. When BB asked why more blood was needed, he said that he didn't order the tests, he just drew the blood. And he drew a lot, something like five tubes. Here's the other thing. When Gensu Li questioned me, I asked about why we were going to Singapore or something like that. As I recall, he answered that he didn't give the orders, he just followed them. It was the same type of response. Bry…" He interrupted her.

"I see where you're going; you think they already have your blood."

"I do."

"I think you could be right. And if they have your blood, they have your genes and who knows what kind of experiments they are doing. But…" He paused to think it through a little more, almost as though he was thinking out loud to himself. "…but if they needed more sample, and that's why Li came after your hairbrush, that means they don't have enough… and that means you better watch your ass, so they don't get any more."

"I hear you. Like you sometimes say, I'm working on it." Tomorrow, she would request a double session in self-defense.

46

Taking candy from a baby represented more challenge. Charles God-fried, aka Claus Gorman, faced his most difficult task in getting transportation from Athens to the Temple of Hygeia. He had done his home-work; hacking the reservation database for the spa was a piece of cake or as he liked to put it, "piece-a-pie." That made him realize how hungry he felt, so he asked the driver if they could pull over somewhere to get a quick bite. The driver responded that in Greece, fast food was not so popular, but there was a McDon-ald's along this route in another fifteen kilometers. Charles felt no need to rush, he just needed to confirm what he already knew and get more information. He opted for something slower, even offered to buy lunch for his driver.

Seated in the back, stomach pleasantly full, enjoying the Greek coastal drive, he reviewed certain details. Following a botched attempt in Perth by Li's people to acquire Serena Mendez, the target seemingly disappears. Her intended destination, the airport in Athens, has more bodies from Onassis operatives than an anthill, but no one spots her. *If they had an ounce of brains among them, they would have realized she took on a new identity...duh! Friggin' pathetic incompetents!* Once he had intel that this spa in Epidaurus was the final destination and had cross-referenced the rough date of departure and travel times from Aus-tralia against the reservation data at the Temple, there was only one person this could be—Chanda Patel, aka Serena Mendez. Not only did she book the day her stay began—unusual as most people plan these fancy vacations in advance; she even left before her scheduled stay had finished. Chanda Patel was his girl, he was sure of it. He only needed to confirm it with Agape. He would show her Serena's picture, ask about Chanda; unless Agape was immune to interrogation, her body language would give her away. *I just need to extract intel on where the girl went after she left the temple.* He leaned back, put the window down, and let the breeze relax his facial muscles and tousle his blond hair—*piece-a-pie.*

"Mr. Reynolds, this is Charles Godfried calling as instructed to report on the status of your latest assignment." While he waited for a return call, he reflect-ed upon what a nice place the spa looked like. He revisited the look of horror on the director's face after he had shown her Serena's picture and casually mentioned the name "Chanda Patel." The look was way better than one of those credit card commercials—priceless! He almost felt sorry for the woman; she really seemed like a nice person. His cell rang, cutting short the reverie.

"This is Charles."

"What have you learned?"

"I have the false ID Serena Mendez used—Chanda Patel—and have confirmed it as the girl. As to where she went after leaving this Temple of Hygeia, that information I am still working on. I can go and interview the director again and be more persuasive if this is how you want me to proceed."

A moment passed as Mr. Reynolds considered the new information and what the best next step should be.

Claus drummed his fingers. "I can be most persuasive. It is supposedly a place of healing; I'm sure the Temple staff will be able to fix any damage." An almost diabolical smile ensued.

"No, I think not. Li created this mess. He's the one who wants the girl; let him figure it out. Onassis is his hotshot cousin in Greece; the two of them can work on it together and either mess it up some more or get it figured out. I'll give him the girl's false identity and pass it back over. He wants to pin this on me, but I don't think so."

"So, what do you want me to do?"

"Screw Greece. I need you back here. I know I promised you a spa vacation but that will have to wait. I'll make it up to you."

"Yes, sir." He sighed, lamenting the short stay and inability to enjoy a nice long mineral soak. As he searched for the driver's card to arrange a return to the airport, he took solace in knowing his boss would well compensate him.

"Focus!" The order came a fraction of a second before the kick landed to her left leg, temporarily causing her to lose balance. She recovered quickly, but her instructress was merciless. It was Chanda's second session of the day. Her muscles screamed, but she would not give up. Her return punch missed as the trainer easily dodged.

"FOCUS!"

Whether from fatigue, the product of her combined physical efforts of the last few days along with the mental discipline of channeling her *prana* or *sekhem* or whatever you want to call it, or some combination of all the above, time slowed and a fog either lifted or descended. She lost sense of the separation between body and mind.

"Focus." The words came through, but they were distant, muffled. Perhaps it resulted from too many blows to her head coming during the double workout session, coming on top of her head injury during the storm. While her thoughts receded into the shadows, something remarkable happened. She felt totally one with her body and mind, with the floor below and air around her. The martial arts instructress, moving, dancing, weaving, attempting to dodge blows and land blows, became another extension of herself. Energy surged up from the earth, through her root chakra, up her spine, through her *djed,* up her *central pillar,* distributing to her chest, her breath, her heart, her arms and legs. Fatigue vanished in this surge of energy and suddenly Chanda moved almost effortlessly, floating over the floor, easily evading the trainer's hands and feet, landing kicks and punches at will.

"Enough!" The instructress, Elaina Tarsef, removed her head pad and hand wrappings trying to catch her breath. "Enough for today."

Chanda, sweating but otherwise breathing normally, looked a bit stunned.

"I've never seen anything like that before." Elaina's breath had normalized. "How did you do that?"

"I'm not sure. You kept telling me to 'focus' but it was more like I had to unfocus. For moments, I felt as though you moved in slow motion."

"The zone…you were in the zone. Except, you were really in the zone. I have been there at times, but not like you just were. That can't be taught—either you have it, or you don't." She rubbed her arm where a large black-and-blue bruise had sprouted. "Apparently you have a lot of it."

Nalini appeared, holding a sheet of paper. She looked concerned when handing the paper to her sister.

Chanda scanned it—not good! Agape had contacted the Pyramid leadership. An American had arrived seeking information about Serena's whereabouts. He had pictures. He knew of her false identity. Of course, Agape had told him nothing and he left, but they were in danger. Revisions to both of their schedules—they were leaving this safe house for another in one hour. The document needed to be destroyed.

They traveled in an unmarked car, two security agents from Pyramid Communications in the front and the two women in the back. All wore civilian clothes. A somber mood pervaded the vehicle.

Nalini spoke. "Remember, sister, the Candelaria have been hunted. You may need a new identity to evade your pursuers."

"You said the Telesti had knowledge, they had power. What else did you learn from the Candelaria book and your research? What was not included in the summary you prepared? Why would the enemy want my blood?"

"Slow down, child. I only included what I saw as most relevant. What I can tell you is the Gnostics in general were the followers of an approach and an understanding of reality. Their scholars were the Telesti. One of their greatest teachers was a woman named Hypatia. She taught what they all taught—within each human is the spark of divinity. To bring this spark to a flame, you must travel within and come to know the creator from this place within. The power of life, of creation itself, is found within. They taught techniques, similar to what we teach today, to find and access this vital energy. She, along with many other great Gnostic teachers, master alchemists, and followers of these mysteries, was sought out and killed. Many were killed by the emperor Constantine when he converted to Christianity."

"But why, why kill people who are just trying to know the essence of divinity which lies within?"

"Because organized religion wants the path to salvation to go through them, through their priest class, through their hierarchy. If they are the keepers of sacred knowledge, it gives them power and dominion over the masses to control such knowledge, to control access."

"But the Gnostics didn't need the priests."

"Precisely. For this reason, they were slaughtered."

"Open-source spirituality."

"What?"

"It's like open-source computer programming." *I sound like Bryson!* "Free access to anyone once you are given the source code. The Telesti simply taught you the code."

"Yes, you could put it that way, but I do not care for the technology metaphor. Only because technology is one of the chief weapons used by the enemy. It gives them a mass market to distribute disinformation, to promote fear and anger, some of the mind control techniques to keep people repressed and turning to their own power elites for answers."

"But can't we use technology against them?"

"In some sense, Pyramid Communications uses the same technology to distribute truth, but it represents only a small eddy in a powerful stream of consciousness, a stream whose current runs strong with beliefs, values, and dogma that are very difficult to counteract. Besides, technology distances us, alienates us from the natural world. If nothing else, the Gnostics aligned themselves closely with nature. To them, the earth herself manifests divinity through a goddess, Sophia, and the planet itself is alive. This too put them in opposition to alternative teachings about deities who sit somewhere above and pass judgement on the actions of humanity."

"So basically, they came up against powerful cultural elements," the anthropologist in her erupted, "and their ideology of a sacred feminine deity could not coexist with a male-dominated hierarchy whose power and influence were threatened."

"Yes."

"Okay, enough history lesson. That does not explain why they want me. I am not teaching large groups of people. I am at most a small voice speaking against the establishment, respecting the planet, trying to get by in my own simple existence."

"In this way you are not a threat exactly…or at least not yet. To answer your other questions, your genes are unique, this is true of anyone. If you carry the Candelaria bloodline, it is a purer genetic profile, one that perhaps can be used to breed a better human, one that perhaps can strengthen the old bloodlines of the power elites, weakened by inbreeding."

"So that is why they want me."

"Quite possibly, but there is another possible reason—one that I uncovered in my research of the Candelaria, one that made their fellowship more of a threat. As I have told you, they were powerful in the voice, and powerful in gnosis or deep knowing. They also had immunity to lies and falsehoods. In other words, they were resistant to the mind control techniques of the time. They could see the truth. For those who peddle falsehood, even one strong voice of pure truth represents a threat. The truth not only can set one person free, it can liberate the bonds of the masses.

"This, my sister, is why you must complete your Circle and why you must be protected. If the flame of truth within you can be lit, it can overcome much darkness in this world. Such light would dispel and neutralize the venomous lies spewed by the dark Brotherhood. Such light could illuminate the higher reality available to all mankind."

Serena stared through the smoked glass of the car. She saw children playing, pedestrians walking, people just making their way through the day. *Can I handle this destiny?*

A mile of silence elapsed before the next question. "What about the seven messages on the robe of the Virgin of Candelaria? Gurumarra in Australia told me they were in an ancient language, one no longer spoken. Agape told me her intuition pointed to these as having something to do with the seven planes of existence. What do you say?"

Nalini's lips parted in astonishment. "Good, even remarkable! You have learned in weeks what has taken me years to discover. The words are not in any language in use today. One of the reasons I remain in Egypt is to learn more from their teachings. Is this the old tongue of Atlantis? Do hermetic texts and scrolls provide a clue? It is in my Naga blood to search until I find this out and learn the truth. As for the words themselves and the actual messages, I believe Agape is correct. They are the names of the seven sacred seals that govern transit along the seven planes existing on the continuum of spirit and matter."

The car pulled into an ordinary house somewhere in the suburbs of Cairo, away from the city noise and congestion, a quiet neighborhood. Nalini leaned forward whispering urgently, "It had not occurred to me, sister, but knowing the words of the sacred seals and speaking them with the full power of the voice…" She shuddered. "I don't know what could happen—mass awakening, mass ascension, destruction, apocalypse? I don't know…"

This safe house wasn't all that different from the one she had left. Different resident cook, but similar layout—kitchen, dining, some sleeping quarters, a library/study of sorts, and an area for training and meditation. The two guards who had driven them remained, armed and alert while taking six-hour shifts. Despite their stoic presence, Serena did not feel safe.

47

It was a big car—a limousine, American-made, a customized Lincoln sporting black bulletproof glass, a full bar, and an entertainment system with a quality big-screen LCD. It even had that new car smell. He hated it! *What were those Greek Onassis idiots thinking? Do they think I'm Kato driving around the Green Hornet?* The vehicle, which handled like a school bus, had only two merits. With the diplomatic plates he could drive anywhere, and no one would detain or question him. The staff at registration seemed to be impressed when he stopped to make arrangements for an important minister to stay at the spa. Tomorrow he planned to call and cancel the booking due to a change in state plans. He liked to impress people, but the Bugatti he drove in Hong Kong was much more impressive, and it handled so much better. The other beauty of the vehicle—the overly large trunk.

Gensu Li scouted along the coast, looking for a poorly lit stretch where he could pull over. *Perfect!* He drove further down the road and doubled back, easing the car into park. He had stopped at a side street, more for small boating access. At this time, it was vacant, lit only by a half-moon. There wasn't any sand which was good. He didn't want to have beach sand contaminate the vehicle or his Salvatore Ferragamo Oxfords. He hadn't packed another set of shoes. After waiting, satisfying himself there wasn't any street traffic, no joggers, or lovers out for a stroll, he opened the trunk, lifted the body, and easily carried it to the rocky shore. With a heave, he watched it splash then drift along with the gentle tidal surf. *A pleasant resting spot,* he thought as the white tunic, stained with blood, disappeared into the soft moonlight.

Looking in the now empty trunk, marveling at how spacious it was, he noticed just a couple of drops of blood. Closing the lid, starting the engine, he reentered the sparse night traffic with two thoughts: *Maybe I should upgrade to the bigger Bugatti, the one with a larger trunk; a shame about the blood... Onassis and his people can clean the tiny little mess and tidy up... I'll be in Egypt.* A third thought followed: *Good thing I didn't get any on my shoes; perhaps I should buy another pair before I leave tomorrow...*

Bryson had just toweled dry, zipped up his jeans, and laced his shoes when the alarm sounded. *WTF? It's the perimeter. Could be a bear.* But it wasn't a bear, or a large animal. He studied the monitor just long enough to confirm—*SWAT team, Homeland with NSA field agents!* While his initial knee-jerk reaction resembled something along the lines of "Shit, I'm screwed!", he merely jumped into hyperdrive and initiated a plan he never envisioned needing.

He grabbed his laptop and quickly replaced it with a dummy pulled from a desk drawer. *They are just going to love forensically pulling this baby apart.* Downstairs he gloved but did not gown as he hurried into the server room and began a complete data dump. That would take time. He had it all backed up at two secure locations each over five hundred miles away. He needed to create a little time, a little diversion. He manually programmed the fire suppression system on a one-minute delay. That would keep them out of the server room an extra few minutes and they would need to deal with the fire department who should show up promptly. Hell, he paid extra for that monitoring service. When he was in his hideaway, he could remotely trigger a fire in the mainframe and melt the core. *Oh, how that will really make it hard for the boys over in forensics.*

A loud crash, probably a battering ram, sounded above. The door splintered and footsteps followed amid shouts of "Federal Agents! Come out with hands over your head."

I don't think so, boys and girls. I plan to miss the party. He pulled back the concealed panel in the storage locker where he kept the masks, gloves, gowns, and a handheld fire extinguisher. As he entered the underground room, his hand reached back to make sure the boxes in the locker remained neatly arranged. He closed the back panel. Eyes adjusting to the dim light, too dim and diffuse to possibly leak through to the other side, he slid the steel barricade in place.

Bryson looked around; he hadn't been inside this room in a good year. Everything seemed in order: food rations for a week, a cot, a composting toilet, limited internal and external surveillance monitors hooked into his system, an independent solar/battery power supply, totally silent and untraceable. His only link to the outside was through an underground cable that ended in a small cell tower installed on the edge of his property, the far edge away from the road. Through it, he could connect wirelessly, but there was some risk as the signal could be pirated. *I have plenty of time before they even begin to think of that.* The fire alarm sounded. *Wow, that's pretty loud!* Even shielded in the safe room the noise pierced his ears. On his internal monitor, he watched the agents scurrying. When the first one got to the stairway, he triggered the fire. He couldn't say whether the core ignition would prevent the data dump from finishing, but the computer equipment would be toast by the time NSA got to it.

Not four feet away, no doubt standing in the entry anteroom, an agent radio communicated, "Found it, there's a fire in what looks like a server room in the basement... Holy fuck!" Bryson felt pretty sure that last bit of talk wasn't radioed. He smirked in satisfaction.

Five minutes later, he heard distant sirens from the fire department truck and watched the drama unfold on his screens as the fire department and Homeland Security tried to sort things out. He looked around. This little room, a tornado shelter on the building plans, would be home for the next few days. *I'll be playing a lot of Zelda.*

Powering up his laptop, Bryson typed the first of three emails.

"PTG, an unexpected storm has caused a power outage. It will be about three days before you hear back from me. Don't worry, I am doing just fine." He sent it off.

Next message needed some research. He called up the US Federal Marshal's list of most-wanted criminals. *Oooh, some real badass dudes here. Hey, a not very ladylike group here either.* He scrolled through a list of fugitives; he wanted someone with drug cartel ties, someone who might have bodyguards and lots of guns. *Fernando Garcia, age thirty-six. Do not attempt to apprehend. Oh yeah, he is my man.*

A brief but very specific anonymous email tip then followed to a hotline at the US Marshal's Headquarters. It informed them that a covert meeting at 8 PM Mountain Time in Taos, New Mexico, in exactly three days, would include Fernando Garcia as one of the attendees.

That should be about when only a few remaining NSA field agents are poking around. After NSA left his home, it would have so many bugs Bryson would need to call the Orkin Man. Bryson left his home address to conclude the snitch and notification to the hotline.

The last email needed a bit more panache. He tried a couple but didn't like the sound; at last, he had it:

Dear Barrister Fulbright,

Apologies for the short notice, the mistress I serve can at times be a bit capricious. She informs me today, but I must warn you that her sentiment may change tomorrow, that she is prepared to sell the Candelaria necklace.

Her proposed opportunity to have you view the merchandise and verify the authenticity is in three days, at the home of a personal friend who has offered to open his home to you and any jewelers or appraisers you might choose. Her only stipulation is that you limit your retinue to no more than five guests.

The proposed time is 8 PM Mountain Time at the following location: #518 Hillside Summit Pass, Taos, New Mexico.

Cocktails and light hors d'oeuvres will be served. If these arrangements are acceptable, please notify me at your earliest convenience.

Cordially yours in the light,
Alex Stark

That last tidbit on the closing was just a hunch, something he pulled from Raleigh Jones's research. Bryson was curious to see if Sir Dalton Fulbright took the bait. He sent the message off with a copy to Monsieur Rene Dubufet. *Won't he be thrilled,* he mused as he closed the laptop case, found his old gaming console, and fired up a game of *Zelda*. It wasn't as much fun muted, but with earplugs it still provided entertainment.

The real entertainment is going to happen in three days. Now, he waited.

48

Day one in the new safe house passed relatively uneventfully. She had trouble interpreting the cryptic message Bryson had sent her, but he sounded as though he had things under control. The routine here was pretty much the same. She enjoyed her dialogue with Nalini, and learned that the Virgin of Candelaria depicted in the picture of her appearance to the Guanches represented an etheric apparition. It required powerful *neter* and great mastery to return to the physical plane in the subtle body form. Mary, according to the teachers of the Isis Order, had not only trained in the Egyptian techniques of channeling *sekhem,* she had reached the highest levels among their ranks.

After Chanda's initial transit to the "zone," her instructress today explained how energy from the root chakra flows to distribute vital energy throughout the entire chakra system. With practice, Chanda learned to access this flow state. She could enter the "zone" almost at will. Supercharged in this fashion, her Shakti yoga, her martial arts training, and her general sense of being aware and alive all became elevated. She felt potent and empowered as never before.

"You learn quickly, Chanda, and excel," Moon 5, her instructress, complemented the student. "Soon you shall be ready to have your fifth chakra opened. The true strength of your voice will not be known until the sixth is opened. As you have heard in the teachings to your sister Nalini, channeling your kundalini up to your third eye and sending it back down is how true force is expressed. The three lower chakras are important, but more for gathering and storing your energy. When you redirect the energy down from the third eye through and out through the fourth heart chakra, this is how you achieve great healing. When it is through the fifth," she closed her eyes, spoke words unintelligible to Chanda, and books flew off the bookshelf, "you use the voice with power."

Nalini and Chanda looked at one another, startled at how Moon 5 had done this. "But such tricks are frowned upon. We dedicate our voice to speaking the truth with authority. In this manner, it has the energy to pierce the shadows of doubt and confusion."

Surprise came a moment later. As the teacher picked up and replaced the books on the shelf, a new unmarked vehicle pulled into the drive. Chanda watched through an open window as the driver exited with gun drawn; he scouted the area.

"All clear."

A woman emerged from the back seat; she wore the uniform of Pyramid Communications.

"Thank you, Fahim."

Chanda recognized the voice as the pilot who had flown them from Greece; the scars on the woman's face left no doubt. And those same scars did little to mask clear distress; the woman appeared rushed and pressured.

"Everyone put your vests on and keep them on even when you sleep." The woman turned to one of the house guards. "Ibreham, you are to accompany me with Chanda… Hurry, gather your things… Jared, you are to remain at the house with Nalini. Issue her a weapon. Reinforcements are on the way." The tone and commanding authority in the woman's voice left no room for questioning.

Within minutes, leaving in the other car that had been parked in the drive, Chanda sat next to the woman. Fahim drove, seemingly circling through and around the back streets of this suburban neighborhood before exiting to a main road. Ibreham sat adjacent with an assault weapon readied. As the woman made a series of phone calls, speaking rapidly in Arabic, Chanda steadied herself with breath exercises. Her mind remained clear. The call ended and the woman shifted her cell phone to her prosthetic hand. Chanda noted the woman's facial scars and creases deepen.

"Please accept my apologies for the abrupt change in plans. Your safety, and the safety of our people, are of utmost importance."

"What danger are we in?"

"Chanda…Serena…" Sadness darkened her face; she reached out and held Serena's hand. "I am so sorry, child! A short while ago…" A tear welled in her eyes. "…Agape's body washed ashore about five miles from the Temple of Hygeia."

Serena gasped, gripping the woman's hand more tightly.

"The report claimed she had drugs in her system; they are ruling it a suicide." Above Serena's rising protest she added, "We know this to be false, but such is the power of the enemy. They control the press. This is the lie they tell."

The woman continued as Serena struggled for composure, struggled to set aside emotion and focus on the implications. "We have to presume your location here in Egypt is compromised as is true for our personnel at Pyramid and at the schools. The tentacles of the Brotherhood reach deep. None of us are safe."

"Where are we going now, another safe house?"

"No, we are going to a secret initiation spot. It is seldom used but should do."

"Do for what?"

The woman reached into a bag and removed a richly colored and decorated long fabric strip of some sort. She handled it reverently, as she did with the leather-bound book adorned with symbols that she now produced. The vestment resembled something Serena had seen priests wear; she studied the gold-embroidered symbols and fringe—a stole.

"To open your fifth. To release your voice." She barked an order to Fahim who veered sharply to the left.

"My fifth chakra?" It all seemed to be happening too quickly. "Am I ready?"

"That is for Isis to decide."

"Wait… I don't even know your name… Who are you?"

They locked eyes. "I am Moon 2, Abbess for this Isis school."

Serena looked out the window, swallowed, and tried to process this new piece of information. The car had entered a gated entrance to a cemetery. After several turns ending at a dead end they stopped, waited till given the clear signal from Ibreham, and got out of the car. The sun was setting. They stood in front of a mausoleum.

"Fahim, turn the car around. Stay sharp. We should be no more than thirty minutes. Ibreham, follow with us, please." Moon 2 seemed clear in her orders and her plan. She produced a key ring from some hidden pocket, selected a key and unlocked the door to the mausoleum. Inside, amidst the urns and darkness, stood a second doorway. The priestess produced another key and opened this door which led to a stairway down. Stale, musty air rushed outward.

She lit a candle and positioned the security guard in the mausoleum. He shut the door behind them. In silence, they carefully stepped down the stone stairs. Curving slightly, the stairway ended in a circular underground chamber measuring perhaps twelve or fifteen feet in diameter. Two doors flanked each other. Moon 2 placed the candle on a stone altar of some sort and opened one of the doors. From within this closet, she removed a bowl and a jug and placed these on the altar as well.

Remaining silent, her eyes having adjusted, Serena watched as the Abbess made preparations. The single candle flame stood erect, illuminating the entire chamber in soft steady light. The elder woman murmured prayers or incantations as she poured oil into a bowl and motioned for Serena to step toward her.

As the Abbess continued with her chanting, Serena began to feel tingling, then an intense burning traveled up her spine and forward into her abdomen and chest; it stopped at her throat.

"Now child, I have set the preparations." She anointed Serena's throat with the oil and reverently placed the stole, not around herself, but over Serena's shoulders, crossing the symbols over the initiate's heart.

Subtle, almost barely perceptible, the candle flame flickered and wavered toward the stairway. Moon's eyes grew wide in the candlelight and she shouted, "DOWN!"

Serena obeyed instantly and looked up to see a glint of metal flash through the air, landing with a thud into Moon 2's chest. A shadow grew in the stairwell, and Serena heard the priestess speak foreign words. A fierce gust of wind swept through the chamber leaving only the red glow and trailing smoke from the wick's top. Darkness immersed them.

The drama unfolding at his house had subsided as the agents scoured, examined, and impounded all sorts of things. "Operation Mesa Gold," as the agents called it, settled into standard operating procedure after the fire department had left.

"Probably something in the security system triggered a circuit overload in the server leading to the fire." That at least was the explanation the fire chief had satisfied himself with. "No, I don't know much about the owner of the house. I hear he is some kind of genius. No, the department has not had any previous calls. No, I have never seen the owner, don't even know what he looks like."

Once the agents had interrogated all the fire department personnel and dismissed them, conversation was minimal. It almost broke Bryson's heart as he watched the team dismantle his server, mainframe, and the other components of his system. The main unit didn't look as melted as he had hoped. Still, he felt confident nothing on the unit would land him in prison. The only odd thing was a bookish-looking young woman who didn't seem to do much other than walk around asking questions.

Definitely not a field agent. She looks like an analyst. It's not a bad idea to cross-train some. The thought had just entered his mind when the email response came in. The corners of Bryson's eyes crinkled.

Mr. Stark,

These arrangements you have suggested are fine and our buyer is pleased at the owner's willingness to sell. I look forward to meeting you at 8 PM Mountain Time in less than three days.

May the light guide you,
Sir Dalton Fulbright

Fortunately, the other chamber door opened to a tunnel. At least that was Serena's conclusion. There was nothing to block the door and in total darkness, searching for something proved fruitless. The intruder would have to follow them blind.

Moon 2 held her hand and softly counted strides and side passages. Periodically, she paused to listen, to see if a pursuer followed, but the only sound was the muted breath of the two women. Eventually, they turned to a side tunnel, climbed steps and stood blocked from further progress. Moon 2 located a handle, door hinges creaked, and they exited to another mausoleum, grateful for the subdued light within.

Closing and locking the door, Moon 2 took out her cell, muted the sound, and began texting a series of messages. Serena noted a metallic starlike object embedded in the woman's vest. She continued to text. Eventually she put the phone down and removed the star—a shuriken, used for centuries by ninjas. Moon held it in her prosthetic hand, cautiously tasting an edge with her tongue then spitting.

"Poison," she whispered, then cursed, gingerly wrapping it in a portion of her shirt that she tore off, placing the weapon in her pocket. Carefully, she removed the stole around Serena's shoulders, cursing as she noted the badly soiled vestment.

An unmistakable explosion sounded in the distance and momentarily the light flared. The car, and presumably Fahim, smoldered. The Abbess fumed. Even in the fading light, Serena saw the woman's eyes on fire. Silently, she mouthed prayers—prayers for the dead.

Twenty minutes later a vehicle pulled up; they both heard the engine kill. The password of the day and response were exchanged through an open transom of the mausoleum. Moon 2 handed a key through the opening and a security guard for Pyramid Communications unlocked the door. It was Youssef.

"Are you harmed?"

"No. Were you able to reach Fahim or Ibreham?"

A pause followed. "We have not been able to contact them." They entered a vehicle and left through an exit on the far end of the cemetery. A series of calls ensued; Serena learned they were headed back to the company headquarters.

"I'm...I'm sorry!" Serena, unsure how to start, examined the taut lines in Moon's face that accentuated her scars.

"As am I. Sorry that I cannot protect you, sorry that blood has been spilled. Sorry that you did not feel the embrace of Isis in the opening of your chakra." Moon 2 held up her prosthetic hand. "The high priestess of our order has told me I have no power for healing. My heart chakra is too closed. But I do have some small power in the voice. For this, child, we should both be thankful. The enemy lurks in the shadows. We must ever be on our guard."

To Serena's great surprise, she reached into her bag and retrieved the sacred book. Somehow, she had managed to grab it from the altar. "We should finish what we started."

There, in the back seat of the company car, with Youssef seated in the front and driving, Moon 2 gathered herself, gathered her *sekhem,* and softly sang and chanted from the text she held in her prosthesis. Somehow, the headlights, the road noise, and the traffic all faded to obscurity in Serena's conscious awareness.

With Moon 2's hand held over her neck, still oiled but now slick with sweat, the young woman again felt the burn rise from within. She swore she saw a snake emerge from the priestess's open palm as something slithered around

Serena's shoulders and coiled around her neck. This was no gentle caress. She imagined a python squeezing while wrapped around her throat, constricting her, squeezing with power. Serena tried to raise her hands, but they remained immobile, beyond the reach of her will to move them. She was choking... She couldn't breathe!

The priestess spoke, the words came through clearly and with power. *"Seh Ka Paress."*

Something tore a hole in her throat. Serena gasped for air, worse than a swimmer held underwater for too long bursting forth to inhale. A sound came forth, a howl, as with wind forcing itself through a narrow opening, as with air rushing to fill a vacuum void. Serena gasped then breathed out: *"Ka Paressti Onnanesh."*

Where those words came from, what they meant, or how they worked didn't matter. Serena breathed, she spoke...and the fire burning within seemed to fill the entire cab with heat as it dissipated. A snake image, circling her neck like an open necklace, glided over her skin. The serpent raised its head and looked at Serena. As it withdrew back into Moon's still open hand Serena had no doubt—the serpent smiled!

49

"Boss, I know I shouldn't laugh, but the surveillance footage from your nephew's place is comical. Homeland Security pulled a joint raid with NSA; I'm digging into it a little more with some of our contacts there. Fire department showed up—total chaos and confusion."

"Did we have anything to do with the raid?"

"Not as far as I know. Bryson is sharp, but somewhere along the way he must have left a trail. Anything involving international correspondence, these days the NSA is on that stuff like flies on shit."

"So, what do you think we need to do?"

"Hard to say. Not likely your nephew will show up anytime soon, so I'm working in the dark again. Haven't turned up anything on the girl either. I could poke around down there; see if the agents on-site reveal anything in their conversation. Right now, my listening post is too unidirectional. I would need to manually reposition the dish to get the agents' chatter."

"Okay, head back down and scout it out; see if you can't locate him and track him down some way. Are you monitoring his accounts?"

"Absolutely. Homeland will probably freeze them, but I'm on the scent."

"Okay, Claus, do what you have to do. When you find him, let me know. I don't like the idea of him being on the run, so if you locate him, be ready to take him in. I don't want federal authorities to find and apprehend him before we do…and certainly not Li!"

"Understood."

"Do you need additional personnel?"

"Boss, I fly solo. If I need help, I'll let you know, but it's not likely."

"I've included something extra in Charles's next paycheck. Keep me informed."

The Abbess spent most of the time on the phone. Youssef assured her the cell phone conversations could not be pirated thanks to the jamming device in his bag. Serena kept rubbing her throat and swallowing; anything she tried to say came out as a hoarse whisper.

"That is only temporary." Seeing the young woman's distress, Moon 2 spoke in between calls. "The activation of your throat chakra strained your voice box. You have laryngitis, but it will clear."

"Thanks," she croaked harshly. "What happened?"

"Isis, Foundress of our Order, embraced you tightly." A sigh followed. "Each time I have witnessed the opening of the fifth has been different. In your case, I sensed your voice was just waiting to be released. For the moment it is wild and untamed. Unfortunately, we cannot complete your training here."

Her voice cracked. "So where do I go?"

"I don't know, Chanda. You must leave our soil. I am making arrangements."

Pyramid Communications took security very seriously. The compound lights and patrols revealed how seriously. They cleared the dogs, outer, and inner security. She sat in a room, the same one where her debriefing had occurred. The place buzzed, a hive of activity, but she sat alone. *I'm like a mushroom, left in the dark.*

Somehow Bryson's words about trust percolated to her consciousness; however, that only heightened her frustration. *I can't even contact Bryson at the moment. For someone who is supposedly filled with light, it seems I am surrounded in darkness...*

Someone brought her a Pyramid uniform to change into. She packed her dirty clothes among the rest of the belongings in her bag. Wherever she went next, she would be traveling light. Another staff person arrived and wordlessly delivered a printed news clip about Agape. *Bastards!* Bad enough someone had murdered the loving disciple of Hygeia, but including the blatant lies implying she was a drug addict who took her own life, that was blasphemy. She bristled. *There's no justice, and it's the same bullshit going on for centuries. Hypatia was murdered for teaching...teaching, dammit...and those responsible got away with it! Agape is killed simply to get to me... WTF is that all about?* Her throat burned, she wanted to shout out against the injustice, shout out against the powers suppressing justice, speak out against the venomous lies and untruths. The more the thoughts swirled then gelled, the angrier she felt, the more her throat burned. Throwing the paper down, rejecting the news and lies about Agape, she found herself shouting, yelling, "NOT IF I HAVE SOMEHTING TO SAY ABOUT IT!"

At that moment Moon 2 entered the room. "I see you have found your voice."

With clear and stubborn determination, she stated emphatically, "You're damn right I have!"

The Abbess handed Chanda a paper containing the familiar instructions to shred after reading, but she verbally summarized the contents. "You're going to Lisbon. There have been demonstrations there protesting the government's immigration policies. You'll travel as a journalist working for Pyramid as 'Chanda Patel.' We are not concealing these plans because we need the enemy to be aware that you have left the country. You will stay in a hotel connected to the airport. Youssef accompanies you; he will keep you safe."

"You need to protect the rest of your people. I endanger all of you."

"Yes, I am sorry to send you off in this way, but my duty and responsibility is to our Sisterhood and this company. I'm also sending Nalini back to your sisters in India. I believe she will be safe there."

"Understood."

"There is more…" Moon 2 explained that Pyramid had made arrangements for Chanda to next travel to India by herself the following day; however, she strongly advised Chanda to miss that flight and instead make travel arrangements under the name of Serena Mendez on her own, and to leave Lisbon before the flight to India. She recommended traveling to a country where the name "Serena Mendez" was common. It made sense. If someone was tracking her travel, she would have left Lisbon under a different name to a place where she could hopefully blend in and disappear. The Abbess also cautioned Serena to tell none of her staff or the hotel staff of the actual travel plans she decided upon.

"People cannot reveal secrets they do not know." The implications of this reminder needed no further explanation.

"Another thing, you arrive in Lisbon tomorrow morning; two rooms are booked for you and Youssef for tomorrow night. I have instructed him to switch rooms with you. He will order room service. Interact with as few people as you possibly can."

The door opened, and Youssef arrived carrying some luggage and two printed boarding passes. "The helicopter is ready."

As they flew over the lights of Cairo, Serena's thoughts whirred in her head and made more noise than the blades of the craft. She was glad to leave Egypt, a region fraught with turmoil. She felt concerned but not worried about Nalini, and both impressed by and grateful for Moon 2 and her people. Once she had left the country, whoever hunted her would have a new trail to pick up, a trail that she was determined to run cold on her pursuers.

Whatever arrangements Pyramid Communications had for the expedited processing of their press corps through customs gave the two an edge. While Youssef was allowed to carry his handgun on the helicopter, he lacked the authorizations to transport it on the commercial flight to Lisbon. Mentally, Serena reviewed her self-defense training and quick entry into her flow state. A deceptive appearance as a young, petite, and vulnerable woman represented a decided advantage.

Her goodbye to Moon 2, once again their pilot for this short nighttime jaunt, lacked all the things she wanted to say. Serena hugged her, kissed her scarred face—first the left cheek, then the right—and thanked her.

"Be safe, child." A pause followed as the woman unexpectedly reached up using her good hand and removed something from her opposite arm—an upper-arm bracelet in the design of a snake. She handed it over. "You wear it on the left. In our tradition, you receive this upon the opening of the fifth chakra. When the sixth is open, you are given one to wear on the right."

Appreciatively, Serena slid the cuff bracelet and tightened it to fit her slender arm.

"You are not of the Black Snake Sisters, but we all serve the same cause." She slid the silver snake from Serena's arm. "Pack this away in your carry bag for now and keep it safe. Perhaps someday I shall give you one for the right arm... May you become all that you are."

Once they were in the passenger terminal at the boarding gate, Youssef close at hand, Serena steadied herself using the breath and meditative practices she had honed over the last several weeks. Bryson remained incommunicado for the time being. Her security guard would be doing something else in less than two days. She needed to plan her next step.

She removed her tablet and searched. *Let's see, where do I want to go?* She browsed travel sites, then a different idea popped into her head. *Quetzalcoatl... Aztec...Mayan... Hmmm, lots of Spanish names in that part of the world. I can do this...*

50

All of her recent travel dulled her to the particulars. Their flight on Turkish Airways routed through Istanbul on the way to Lisbon, a ten-hour trip. She slept on and off, waking to rub her throat which still felt sore. Thoughts stirred about injustice and how most people are blind to what is going on around them in the world, complacent, unwilling to challenge authority or to question who is pulling the strings. *Why should they? If they have a place to sleep and food in their bellies, they are grateful and tolerate the oppression.* She questioned if the Illuminati actually had it right—most people are not able or willing to critically evaluate the world and therefore they depend on others to do it for them. The power elite exist to make the hard decisions, to shepherd a large flock—the great unwashed masses. In the end, she settled the debate in her mind decisively.

We are not here to do someone else's bidding, to let someone else exercise our free will for us, to deprive us of our birthright. If we have all the facts and decide to hand over decision-making to others that is fine because we do so fully informed. But if we remain ignorant, if we are fed lies, IF WE REMAIN IN THE DARK, we are manipulated and controlled and are fettered in our ignorance. As her sleeping and dozing mind brought all the pieces together, so she could see the big picture, it all seemed so clear. Clarity and focus emerged. Somehow in this big mess, she was supposed to shine with the light of truth.

Illuminati, bloodlines, Candelaria, Gnosticism, chakra openings—she was simply a warrior-in-preparation to fight in this great war between the two serpents. She considered great leaders who fought on the side she imagined herself—Christ, Buddha, Gandhi, Mother Teresa, Martin Luther King, Nelson Mandela. *There aren't many women on my list.* The reason underlying this gender inequality flashed in a moment of insight—suppression of the divine feminine. Hypatia became her role model, a historical figure she wanted to emulate, except for the assassination part; she didn't care for how that particular story ended. *My story is just at the beginning…*

In Lisbon, after clearing customs, they changed into civilian clothes. Should she wear her burqa? Youssef advised against it. Anti-Muslim sentiment fueled some of the demonstrators. The two had no plans to cover any of the demonstrations as journalists; they wanted to maintain a low profile. So, they spent the time browsing shops, picking up some toiletries and other needed items. They checked into their hotel without incident. *So far so good.*

Serena spent the time sorting through travel options and conducting research. The next picture-symbol in her Circle was Quetzalcoatl, god figure of the Aztecs. Not only did history claim he had blue eyes and fair skin, not only did some scholars claim he was Atlantean, the big surprise came as an almost shocking discovery. Quetzalcoatl was actually Thoth! *So Thoth, Hermes, and Quetzalcoatl were all the same dude, and he apparently set up mystery schools in at least three areas of the world to teach the ancient wisdom of Atlantis. Makes sense.* She filed a note to herself to make sure she shared this insight with Bryson.

She made a decision. Tomorrow Serena would fly to Madrid on Iberia Airline, well before the scheduled departure to India booked for Chandra Patel. Her efforts focused on finding a charter tour to Mexico visiting Mayan ruins that departed from Madrid. A charter flight would be less obvious to investigate in the event someone tried to follow her. She reasoned that a vacation travel tour would be a good choice. As Moon 2 had warned, Serena did not even look to Youssef for advice. On her own and left to her own wits, she called three tour companies who met her specifics, but the response was always the same—the tour had been filled months ago; they could place her on a waiting list should there be an unlikely late cancellation.

Youssef ordered a meal for each of them delivered to his suite though neither of them felt hungry; they ate in silence in his room. He insisted on tasting her food before allowing her to try it—rather extreme in her judgment, but she didn't complain. The knock on the door of the adjacent room stirred them both into instant awareness. He motioned her to the floor, entered the adjoining room, and peered through the doorway. A courier in uniform held a package.

"Who is it?" The Pyramid security guard stood to the side of the door.

"Package delivery for Chanda Patel."

"Leave it at the door, then exit." The courier held a book-like package wrapped in brown paper.

"I am sorry, sir, but the delivery instructions are very specific. They say I am only to leave the package for Chanda Patel and only after she answers the following question correctly. I doubt that you are the correct recipient."

Serena overheard the exchange. She got up, then stood behind Youssef. "Ask your question."

Her voice convinced the courier to proceed. "I love the gift you sent Jolene."

Shit…yesterday's password exchange, but this was a new day, and there should be a new password, but they'd had no contact with headquarters. She looked at Youssef and he shrugged.

She responded, "I was worried it wouldn't be the right size."

Her guard looked through the peephole as she answered, watched as the courier leaned the package against the door to the room and left. Cautiously,

Youssef opened the door, retrieved the package and looked at it, smelled it, listened for anything unusual before he sent Serena back to the other room.

As she remembered the Abbess's prosthetic hand, the result of a package bomb, she prepared for the worst. Moments later tearing paper preceded a nervous laugh. "It is a book."

He'd unwrapped *A Separate Reality: Further Conversations with Don Juan*, by Carlos Castaneda, and within it a note:

> Dear Sister,
>
> I cannot complete your training in that which I myself have not attained.
>
> Ooljee instructed me to give this book to you upon the opening of your fifth chakra.
>
> Be safe.
>
> Namaste,
> Nalini

She thumbed through it. Carlos Castaneda, an anthropologist who studied with some old Mexican shaman, used hallucinogenic plants, and wrote about his experiences. She remembered seeing a book by him on her parents' bookshelves. *Wasn't he mentioned in one of my anthropology lectures about myth and symbolism? Maybe he popped up somewhere in Bryson's data program.* She tossed the book into her bag thinking there would be plenty of opportunity to read through it and hopefully understand what her *shibízhí* had in mind, where this piece fit in and where it would lead. Her more immediate concern—getting through the night and out of Lisbon incognito.

Chanda Patel, her false identity, remained for all intents and purposes still checked in at the hotel in Lisbon. Youssef would handle the checkout before he flew back to Cairo. Everything that remained of her alter ego—a fake Indian passport and a muted brown burqa, lay packed in her travel bag. Serena felt glad to have shed the false identity and to fully embrace her true self. Her hair, thick and dark, now measured about one and a half inches. She had no plans to shave it again. Serena Mendez, on a mission of faith and destiny, fully committed and determined to complete her Circle, sat back in her window seat and looked down at the Iberian Peninsula below. There was only one slight problem—she remained clueless on where to proceed next on her journey. She cracked the spine of *A Separate Reality: Further Conversations with Don Juan*. Part of her wondered why her great aunt couldn't be more forthcoming in messaging her intent. *There are clues here. I just have to find them.*

The pilot's announcement that the plane had begun its final decent startled her from sleep. She must have fallen asleep less than a chapter into the book. Not yet fully awake, dream images flashed in her mind: a fire billowing smoke over dancing flames, a bright moon overhead surrounded by desert or was it forest, or jungle, or savannah? The background of the image itself seemed to shift and change each time she blinked. Sitting across from herself at the fire was her *shibízhí* or was it Gurumarra or Don Juan the Yaqui sorcerer? The dream images began to fade, but the final image in her mind stuck a moment longer. Sitting across from her at the fire, unmistakable as an image in a mirror—herself. She blinked, shook her head and fastened her seat belt.

Powering up her cell phone she noted a voice mail from an unfamiliar source. Who could possibly be calling her?

"This is Garbiñe from Aztec Gold Tour Company; we spoke on the phone yesterday. A couple has unexpectedly cancelled their booking due to a medical emergency. I know it is short notice, but if you are still interested in the eight-day/seven-night tour of Ancient Mexico, please call me back as soon as possible. The flight leaves Madrid at 3:30 PM."

Her racing heart made waiting to deplane a test of patience. Deep breaths. Finally, she found a quiet spot to return the call. Whether Garbiñe felt more surprised by Serena's ability to plan to be at the airport in time to join the tour, or Serena herself, who grappled with the synchronicity, would be difficult to say. She hung up, linked to her e-board pass, captured the image on her phone, and negotiated her way through the terminal. Local time of 1:00 gave her plenty of opportunity to leisurely make her way to the gate and grab a bite to eat.

Destiny had spoken. When the student is ready, the teacher will appear. As these thoughts mulled between tapas, her only concern lay in covering her tracks. She sipped the iced brown liquid masquerading as coffee. The flight and tour package strained her remaining funds; soon she would need Bryson to transfer more money to her debit account. But she dared not contact him until he initiated contact again. If something happened to her, no one would know where she was or where she was headed. Realizing that she was totally on her own no longer bothered her. She flexed her arms and shoulders; the new Serena Mendez could take care of herself just fine.

51

S nake whores! Witches and whores—I hate them! Gensu Li ranted. His uncle would not be pleased. Hong Kong seemed more and more desirable over Singapore. Yet, the corporate jet flying him out of Lisbon would land in Singapore, and he would have to explain himself. No doubt the girl had help. *Pyramid Communications,* his lips curled in a sneer; he wanted to spit, *the serpent sisterhoods all align against me. But Gensu is one of the Dragon Brothers;* he rolled up his sleeve and studied his tattoo. This was no longer just business; Serena Mendez had twice eluded him. Now it was personal. *An angry dragon is not to be messed with.* If this wasn't already an old Chinese proverb, he decided it should be.

Oh, this is just too good to miss! If what I think is about to happen is going to happen, I am definitely staying put. Claus Gorman sat in the high hide stationed at his lookout perch. He was not hunting elk. Not much had happened yesterday while he monitored the sting operation at Bryson Reynold's house. Homeland Security, no longer adorned in their assault unit gear, had left the premises. Electronic equipment and assorted other items from the house had been boxed and carted away. A crew from NSA seemed to be strategically placing electronic bugs and other surveillance equipment. They were oblivious to his presence, a fact he took some pride in. Based upon their conversations that he had intercepted, they were planning to finish up their little sting sometime tomorrow. *Operation Mesa Gold—sounds like a brand of tequila.*

That last thought reminded him that he was hungry, thirsty, and could use a stiff drink. He would have wrapped up his efforts for the day were it not for the helicopter runs. Three passes in the last hour, and two earlier—late this afternoon and at dusk. He had been around long enough to realize something else was in the works and he sat somewhere right in the middle of it. When agents from the US Marshals Service, readily identified in his binoculars as daylight waned, crawled into position, he wasn't sure what to expect, but he knew he needed to hang around. Besides, it would be difficult to explain his presence. So, he sat in his perch and watched through his night vision monocle as a black limousine slowly crunched its way down the long gravel drive. It was five minutes before 8 PM—showtime!

Within the vehicle, Sir Dalton Fulbright turned to one of the other members of his party and commented how out-of-the-way the location seemed. "Not nearly as fancy or prestigious as I had imagined."

The response came back: "Puzzling too at how few vehicles are here. The plates on the cars are more than peculiar—US Government. Mr. Stark alluded to his employer having some eccentricities." They pulled into a clear area in front of the garage.

The party of five men—Barrister Fulbright, along with a jeweler, an authority in religious artifacts, Monsieur Dubufet, and the chauffeur exited their vehicle, leather and titanium briefcases in hand.

"FREEZE! HANDS UP… ON THE GROUND… NOW!"

As fifteen agents materialized from the blackness—fully armored and carrying assault weapons, wearing helmets and having the undeniable authority at the moment, the five men readily complied. Two sets of tire spikes and a portable barrier suddenly and neatly pinned their vehicle. The jeweler, lying face down on the driveway gravel, wet his pants. Most undignified!

Storming the porch, the still splintered door from the Homeland Security battering ram offered no resistance. Eight US Marshal agents entered the home, shouting commands to come out with hands up.

Watching from his surveillance nest, Claus saw the scene unfold, thoroughly impressed at the professionalism and precision of the raid. The five men who had arrived in the black limousine stood cuffed and immobilized in the driveway while Claus tried to make sense of the driveway conversation—something about a private showing of some rare necklace, no they did not know the owner's name. It was hard to say who was more confused, the agents or the people they had apprehended. No, they had never heard of Fernando Garcia. Who is he?

The field agents from NSA mopping up the end of Mesa Gold were even more confused. As the Marshals led them one at a time out from the dwelling, Claus listened: "We ran a sting here three days ago with Homeland. Some previous government operative went rogue with cyber-espionage. Fernando Garcia, fugitive cartel drug trafficker? Never heard of him."

From within, Bryson watched it all on his monitors. While the amusement value was certainly there, he didn't have time to enjoy it. For his escape to work, he needed to execute it just right. Leaving his safe hideaway and carefully repositioning the back panel, he held his backpack with his laptop showing. Within it, he carried his real passport, a fake ID and passport, ten thousand dollars emergency money, and one last surprise. A white lab jacket, standard attire for an agent doing mop-up at the end of a sting, along with his old NSA photo-badge affixed to his front pocket completed the deception. *Don't know what possessed me to store my old jacket in the hideout but I'm glad I did. Damn, I am tired of playing Zelda!*

Hands overhead, sounding afraid but feeling pretty cocky, he slowly walked up the stairs saying, "Don't shoot. NSA. Was downstairs in the server room."

When the first Marshal he encountered told him, "Okay kid, you can put your hands down," they hadn't quite made it to the porch beyond. That's where the rest of the NSA team had been herded.

Perfect! Bryson palmed the remote. Pressing the correct sequence first released several gas canisters from the eaves of the house. The second sequence cut the power to the house including the outdoor lights.

In the chaos and confusion that followed, amidst shouts, cries, coughs, sputters, blinding smoke, scrambling to find lights and some gas masks, the US Marshals suddenly appeared hopelessly and pathetically overmatched.

Bryson reached into his pack, removed his last surprise, donned the gas mask, and quietly walked to the back of his property. From a storage shed, he got out his bicycle and silently pedaled his way to freedom. A half mile into his escape, he stopped, removed the lab jacket and stuffed it into his backpack. Once he was out to the main road, he would need to hitch a ride to Santa Fe. With any luck, he could still make the last Rail Runner into Albuquerque. It felt good to stretch his legs. The temperature was perfect. The night air against his face felt wonderful. He took a deep breath, glad to be free from the confines of his secure space.

No one at 518 Hillside Summit Pass was taking a deep breath. Of course, there weren't enough gas masks to go around. Teary-eyed and coughing, the contingent from overseas had at least been uncuffed. The NSA agents still had work to complete and now they were without power. That made the job a lot more difficult. Total cluster fuck!

As the US Marshals tried to reestablish order, Claus Gorman climbed down from his nest, unaffected by the tear gas at his location. In his night vision monocle, he had seen the tall figure slip away and ride off on a bicycle. He had a newfound respect for Bryson Reynolds. *That kid's a genius. I'm sure I would not have conceived of such a well-thought-out escape plan. Uncle Peter will be so proud!*

52

Something she had missed in booking the tour with Aztec Gold, a minor detail she had just somehow overlooked—this particular tour package catered to the golden oldie crowd. As such, Serena found herself to be the only American and the youngest by at least thirty-five years. It did give her more time to herself, more frequent rest stops as the tour bus wound its way across the Yucatan, and more opportunity to hone her Spanish—the true and pure Castilian; her New Mexican Spanish sounded like a poor bastardized cousin. Many of the other tour guests spoke English as well. She simply let them know she studied anthropology and was going to various places of interest throughout the world as she tried to figure out what she wanted to do with her life. In maternal and paternal fashion, they freely shared what they thought a smart, attractive, and determined girl such as herself should do. More often than not, it involved having lots of babies. Of course, she also endured a relentless display of family pictures, mostly of eligible grandsons. For all she had been through lately, it represented a welcome distraction. By day two, they had accepted her, and she had accepted them, and they all enthusiastically learned about the ancient civilizations from this part of the world.

She missed Bryson—his encouragement, his super sleuthing, and his quick wit would be the perfect companion on this tour. His interest in ancient peoples focused on Greece and Rome, but she knew he would delve right into Aztec and Mayan culture and become an expert in no time. *He would probably drive the tour guides nuts!*

Day one consisted of travel. They arrived in Mexico City at night given the time zone change. The hotel accommodations weren't luxurious, but they were more than adequate. Day two had them in Teotihuacan. At one time, centuries before the Aztecs, it stood as one of the greatest cities in the world. The Jaguar Palace took her breath away until visiting the Temple of the Plumed Conch Shells. Her ignorance that such a beautifully named and incredible archeologic treasure had previously been unknown to her swept her with the desire to resume her study of anthropology—not at the university, but by visiting the sites themselves and experiencing their beauty firsthand. The Pyramids of the Sun and the Moon followed. She strolled along the Avenue of the Dead, all the while snapping pictures and collecting brochures. How could she have missed this all these years?

That night she finished *A Separate Reality* and began to dig into Toltec teachings, entheogens, Don Juan, Quetzalcoatl, and anything else that seemed relevant. Basically, most of the book struck her as being instruction in the way of the Warrior. This way required intention and dedication. While it made sense to her that her *shibízhí* would want to share something to do with training a warrior, Serena saw no connection to opening the sixth chakra, her third eye. Although Don Juan insisted that Castaneda must learn how to "see," he never explained how this learning occurs.

Day three took them to Oaxaca; unfortunately, the entire morning was spent in the tour bus. She would have liked more time here. Some of the other guests felt the same way. The Monte Alban pyramid complex would require days of investigation for her to feel satisfied. But the disappointment vanished with the fabulous food accompanied by music and dancing that evening. This Mexico enthralled her. Everywhere she had been in the last two months had unique culture, food, customs, and charm. But here, in the Yucatan, she suddenly felt at home, much more so than back in Santa Fe. She resolved to return some day and complete her exploration of the ancient ruins at a site dating back to 500 BC. Too tired for any online research she crashed.

Her cell ringtone stirred then snapped her from sleep at 12:36 AM—it was Bryson!

"Hey…OMG! Great to hear from you! Is everything okay? Where are you?"

"Well, at the moment, I'm on the last Rail Runner headed toward Albuquerque."

"What? Why? What's been going on?"

"Long story, kind of exciting too." He didn't want to admit to himself how cool he felt outsmarting his former employer by setting things up with a different government agency, but he did want to show off a little. "I'll get to it in a moment, but I should let you know, there could be a little problem with trying to sell your Candelaria necklace. First tell me, what's new with you?"

"Well, at the moment, I couldn't care less about the stupid necklace. As to what's new since the last time we spoke, how much time do we have? Oh, and I'm in Mexico right now."

"Mexico! I can't believe it; that's where I'm headed. Um…I'm kind of a fugitive making his way out of the country."

After placing a bet with each other on whose story over the last few days was better, the two proceeded to tell each other the details of their lives since contact went dark. There were multiple oohs and aahs, as well as "awesome!" and "no shit" comments, exchanged. In the end, they called the bet a draw.

"I can tell you this, *Zelda* used to be a lot more fun. I have met my lifetime quota playing that game. Hey, I'm almost at my stop." They had been catching up for forty-five minutes.

"Okay, I have to look at our itinerary and see where would be good to meet up in a few days. I think I'll be close to Cancún, so rough out the travel times and I'll call you sometime later today. First round of tacos is on me. Shit, that reminds me, my card needs a recharge."

"That could be a problem, PTG. I haven't checked, but there's a good chance my accounts are frozen. I've got cash on hand, so you might need to wait until I get there." He swallowed. "Assuming of course I make it over the border."

"Remember, trust! That's what you have been telling me and it's worked so far. Besides, they don't care when you leave, it's when you try to get back in. Changed my mind; first round of tacos is on you, Snowman."

"Deal."

"Deal. Drive safely."

She hung up. *He's coming down to Mexico. I can't believe it!* The excitement about seeing Bryson, about showing him some of these incredible Aztec and Zapotec ruins, and…well, just seeing him… This unexpected good news displaced all thoughts of chakras and completing her Circle and the bad people chasing her. It took a long time to fall back to sleep.

Palenque, their day four stop, had an intriguing description on the tour itinerary: "Palenque is magical—mysterious Mayan ruins rise from a backdrop of lush jungle. Read from the Temple of Inscriptions. Stand at the Observation Tower, unique among known Mayan buildings, constructed to view the winter solstice…" The description went on but didn't do the site justice. The exotic jungle birds with their haunting calls, the magnificent stonework and mysterious pyramids—the site vibrated with sacred energy. A power spot definitely lay beneath these ruins. All her chakras opened; she felt overwhelmed by bliss as she walked reverently amidst the vegetation, flowing water, and palace stonework. Again, she found herself transposed and transfixed by an ancient advanced culture and civilization.

The next day and a half, Merida provided a base for them to explore the nearby Dzibilchaltun ruins. Serena felt curious about the Temple of the Seven Dolls at the site. Seven Dolls; did they each guard the seven sacred seals between the planes of existence? But the secrets of the site were not revealed to her. Again, the time seemed too short. Perhaps that is the nature of such tours—a whirlwind taste just to make you hungry for more. To her delight, the Cenote Xlacah, where the Mayans gathered and stored fresh water, permitted swimmers to enter the freshwater pool. She didn't have a suit; undeterred, she entered in her clothes and bathed in the cool refreshing water. Soggy, but happy, she sat in her seat on the bus, laughing with a widower from Barcelona who himself had bravely taken a dip, but only to his hips. Life and the joy of being flowed from her, from the earth, the sun, the air, the water. In all her life, Serena had never felt so alive.

The following morning at Chichen Itza, also close to Merida, more fascination waited—the Castle Pyramid, the Group of a Thousand Columns, and the Sacred Cenote. She took videos and sent them to Bryson. She wished he was with her to witness these marvels and share them together. They traveled to Valladolid arriving midafternoon. Scheduled downtime provided a welcome break for all the tourists. They would spend the night there; the guide said their restaurant that evening was among his favorites in all the places he traveled with the company.

Serena had no desire to shop; besides, she was out of *pesos*. Instead, after settling in at the hotel, she asked at the desk about local salons. The scar on her scalp had some uneven patches of hair sprouting in haphazard fashion; it accentuated how untidy her hair looked while regrowing from bald. Last peek in a mirror confirmed that the wild growth exceeded even her modest requirements for self-respect. She needed to tame it down and to clean it all up, even if it meant a small charge to her regular credit card. She had been carrying it around for months with a zero balance. *Visa probably thinks I switched to a different card since paying it off. Time to make myself look good for the Snowman.*

53

She loved her new do—sculpted on the sides, shaped on the top, a nice stylish pixie cut. Sexy too. The sunlight reflected on her snake arm bracelet. She knew she looked good—tan, fit, confident. Serena had maintained the discipline to spend an hour each day training her kundalini energy through the Shakti yoga techniques and the Egyptian *sekhem* exercises she had learned. She also sparred with imaginary adversaries during the freestyle kickboxing training moves she continued to practice. She had taught herself to enter the "zone" at will.

Sitting at a café table, one of several scattered throughout a small plaza with a few shops and even fewer shoppers, she glanced at the clock in the bell tower of the church at the other end of the square. A sign labeled it a cathedral, but it looked more like a church to her. Ten minutes before six. The hotel was located nearby; they needed to gather in the lobby at 6:30. She figured in another ten minutes she should head back. The guide's ongoing praise over tonight's planned meal left her full of expected gastronomic delight.

She sipped her ice water. The heat from the sun radiated from the stones below. The air felt thick. The past hour she had forced herself to once again read from *A Separate Reality: Further Conversations with Don Juan.* She scoured the words for clues. A crow scolded her, perched on the stone wall behind. She wrinkled her nose and squawked back. Whatever insights her great aunt had hoped for by instructing Nalini to deliver this book completely eluded the young Candelaria. She had been through it twice already to no avail. She had researched the third eye and pineal gland, the Yaqui Indians, hallucinogenic plants, and Toltec Nagual Shamanism. Bryson was also stumped. Other than some ideas about DNA that he promised to elaborate upon, he seemed to be as clueless as she.

Sometimes, you need to set something aside while your unconscious plays with it, let things gestate before it births insight. It seemed a poetic approach. She put the book down and idly looked around the plaza. An old man stood thirty feet away; he began to play the pan flute. A straw hat set in front had no coins and would likely remain empty. Other than two youths kicking a soccer ball, there were no tourists and no shoppers to reward the old man's efforts. She closed her eyes.

The exquisite music captivated her, and she felt herself soaring on a mountain breeze. Llamas grazed amid lush vegetation. The setting sun cast shades and hues of soft orange, pink, and red. She wished she had a few coins to give the musician. The imaginary mountain wind chilled her, and she felt goosebumps. While she drifted in the magical music something banged her leg, startling her. A soccer ball wedged between the foot of her chair and the table.

"Disculpe me!" The two locals smiled at her and motioned to the ball. Their torn clothes looked dirty, even more so than the muddy, torn, and scuffed soccer ball.

"No problema." She couldn't say why, but a danger sense tingled within. She didn't move to get the ball, and they didn't move.

"Eres muy guapa!" It was the smaller of the two; she guessed about thirteen or fourteen. He stepped toward her pointing at the ball.

She continued to study the situation. The taller one, speaking in broken English, smiled. "My brother tells you that you are very pretty."

Pretty yes, but not stupid. She saw the sunlight glint off the small blade. I bend down to get the ball and one cuts my belt while the other grabs my purse. With one hand holding her belt purse, she eased her chair back, warily watching the two boys. *"Gracias."*

A stream of loud Spanish erupted from her side. The old man had come to rescue her. He let out a torrent of rapid words; the only one that caught her attention was *lagarto.* The two boys looked at each other but did not move. A second litany from the old man followed as he waved his hands gesticulating menacingly at the two youths. Frightened, they dashed off. The ball still lay wedged under the table.

The old man smiled, showing her his yellow-stained cracked teeth. He removed his straw hat and bowed with the exaggerated grace of an old-world Spanish aristocrat. Yet, he didn't look Spanish; he looked native, maybe *mestizo*—it was hard to say.

"They were right to say you are very pretty." He spoke in perfect English. Seeing Serena's momentary puzzlement, he pointed. "The book you are reading is in English, *Señorita.*"

"The music you play on your instrument is most beautiful. I am sorry I have nothing to give you for your noble rescue, Don Quixote." She smiled at her knight. "And sorry that I have no time to listen to more of your beautiful music." She looked up. It was one minute before six.

He held the hat and sat across from her. "There are more important things than money, *Señorita.*"

She sensed a double or hidden meaning in that response. She still had more than enough time to meet back at the hotel. "What did you say to them?"

"I told them can't you see this is not a little girl but a powerful Nagual sorceress? If they weren't careful, you would turn them into lizards. When they seemed unsure, I told them if they didn't leave you alone, I would put a curse on them to make them sterile."

"Would you?" The old man's silence intrigued her. *There's more here than meets the eye.*

He smiled. There was something strange about him. When she cocked her head and looked at him with her peripheral vision, he seemed to shimmer slightly, almost appearing out of focus. It was strange. She noticed he didn't answer.

"*Señorita*, you are either very early or very late."

"What do you mean?"

"The festival is in February."

"What festival? I am here on a tour."

Again, he smiled—mysterious, Mona Lisa-esque, half-smiling half-knowing something he chose not to reveal. "On a tour, or on a journey…? The *Dia de la Candelaria*…it is a big festival here in Valladolid…a procession of candles… it lights the town and starts right there." He pointed to the cathedral across the plaza. "Still, the festival here is nothing compared to my country."

Serena spoke slowly. "You seem to know certain things. Are you Nagual?"

Now he laughed. "Like the great Don Juan in the book you read?" She shifted her gaze to the book on the table while he continued to look at her, or through her. "He was a great Toltec sorcerer, a shaman, a Nagual warrior." He looked at the girl with dark deep-set eyes.

For a long moment, neither spoke. "Yes and no. I am more like my countryman, Castaneda. He was from Peru, but closer to the sea, where the mountains rise up. I am Yaminahua, from a place close to Bolivia." He held up his pan flute. "Where we sing to the spirits, our *koshuiti*—songs in the dreams of ayahuasca. Without the sacred plant, the songs cannot be fully appreciated." He ran through melodic scales on his instrument then put it down with a mournful shrug.

"So, you know of my journey, my mission?"

"There are many things I know, *Señorita*, many of which I cannot speak. This I do know. Here is not the place for you. That which you seek will not be found here."

"How do you know this? Where should I go?" If the questions sounded desperate it was because she felt desperate.

"Until the eye is fully opened," he pointed to his forehead, "there is much that remains unseen. How do you decide what is truth and what is illusion?"

She rubbed the spot between her brows, something itched. He nodded. "You must go to Peru."

"Where in Peru? It is a big country."

"Learning comes through the journey not the destination, *Señorita*. Still, I cannot say. There is a Temple of Light where great *Shipibo* healers practice. They are *ayahuascaros*; perhaps they can answer. There is a Temple of the Moon where you can go and pray, and in the power of your dreams the answer could be revealed. We have powerful *Xamanicas* among my people; they speak the twisted tongue when they drink from the sacred twisted vine. There are many hidden answers in the language they speak, in the language they sing." He paused and looked intently; he seemed somehow iridescent. "Or, you could visit the place of Castaneda."

He reached forward to grab the book, instead pushing it off the table. It landed with hardly a sound. Serena bent down to retrieve the fallen book, next to the wedged soccer ball. When she straightened, he was gone! The old man had vanished! A crow cawed—it was the same one that had scolded her earlier. She looked up and sunlight danced on black iridescent feathers. A second caw followed, long and melodious; it sounded like whispered laughter fading on the wind.

As she sat there in stunned disbelief, holding her copy of *A Separate Reality*, the bell in the clock tower tolled. She looked up—six o'clock. *What! How can that be?* As the bell chimed, notes in her mind resonated in words answering her own question: "Until the eye is fully opened…gong…there is much that remains unseen."

54

Another forty kilometers and he would finally be in Valladolid. What an ordeal! Still, several things that could have gone wrong didn't. Bryson had spent the first night in Los Lunas, next-to-last stop on the Rail Runner. Then, he turned in his bike at a Goodwill store and rented a car that he drove to El Paso, Texas. He paid cash and used his fake ID. In El Paso, he rented a different car at a different agency and paid extra insurance allowing him to drive into Mexico. He used his real name for the second rental. Eventually, he wanted to return back to the US. He had not committed any crimes but using a fake ID to cross the border could get him into trouble. Passing through at the small Tornillo, Texas border crossing driving a car with Texas plates would not raise any eyebrows. If asked, he had the proper IDs and paperwork and planned to explain he was meeting friends in Cancún and that he was afraid of flying. Nobody asked. Serena had called it—they are only concerned about who is coming back in. When NSA forensics and their analysts realized the raid gave them no credible evidence, he could safely return. For the moment, all the misery of driving the past few days, the discomfort of sleeping in obscure motels with a bed barely accommodating his tall frame, and the stress of constantly watching the road for state police and other official vehicles evaporated with the anticipation of finally seeing Serena. He couldn't wait!

She had given him the name of the hotel; her tour group had left, but she would wait for him in the lobby. It would have been nice if he had the Aussie bush hat she had sent or if he had thought of picking up a present or something to give to her. Instead, his Goodwill attire and the contents of his backpack would have to suffice. In that laptop and in his photographic memory he had some new data and information. Bryson thought he may have solved the rest of the puzzle. He only needed to wait a little longer to share his conclusions with Serena. At least he had shaved and showered. He pulled into the hotel parking lot, stretched his legs, and ambled to the front lobby entrance.

Through the glass he saw PTG seated, then standing and waving at him excitedly. He couldn't help but notice how great she looked—leaner, fitter, more alert. *Whoa she looks great! Is she taller? Look at the way she moves, like a jaguar... Awesome!*

Moments later, he engulfed her in his lanky arms, lifted her a foot in the air and held her in long embrace.

"It's good to see you, girlfriend!"

She had planned to say something witty, something cute about missing him; instead, hugging him back, choked up, all she managed to say was "Ditto!"

He kissed her forehead. "You look great...different. Not sure if it's the hair or the new toned tan look, but somehow you look taller."

"Really?" She stood on her tiptoes, almost did a backflip she felt so giddy, then regained her composure. "You look the same." She sniffed the air. "Did you take a shower today, stinky boy?"

"Yes." Feigning indignation he added, "It's good to smell you too!"

Following a brief reunion in the lobby, they got in the car and discussed strategy. They needed a plan. Serena updated him on her encounter with the mysterious old man. She handed him her copy of *A Separate Reality* but he pushed it back, reached into his backpack, and pulled out the copy he had already picked up in El Paso.

"Don't you just love the way Castaneda describes the warrior's path? He says that as the warrior gradually becomes more aware, he has to leave normal life behind and adopt a new way of life. Are you ready for that, PTG?" Then he added, "Not that either one of us is normal to begin with."

After making spooky *Twilight Zone* noises and poking her in the arm, he got serious. "I don't know what any of it means for certain, but some things are making more sense. I'm not sure about Peru, but the whole Circle training with the opening of your chakras is your training gig to become a warrior woman. I'm positive about that."

"Yeah, I kinda figured the same. What I don't understand is why my *shibizhi* didn't just come right out and say that from the start."

"It doesn't work that way, Serena. Don't you see? That's too rational, too left-brain." He pointed to the left side of his head. "These clues and the mystical experiences are part of your right brain absorbing and playing with the information. You can't just open your eyes and see it. It takes time to develop the sight."

"I like the way you put it. In a way, I know it…feel it, but I still don't fully see it. Still, it's coming into focus. At times I catch a glimpse, like when you are waking up from a dream but don't quite realize it yet. Bits and pieces swirl in my mind. I'm hoping Peru unlocks the last piece until I really see the whole picture."

"That's a long drive, PTG."

Her steely gray eyes bore down. "Who said we were driving?"

"Oh c'mon, you know I don't do flying."

"Man up, boyfriend. You can do this. What happened to the brave warrior archetype? It's not a video game, Bry. This is as serious as it gets. Don't think I'm not a little afraid. Believe me, I am, but I need you with me to continue this journey. You are in it with me. And we are in it to win it. I know it's outside your comfort zone, but sometimes you have to push the envelope."

He looked back at her, saying nothing. She watched his Adam's apple slide with a hard swallow. "Okay…let's do it."

He sat and stretched out his long legs. LAN Airways did not meet luxury standards, even in the first-class cabin of the Airbus A320. But he had a good seat from where he could watch the other passengers in first class. Charles Godfried always traveled first-class on his business trips. Now, poised for takeoff to Lima, Peru, he watched as the other passengers boarded. In front of him, his laptop was open showing a game of Yahtzee while he casually scrolled through images on his cell phone.

Tracking both Bryson's and Serena Mendez's accounts for activity was a piece-a-pie. The hairdresser in Valladolid responded informatively to a pittance—five hundred *pesos*, less than thirty bucks. Finding the hotel where the tour from Aztec Gold had stayed also yielded helpful intel; it didn't even cost him. He just said he was supposed to meet his younger brother and his girlfriend who had been on the tour. He tried his brother's cell, but there was no answer; maybe he'd dropped it. Heck, he was tall and so was Bryson, so it was more than plausible, even though a considerable age difference separated them. He showed a picture to the clerk. Yes, the tall American had met the much shorter girl, but the tour group had already left. Maybe the two were driving to Cancún to rejoin the tour.

The clerk at the hotel looked a little worried. Charles put her at ease by saying what a nice place she worked at and how lovely the city was; if he returned, he would be sure to stay there. That's when she dropped the bomb. Another man had been in earlier. He said he worked for the US Government, but he looked Chinese. He said the girl was a fugitive wanted for drug trafficking. Maybe she should have said nothing. She hoped his brother's girlfriend was not in any trouble; she seemed like a nice young woman.

The rest had been easy—checking flights out of Cancún with passengers named Bryson Reynolds, Serena Mendez, or Chanda Patel. They must be getting sloppy. The credit charge at the salon was more than a rookie mistake, but stuff like that put bread on his table. Bryson slipped a cog booking a flight under his real name. But the best part came as images continued to flash on his cell. The Asian man seated two seats ahead matched the picture on the phone. *Gensu Li, recently appointed head of security at Advanced Bionics. Snappy dresser!* It was a long enough flight and there would be plenty of opportunity. He fingered a tracking button. *An aisle seat too! Piece-a-pie,* he thought as he powered down his cell and read through what he had printed out earlier on Cajamarca, Peru. The name meant "town of thorns" or "cold place" depending on how you translated the native word. *Not exactly inviting to tourists,* he thought to himself. *Why are they headed there? It looks like a dump.*

55

Truthfully, it just didn't make sense. Bryson knew it did not make sense, but he still could not figure it out. He blamed Serena.

The flight over had been long, but cozy. She nestled against him and slept. After getting over some initial fear, he found a comfortable position resting his head on hers and slept a good part of the way. They talked…a lot. He explained everything he knew about DNA—its microcrystalline structure, four nucleotide bases linked according to specific rules in a double helix, sixty-four base pair combinations, etc. It was a remarkable molecule that emitted biophotons and could absorb light energy. Same was true of sound energy. The genetic compound responded to harmonic resonance as its structure was effectively an antenna. It operated like a dual oscillator that could both receive and transmit sound energy, as well as scalar electromagnetic waves.

From the perspective of a computer programmer familiar with coding principles, DNA was nothing less than phenomenal—a data and information repository unparalleled by even a supercomputer. Quantum computing might someday achieve this capability, but Mother Nature was years ahead of current information-storage technology. A thread of DNA is a billion times longer than its width. A typical person had DNA threads wiring their body on the order of 125 billion miles. You could store a mess of data on an information highway that long. Truth be known, scientists didn't know what most of the DNA did.

They labeled more than ninety-five percent as "junk." Mother Nature might disagree with that label. Anyway, he was still researching things. He had bought a copy of *Gene Keys—Unlocking the Higher Purpose Hidden in Your DNA*. The book kind of popped out at him when he was in the Barnes and Noble in El Paso; it looked interesting and relevant.

Serena had been doing research of her own. She explained that Quetzalcoatl meant "feathered serpent," although a different translation came up with "magnificent twin." In either case, it suggested a marriage or joining of earth and heaven. In Peru they named him Kukulkan and referred to the feathers as emerald plumes, a possible tie into Thoth and the emerald tablets. She told him about the sixth chakra and its relationship to the pineal gland, that the gland had a type of cell like those in the retina that could sense and respond to light stimulation. It produced melatonin that helped to regulate our sleep-wake cycle and tiny amounts of DMT, the so-called spirit molecule present in some hallucinogens. When she went on about Castaneda, how she had overlooked him and concentrated on the story he had written rather than the author himself, that's when things tickled Bryson's mind. That's what he blamed Serena for—a tickle he couldn't scratch that drove him crazy. There were dots there screaming to be connected.

She wanted to pick up the next book in the series, *Journey to Ixtlan*. It was a place in Mexico, but she couldn't make any definite connections just yet. That was it: "Ixtlan" was just a funny word to him. He didn't know why, but he just knew it. His mental itch intensified every time she mentioned that word. If Castaneda, and undoubtedly he represented the key, was traveling to the next place beyond *A Separate Reality*, shouldn't it be a mystical otherworldly place? Ixtlan, Mexico didn't seem to fit the bill.

Bryson had trained in cryptography theory from old Roman times through to present mathematical models and methods—substitution codices, transposition ciphers, cryptanalysis, elliptic curves, asymmetric-key cryptosystems, the list went on. NSA training and cybersecurity required extensive knowledge of cryptography. Castaneda used that word for a reason. Bryson was certain it contained an encrypted clue; he couldn't sleep.

His bed was comfortable enough, even for his height. The Costa del Sol Hotel had a nice central location and an airport shuttle. Their room included a cozy balcony overlooking the streets below. He opened the slider and sat with his laptop, entered "I-x-t-l-a-n" into several encryption decoding algorithms. Working through the comparatively slow processor in his portable computer, the analysis would probably take hours. The night air felt cool and refreshing. Mountains stood silhouetted in the half moonlight. He took out *Gene Keys* and read—interesting, but nothing clicked. *Maybe I should just call it a night, turn my brain off and let it recharge.*

When he woke, he found Serena busy doing yoga, or was it Tai Chi, or some kind of kickboxing? In his dreams he had flown to the sun, swam as a great sea serpent, and stretched from the earth to the stars in some crazy Tesla coil. The dreams were weird. He had a headache. He found his laptop. The decryption analyses had compiled absolutely nothing intelligible—a dead end for the moment.

"Where do you think we should start? I was thinking maybe the city hall equivalent where they keep municipal records." Bryson felt eager to begin their detective work.

"I'm game. I am feeling a little clueless. Maybe we could find Castaneda's old house or wherever he grew up, track down some cousins or relatives." She toweled the sweat off her lithe body.

The Ministry of Records had a birth listing but nothing more. They already had that information from biographical details on the web, although a lot of details about the author were murky, including information about his life and death. Their web research on the famous man revealed a shroud of mystery. Nothing in the municipal records showed what part of the city he may have lived in. Among phone listings, there were hundreds with the last name "Castaneda." They decided that could be a waste of time. The hotel clerk offered no suggestions, but he knew of a bookstore in walking distance. They could probably find English language versions of Castaneda's books there.

"*Libros De Cabra Con Barba*"—Serena translated for him: "Bearded Goat Books." The shop had some new, but mostly used books. It also had incense, crystals, tarot cards, and all sorts of arcane-mystical items. It reminded them of shops in Taos and Santa Fe. A woman in her thirties holding an infant tried to assist them, but the baby was fussy, cranky. "He is hungry," she explained in broken English.

"Abuela, tengo que alimentar al bebé; tenemos clientes." She exited to a curtained back room as an old woman using a walker made her way toward them. Her face had a thousand wrinkles; she was almost deaf.

Serena did her best to explain what they wanted, but the old woman was hard of hearing. Serena felt bad that she had to yell at the woman. They were looking for books by Carlos Castaneda. The old shopkeeper grew a little animated as they asked; she hobbled toward a section in the back of the store. She explained, and Serena translated for Bryson. Castaneda enjoyed some notoriety as a celebrity, mostly years ago, not so much now. When she had first opened the store, when she was much younger and much prettier, she had met him. He liked her store. The old woman paused and basked in memories of her youth.

They found a used English copy of *Journey to Ixtlan.*

"Después de él, él nunca volvió." She looked mournful when they were paying for their purchase.

"¿A dónde fueron?"

"Después de él habló al que sueños con los ojos abiertos, se fue a América." The old woman sighed; the granddaughter returned.

"¿Quién es esta persona que sueña con los ojos abiertos? ¿Dónde está?" Serena spoke. Bryson sensed hope and excitement in her voice, but he had no idea what she was asking.

The granddaughter escorted them to the front of the shop and pointed in the distance. Her child slept contentedly. In her broken English, she communicated that he lived somewhere near the top of that mountain in a cave. *"Él es un* shape-shifter. Some call him *el gran cóndor que mira hacia abajo desde arriba."* She clutched her young son as though fearful a great bird would swoop down and snatch him from her. Frightened, she turned to her grandmother, who nodded.

How the old woman heard her granddaughter's speech, despite near deafness, occurred to neither Serena nor Bryson. She muttered, «*Mientras tomaba Carlos.*"

They stood outside, and Serena pointed to a distant peak. "That's where we need to go." She spoke authoritatively.

"Excuse me. But could you share with me what the hell that was all about?"

"Sorry. The old woman knew Castaneda a little. I have the sense she was attracted to him or something. Anyway, he left for America after he spoke to some kind of a shaman who lives in a cave up there." She pointed again. "Her granddaughter called him a shape-shifting condor who looks down from above or something like that. Did you see the way she held her baby?"

"I saw that she looked afraid."

"The old woman claims he took Castaneda. Oh, she also called this shaman a different name, 'the one who dreams with his eyes open.' I'm thinking he's our man."

56

They had a plan. The two friends finished dinner, a wonderful medley of local cuisine with many fabulous cheeses. Cajamarca had fertile soil and the local dairy and agricultural offerings from this high Andean city were fantastic. And the coffee... Serena quickly decided the Peruvian roast at this small *cocina-café* was possibly the best she had ever enjoyed. She sipped a third cup.

Armondo, the front desk attendant at their hotel, overextended hospitality in answering their questions and offering suggestions. The mountain they wanted to visit, Cerro Colpayoj, was only fifteen or twenty kilometers away. They could walk there and enjoy the hiking trails. If desired, he could pick them up early tomorrow and drive them to the hiking trails before his work shift started. They could walk back or call him, and he could arrange to have them picked up. Or they could rent bikes and travel that way, maybe continue to visit Llullapuquio, a very nice town to the northwest. They could even stay overnight at a campground, but he did not recommend that as it might get cold at night. He could put a hold on their room.

They decided on the bikes and had already rented them. The bike shop the clerk had sent them to gladly rented overnight; they had left the rentals safely locked in their hotel room. Tomorrow they would get an early start—maps, plenty of water, some power bars, and fleece pullovers—all packed and ready to go. Armondo laughed when they asked about *"el gran cóndor que mira hacia abajo desde arriba."*

"The 'great condor who looks down from above'—a tale to scare little children when they misbehave. My mother used to tell it to me. Unfortunately, *señorita,* it did not stop me from getting into trouble." When he laughed, it had the honesty and musical sound of someone who is carefree and happy, much like all the people they encountered in this marvelous city.

"I have heard there is an old hermit who lives in a cave there, but that too may just be a story. There are many stories in this land."

"Thank you, Armondo. Is everyone in Cajamarca as happy as you?" Bryson popped a mint from a bowl on the front desk into his mouth.

"Si, señor, it is the fresh mountain air and beauty of this region. How can we not be happy amidst such blessings?"

They paid for their inexpensive meal in *soles* and walked back to the Costa del Sol. The Spanish colonial architecture, the agave and prickly pear cacti, and the hilly, high elevation reminded them both of home. For Serena, it seemed ages ago since she had been in New Mexico.

"When do you think we can go back home?" She held Bryson's hand as they leisurely strolled, enjoying the twilight.

"Part of me thinks it would be nice to stay here as long as possible, but that's selfish. I think I'll be cleared of any foul play within a week. I'm more worried about you."

"We should just take it one day at a time. Tomorrow we try and find the shaman. If there's still time, I want to check out the Inca baths close by."

"But what then? You are safe for the moment, but don't think these Illuminati types, or whoever they are, aren't still trying to hunt you down."

"I know. I try not to think about it."

They sat on a bench. "I've been thinking about it a lot. I've been asking myself some questions lately about why your great aunt would send you on this Candelaria mission to get chakra openings and training. Why she would probably have you as an apprentice if she had lived. Hear me out and see if it makes sense to you."

Bryson shared his thoughts. He worked off the premise that a Candelaria had a special genetic profile but that it had to somehow become activated. The chakra openings were part of the activation process, but Ooljee would have to have a purpose behind mentoring Serena along the path. Put in the dual context of some ancient historical alteration or corruption of DNA and some battle between a group wanting to withhold information and another group wanting to share information, Bryson speculated that once the Candelaria genetic potential became fully activated, maybe it gave them special powers or abilities such as the voice.

"But what good would that really be? One very powerful person against an entire group opposing that single individual? There has to be more and here's what I am leading up to. This Thoth person, apparently from Atlantis, seemed to live a very long time. We know he had major influence in Egypt, Greece, and Mesoamerica. It looks as though he spread out pieces of knowledge, ancient technology, and wisdom through these mystery schools that he set up in different places."

"I'm following you, but I don't quite see where you are going."

"Think about it. A lot of advanced healing seems part of what they taught at the Temple of Hygeia. In Egypt, they were apparently masters at controlling this life force energy. I even read that Isis could supposedly stop a person with just the command in her voice. That's just one way they harness this life energy. Often, it's priests and priestesses that hold these arcane teachings. What is different here in Peru and in Mexico? It isn't priests or priestesses, it's shamans who hold the wisdom. In fact, that's true worldwide; you saw it in Australia. Same goes for your *shibízhí*. They are the masters of the dream world and altered states of consciousness. Sometimes they get there using sacred plants. The separate reality, 'Ixtlan,' wherever that truly is and how to journey there, is just another part of what Thoth felt was important for people to learn about."

"Sure, I get what you're saying, everything you have said makes sense, but what happens when you have all this ancient knowledge?"

It wasn't the smile on his face; it wasn't the intense look in his blue eyes; rather, it was the conviction in his voice. "Those pyramids in Egypt, probably same as the ones here, they are more than burial tombs. Everything we now know points to Egyptians being obsessed with immortality. How many thousands of years did Thoth supposedly live? What if completing your Circle training enables you to access all this Atlantean wisdom; what if it somehow gives you some kind of immortality?"

He stopped a moment to study his companion. "I'll tell you what, warrior girl; you could do some serious damage against the forces of darkness if that is what your *shibizhí* had in mind. One powerful person fighting for truth over hundreds of years would be a force to be reckoned with."

Serena looked with an unfocused gaze while absently staring at Venus, the evening star. She carried a burden that she didn't comprehend. "Thanks. We better get back. Tomorrow could be a big day."

They got up from the bench. After walking a dozen yards, Serena stopped, faced Bryson and said, "I didn't ask for this… I wish my great aunt was still around to tell me what I'm supposed to do… I want it all to work out according to plan, even though I don't know what the plan is… But I do know one thing. I know I'm glad you believe in me, and that you're right here with me."

She stood on her toes and kissed him—not a peck, but a soulful joining between their lips, locked a moment in embrace. For that moment, heaven and earth met, time stopped, and then they continued back to the hotel, each lost in the silence of their thoughts.

57

He jumped out of bed. *Of course, why didn't I think of that sooner?* Bryson entered a new sequence into the decryption program and tore open *Gene Keys: Unlocking the Higher Purpose Hidden in Your DNA. Of course! How did I miss this?*

"PTG, wake up," he whispered, but got no response. "Hey, you, wake up. You're gonna love this!"

Bleary-eyed, Serena murmured, "What time is it?"

"I don't know, two o'clock or something like that."

"What's so important at two o'clock in the morning?"

"It popped into my head during my sleep. It's all right here."

"Bry!" She sounded annoyed. "I can't read your mind. What are you talking about?" She could see his nerd-boyish enthusiasm on full display. It softened her. "Okay, Mr. Genius, you have my full attention."

"Ixtlan is really Ixland—they sound the same."

"Yes, they do…so?"

He felt awfully proud of himself at that moment. He grabbed a piece of paper, writing in capital letters "IXLAND." "If you spell it backwards, what do you get?" "DNALXI"; he turned the paper toward her.

"Yes, that is 'Ixland' spelled backwards and I still don't see it as worth being roused from a deep slumber." An annoyed yawn followed.

"Ahh, Grasshopper…observe." He drew a line separating DNA from LXI.

"Yep, that clears it up entirely—DNA/LXI… Not!"

"The DNA part is clear. The second string isn't a word; it's a number—Roman numerals, actually. DNA 61." He grabbed his gene book. "Would you like to know a little more about the sixty-first gene key? That's why I woke you up."

Now he had sparked her attention. "This *Gene Keys* book explains what is unique and special about each of sixty-four different genetic keys. Each gene key has unique characteristics that affect personality, development, strengths, weaknesses, and a host of other attributes both physical and metaphysical. The sixty-first is remarkable. It attunes us with the true nature of mind and how we perceive reality."

She yawned again. "My current reality is that I'm beat, and we have a busy day tomorrow."

Undeterred, Bryson continued. "This gene has something to do with human awareness. You can read the details in the book later, but the author is very specific. It controls the communication between the left and the right hemispheres of the brain. It all centers on the pineal gland which acts as a type of doorway to open awareness and allow us to perceive the infinite. The sixty-first gene key is another corner piece to the puzzle. Don't you see that?"

"Not really. You seem convinced. Other than the pineal being associated with my next chakra opening, I don't see the connection... Wait!" She jumped out of bed. "The crow...the pan flute player in Mexico..."

The Nagual musician's words returned with the clarity of the cathedral bell. "Until the eye is fully opened…gong…there is much that remains unseen…gong… How do you decide what is truth and what is illusion? Until the eye is fully opened, there is much that remains unseen."

"That's it. In order to distinguish truth from illusion, you must activate the pineal. You're brilliant!" She pulled him forward and kissed him on the cheek.

"Yes!" Bryson pointed first to his own, then to Serena's forehead. "This is the place where all Western and Eastern mystical traditions arrived—enlightenment, Samadhi, nirvana, etc." He shut the book. "It's what the Gnostics taught as the way to the divine. The opening of your pineal gland—the third eye, your sixth chakra, is tied into this gene. I'll bet you a thousand tacos the sixty-first gene is the one that got messed around with at the time of the second breaking. That genetic engineering prevents us from advancing to enlightenment. Not that enlightenment still can't happen; it's just a lot harder. Besides, powermongers could never control or mind-manipulate people who were enlightened at this level. This is awesome! It's how you consciously become aware of matter and spirit and how they dance with each other—all the things your great aunt referred to. The 'Journey to Ixtlan,' or getting there, requires you to open your third eye."

His laptop chimed: "Analysis complete." He smiled as he positioned the screen for her to read the result: CCASTENEDA = CANDELARIA. He watched her expression; it defied description.

"Holy shit! Do you think my *shibízhí* knew that?"

At the knock, Big Mike swiveled his desk chair away from the monitor on his side table. The report file remained open.

"Come on in."

Roberta Reardon entered timidly. Fingerprints smudged her horn-rimmed glasses. "You wanted to see me, sir?"

"I just reviewed your final report on the Operation Mesa Gold fiasco. Have a seat." He motioned to a chair.

"Yes, sir." She withered into the chair.

"It says that somehow the computer mainframe caught fire and essentially nothing could be recovered. Do you really think the home security system triggered a circuit overload?"

"That was the opinion of the fire chief. I cannot offer another credible explanation."

"How about something *incredible*?" He leaned forward. "Speculate. Think outside the box."

"It could have been done intentionally if there was some security link access and an operator triggered the meltdown at the time the raid breeched the interior."

"Good. Next time put that in your report. How about the laptop we confiscated?"

"Probably planted there. Nothing of value. I put that in the report."

"What about the way things ended? I know you had left the previous day. Do you buy the booby traps with tear gas? Do you think the power cut off by mistake? Do you think someone tipped the US Marshal Service off that a wanted criminal would just happen to be arriving at the same time as this foreign delegation from Britain, this…" He looked back at the computer screen. "Barrister Fulbright?"

He studied the young analyst. "What do you make of it all?"

"Sir, I read the file on Bryson Reynolds. I'm sure you have as well. Did you really want me to put in the report that he outsmarted three government agencies, if you include Homeland, and some wealthy influential foreigners? I could have put that in writing, but it makes us look bad. It makes our government look bad. It makes you look bad since you sent me over as part of the team. I didn't say all those things, but that doesn't mean they didn't occur to me." She crossed her arms and locked eyes with her boss.

"What did you learn?"

"Field work is okay, but being an analyst is where all the excitement is. I want to be as good as Bryson Reynolds one day. I know he doesn't work for us anymore, but the guy is a genius!"

"Good."

"You mean you're not angry with me?"

"Not at all. I like the way you reasoned it out and also appreciate the sensitivity of not embarrassing a whole lot of people. It's good, Roberta. We need bright people like you. Now get back to work."

She left. He swiveled back and closed the file. *Goddamned waste of taxpayer money!*

58

They left before breakfast. In no time they had biked out of the city proper and found themselves in the high Andean countryside. A cool mountain mist evaporated in the early morning sun. The world felt alive and refreshed. People on horseback waved or smiled. They passed children who tended small herds of sheep lazily foraging the hillside vegetation.

"How come we hardly ever do this when we're back home?" Serena gulped some bottled water. They had pulled over at a grassy bend and rested beneath some kind of tree neither recognized.

"What do you mean? I went biking less than a week ago." He joked about his nighttime escape from the government raid. He pointed to the mountain, still shrouded in mist but now much closer. "It wasn't nearly as beautiful though."

"It seems everywhere I've been the last couple of months I've fallen in love with. Well, Egypt not so much, but that's only because of circumstances. I will go back there some day and see the sights, meet the people. I'm sure they're wonderful, just like everywhere I've been."

"Well, I haven't traveled much, but now that I've learned you can fly safely and how beautiful the rest of the world is, I think I'll come out of my little bubble."

"You're not the only one who has been living in a bubble."

"When everything settles down, maybe we can do some traveling together." He placed his helmet back on and straddled his mountain bike.

A tingle erupted just above her saddle; it wasn't from the seat. "I'd like that." She pedaled on ahead with extra vigor.

Cerro Colpayoj stood at 12,159 feet. Horse trails and old mining roads made this a biking heaven. They passed a camping area, but few other riders. The problem was the many trails were mostly unmarked. They asked hikers if they knew about the hermit in the cave, the one who dreams with eyes open, the condor who looks down from above. Unfortunately, the group was German; they had never heard of him. An old peasant tried to coax a cow to leave a patch of grass and join the rest of the herd; she knew the stories. As to where to find the shaman, she shrugged, explaining it was only possible to find him if the shaman wanted to be found.

Three hours since starting, the air still felt crisp, but they were both sweating from exertion. Even coming from the high desert elevations of back home, they needed to rest and catch their breath. No trails led to the summit. They figured they had already zigzagged around the mountain once. A stream trickled nearby.

"I wouldn't mind getting my feet wet a little." Serena explored for the stream. "Found it." A goat bleated. "Looks like someone else found it too."

Bryson joined her, and the goat bleated again. "Hey, do you mind sharing?" he asked, but with a quizzical look and a long "baa," the goat jumped to the other side of the stream and disappeared.

With pant legs rolled up and feet dangling in the water, the two silently reveled in nature's beauty. Wordlessly, Bryson rose, took two or three gawky steps to cross the water, and put on his hiking boots.

"What are you doing?" Serena still sat on a rock.

"Just a hunch. I'm going to follow the goat. There's water here. Looks like there could be caves over there." He pointed. "Be back in a few minutes."

"I'll watch the bikes." But he had already disappeared.

Seated in lotus position she quickly entered a deep meditation. Fifteen minutes later, Bryson returned.

"Let's get the bikes. I found something." It was about 11 AM.

On the side of the mountain, a small clearing showed a fire pit, clothes drying in the sun, a small herb garden, and a goat. The clearing ended where a steep ravine showed below; beyond that, the distant rooftops and streets of Cajamarca lay flanked by hills and farms. A cave opened at the back end.

"*Hola,*" Bryson called tentatively as the goat looked on while contentedly chewing a shrub.

Perfectly good English responded, "Come in; it's open." A chuckle followed. "I thought you would never get here." The two looked at each other. "Carmelita grew tired of waiting." The goat bleated again. "She went out to look for you."

Serena whispered to Bryson, "I think we found him."

As they entered, a man not much taller than Serena stood up from the only chair, more of a stool, something hand-hewn from a log. A small table had a burning bowl with curls of smoke drifting in the dim light; an unfamiliar smell greeted their nostrils. He was old—white hair, hobbled gait, thin and frail. Yet, his eyes shone with power and energy. Deep, dark, intense, he stared at the two. As he studied them, each felt stripped down and naked in front of the old shaman's scrutiny.

Finally, he spoke. "A crow whispered in my ear a few days ago. Last night I dreamed a red dragon came to visit, but a scorpion kissed him with its tail and he fell down dead only to be eaten by wolves, his bones picked clean by vultures."

They remained silent at first, unsure how to respond to that opening. Eventually they introduced themselves. He seemed amused at the formalities.

"I have many names; some I have forgotten; some I still remember. You can call me Sam."

"Sam? It seems a surprise."

He shrugged. "Easy to remember."

From outside the cave, Carmelita bleated, "Saaammm."

"Easy to pronounce too." Another chuckle echoed in the cave.

He explained a little about himself, how he rode the currents of thought and time and heard the whispers on the wind, his initiation into shamanism, and so on. He covered a lot of mystical ground. Some of it made sense, much of it did not, but he continued undeterred with no offer to explain further. He seemed to like to talk and did not like to be interrupted. It was past noon. They took out their power bars, but he confiscated them and threw them with force into the fire pit.

"This is not food. Besides, you must fast for the opening."

They looked at one another, not challenging the old man.

"Opening?" Serena asked.

He ignored her question. "You have not had any alcohol or sex for at least three days. This is true, yes? Otherwise, we cannot have the ceremony."

Bryson and Serena both shook their heads emphatically. They both blushed a deep shade of crimson.

"Good. It's important to abstain and fast from certain things to be properly prepared, but you can have tea." At that moment a kettle whistled on a tiny cookstove, and Sam produced three clay mugs.

Bryson whispered to Serena, "This isn't a cave. It's a rabbit hole and we've gone way down deep."

As they sipped tea, Sam continued to speak. He was surprisingly talkative, perhaps because he seldom had visitors. They had not even told him about why they were in Peru, but when he poured himself another cup, they had just enough time to give him a brief summary. They politely declined a refill of the bitter brew. He seemed bored as they recounted the scantest details.

He held up his hand to silence further storytelling. They had not even gotten to the part about opening the last chakra. "This great snake war—so foolish, so unwise. A waste of time! The great teachers have told us all we need to do and given us all the means to do so." That was all the explanation he offered. Instead, he launched into a series of dreams. It seemed much of his knowledge came from dreams and dream interpretation.

> "I dreamed once when I was a young man, that I was a condor sitting high atop a tree watching the moon rise. As I stared at the moon, a black dot appeared and grew larger and larger until I could see it was an eagle from the North. She was young and beautiful and saw me high in the treetop. When she came, we made love as stars sprinkled drops of light upon our feathers.
>
> In the day, we flew together to the highest mountain top, where the earth and sky come together, and we looked down upon the world below and we looked up upon the world above. We stood perched between the two worlds and we made love again.
>
> That was a special day for the moon overcame the sun in shadow, and complete darkness surrounded us. Where sky ended and earth began neither of us could say. The eagle turned to light, kissed me goodbye, and flew back to the moon. I watched

as she grew smaller and smaller until she was only a dot of light against the black moon.

When the shadow gave way to the light of the sun, I flew back to my treetop and pondered this dream."

He looked at Serena. "You remind me of that eagle.

"A young man came to me once and I saw that he flew as a condor, a younger brother asking me what his dreams revealed. We drank the sacred medicine and he dreamed he flew to nest among the eagles in a giant cactus. I told him to seek a great warrior among the Nagual and to learn the sight from above so that he too would become a great warrior.

"You remind me of that man." He looked at Bryson who was evidently surprised by this. "Do not look so confused.

"Long ago, I dreamt of a young snake who came upon a young eagle, not ready to fly. Afraid the bird would eat it, the snake bit the eagle on the leg. But the bird did not die; instead, it fell into a deep dream sleep. When it awoke, it could fly higher and see further than any of its kind."

He addressed Bryson again. "You remind me of that eagle." Then he turned back to Serena.

"In my youth, the snake mother came to me in a dream and told me to learn the tongue of the eagle, for this was the time of the eagle, but the wheel would turn before I took my last flight and the condor would soar again. The wheel of time has turned. A few weeks ago, I dreamt a great ibis flew from the place of the pyramids, not those we have here, but the place of the first men. The ibis carried a baby snake and placed the snake at the foot of my cave and flew away."

He stared at Serena. "You remind me of that snake."

Abruptly, he got up, and they followed the shaman outside. "Now it is time for your gift."

"Gift? I'm...I'm sorry; we didn't bring any gift." Silently, she kicked herself. *You seek out a holy man in a cave; shouldn't you bring some kind of gift or tribute?*

Sam waved his hand. "Bah, of course you did. You brought him." He turned to Bryson who looked more confused than ever. Sam escorted the young man to a nearby tree and pointed to a branch overhead. "That is my walking stick. A man as old as I am needs help sometimes. The tree said I can have it if I can get it, but I am too short. I think she mocks my height as she is so tall." He waggled a crooked finger at the tree.

Even with his tall frame and long arms, Bryson could not reach the branch. It grew straight and looked quite sturdy, and probably would make an excellent walking staff. Maybe he could jump up and yank it down.

As he studied possible solutions, the old man disappeared and returned with his chair and a short ax. "Here, use this and try not to hurt the tree. I like to perch in her branches sometimes." He handed Bryson the ax, placed his hands on the tree, and whispered something in a foreign tongue. The leaves rustled.

Moving right down that rabbit hole a little further. I wonder how deep it goes? Bryson stood on the stool and took a swipe at the branch making a first cut. The leaves shook again. He winced. "Sorry!"

59

Sam busied himself with preparations. The ceremony had to be at night. He had become strangely silent. When Serena asked about what the ceremony was for, he looked at her sternly, thumped her between her brows, and muttered something about third eye. Periodically he went inside and sang softly to some concoction simmering on the cookstove. When she asked him what was brewing, he looked at her as though she was speaking a foreign language. Shaking his head disapprovingly, he muttered, "Ayahuasca." They would be awake most of the night, so he encouraged them to rest. He brought out two woven straw mats and two shallow clay basins, placing one by each mat. She asked about the clay basins and again, he looked at her as though she was hopelessly dense. This time he shrugged and again repeated, "Ayahuasca." He smiled a moment before he added, "You will see."

Bryson had returned with the branch, chair, and hatchet. When the old man held the future staff, he nodded his approval, went off to the tree, pressed his hand against it, and sang some words. When the sap running from the fresh cut stopped, he returned to the cave.

Serena lay on a mat, hands behind her head, but she didn't feel at all tired. She turned to Bryson on the adjacent mat. "What do you know about ayahuasca?"

"Not much. I remember some of the free-spirited guys I worked with in Silicon Valley were talking about heading to the Amazon and trying it. It's hallucinogenic. I wasn't too keen on messing with my mind. I figured when I got bit by that snake when I was young, I had enough hallucinations to last a lifetime."

"I don't know much either. I read that entheogens can open the sixth chakra, but I feel the same way as you. I'm not keen on hallucinating. I spent years with shrinks trying to not be crazy."

"Why are you asking? We're supposed to be trying to get some sleep."

"Because, Bry, that's what Sam is cooking inside the cave. We're supposed to drink it tonight during some kind of ceremony."

"What!" He got up and checked his cell phone for service, but they were out of range. Bryson was accustomed to having information at his fingertips. He didn't like venturing into the unknown. "Are you going to try it?"

"I don't know."

"Do you trust him?"

"I don't know."

Strangely, Bryson warmed to the possibility. Yes, it was outside his comfort zone, but the same had been true about flying, and that had turned out okay. He faced Serena, looking at her gray eyes, and whispered, "I'll try it if you will too."

"Really?" She drew courage from his willingness to head into the unknown.

His nose sort of wrinkled. "How bad can it be?"

"Let's do it." She lay there staring at the clouds, watching animal shapes form and dissolve. To her surprise, Bryson began to snore on the mat next to her. It was about 5 PM. Although she had been hungry earlier, she had lost her appetite. She practiced meditation to connect to her stillness within. *It will be fine. Everything will be fine. Trust...*

Finding the hotel where the girl stayed had taken longer than expected. The desk clerk there said he put a hold on the room, but they were expected back later. He got to the bike shop just before closing. The bikes hadn't been returned, and the shop owner worried the two Americans might have stolen them. Fortunately, GPS locators were on all the overnight rentals. The owner knew exactly where the bikes were and didn't need much convincing to share the information. It was getting late on the mountain. Unlikely the two Americans would go anywhere tonight. Tomorrow morning, Gensu would surprise them. Now, he had shopping to do.

It wasn't difficult to find stores still open that had what he wanted. A short while later, Gensu Li liked how he looked in his new Patagonia Elite Defense M10 jacket. The sleeves were a little long, but the camo motif would do just fine. He admired the curve of his new Condor Parang machete—positively elegant, almost like a samurai blade. His final item did not require an open store. A few phone calls, a rendezvous spot, followed by a generous cash exchange, and he held another new purchase. The Glock 40 Gen4 10mm sported a nice balance. Two loaded magazines gave him thirty rounds. The pistol and accessories would go well in his collection. Tomorrow, he planned to do some hunting.

❖   ❖   ❖

Across town, Armondo had come on for night duty. Claus Gorman, posing as Charles Godfried, pretending to be the older brother of Bryson Reynolds, used the same story about hooking up with his brother and girlfriend. He was supposed to meet them here at the Costa del Sol, but Bryson wasn't answering his phone.

"*Señor,* that is likely because there is no cell service in the mountains. They went biking over at Cerro Colpayoj. They were expected back today, but they must have decided to spend the night. Not a problem, we are holding their room." He laughed.

"Why is this funny, Armondo?"

"Oh, I am sorry, *señor;* they were looking for a hermit, a powerful shaman, who lives in a cave on the side of the mountain. I think it is only a myth, but who knows? Maybe they found him."

It took a while and quite a few questions, but eventually he found someone who claimed to have visited the *ayahuasquero.* He gave enough information about where the cave was located that Claus thought he could find it tomorrow. He packed his gear and checked his rental jeep. Back in the hotel room he monitored Gensu Li with the tracking button he had planted on his adversary's jacket. Gensu had booked in the best hotel in Cajamarca; or at least that's where his jacket was.

60

They both had been dozing when Sam announced the time had arrived. A fire crackled; it bathed their wide-eyed faces with warmth.

"First, you should know that I am here to guide you and also to protect. No spirits will enter you as long as you remain pure in your intent and I remain with you. Do you understand this?"

They spoke simultaneously. "Not really."

"Good; an honest answer. You will do fine. The first opening is always the most difficult. When you enter the dream and spirit realms still awake, it is hard for your awareness to comprehend. It is best to just look and listen and absorb what is. Remain in the clearing." He pointed to the edge adding, "It is a long way down."

They nodded their understanding.

"What do you seek in the opening of the eye?"

"Wisdom." It was the first thing that popped into Bryson's mind.

"Truth," she responded.

His yellow teeth looked orange in the flame's light as he smiled with approval. "The code of the warriors." He picked a brand from the fire and lit a pipe that he passed to each of them before inhaling a long draft. He exhaled, "*Toe.*"

Neither knew what *toe* was; it wasn't harsh like tobacco, sweeter. They had no clue what the *toe's* effect would be. They simply did as instructed. Despite the anxiety and uncertainty about what would occur next, they felt a calm clarity. The shaman instilled confidence. He passed around a cup, announcing, "Ayahuasca, sacred medicine taught to us by the old ones." Each drank half; he instructed them to sit on their mats. The reddish-brown liquid tasted horrible. Clouds drifted past the starry sky. It was about 9:30. He began to sing.

A few minutes after sitting, intense nausea gripped Serena; she grabbed the clay basin and retched violently. She turned to Bryson and saw him heaving. The singing stopped for a moment, and they heard Sam say, "We have another word for the sacred medicine—*kamarampi*—that which causes one to vomit. It is how we clean out the old to open way for the new." The singing resumed…and the world began to change.

Scintillating sparkles seemed to be all around, and for a moment, Serena thought all the stars danced and twinkled around her in some pyrotechnic kaleidoscope of light. The singing had become angelic; a chorus of musical notes and voices surrounded her in sweet melody. She looked at Sam, but he had transformed. There was nothing feeble in the old man's appearance; he looked vibrant, strong, and he brimmed with power. Threads of light emanated from him, to him, and through him, and she could see his aura or energy surrounding and enveloping him like some translucent multicolored misty egg, amorphous yet formed. When he looked at her, the thought erupted in her head: walk around.

She didn't really want to walk around as there was so much to see, feel, and listen to just seated, but she followed the command. A plant she hadn't noticed earlier seemed to call out, and she bent forward to examine it. The leaves shimmered in luminescence; the plant emitted a unique sound, part of the chorus of music surrounding her. Everything teemed with life. Carmelita the goat stood bathed in light, looked at Serena for a moment, and it seemed for an instant as though they were one. She felt what it was like to chew the brambles, watch for wolves, feel thirsty, and find refreshment at the stream. She turned to the tree whose branch Bryson had cut, walked there, and gently placed her hands on the bark, caressing it. The tree had a feminine nature, she couldn't say why, but she knew it. The spirit of the tree reached out in song and Serena understood what it was like to have the rain upon her leaves, the birds nesting among her branches, storms and sunlight and wind and mountain mist feeding her, testing her strength. Everywhere she looked, everywhere she touched, seemed alive, radiant, and filled with song. Suddenly, she threw up again, and the vision subsided.

Bryson looked around; nothing made sense. The world pulsated with light and sound. He could hear Sam singing, but it seemed far away. Then he realized he was floating—or was it flying? The world below grew smaller, then he caught sight of a rope, or was it a vine? It reminded him of Jack and the Beanstalk, except it was a ladder, a glowing twisted ladder down to the earth below and extending to the sky above. He grabbed hold and climbed. As far as he could see the ladder continued spiraling out to the stars. He was among the stars; they sang to him. The earth below was bathed in a soft rainbow of light. He clung to the rope ladder; it was alive and singing to him as well. He sang, joining in the cosmic symphony of light and sound. He looked at his hands and feet and they were alive with light; every cell in his body seemed awake. He wanted to laugh and dance; instead, he began to vomit violently. He was falling, falling back to the earth which grew larger and larger, closer and closer; then a giant bird, glowing and bathed in light, caught his fall and they descended gently. The bird sang; it was Sam's voice telling him to lay still and rest. He retched again and lay still.

For a moment, Serena saw Gurumarra, but it was just his head. His body was a crocodile, but he wore the same stovepipe hat, had the same toothless smile. He whispered, "Galinawa," and then he swam away. A great luminous snake, fifty or a hundred feet long, approached. Serena knew it was the spirit of Gaia herself. They looked at one another and Serena recognized her mother, for she herself had transformed to a baby snake. Happily, she slithered and undulated. Suddenly, a firm hand grabbed her in a talonlike grip. She was at the precipice, at the edge of the clearing. Sam guided her back. Spirit beings rose from rocks talking among themselves, speaking to her, but she did not understand them. Lying down, a bug flew down next to her. It was beautiful. She studied it, some type of beetle; it too sang to her and then it lit up in a flash of light—a lightning bug! She heard her Ooljee laughing. "Welcome, *ch'osh bikq'i*." Her laughter sounded like the most beautiful wind chimes she had ever heard. Serena looked again, but no one was there, and nausea again overcame her in fierce waves.

Everywhere he turned Bryson saw snakes—snakes in the plants, snakes in the insects, snakes in the trees and animals. The world was full of writhing, slithering snakes and then he saw they were all dancing. A music and melody choreographed the dance, and the movements produced a harmony; everything sang and danced in an ecstatic snake rhapsody. Then Bryson turned into a snake, joined in the rhythm, adding his song to the symphony. A great luminous serpent smiled and sang to her children. Lights and sounds enveloped him. The beauty and harmony of an infinite music surrounded him, and he was just a part of the great celebration. It ended abruptly with repeated heaves. He felt his insides retch until he thought there was nothing left in him that hadn't spilled out onto the ground or into the bowl. It didn't matter.

For at least six hours Serena and Bryson vacillated between this world and another reality, broken by violent spasms of emesis. All the while, Sam sang to them or whistled sweet music until the visions of color and light and sound and spirit forms faded. They slept.

61

A bleat and a nudge by Carmelita stirred them. The bright morning sun hurt their eyes. The basins had been removed, and Sam was nowhere to be seen. Serena attempted to rise but immediately lay back down, pushed back by weakness and thirst. Something cooked in a cast-iron pot over the fire pit, but the smell caused her to dry heave.

Not quite ready for breakfast. She used her sleeve to wipe some spittle. "I puked my guts out last night." As soon as she spoke, a burst of color filled her mind.

Bryson had no intention of getting up. "Tell me about it. If I ever need to purge, I'll just think about *kamarampi.*"

A similar burst of color flashed in her visual field when he spoke. "What did you say?"

"I said if I need to throw up, I'll think of this ayahuasca adventure."

"That's totally weird." A blue-green bubble burst. "That's totally weird." A second blue-green bubble formed and burst. "Every time one of us speaks, I hear the words but also see an accompanying flash of light or color, a shape." As she spoke, a rainbow image of light formed then fled.

"There's a word for that. It's called synesthesia; it's when two senses simultaneously react to a stimulus. In your case, sound is activating part of your visual cortex or something like that. Watch, err, I mean listen…actually both… 'Serena Mendez'… What did you see?"

"Kind of a yellow pear shape, then a circle of red."

"Try again… 'Serena Mendez'… What did you see?"

"Same image, shapes, and colors as before. It only flashes a moment. It's really weird."

"I hope this psychedelic stuff we drank didn't mess up our brains too much. I feel drained, but otherwise okay. How about you? How do you feel, what did you see last night?" He looked at her as he tried to shake the cobwebs from his head.

They compared notes. Each time Bryson spoke, or another sound occurred, such as a howl of wind, she experienced some associated light or color. They both tried to process their experiences.

"Do you think this sensory crossover, this synesthesia, will fade or do you think it's permanent?"

"It might," Sam answered. He arrived carrying roots and leaves. He added them to the pot and stirred. "If you received the sound-sight, that is a rare gift. Sometimes it stays, sometimes it does not. For now, see how sound and light are related; they are in everything you see and everything that you do not see."

Serena tried to sit up cautiously and promptly collapsed back down. "Last night, everything I looked at seemed to have some sound frequency or vibration connected to it. Lights and colors were all over the place."

"Same for me," Bryson chimed.

Sam looked at the two of them as a parent might look impatiently at a young child. "Of course! Sound and light make up creation. This has been known to us for thousands of years, but people have forgotten." He shook his head. "What do they teach you in school?"

Serena answered, "Language, arithmetic, reading, art, history…"

He stopped her with a scowl and a wave of his hands. "You know nothing of history."

Bryson changed the subject. "How about snakes? We both saw a lot of snakes and some of them talked."

"Of course; snakes are in everything!" He sounded exasperated, even angry. "Without snakes we would not be alive."

Serena countered. Somehow, she managed to put the color flashes and shapes into the background. "But last night even the rocks spoke to me, the mountains, the wind, and the stars."

The shaman nodded. "Yes. Everything speaks, actually sings, and in this sense is alive with energy. But snakes are part of what lives in the plants and animals; part of their spirit beings." He gestured all around them. "The creator has marked them such... I need a certain mushroom. The ones close are not ready so I need to go across the ravine. Water only until I return, then when you break your fast with my soup, you will feel much better." He stirred the pot again and walked into the cave.

Trying to brush away spikes and nettles, he moved slowly and cautiously. *I know why they call this the town of thorns. Why would anyone want to live around here?* Something poked through his sleeve as he lifted his field binoculars and surveyed. He couldn't wait to get back to Chicago. He dreamed of some nice chicken cacciatore. Claus Gorman had never been a big fan of cheese; it gave him gas. The locals here seemed offended when he turned down their offerings. "Ouch!" He pulled a thorny pricker from the side of his leg. *Damn, I hate this place!*

He hushed and reminded himself to stop being a wuss and focus. He could see bits of the clearing with the two bikes and a goat, but he couldn't see anyone else. He felt leery; another car had parked on the side of the road at almost the same spot where Claus stopped to continue the rest of the way on foot. The hood of that other vehicle still felt warm. It could be a coincidence, but then again maybe not. He reached his weapon, slung over his back, and brought it forward to his shoulder. He inched his way forward. Finally, he saw them both. Bryson sat on a straw mat, and the girl lay on a mat close by. Neither spoke. Close enough. He folded back the shoulder stock and waited.

Someone spoke from the side of the clearing. "Well, well, well...what do we have here?"

Claus swung the binoculars to the sound of the voice.

WTF! Not good! He must have left his nice jacket hanging in the hotel closet. Through his binoculars, Claus saw Gensu Li approaching his quarry. He brandished a wicked-looking machete in one hand and a formidable pistol in the other. A shit-eating smirk adorned Li's baby face. Adjusting the focus on the binoculars, Claus examined the sidearm. *Glock 40, I wager, fifteen rounds in the magazine. Could have picked one up black-market yesterday from that dealer. Instead, I got this baby. Those Czechoslovakians know how to manufacture a gun.* Claus stroked his semiautomatic tucked back and steady on his shoulder.

"Serena Mendez, I'll bet you're surprised to see me. Maybe even shocked! No more cigarette tricks, witch. They say revenge is a dish best served cold." Gensu took a few steps toward Serena and Bryson.

"What do you want?" Bryson spoke protectively.

A bullet blast followed, and Bryson collapsed in agony grabbing a bloody leg. With a rush of adrenaline, Serena rose to comfort him, the neon-green splash in her mind from the blast noise still fading.

"Speak when spoken to. Now to answer your question, she is coming with me to Singapore. Uncle is impatient. He said alive if possible but in pieces could work out, although it would be less desirable." He waved the machete menacingly.

Bryson moaned, holding his leg.

"He's bleeding. I'm not leaving him here."

"Your choice: bleeding alive boyfriend," he pointed the gun toward Bryson's chest, "or not."

Could she somersault, take him down, surprise him with a lunge? Not a chance.

"I'll count to five."

Serena couldn't think. Her mind still fuzzy from the hallucinations last night, confused with colors and images provoked by everything she heard, weak from vomiting and dehydration. She tried to shake sense into her head, enter the zone.

"One."

Bryson lay there groaning in obvious pain, an enlarging pool of blood soaking into the ground below.

"Two."

What could she do? Li had the upper hand and a gun that he wasn't afraid to use.

"Three"

"Shit! Bry, what should I do? What should I do?"

"Four."

Carmelita bleated. A shot echoed as neon-green exploded in Serena's mind. She screamed.

62

E verything happened in slow motion. Bryson yelled and tried to throw himself over Serena. Gensu Li looked down, perplexed to see red staining his new camouflage jacket. His jaw dropped along with his pistol and machete. Sight and sound erupted, short-circuiting Serena's brain as the scene unfolded before her. She managed a lunge.

Li collapsed and Serena pounced on his gun. She had never fired or even held a gun. She waved it while looking for cover.

From the near edge of the clearing, a tall man holding a compact semiautomatic emerged. He had blond hair.

Bryson squirmed. "It's him! Shoot him!"

Serena hesitated.

"It's Godfried, Gorman," he moaned. "FROM CHICAGO!"

Claus Gorman approached, weapon raised. They looked outmanned and outgunned.

"Put that thing down!" Claus commanded.

Cautiously moving away from Bryson, drawing any potential fire away from him as a target, Serena circled to the side, not even blinking as her eyes remained locked on this second assailant.

The blond man barked, "Do you even know how to use that? Do you?"

"I'm a fast learner." She steadied the firearm with both hands.

"Look, Bryson is hurt. He needs help, so why don't you just put the gun down?"

"Not a chance, buddy…at least he's still alive…not a chance. Maybe you should lower your weapon."

"Okay, okay… Nice and slow, see?" He placed the gun on the ground and put his hands up.

"Kick it to the side."

He toed the weapon and kicked it. It slid toward Li and nestled against the dead body. Claus looked a little confused. "I think there is some kind of mistake."

"Really? What makes you say that?" She cautiously kept her distance, and the gun pointed at Claus Gorman.

"Do you know who I am?"

"Sure do. You're Claus Gorman, aka Charles Godfried. You work for Peter Reynolds, Bryson's uncle. I don't remember the name of the company, but it's in Chicago. You snooped in my apartment back home."

"Great! So why are you still pointing a gun at me?" Serena looked puzzled, so he continued. "I'm the good guy, sent by Mr. Reynolds to rescue you, or at least make sure that Li, Asian bastard that one, didn't get to you."

Now Serena looked really confused. Bryson had lost consciousness. "I'm the freakin' cavalry, girl!"

At that moment, a bird screeched, wings flapped, and from nowhere Sam appeared. He held a handful of mushrooms. No one spoke. He walked over to Li's body and kicked it gently. He bent down to look at the semiautomatic on the ground and examined it, Czechpoint VZ. 61 Scorpion tactical assault gun.

"Humph, I wondered about that part of the dream." He turned to Serena. "Oh, put that down, would you please?" He pointed to Claus while still addressing the girl. "Can't you see? He stung the dragon! He's the scorpion from my dream." Sam went to the soup, put the mushrooms in, and turned his attention to Bryson. Placing his hands over the leg, the shaman sang something barely audible. The oozing stopped and Bryson regained consciousness.

"He'll be okay, but he'll need some medical attention. Let's tend to business first." He picked up the machete, eyeing it appreciatively, and turned to Claus. "Can you give me a hand?"

If Serena looked perplexed before, double that for the look on Claus Gorman's face. He found Gensu Li's cell phone, removed the battery, and collected Li's wallet and any other personal effects. Under direction from the smaller, older man, the much taller and much younger man dragged the body to the edge of the ravine. Serena, Bryson, and Carmelita watched in silence.

"Time to feed the wildlife." With a heave, the two men launched the body down the ravine. Sam was surprisingly spry and strong. He made a long, throaty, howling noise and waves of deep blue exploded in Serena's mind. "That accounts for the rest of that dream-vision from the other night."

"Now, time for some soup." As though nothing unusual had happened, the shaman left to find bowls and spoons in his cave.

Flabbergasted, Claus strode to Serena and whispered, "Who is this guy?"

"Saaammm." The goat replied.

"Long story…"

Two hours later, a lot had transpired. Claus helped Bryson hobble into the jeep. Before leaving, Sam pulled Serena aside and offered his advice. With time and practice she should learn to control the sound-sight. He cautioned her against traveling to the spirit realm without a trusted guide. He warned, "There are many dangers in that place of true reality, especially for a mind conditioned by illusion."

The soup hit the spot. After a bowl and some sort of medicinal tea Sam brewed separately, Serena felt strong. Her mind felt clear. She asked him about the Candelaria messages regarding the seven seals guarding entrance to the seven levels of spirit's transformation to matter. His answer struck something in her truth resonator, an internal guide that sharpened with each chakra opening.

"There are many myths related to the Candelaria; especially here in Peru where myth has been confused and clouded by traditions. I have heard myths about the Virgin's message, but nothing of which I am sure. Of one thing I am certain—all transformation is achieved through manipulation of sound and light. That is why your gift is so important, child. Learn to sing so your light may shine."

Learn to sing…that sounded right to the young Candelaria warrior.

❖   ❖   ❖

Their whereabouts needed to remain unknown. Claus rented a room in a cheap motel, the kind with no security cameras, a place where no one asked questions. Their cover story about an older brother camping with his younger brother and his girlfriend, and Bryson slipping and getting impaled by a nasty San Pedro cactus, was more than plausible. Why did they name such a devil of a plant after a saint? The desk clerk couldn't care less; his only interest rested with the cash paid for the room. Serena wondered how much the proprietor would get.

The knock on their door came a few phone calls and an hour or so later; a doctor and a muscular security guard arrived. Neither spoke English, the guard could have been mute as he spoke not a word. Claus left to return the bikes and paid an extra late fee. The shop owner seemed satisfied. Afterwards, Claus checked out of his own hotel, casually mentioning heading down to Chile for more adventure. He thought Li probably worked solo, but he took no chances; diversion and skillful misinformation seemed prudent. Tomorrow he would return the jeep.

Bryson winced as the doctor probed and examined the wound. He drew up some morphine and readied his instruments. Serena held her geeky friend's hands, offering to give him a bullet to bite on. That brought a weak smile, but as the narcotic took effect, the biggest and happiest grin she had ever seen spread across his face.

"I love you, PTG; you are so awesome, dudette!" The words came out garbled and singsong, but the smile stayed as he slipped into a drug-induced stupor.

The doctor carefully cleaned the wound, extracted a bullet, probed the bone, and then sutured and bandaged the injury. Claus returned with a set of crutches just as the doctor snapped his gloves off. Another injection, some kind of antibiotic, followed. The doctor left pill bottles containing more antibiotics and pain meds. He gave instructions in Spanish and Serena wrote them down. Lastly, he took out an inflatable air cast. He didn't think the bone was broken, but advised an X-ray to be taken to make sure. If Bryson wore the cast, there was no rush to get an X-ray.

That was it. The doctor took cash payment. The guard took payment in an untraceable Glock handgun—a very generous compensation. They left. Claus made calls to arrange travel back; Bryson slept. Serena needed to practice her yoga, practice channeling her kundalini all the way up to and through her six open chakras. The exercise both energized and settled her, leaving her feeling balanced, in tune, and firing on all cylinders. She wanted to go back home.

63

I n heavy rains, a cab left them at the airport. Bryson got soaked as he still had trouble getting around even on crutches. Their gate stood at the furthest end of the international terminal. They could see a small jet being fueled. It had no company markings.

"I'm impressed!" Claus whistled; turned out he was quite a decent fellow. "That's the boss's private jet. I've only flown in it once before…very smooth."

Negotiating the metal stairs proved a challenge with crutches until Bryson put them aside and hopped on his good leg. Both men needed to duck to enter the craft.

"Hello, nephew. Claus tells me you are making good progress on that leg."

"Hi, Uncle Peter. Thanks for sending him down our way. Didn't mean to cause so much trouble." Bryson didn't feel cheery; he spoke cautiously. He still didn't trust his uncle.

An awkward silence followed. Neither man knew how to bridge the gap between them.

"You must be Serena." He extended his hand and turned toward his nephew. "Actually, she's the one who's been causing all the trouble."

That comment, the firm grip of his hand, and the sharpness in his blue eyes all left a favorable impression on Serena. She studied Peter Reynolds before releasing her grip. Almost as tall as Bry, but with thinning hair and many worry lines that creased the man's face. She could read his energy field slightly and she detected a resolute determination. Serena had already mastered keeping her synesthetic images in the background.

"I would say you two have a lot of catching up to do." She offered to take a seat away from them so the two could speak in private, but both men insisted she be part of the conversation. She buckled in. The jet taxied to a runway.

"It's a long flight and we do indeed have a lot to discuss. I had hoped to protect you from these truths, Bryson…"

"You seem to have made a point to remain pretty much out of my life. Is that what you call protection?" Bryson still hadn't warmed up to the older man.

A long sigh followed. "Believe me, I have revisited the decision to keep my distance a thousand times. Circumstances have transpired against that approach. Despite my best efforts, you have wandered into dangers you cannot begin to know. Dangers that even I don't know, but I have my suspicions. Give your uncle a chance to explain before you pass judgment on my actions." Sadness in his uncle's voice softened Bryson.

Serena nudged her friend. "C'mon, Bry, give him a chance. There's something going on here, maybe some new pieces to the puzzle."

His leg throbbed, but he figured out a way to position it propped-up on some kind of footrest. "You're right, PTG. A lot of water has gone under the bridge and there's nothing that can be done about it." He turned to his uncle. "Okay, let's hear what you have to say, but first, I want you to tell me about Dr. Kenseiko Li… I want to know what happened to my parents."

"That's as good a place to start as any. Li is a ruthless monster…"

For the next three hours, Peter Reynolds summarized in lengthy and often disturbing details various facts about the Reynolds family and their genealogy, information about the Illuminati, information about Serena's *shibtzhi* that neither had suspected, and basically everything that he knew about Dr. Kenseiko Li.

"I tried to dissuade your father from going to Singapore, but he was too idealistic to listen. Once he gathered the general gist of what he thought Li was trying to do—alter human genetics, build a master race—he wanted to try to stop him. I assure you that Li orchestrated the plane crash, but I can't prove for sure they are dead. For all I know, Li wanted some Reynold's DNA to experiment with. And your poor mother, she was just an innocent bystander in all of this."

"But why did you keep your distance from me and why haven't you gone after Dr. Li?"

"I figured if I brought you close, Li could very well target you. He and I have a somewhat strained relationship. Suffice it to say that the larger organization, and certainly the heads of the thirteen families, are evil. They want Li to succeed. They see their power and influence being challenged by truth seekers such as the two of you. The world has become unruly, even for the great and powerful Illuminati. They can consolidate their power by reducing the population and by promoting even greater amounts of fear."

"You still haven't explained why you are part of this organization. You admit they are evil." Bryson questioned him, "Why do you hang around?"

"I didn't ask for these genes and not all the Illuminati are evil. Your father wasn't, and neither am I. Most don't know the full extent of the plans. I don't know the full extent of the plans; it's above my pay grade. But working from the inside, I figured gave me a shot at stopping them. That, and not ending up like your father."

Bryson pressed him. "Have you been to Bilderberg or to Bohemian Grove?"

"Bilderberg, no, but believe me that group is a shell compared to the real influencers and power brokers. The entire monetary system is rigged to create and sustain debt. That's one of the ways they control things. As for Bohemian Grove, I did go once, but I didn't see or attend anything with sacrifices, satanic rituals, that sort of thing. That isn't to say those things don't go on; I just don't know for sure. If I had to guess, I suspect the stories are true."

They took a break. Peter Reynolds had confirmed much of what Serena and Bryson already knew about the history of the war between the two serpents, how one faction wanted to share knowledge and information freely—that faction loosely called themselves Luminaria. The other faction, composed of elitists, wanted to control, dominate, and maintain a certain genetic purity by inbreeding among selected bloodlines. They used fear and misinformation to manipulate the great mass of humanity and had done so for thousands upon thousands of years. Modern technology had given this faction even more powerful tools to shape public opinion and to increase the wealth and power of this tiny group. Dozens of conspiracy group meetings and talks Serena and Bryson had attended in New Mexico had most of it right. Doubtless, such groups worldwide challenged the authority of these Illuminati. Collectively, that challenge seemed meager given the extent of control and corruption the Illuminati exerted throughout governments, corporations, financial institutions and so on.

The frightening part wasn't so much the past or even the present; it was what lay in store.

"You talked about creating a master race and about plans to reduce the population. I want to know more about that." Serena felt electricity shooting up and down her spine.

Peter Reynolds shook his head. "I wish I knew for sure. They have the technology to control the weather and could initiate all sorts of climate upheaval. Drought can strain food resources, lead to war. Clean water will become an increasingly valuable commodity, I am sure that's part of it. We're on the threshold of collapsing food production as they have structured a lack of biodiversity into plant and animal stock. Remember the Irish potato famine? There is no genetic diversity in the corn, rice, soybean, and wheat lines that are responsible for something like 90% of agribusiness and the world's food supply. A fungus or a virus or two and the entire system could topple. There's next to no diversity in meat production also, but take away the grain, parch the grasslands—people starve to death and go to war over scarce resources. They like war; it consolidates their power."

"That's just one scenario. Pandemic flu, a modern Black Plague—don't think Li and his team of geneticists haven't created superbugs. A global economic collapse? I could think of half a dozen other ways, but the problem is I don't know how they plan to do it. I know they want to create a New World Order; I just can't give you the details." He smiled; it was grim, not happy, and filled with irony. "The devil is in the details."

"What do we need to do to stop them?" The tingling in her spine intensified.

He shrugged. "To stop the plan requires that you know what the plan is and where the weak links and vulnerabilities are. That's not to say we can't work on finding those things out, but at the moment, I think we need to make sure the two of you remain safe. That's the top priority."

Peter Reynolds had limited information to share about Ooljee. Though he had never met her, his younger brother had. Bryson's father had always been interested in shamanism. The Navajo woman told him about the great war between light and dark and that he played a role in the war. As did she. "My brother didn't share a lot about her with me."

He turned to Bryson. "I didn't know why, but he told me to keep an eye on that Navajo woman. He reminded me of that before he took that last vacation. So, I did. I pieced together a few things, learned a little about the Candelaria and recognized they were one of the Luminarian sects." He turned to Serena. "But I didn't know anything about you. And quite frankly, I don't know what is special about you, but I know Li wants you badly. That by itself convinces me there is something unique about you. Maybe if you can tell me more about why you have been all over the world and what you've been up to, I can puzzle it out."

Other than pausing for restroom breaks, over the next two hours Bryson and Serena shared what they knew with Peter Reynolds. Hard-to-believe harrowing escapes, piecing together clues, synchronicities, etc.—they laid it all out. The incredible chakra openings and the amazing people Serena had encountered while completing her Circle journey all comprised an astonishing tale. In truth, the two were lucky to still be alive. In the big picture of this endless war, many had sacrificed their lives.

Peter asked pointed questions. He took out a scratch pad and all the while took notes. He scoffed and confirmed Rothschild as most certainly the Candelaria necklace buyer, remarking how pompous and full of himself the man was. He chuckled hearing the inside version of his nephew's evasion during the government raid and Bryson's eventual escape. Proudly, he commented that the Reynold's genes did connote a certain intellect. But it was more Serena and her experience that intrigued him.

When the two were done, they all had prepackaged food heated. It wasn't gourmet, but it wasn't half bad. Same with the coffee. The elder Reynolds reviewed his notes.

"Well, it's clear to me your Candelaria genes are associated with some unique abilities. I suspect Li wants them for his master race, but it could be more than that. Your sect seems to have suffered more persecution than other Luminarians. Could be you represent a threat."

"We drew the same conclusions, Uncle Pete."

"Unfortunately, Li has his fingers on anyone and everyone who is prominent in genetics. I don't know anyone we could even approach to get to the bottom of this."

"But I do…" Serena chimed in. "Beangagarrie Brindabella; I told you about him. He seemed to have discovered some important piece of genetic information, then had his work ridiculed, purged, and outside forces professionally destroyed him. He's pretty sure those same forces murdered his wife."

"That sounds like Dr. Kenseiko's modus operandi. Do you think this BB fellow would be willing to get back in the fight? I could outfit a lab for him—all state-of-the art."

"I don't know. He's tough to get ahold of. I can ask."

During the remainder of the flight, they made short-term plans. Bryson needed further medical attention. Peter assured Bryson that he could reenter the country safely. Some things needed to get cleaned up in Taos—but nothing Claus couldn't handle. They needed to remain invisible until Li felt convinced they were either dead or couldn't be found.

"Claus?"

"Yes, boss?"

"Can you entertain some houseguests for a little while? I need to work out some logistics for a few days."

"Providing the young lady here promises not to shoot me, piece-a-pie."

"Great, we'll land in Chicago in a few hours; let's all try and get some rest."

64

Dr. Li weighed the recent turn of events: Brindabella had disappeared, melted into the wild Australian bush; Gensu had not reported in four days; Onassis was still upset that his precious vehicle had blood in the trunk; and some Egyptian news agency claimed the report of drugs being found in the Temple woman's system was a hoax, a cover-up. Messy! Even Rothschild had wind of the girl—something about a necklace. *Pompous fool is worked up about a piece of jewelry. I'm trying to reengineer humanity. They're all clueless!*

Reynolds had been less than useless; his nephew Bryson had apparently skipped town or the country. In Gensu's last report, he claimed Reynolds's nephew and the girl had both escaped to Peru. Kenseiko picked up the secure line and dialed to England. Any family head could call a meeting, but it was always best to work through the chair.

"Dr. Li, what occasion affords me the pleasure of your conversation today?" It all reeked of fake British high-society good manners.

"Consul Rothschild, I am sure you have been following some recent developments involving the Candelaria Cult. A witch has resurfaced after so many years."

"I am aware."

"I am wondering if perhaps the family heads should gather to discuss this new circumstance."

"Convene the family heads to discuss the Candelaria threat?" The words sounded indignant, derisive, demeaning.

"You could put it in those words, Illuminated Chairman." He smiled to himself. "I rather prefer to use the words 'Candelaria opportunity.'"

"I shall consider it. Remain in the light, Li."

"May the light shine upon you, Consul."

He hung up the phone while still holding the receiver in place as he studied the enlarged patch of gray skin on his hand. *That will be cleared up soon.* He rubbed the back of his hand and lifted the receiver, this time dialing the United States.

"Peter, I haven't heard from you in over a week; I hope you haven't forgotten about me."

"Dr. Li. What a pleasant surprise."

"I trust you are well. How about your nephew? How about the girl, Serena Mendez? What have you learned? What are you not sharing with me?"

"I had my best man trace them to Peru, but the trail went cold. Somehow, they slipped away. Who knows, they might be dead."

"You don't sound so upset."

"I've never been close to Bryson, and I don't know anything about the girl. Why is she so important?"

"That is my business, Peter."

"With all respect, South America is out of my jurisdiction. Besides, don't you have people of your own to try and find the two?"

"I sent my very own nephew to look for them; he's not reported back to me in four days."

"Sounds as though you need to send a search party."

"Careful, Peter. It seems we have both lost a nephew, at least for the moment. I'm sure you will keep me posted as to your family's whereabouts. It would be a shame if a family member should simply vanish and never be heard from again."

The thinly veiled threat pushed Peter Reynolds to the limit of his composure. "Live in the light, Dr. Li."

"May the light protect you, Peter."

"Cool!" Bryson hobbled on one crutch. "You say Baxter manufactures this?"

"Not yet. This is still a working prototype." Claus handed the device over for inspection. It looked like a pyramid with an egg sitting on the top, a pretty nondescript silvery metallic compound covered whatever was inside.

"What's the skin made of?"

"Niobium superalloy."

"What's inside?"

"Quartz crystal, magnets, nano-circuits. The techies could tell you more. I just care that it works."

"So, you think this micro EM burst will knock out all the bugs NSA planted at my house?"

"Their bugs, your bugs. This thing is a freakin' exterminator. I'm going to power down my listening post before I give the rest of them a zap. Then I'll power it back just to make sure that we'll have eyes and ears out if the government decides to invade."

"Good plan. Then I can go back?"

"I think you should wait at least a month. And by the way, I want to go over your perimeter defense and drone vulnerabilities before you relocate. You have some defensive gaps."

"Thanks!"

"Anything you need me to do while I'm there, pick up something important?"

"If it's not too much trouble, can you empty the perishables from the fridge? That and I'm missin' my Star Wars action figure collection. Can you bring that back?"

"Roger that." They both laughed.

The two had become good friends during the week Serena and Bryson remained as houseguests. Claus and Bryson had a lot in common and many similar interests. Claus had copied the Homeland/NSA raid and also the US Marshal's visit to the homestead. Bryson must have watched those clips twenty times and still laughed his ass off.

Serena felt bored. She itched to go back home but knew she couldn't do that yet. They planned to leave when Bryson could put a little more weight on his injured leg. She and Bry would use the hogan as a base. Fortunately, the X-rays were negative. He just needed a little more time.

"You're sure I can't convince you two to stay? I can get you both set up here or someplace else if you prefer. You would have new identities, new lives."

"We're sure, Uncle Pete." They hadn't seen him in a week. He looked drawn and weary. "We need to get back; there's more work to do."

"We all have work to do. Li has called some kind of meeting for the family heads. Of course, I'm not invited, but I've got some contacts. Something is brewing; that's for sure."

"I'm sure it's nothing good. From all the things you've told us, calling him a 'monster' is too kind."

"It's an open offer in case you change your mind." He handed over his nephew's backpack; they were ready to board his private jet. "Has Serena reached her Australian contact?"

"Not yet, Uncle Pete." She had taken to calling him that. "I did reach my friend Djalu who is one of BB's tribesmen. He'll find him. It might take a while."

"Keep me posted and stay safe. Claus will drive with you back to your great aunt's hogan. He's bringing along some equipment. After it's all set up,

I need him back here, so you'll be on your own. Well, not really... I'm just a phone call away. Cuch is there too if you need him." They hugged and kissed. "Oh, by the way, there's a little surprise waiting upon your arrival in Arizona at the airport." His blue eyes twinkled.

65

C laus hooked up a scandium-oxide fuel cell, and the hogan had all the power it needed. A wireless signal booster and repeater installed on the highest local peak, both with ultra-sophisticated encryption technology, completed the setup. He had left two days ago in a rental. Uncle Peter's gift, a brand-new white Ford Explorer, registered to one of the Reynolds's family of companies, remained behind. Bryson worked off a new desktop.

"After reviewing your *shibízhí's* Circle," he pointed to the artifacts and symbols still hanging on the wall, "double-checking for hidden codes or messages, and trying to use both my left and right brain, here's what I've come up with so far. You've got another chakra to open, PTG, but I don't know how that's supposed to shake out."

"I know. I have an idea about how to do that."

"Was this an idea you planned to share or am I supposed to guess?"

"I'll let you know soon. I'm still thinking it over."

"Okay, another mystery for me to figure out." He let go a soft chuckle. "The rest is all about DNA. If BB can help us localize the part of the DNA that's been altered, and we can fix it, my working hypothesis is that the Illuminati will not be successful in establishing a New World Order. People will expose them for the power-mongering fakes they are and move beyond their mind control methods."

"They do say you need to cut a snake at the head. I think it's a great hypothesis. How do you propose we fix the DNA?"

"I'm workin' on that. One thing I have learned, there is a lot of information about DNA responding to light and sound. There are dozens of things I've been researching on the internet and some hard science to go along with DNA repair. Here's where we have a secret weapon."

"Secret weapon?"

"You. You're our secret weapon, Candelaria Warrior Girl. I might have to start calling you CWG instead of PTG, even though your hair has almost grown back."

"I think you've been watching too many *Mission Impossible* episodes."

"You can do it. I'm sure of it. We just need to unlock the DNA code. By the way, I happen to be a coding genius, so I guess the two of us combined are a secret weapon."

"What happens if we decode the DNA?"

"Theoretically, the right combination of light and sound should be able to fix it. Once we have that, we build an app, broadcast and message it around the world. This way we turn technology and media against them. Kind of like aiki-do." She looked confused or distant. "It's a Japanese marshal art where you use an opponent's own power against them." She continued to stare.

For a moment, Serena seemed off in a faraway place. Her spine and forehead burned. She was trying to remember something buried in her unconscious. "Where did I hear that?" she mumbled out loud to herself, then her teeth emerged behind a sly smile.

"Solfeggio." It came out as a whisper.

"What?"

"Solfeggio. Didn't you go to the meeting our group held on the topic of Vatican conspiracies?"

"No, I missed that one."

"The Solfeggio scale had been used in composing a lot of Benedictine chants and other music, but the Vatican banned it. Supposedly, the harmonic resonance," the lecture talk had surfaced to the forefront of her consciousness, "was so powerful that people listening had mystical visions and experiences directly of God. They had spontaneous healings. It threatened the power of the church, so they suppressed the music, and that's pretty much all I remember. I'm sure we can look up more."

"I just did. There's a ton on the net about it, including stuff on DNA repair. Good lead." He stood up, went over and kissed her on the forehead. "You're a genius! Together we are a good team!"

"Yeah, it's the together part and combination you mentioned that I wanted to talk to you about…" She looked him in the eyes. A distinct throb and tingling of her second chakra sent kundalini energy snaking up her spine.

"You're sure?" Her voice matched her name—totally serene and tranquil.

Bryson responded, "Positive." The single emerald green candle, the one Ooljee had left, provided the sole light within the cave.

They both stood naked and completely open in trust to one another, water up to Bryson's navel and up over Serena's breasts.

"When I was in Egypt, one of the Isis mystery teachers explained the dance of the four snakes to Nalini. I listened. As I understood it, advanced initiates in the order are taught this as the most complete way the masculine and feminine can unite into one combined and unified energy."

"I've been practicing the exercises you taught me to gather and raise *sekhem*. I'm ready when you are."

As the two held, touched, and caressed one another, wrapping their bodies together, the light from the candle seemed to glow with ever-increasing brilliance. Their union became not a sexual act so much as the complete joining of consciousness into a singularity. They entered pure source consciousness as both their crown chakras opened fully and completely. The godhead within joined with the universal godhead in cosmic bliss. It went on for a time neither could comprehend. The energy from the celestial heavens beyond and the grounded energy of the earth below met in the sacred space of the two-as-one. Their combined kundalini snaked from earth to sky. The entwined black and white wick of the green candle cast a brilliant light as earth, air, fire, and water all danced a cosmic dance.

As their minds, bodies, and spirits melded into the oneness of all creation, Bryson's life experiences, his memories, hopes, and dreams became hers. Serena's life experiences, her memories, hopes, and dreams became his. As the dance of the four snakes slowly ended, they continued to hold each other in ecstatic bliss. The candle sputtered, and the cave went dark.

In the light of their fully open crown chakras, neither one noticed.

66

S erena set her *shibízhí's* note to the side. "I don't know, Bry, I've read this umpteen times. It says when I complete my Circle training my Candelaria strength should become known—healer, dreamer, or speaker. What am I and how do I find out?"

Yoda answered. "Impatient you are, my young Padawan."

Gregorian chants filled the hogan with added reverence. A Mandelbrot of ever-changing geometric forms and colors played like a screen saver in her mind's eye. "You're not helping. I'm looking for suggestions. Who's the genius here?"

"Have you contacted Nalini at the Naga Sanctuary? Maybe that book you left behind says something about what happens after all the energy centers are opened."

"I'm trying to stay incommunicado."

"Oh, I can help there. We can encrypt a message that would be impossible to trace back. You just give the word, PTG."

"I think if dream-walking is my strength, like Ooljee's, I would already be communicating with her and Nalini and Gurumarra and a whole retinue of dream spirits. I've had some weird dreams, but nothing makes me believe that's my gift."

"Any miraculous healings? I can cut myself and you can chant over the wound. We'll see what happens."

"Stop. You're not helping."

"Okay. You're overthinking it in my opinion. Candelaria had a reputation for speaking truth with power. That's what got them into trouble. I think it's pretty clear. You told me about Moon 2 and the Isis mystery school instructress each speaking some words of power—winds blow, books fly, Moses parts the Red Sea. Pretty clear to me. You need to learn that language and charge up the vocal cords."

As Bryson spoke, Serena's throat tickled. She tried to clear the sensation, but it persisted. "Egypt? Maybe you're right. Maybe you speak truth." They both smiled. "What about the seven messages on the Virgin's cloak?"

"I'm working on it. Seven seals binding the planes of existence between spirit and matter. Not a day goes by that I'm not trying to figure that out. No new ideas yet. At the moment, I'm doing a crash course on DNA and genes. That way when BB arrives, I can work closely with him to help unravel the puzzle a little more."

"Sorry. I'm just feeling frustrated and impatient. I want to understand what I'm supposed to do as a Candelaria warrior. Is that too much to expect?"

"For the immediate present, I think you're supposed to turn the music down and get some sleep."

A strange dream…odd…disturbing. Lying in bed, Serena saw them in her mind's eye—somewhere, deep in the Himalayas near Tibet, but far underground. Dr. Li stood next to the other who towered above the Asian man. Dim light from a source she could not identify illuminated the two in pale shadows. Scaled skin glistened in the dim light. They spoke without using words, only thoughts shared between them.

It will be enough?

Yes, the blood and the hair are sufficient.

And the cull?

We have already started.

It will be like the old times. It seems like so long ago, even I have almost forgotten.

Serena rose, and the strange dream faded. She stared at the Circle-journey symbols, focusing on the painting of the Black Madonna appearing to the Guanches. In the pale moonlight, she looked completely transformed from the young woman who had first gazed at the same picture months earlier. What started in the hogan brought them both back to the same place, back to the beginning. Where does the Circle end and where does it begin?

"Bry, are you awake? I just had a strange dream."

"Right here. I think I had the same dream—Kenseiko Li and a big scaly guy?"

"Do you think it's possible the Candelaria weren't persecuted and hunted down so much as they allowed it to happen?"

"What do you mean?"

"I don't know. What if they didn't want to expose themselves to being captured, to prevent the enemy from using their blood and bloodline?"

"Well, I hadn't considered that, but I guess it's possible. They realized they had something they could not let the enemy get their hands on."

"You saw them too, heard them even though they weren't speaking?"

"Yeah, except it didn't seem like a dream, more like some kind of a premonition."

"What are we going to do? A cull? Like humanity is some herd of animals?"

"Uncle Pete didn't put it so bluntly, but from what he told us, that sounds like the plan. I don't like it and I sure would like to stop it, but at the moment, I'm fresh out of ideas."

She removed the picture at the top of the Circle from the wall. Funny how she had never thought to do this before. Unmistakable on the back, even in the pale light, Serena read Ooljee's flowing handwriting:

"And the spark shall become a flame…"

"Bryson, I just realized something." She hung the picture back on the wall.

A cloud blotted out the moon and stars; it cast the hogan into total darkness. Bryson blinked. He couldn't see Serena, but he felt her presence. He couldn't see anything. Her slow steady voice pierced the pitch-blackness. Her words carried conviction, but there was something more…something ominous. Her words held power. Inexplicably, a wave of fear and anger washed over him.

"A candle emits more than just light… They are gonna burn… They are gonna burn…"

ACKNOWLEDGMENTS

I feel a deep debt of gratitude to the Gaia television network. The network's content is full of thought provoking and stimulating content. Much of this explores esoteric, mystical, mythological, and spiritual themes essential to the fabric of this novel. Thank you!

Three of their network hosts: Regina Merideth, David Wilcock, and George Noory are in my mind true Luminarians—my designation for Lightbringers. Many of the guests interviewed by these hosts have provided research findings and substance that is represented in this work of fiction. Many resources available on the internet also provided material and inspiration for this novel.

I further wish to acknowledge the following scholars and Luminarians: Greg Braden, James Charlesworth, Graham Hancock, David Icke, Tom Kenyon, John Lamb Lash, Jeremy Narby, Mark Amaru Pinkham, and Richard Rudd. They have collectively given me much to ponder and speculate upon in the weaving of this tale. I am grateful for these and all Luminarians both past and present.

My family and friends have been unwavering in their support and encouragement. In addition, they have often provided valuable feedback. Special thanks to my wife, Regina, and to my sisters and brothers Elisa, Mary, Michael, Tom, and Tony. I also recognize the special help from my friends Charlie, Kirk, and Shelly. I am particularly grateful for my dear friend Louie. We frequently discussed the underlying story content for *Serpent Rising*. In the early stages of formulating this novel, I wanted to have a character who acted as a Lightbringer. Part of our conversation one day included discussion about his deceased mother. When he first mentioned her maiden name, Candelaria, a light within me ignited.

I wish to thank my publishers Joni and Vern Firestone along with their staff at BHC Press for their expertise, skillful efforts, and support in moving this project forward. I expressly thank my editor, Jamie Rich, for her outstanding work. Finally, I am grateful that fellow Brooklyn native and author colleague Gary Morgenstein recommended BHC Press.

Finally, I am thankful for all the readers of this novel.

ABOUT THE AUTHOR

Victor Acquista has become an international author and speaker following his careers as a primary-care physician and medical executive. He is known for "writing to raise consciousness." His multi-genre works include fiction and non-fiction and often incorporate social messaging to engage readers in thought-provoking themes.

He is a member of the Authors Guild, the Mystery Writers of America, the Florida Writers Association, Writers Co-op, and is a Knight of the Sci-Fi Round-table.

When not pondering the big questions in life and what's for dinner, he enjoys gardening and cooking. He lives with his wife in Ave Maria, Florida.

Revelation, the final installment in the two-book series The Saga of Venom and Flame, is slated for publication in 2021.